MW01064698

THE SERPENT SLAYERS

Integra Press

Phoenix, Arizona

Other Titles from Integra Press

Novels in *The Shaman Cycle* by Adam Niswander
The Charm
The Serpent Slayers
*The Hound Hunters**

Novels of the Merchant Marine by Larry Reiner
Minute of Silence
*The Other Shore**

*Forthcoming

THE SERPENT SLAYERS

A Southwestern Supernatural Thriller

(A Novel In the Shaman Cycle)

by

Adam Niswander

Integra Press

Phoenix, Arizona

The Serpent Slayers
Publisher: Integra Press
        1702 West Camelback Road
        Suite 119
        Phoenix, Arizona 85015

This is a work of fiction. The events described here are imaginary; though many actual settings and institutions do exist, the portrayal of these settings and institutions is strictly fictional; the characters are fictitious and not intended to either characterize the places or represent living persons. In other words, this is all made-up stuff.

Copyright © 1994 by Adam Niswander

All rights reserved. This book or parts thereof, may not be reproduced in any form without permission from the author.

Cover Painting and the Special Edition Frontispiece by Armand Cabrera
Printed in the United States of America
First Printing: 1994
1 2 3 4 5 6 7 8 9 0
Library of Congress Cataloging-in-Publication Data
Niswander, Adam, 1946
    The Serpent Slayers; a southwestern supernatural thriller
    by Adam Niswander
    320 p. cm.
ISBN: 0-9626148-2-3: $21.95
1. Indians of North America—Southwestern States—Antiquities—fiction. 2. Excavations (Archaeology)—Southwestern States—Fiction. 3. Archaeologists—Southwestern States—Fiction. 4. Southwestern States—Fiction. 5. Supernatural—Fiction.
I. Title

Dedication:

For my Jo
and my mother, Olga

Acknowledgements

Heartfelt thanks to all the following:

H.P. Lovecraft and Zealia Bishop for the legacy of Yig.

New Mexico Herpetology hobbyist Gary Sleater for numerous, serious and helpful discussions of an impossibility.

Minnesota Paleontology Professor Bob Sloan for graciously pointing out the unlikelihood of some of my geology and history, and for making suggestions to correct some inaccuracies. His stuff is the correct data. Mine is, of course, literary license.

My friend and Publisher, Frank Wagner for continuing support.

The Adam's Bookstore Writers' Group for continued good counsel and increasingly sophisticated criticism.

To those writers and reviewers who have been kind enough to offer praise, kind words and comments on this and my other work. This time in particular to Diana Gabaldon.

To Margaret Grady and Matthew Frederick, editors of the quarterly magazine ConNotations, for professional skill and a generous contribution of precious time.

And to friends and fans alike who continue to offer good will and encouragement.

What people said about the first Shaman Cycle Novel

THE CHARM

". . . Niswander's fast-paced, well-written debut . . . invests his characters with colorful personalities, displays knowledge of and respect for Native American culture, and knows how to weave disparate story lines into a compelling whole."
Publishers Weekly

"An intriguing excursion into the mythology and wonders of both the old and new American Southwest."
Alan Dean Foster
Author of the *Flinx* adventures, *The Damned*

"I read the first few chapters, turned to my wife and said, 'He can write!'"
Brian Lumley
Author of the *Necroscope* series, *The Burrowers Beneath*

"First try is a 'Charm' . . . generous portions of Indian legend create an entertaining yarn . . . Strong action . . . a strong plot . . . Niswander writes excellent dialogue and handles subplots skillfully enough for the reader to . . . rush for the ending. Followers of the science fiction genre will see reminders of Dean Koontz, or Robert Heinlein, or A. E. van Vogt. Niswander offers credence to beliefs that a new generation of writers will carry on the genre with strength. He knows the roots of legends that cross cultures and time and is able to weave a fascinating new perspective on the old. His knowledge of Indian legends is impressive."
Jacque Hillman, The Jackson Sun

"Adam Has written a yarn in the great tradition of van Vogt's *Voyage of the Space Beagle,* Williamson's *Darker Than You Think,* and Heinlein's *Glory Road* and *J.O.B.*.. The book's an 'all-nighter;' you'll stay up all night reading it because you'll be afraid to go to sleep until you discover how it turns out."

G. Harry Stine
Author of the *Warbots* series, *The Earthsea Invaders* Trilogy

"Had Louis L'Amour ever tried his hand at writing horror or H. P. Lovecraft considered writing about Arizona, *The Charm* is the sort of novel either one would have produced . . . . A fast-paced, good read, *The Charm* marks the arrival of a coming talent in the horror field."

Michael A. Stackpole
Author of *BattleTech* Novels, *The Fiddleback Trilogy*

"What a debut! And he has promised us more! I predict that Adam Niswander will be the Tony Hillerman of horror . . . I couldn't stop reading *The Charm* . . ."

Thea Alexander
Author of *2150 A.D.*

"If a Native American Thriller is your style, try *The Charm* for a 12-in-one combination . . . Prepare to get hooked."

Darragh Doiron, Port Arthur News

"The story is well-told, the characters are well-drawn, and the Native American heritage, history and customs are true to form . . . Niswander is off to a good start and there are more books . . . Be on the lookout for this one."

Baryon Magazine

Prepublication Commentary on

THE SERPENT SLAYERS

"A genuinely creepy book that pits shaman against snake, *The Serpent Slayers* will slither into your mind and wrap cold coils around your heart. Layered in Indian myth, it twines horror and the occult expertly together."

Diana Gabaldon
Author of *Outlander, Dragonfly In Amber* and *Voyager*

"I predict a great future for this group of shamans . . . the books are real grabbers, have a great plot . . . significant character differentiation, and the second follows well on the heels of the first. *The Charm* and *The Serpent Slayers* are among the best first novels I have read in 47 years of reading SF and fantasy . . . a great read!"

Robert E. Sloan
Professor of Paleontology
University of Minnesota

"The Southwestern United States is the most interesting and exotic part of the country. It is also, strangely, the most neglected by writers, perhaps especially in the science fiction and fantasy fields. Thus it was very good to see Adam Niswander use this setting knowledgeably, sympathetically, and above all, excitingly, in *The Charm*. Now he has done *The Serpent Slayers*, a book just as taut and evocative. How fine that we can look foward to a third."

Poul Anderson
Hugo and Nebula Award Winning Author

Friday, June 28th

Chapter One

Pink Cliffs, Northwest of Snowflake, Arizona

The unmarked truck had backed into the wash, rear doors facing the rock formation directly opposite. The muffled sounds of heavy objects being moved about by cursing men filtered back, sometimes clearly, sometimes fading away.

Agent Curt Duncan of the EPA squatted on the rocky side of a high mesa about one thousand yards to the west of the site, binoculars focussed on the activity below.

The agent fumbled with his parasol receiver trying to catch what the men said. The small, black-screened, inverted disk tapered to dual wires connected to the headset he wore under his EPA ballcap. Crouched in the shadow of a large boulder, he remained invisible to those across the wash.

"Roll that boulder aside," ordered a guttural voice. "You see why this place is so good? All you have to do is move the barrels to the edge, then the slope inside the entrance takes 'em down."

"Jesus! That's great, Skeeter!"

"Been using it for three years now," said the first voice. "No way we'll get caught unless someone comes along while we're here."

"Right," whispered Duncan to himself. He reached over and triggered the still camera on its tripod. The muffled clicks of the shutter as it took a series of six exposures sounded barely audible in the light wind whistling over the rocks.

"Only a dozen this time," said voice number two. "It hardly seems worth the trip."

"These guys pay the same whether it's one barrel or a hundred. Don't complain. We got off light this time."

Duncan saw a man walk out from behind the truck and stand squinting into the western sky. Even though the agent felt certain he couldn't be seen, his nerves jumped. The man held a large rifle with a telescopic sight.

Voices number one and two continued their conversation amidst grunts of effort.

That meant three of them.

Curt shot six more photos as the armed man leaned against the side of the truck and lit a cigarette.

There would be at least one good profile for ID. The agent hoped the other two would come out in plain view as well.

Suddenly, voice number two cried out, "Jesus Christ!"

"What is it?" The man—Skeeter—was drowned out as the scream continued. The amplified sound rang amazingly clear.

"Snake!" shrieked voice number two.

"Aw, shit, Ralph. Why the fuck can't you be more careful?"

A moment of silence followed.

"Ralph?"

The second man did not reply.

"Ralph, don't fuck with me." The guttural voice of Skeeter sounded frightened. "Louie, get over here. Ralph's been snakebit!"

The third man, who had been leaning against the vehicle, threw down his cigarette, picked up the rifle and moved back out of view behind the truck.

A full minute of silence followed before anyone spoke.

"Godammit! He's dead!"

The heavy voice of what had to be Louie spoke with incredulity. "How can a man die like that? What kind of snake kills that fast?"

"I don't know," said Skeeter, panic in his voice. "I just know that ... shit! Ow!"

"Skeeter!" Louie sounded scared. "Oh, shit!"

There were more sounds that Duncan couldn't identify, then silence. *What the hell is going on down there?*

Carefully, the agent rose and began making his way across the slope, heading for the wash and hugging the cover.

The Lieutenant would eat his words over this one. The dumb sonofabitch had refused Curt permission to stake out the suspected site. For this reason, he observed there alone on a Friday afternoon. He would show the asshole real investigative work!

He approached the truck obliquely, his pistol drawn. No telltale sound of crushed gravel or stumbling would give him away.

When he moved around to the rear of the vehicle, he saw the cave in the side of the formation, a large round boulder rolled aside to reveal the opening.

No wonder we couldn't find it.

Skeeter, Louie and Ralph lay unmoving on the sand.

He checked each of the three before moving any closer to the opening. Dead.

Cautiously, he approached the cave.

A steep decline stretched into the darkness before him. He could make out the shapes of fifty-gallon drums scattered haphazardly below. Moving closer to snap a picture, he braced himself in the opening and steadied the camera.

Too late, he heard the warning buzz of a rattle from a rock shelf just next to his ear.

He would hear no other sounds. His life had ended. The snake struck and clung momentarily to the flesh just below his left eye. The venom moved directly into his brain. He died instantly—like shutting off a light.

Chapter Two

City of Phoenix

Gloria Larson, on the fifteenth floor of the Valley Bank Building, had just lifted a cup of coffee to her lips when the tremor hit. For most of the residents of Phoenix, it would be a minor sensation. For those who worked in the upper stories of the buildings lining the Central Avenue corridor, the quake would be memorable.

Everything atop her desk suddenly flew up and to the right. The drawers opened and the spilled contents filled the air, as if gravity had gone insane. Gloria cried out even as others screamed.

People, who moments before had been standing or sitting secure in a nest of timber and steel, found themselves flailing at the emptiness of space, headed for hard landings.

The building swayed and the sharp report of sheared bolts and split beams cracked overhead like heavy artillery. Two windows, stressed beyond capacity, exploded inward, straffing nearby unfortunates with shards of glass. The shrieking of a security alarm added to the cacophony.

It lasted seconds—and seemed an eternity.

When the world returned to normal, Gloria sat wedged in a corner of the room with Harvey Carruthers' face buried in her lap. It would have been difficult to choose the recipient of a "most embarrassed" award. Harvey, at fifty-four, had dedicated his life to the Church of

Jesus Christ of Latter Day Saints. A family man, he found himself extremely shy around young women.

"Mr. Carruthers!" said Gloria, pushing him away and trying to pull her skirt down from where it had crawled up around her hips.

Harvey, his glasses askew and his face flushed, covered his mouth with a handkerchief pulled from the breast pocket of his brown business suit. "I do beg your pardon, Miss Larson," he said, hiding a smile behind the hanky. "I'm terribly sorry."

Blushing an attractive shade of rose, Gloria struggled to her feet and pulled her clothing into place. "Oh dear," she said as she looked at the chaos surrounding them.

"Thank you," said Harvey, then scuttled away, wiping a sheen of perspiration off his brow despite the air conditioned coolness of the room.

"What happened?" Gloria looked at Mildred Stone who brushed herself off and righted the chair at the desk opposite hers.

"It must have been an earthquake," said Mildred, adjusting her glasses and looking around in awe. "We had one here in 1978, but I don't recall it being this severe."

"An earthquake? In Phoenix?" Gloria tried to accept the idea.

"There are a lot of minor faults running through the center of the valley," said the older woman as she sank into the chair. "I saw a map once."

"Should we be trying to get out of here?" Gloria felt cold fear replace the disorientation of moments before.

Mildred looked around at the shambles that had been their office, but the building had stopped moving. Some of their co-workers stood clustered at the elevator entrance across the way, but it didn't seem to be working. Many others still struggled to their feet, brushing off the shards of glass and righting the furniture. "Unless there's a severe aftershock, we've probably seen the worst of it." She looked at Gloria. "Are you all right?"

The younger woman patted herself, checking for injury. The tender spot on one thigh would probably become a bruise, but she felt otherwise unharmed. She brushed back a strand of dark hair that had escaped its pin and now hung in her eyes. She must look a mess! Gloria moved toward the restrooms, turning to speak over her shoulder. "I think I'll freshen up," she said.

Entering the ladies' room, she found Arlene Mays standing helplessly in front of one of the sinks. The mirror above had cracked, but no glass had fallen out.

"No water," said Arlene. "The pipes must have broken."

"Oh great," said Gloria, moving up to the mirror. She looked pale and had dust in her hair. She brushed at it ineffectively. "How are we supposed to clean up?"

The other woman moved over to the window looking down on the street below. The sound of sirens began. "Gee, I wonder how much damage it did?"

As she watched, a fire truck with siren wailing pulled up next to a broken fire hydrant that spewed a tall stream of water into the air.

Joining her at the window, Gloria glanced the activity below. "Looks like there may have been damage under the streets."

"That's all we need," said Arlene. "The damn streets are always torn up anyway. Now they'll have to dig up the sewers again."

Gloria turned and gave her a wan smile. "Just our luck. They finished putting in the new system just last month. Now they get to do it all over again." She shrugged. "It just goes to prove the old adage. You know what they say—the shortest distance between two points in Phoenix is always under construction."

Saturday, June 29th

Chapter Three

Springerville, Arizona

The seedy-looking ranch slouched on level ground eight miles from town. As dwellings go, it appeared to be a poor reason for disturbing the landscape. The main house, comprised of three badly wrecked single-wide trailers propped up on blocks, formed a drunken horseshoe of living space.

Numerous derelict vehicles littered a yard set off by a makeshift fence. Repairs had been made everywhere with rolled tarpaper, bailing wire and cardboard in a random, wandering skirmish line that reeled illogically from wall to post—as if some hapless hobos had stumbled on a junkyard and decided to call it home.

The owner, Jake Roberts, looked neither tidy nor pretty. His face, ravaged in youth by acne and chicken pox, had matured into a lumpy, cratered, road map of scars and burst blood vessels. Only his eyes gave a hint of the craft and wile that resided within the hulking six-foot frame.

He wore a ragged glove on what remained of his right hand. Within the stained black leather resided the only single item he had paid more than two hundred dollars for in his entire life—a prosthesis made of stainless steel and rubber, a mechanical hand. Years of practice had made him expert in its use.

All that remained of the meaty paw with which he had been born was the stub of a thumb, half a palm and the little finger. The rest had been lost twenty-three years before.

Jake did not regret it, though. The loss of his hand and fingers had constituted a rite of passage. It had not only marked his physical disfigurement, but twisted his mind to a new view of the world. It had signalled his loss of innocence and divorced him from humanity.

Mostly, it had shown him his life's work—work he could take pleasure in, work that demanded all the meanness and skill he possessed.

At seventeen, he had enlisted in the Marine Corps—a big, healthy, gangly Arizona farm boy eager to see the world. He had been cycled through the meat grinder they called Vietnam and dumped back out— an expert rifleman, a bronze star winner, a survivor.

After his discharge, he returned home to find his mother and father six months dead after a fire levelled the house in which he had grown up. No one had been able to notify him because he had been shifted through seven different hospitals in the five months of his recovery from the wounds that won him his medal.

The old ranch house had survived drought and flash floods but succumbed at last to a grease fire on the new electric stove. The log structure built out of poplar on a rock skirt had burned to ashes.

No one stumbled across the ruins until after. Isolated in a barren section of the countryside, the house had burned on a fog-shrouded morning while his parents slept. Only the rock skirt and the flagstone chimney he had helped his father build when he was eleven remained. Its blackened and baked pillar rose up between the trailers. The rocks served as a platform for the wheeless hulks that were his present home.

Roberts' hand had been lost the day after his return home.

He had been cleaning up debris from the fire and, while trying to pull a charred fencepost from the hard ground, snagged his jacket sleeve on barbed wire. The noise resulting from his attempt to free the garment without slashing his arm had disturbed a rattlesnake hidden in the stark desert shadows.

When it struck without warning, Jake stared in stupid horror, still unable to free his arm from the tangle. Twice the fangs sank into his hand. Twice the venom flowed. By the time he had delivered himself to the hospital in town two hours later, the flesh had already turned necrotic and started to slough away, exposing bone.

It had been a near thing, but he lived. Despite the days of delirium, the agony, the subsequent surgeries—all at the expense of a grateful if impersonal government—he had new purpose in his life.

With his hand freshly bitten, his arm still trapped by the wire, he had looked into the dark eyes of the snake. It had not fled—even after the second strike. It coiled again and stared at him, its tongue flicking in and out.

In that moment, Jake had seen—or imagined that he had seen—the snake smile. It was a smile of pure, gratified evil.

The war, his wounds, his parents' deaths, the blackened cinders that had been his home, and now the snake leering at him caused something inside to snap. His mind received a single, clear, devastating thought, an emotion etched indelibly into his brain, never to fade.

Frustration, grief, loss, pain, fear, horror—all focussed into one emotional outlet and became cold, deadly hate. And the object of that hatred was the snake that sat coiled in front of him, smiling.

When he ripped his arm out of the wire, opening the wound and shredding his flesh—and, incidentally, saving his life—he had grabbed the rattler with his mangled hand and broken it again and again. Long after it had been reduced to a pile of lifeless mush in the sand, his booted feet continued to smash, crush, batter and pound it.

From that time on, snakes had been Jake's life's work. At first, it had been personal hatred that drove him. The satisfaction of finding and killing the vipers had been a tonic that satisfied his desire to strike back at a world he viewed as insane. Eventually, however, the modest inheritance left by his parents dwindled and the pressure of real world economics forced him to modify his pursuit.

He killed many. He took pleasure in it. His methodical extermination of the crawling reptiles around Springerville ended when he was contacted by a clinic that wanted rattlers for production of antivenin and experiments.

Roberts visited the clinic. The herpetologist showed him the operation. Snakes were kept alive—even well-treated—as long as they produced the desirable quantities of venom required.

Once their usefulness as pseudo-cattle for milking came to an end, they were transferred to another lab where they served as subjects for dissection, testing of extermination chemicals and even ground up and added as protein filler in feed.

They paid a fair amount of money for the stock and Jake found he could make enough supplying them with rattlesnakes to pay his bills and fill the larder.

There were times when the rage inside took control and then there would be no delivery to the clinic.

After the killing, Roberts would wander, his thoughts numbed by the indulgence in slaughter, his body an automaton that moved stupidly without conscious direction. It took hours for his brain to kick back in and function normally.

He knew no sense of shame. The vipers to him were the essence of evil—cold, intelligent, deadly and emotionless. They had to be exterminated, had to be crushed into the earth they polluted.

On this particular day, he travelled northwest of Snowflake into the area south of Winslow and Holbrook. He had just passed Dry Lake and headed up the Pink Cliffs toward Porter Tank Draw when he stumbled upon a nest of rattlesnakes and lost control. Hours passed before rational thought returned and he found himself at an unfamiliar place.

From where he stood on the slope of a small hill, he saw a peculiar formation of rocks, almost pyramidal in shape, yet separated into two distinct halves. Sunlight glinted off a shiny surface.

Moving downslope, Jake saw a truck backed up into the cleft between the rocks. Crouching behind the uneven boulders and keeping to the shadows, he crept nearer. Nothing moved around the truck and no sound could be heard other than the whisper of a gentle wind.

He dashed quickly across the open ground and knelt by the grill on the front of the truck. Flattening his body to the ground, he looked under the vehicle.

He muttered under his breath, "What the hell?"

A body lay on the sand in plain view.

Roberts crawled carefully around the front left wheel and along the side of the truck. He listened intently for any noise, any sign of life, but the desert stayed quiet. Despite the afternoon heat, he felt chilled.

Reaching the rear of the van, he peered across the open expanse. The body on the sand had not moved. With every nerve screaming alert, Jake inched slowly on his stomach out from the cover of the truck and approached. Two more bodies lay nearby.

The closest man lay on his side, turned slightly away. He wore a denim shirt and bluejeans. His feet were curiously tangled together, as if he had fallen while trying to turn. As Jake watched, the body shuddered, but the movement seemed mechanical, not at all reminiscent of life.

Roberts stopped his forward progress. He looked around carefully, but saw nothing move. He rose into a crouch and started silently toward the figure. He had taken only a few steps, however, before he heard the warning rattle. Checking the ground behind him, he backed away, but continued to circle the prone figure.

The area in front of the body writhed with snakes—all sizes. Coiled up within the comma formed by the dead man sat a huge rattlesnake, fully five feet long and four inches across. Around it were others, worrying at the necrotic goo that had once been a human being.

Jake stared in fascination. He felt no shock, nor was he repelled. Instead, he watched with professional detachment. The flesh that had once cloaked the body sloughed away as if melting. It dripped globules of tissue. The snakes fed on it. Underneath what remained of the clothing, he could see movement. Even as he watched, a small rattler slithered out of the corpse's mouth, its scales coated with blood and bits of tissue, its bright black eyes intent as it turned and struck at the remnants of the man's nose.

The large snake curled up at the corpse's midsection did not move, but focussed its dark and penetrating stare at Roberts, almost daring him to interfere. Jake met that gaze and felt, for the first time since his accident years before, afraid. The level of intelligence apparent in those reptilian eyes chilled his heart.

Suddenly, three other snakes, which had been busy feeding, turned and looked at Roberts as if noticing him for the first time. Jake saw the three look toward the big rattler. They held each other's eyes for a long moment and then the larger snake opened its mouth and hissed, as if issuing a command. Without any further hesitation, the other three turned deliberately and began moving toward Jake.

The serpent slayer wasted no time. He turned and fled back the way he had come, toward the hillside.

As he ran, he looked over his shoulder. The snakes still followed, their progress swift and steady in the sand. Roberts felt immediately better as he left them behind. No snake in the U.S. could match his fleetness of foot.

He passed the point where he had become aware of himself earlier and found his equipment only a few yards further on. Looking at it, he had an idea.

He had snake handling gear in his bag. He took out the telescoping aluminum rod with the hook on the end and a rugged burlap sack. He also took his forty-five caliber service revolver. He turned around and started to backtrack his own trail. Twenty-five yards to the rear, the three snakes continued toward him.

He waited until they were close. They never slowed. Like programmed machines, they moved straight at him. With a laugh of glee, he shot two—both of them through the head. The third paused for a second, as if the loud reports and the sudden silence that followed had snapped it out of its mindless pursuit. That second was enough. He slipped the noose over its head and brought it to a halt. He lifted it wriggling on the end of the rod and put it in the sack, releasing the noose from the handle and trapping the rattler within.

Whether the laughter released his fear or represented an indulgence in sadistic joy, it verged on the edge of hysteria.

Then Jake had another idea. Taking his bowie knife from his bag, he doubled back toward the site. He would send the specimen to Myers. He would also send a little surprise.

Chapter Four

Zuniland, New Mexico

Geraldo Vasquez looked at his small canvas bag, his mind filled with misgivings. The day had passed and he felt weary. He dreaded the coming holiday. He made his home in Zuniland. Why should he travel to Arizona to be with these other people? True, they were medicine men, but they were strangers to him.

His predecessor, Pasqual Quatero, had acted without consulting the other priests. Quatero's subsequent death due to heart failure and the reported success of his mission had served to make him a hero when any other outcome might have resulted in censure by the council.

Vasquez had been chosen to replace Quatero. He had dreamed of this honor since childhood—selection as Chief Priest of the Gray Wolf Clan. Now that it had happened, he faced the onerous prospect of leaving the pueblo on the 4th of July and flying on the white man's airplane to Phoenix. Because of Quatero's questionable adventure, Geraldo had been asked to represent his people at a meeting with the other medicine men of the twelve tribes.

The council had told him he should go. In this, the elders acted atypically. Zuniland had become autonomous and kept its secrets to itself, striving to remain pure and untainted on a small island of sanity amidst the chaos of the white man's world. The wise rarely sent one of their own away from the homeland—especially to cooperate with the other tribes.

Geraldo sat on his bed and took the folded invitation from his pocket to look at it once again. His eyes read through the salutation and on to the body of the request.

"Will you honor us and the memory of our brother, Pasqual, by representing your people at our reunion of the Great Gathering?"

The council had puzzled for two days over what they should do, arguing over the propriety of participation in the event. Quatero had set a dangerous precedent when he went to the Gathering. Many of the elders disapproved, but the destruction of the demon remained a positive result they could not dismiss.

The Hopi, Laloma, had reported actually seeing Quatero with the terrible twins. This had been independently confirmed by the one who represented the Tohono O'odham, the woman, Farley. Faced with the apparent support of the beloveds, the elders had agonized over the problem but ultimately decided to authorize Geraldo's journey. They dared not affront the gods.

The priest put the paper on the blanket beside him and closed his eyes.

"Ahaiyuta and Matselema, cherished and adored gods of war, what would you have me do? Oh Children of the God of the Sun, I am only a humble priest. In the morning I will go into the ki-wi-tsin and pray before the altar. Give me some sign that this journey meets with your approval."

He moved the empty canvas bag aside and lay back on the bed. He tried to still the tumult within his mind. He thought of his forthcoming departure from his people and said a prayer.

> "In the coming days, may the father who, from his ancient place, grasps us that we stumble not in the trails of our lives, hold firm of me that all will be well and I may, happily, return to the paths of my people."

Sleep finally came upon him.

In his dream, Geraldo walked a trail that led downslope and away from the Pueblo. He came to an outcropping of rock and sat there to rest. The red sandstone rose behind him, a wall separating him from his people. Cirrus clouds stretched gently across the sky above and an airliner passing far overhead glinted in the sun.

When he looked down again, he saw a stone shape tortured by the wind standing in front of him. It looked like a serpent, the rock spiraling up from out of a coil.

Geraldo knew it had not been there when he first sat down. As he watched, the resemblance to a snake became even more clear. As if sculpted by the wind, the stone changed shape and color, taking on the patina of age. In moments, it had become a finished piece, a polished image of a great serpent with fangs bared. The eyes had taken on depth and the forked tongue extended visibly, cut from the rock.

The priest knew it for a dream, but felt a reality in the scene that lifted the experience above mere dreaming.

Suddenly, the stone snake moved. The coils separated themselves from the bearing rock and slid smoothly across the surface. Geraldo moved back, trying to distance himself from the now mobile threat before him, but the sandstone behind him blocked his retreat.

The snake hissed and the priest saw a drop of venom at the tip of one of the fangs.

Geraldo felt afraid.

The reptile smiled, the mouth closing over the fangs, amber eyes catching the light.

Vasquez tried to edge his way along the rock, seeking the trail that might lead him back to the pueblo and safety. The serpent swayed and cut off his escape.

"This is only a dream," said Geraldo aloud to himself. "It can't be real."

The snake hissed again.

The Zuni felt his heart race, his skin grew clammy and moist. He looked frantically for some weapon close at hand—a rock, a club, anything. The outcrop lay barren of any debris, as if it had been swept clean.

He had no sense of communication with the serpent. It remained coldly alien.

He found himself compelled to stare into its eyes. Like a frightened hare, the intense, merciless gaze held him immobile.

The snake reared back, opening its mouth, preparatory to striking. The Zuni closed his eyes, calling upon the gods.

He sensed a bright flash—bright enough to be seen through his closed eyelids. The air filled with a hot, electric smell, and when the priest opened his eyes again, the serpent had vanished. In its place, lay a puddle of liquid rock that hardened in seconds under the afternoon sun.

Geraldo sat there, stunned, for a long moment. Then, he thought he heard laughter. Turning slightly and looking up the wall behind him, his eyes were dazzled by the sun. Just before he closed them, however, for just a moment, he saw two childsized figures silhouetted against the sky. Geraldo gasped.

The two had held shields before their bodies and their appearance—though he had only the briefest of glances—identified them unmistakably to the Zuni. Geraldo now understood—it had been the fire of lightning which destroyed the snake.

The Terrible Two, the Beloveds, the Twin War Gods, the Children of the Sun, Ahaiyuta and Matselema, had rescued him. The gods had spoken.

With the speed of thought, the Zuni found himself back from rocky wall and once again in his bed. He lay there with eyes still closed, trying to calm his heart and breathing.

Geraldo now knew he must go to Phoenix, that he must do whatever he could to help the other medicine men at the reunion of Quatero's gathering.

He did not understand the symbolism of the serpent, but felt sure it would be revealed to him at the proper time.

Weariness rushed in and overwhelmed him. He passed instantly from consciousness to sleep. The rest of the night passed in dreamless oblivion .

June 30th

Chapter Five

Glendale, Arizona

She awakened at 11:00 am and lay there for a moment, orienting her eighty-two year old mind to another day. She shivered with cold. Her stomach rumbled. Thick sleep and cataracts clouded her eyes. Her iron gray hair lay matted in the usual morning disarray. Gradually, the nagging ache of arthritic joints began to assert itself as it had every morning for the last forty years. Agnes Littlebaum contemplated the necessity of movement.

The sun shone through the window over her bed, already high in the sky. She knew she had to get her body moving or the day would be completely lost—lost as far too many were at this time in her life. She had laundry to do, and dishes, and dusting, and even some sewing if her fingers weren't too immobile. With a groan, she pushed herself to the edge of the bed and moved her legs over the side. Rising to a sitting position, she stopped in order to let the usual vertigo pass.

She blamed it on that damned blood pressure medicine. It upset her equilibrium. Simply walking from the bedroom to the kitchen proved an ordeal. Her bones ached and she had grown lighter now than at any time in her life. No matter how much she ate, the weight kept slipping away. A fall presented life-threatening possibilities. Two of her friends had died within months of breaking their hips in careless, stupid falls in their own homes. Agnes was terrified of falling.

She really shouldn't live alone, but there were no close relatives left now and pride kept her from admitting she needed help. She held a deep fear of nursing homes. She had visited friends there, seen them fade away, their once alert and wonderful minds dulled by hopelessness. Her own mother had languished away in such a place.

Her lip stiffened in stubborn resolve. She would continue to fend for herself. If she fell—even if she died alone in the house—at least she would be independent to the last.

Cautiously, she used the dresser next to the bed to lever herself into a standing position. Using the edge of the top, she moved carefully through the connecting door to the bathroom. Grasping the sink, she looked into the mirror. She blinked and rubbed her eyes. Her vision cleared only slightly. A gray-maned apparition wavered before her, cloudy and shrunken.

Her mind wandered. It often did. She saw, for just a brief moment, her younger self standing before her. The raven hair hung thickly, rich in color and curl. The twinkling eyes of the beautiful twenty-year-old she had once been shone back at her.

She blinked and the vision disappeared. After washing her face and drying it with a towel, she took her teeth out of the jar on the sink top, rinsed them and applied the gel, putting them into her mouth. They were loose. Her gums, like the rest of her, kept shrinking.

She lifted the lid of the toilet, pulled up her nightgown, and sat gingerly. Behind her, the plumbing gurgled as it had since the tremor. The toilet continually ran as if something hadn't closed properly. Something had probably broken. Something always did. Everything around her seemed to be falling apart. She wanted to keep up with it, but she always had so much to do and so little energy these days. Just taking care of her own meager needs taxed her to the extent of her ability.

Then Agnes felt movement beneath her. She spread her legs and looked down into the bowl. Looking back, partially out of the water, a snake lay coiled. Her eyes widened and her throat tensed as the scream began. The viper struck.

She felt the pain as the fangs entered her cheek and she rose from the stool with tremendous energy, adrenaline granting her uncharacteristic strength. The snake, still fastened to her body, moved with her. She took two steps before she felt the paralysis spreading into her hip. As heavily as a tree, she fell to the side, cracking her head on the edge of the vanity.

Mercifully, consciousness fled, never to be regained.

The snake pulled free and struck again.

Some time would pass before anyone discovered the body. By then, there would be even less left of little Agnes.

Chapter Six

The Salt River Indian Reservation

The home of Tom Bear, Pima Witch, sat by itself on the northern end of the Salt River Indian Reservation. For a reservation home, it appeared large and typically ramshackle. It faced East so the old man could watch the sunrise from the wide wooden front porch. A deep ravine ran lengthwise before it and served as a barrier between the house and the nearest neighbor, almost a mile away.

Tom sat on the porch and played with a large striped tomcat who now lay on his side batting at a feather the man held in his outstretched hand.

"Are you ticklish, furry brother?" he asked with a chuckle.

The cat, Useless, had been the pet of the late archaeologist, Jack Foreman, the ASU professor who had been instrumental in the destruction of the wind demon almost a year before—in fact, it would be exactly a year in two short weeks. After the explosion in the volcanic vent just west of Phoenix that took the professor's life, Tom, accompanied by the Yaqui, Juan Mapoli, had gone to Jack's home and taken the cat in order to care for it.

Useless had mourned for a while, as cats are wont to do when they lose their keepers, yet had adapted well to life with the Pima witch.

The big tabby looked slimmer than when he had lived with Jack, but remained an imposing animal, running to sixteen pounds. He had taken to life in the desert as if he had been born to it, hunting in the ravine and exploring the territory that surrounded the house.

The Bear had grown fond of the animal, admiring its self-sufficiency and independence. It preferred being a loner as the old man did, yet Tom privately admitted surprise at how quickly he had begun to rely on the cat for companionship.

Tom's close friend, Danny Webb, now a full-fledged medicine man of the Pima, visited less frequently than before because he had become deeply involved with the Tohono O'odham medicine woman, Lotus Farley.

Now, as the old man tickled the cat with the eagle feather, he smiled to himself in satisfaction. Danny had matured immeasurably in the past year. Though the Pima considered themselves modern people and officially scorned the superstition attached to the medicine way, there were many individuals who came to the boy seeking his services.

This elevation of Danny to full medicine man status fulfilled the old man's greatest hopes. He felt satisfaction and pride in accomplishing the boy's education and in delivering on his promise to Donald Webb, Danny's grandfather and—when he lived—Tom's closest friend. The old medicine man would have been proud of the boy.

The cat paused in his batting of the feather and turned to look down the driveway, instantly alert.

Tom looked up, puzzled, but then heard the sound of a car pulling up along the dirt road that ran from behind the house to the drive.

A blue sedan came into view and the old man recognized it at once as belonging to the Maricopa medicine man, Kade Wonto. He rose and moved to the steps.

Kade rode on the passenger side and his wife, Estelle, drove. Both smiled and waved.

"Ho, Kade!" called Tom. "Welcome to both of you. Come up and sit with me."

"Ho, Bear!" called the Maricopa. "We felt like taking a drive and found ourselves nearby. I hope we have not disturbed you."

Tom smiled and gestured at the feline. "I have been playing with my friend," he said.

"Such a large cat," said Estelle as Kade helped her up the wide steps and Tom ushered them to a comfortable old sofa.

Kade bent and stroked the tabby, who stretched appreciatively and began to purr.

"He looks well," said the medicine man, "but looking at him reminds me of Jack." He shook his head sadly. "I wish I had known him better."

"I know what you mean, my friend," said Tom. "He taught us much about the white man."

"He saved us all," said Estelle. "Kade has told me about the last few minutes in the kiva." She looked at the witch. "Tell me, Bear, why did he stay within?"

Tom shook his head. "I asked Gordon Smythe, the Navajo singer, that same question," he replied. "He told me the demon had linked itself somehow to the white man. Perhaps Jack believed he could not leave without the beast following, or only that imprisoning it once again beneath the rock might not be enough, I do not know. I feared that myself. I think he meant to assure that the beast disappeared forever, so it did not end up underground awaiting another chance at freedom. It took great courage to set off the dynamite and know there would be no escape."

Kade rose and moved to seat himself beside Estelle on the couch. He put his arm comfortably over her shoulder and looked at Tom.

"Jack Foreman has been adopted into the Maricopa and Pima tribes," he said. "That is all we can do to show how much we honor his memory."

"And by the Navajo, Apache, Tohono O'odham, Mohave, Chemehuevi, Cocopah, Havasupai, Hopi, Zuni and Yaqui," said Tom. "All have given him an honored place."

"Almost a year has passed," said Estelle. "It is time for the reunion of the Gathering."

Kade looked at the Pima with affection. "We came by today to offer our help," he said. "There will be a great deal to do if you are hosting all of them here at your house."

"I thought about it carefully for weeks," said Tom. "Everyone knows this place. It was here we all assembled the first time." He reached into his shirt pocket and took out an envelope. "I received this yesterday. It is an acceptance of my invitation from the Zuni.

They will send the priest who replaced Quatero. His name is Vasquez."

Estelle sighed. "I liked Pasqual," she said, "but, from the first, he seemed so frail."

"I spoke to the doctor in Zuniland," said Tom. "Her name is Treadwell. She said his heart had been damaged before he left the pueblo and flew to Phoenix. It is remarkable that he lived long enough to join us at all."

"What do we know about this priest Vasquez?" asked Kade.

"Nothing," replied the Pima, "except that he will attend. I am surprised the Zuni elders agreed at all. They are usually unwilling to mix with others."

"They must have a reason," said Kade. "We will no doubt learn what it is in time."

"That is true," agreed Tom. "Meanwhile, I accept your offer of help with pleasure." He stood. "Come inside, my friends, and let me see what there is to eat."

Kade and Estelle rose and the medicine man followed Tom through the door. Estelle stopped and walked to the head of the steps. Looking out over the desert, she shook her head. She sensed something familiar about the scene, a kind of deja vu feeling that disturbed her.

Estelle had been suffering lately from bad dreams, nightmares in which formless horrors seemed to come up out of the earth. Kade, who knew from experience that Estelle's dreams were not to be ignored, had told her to ask Tom Bear.

"Something is wrong," she said to herself. "I feel it."

"Are you coming in, Estelle?" Tom stood there, holding the door open.

The troubled look left her face and she gave him a bright smile.

"Of course, Bear," she said warmly. "It is good for friends to share bread together."

She took his arm and they went inside.

July 1st

Chapter Seven

City of Phoenix

The herpetologist held the rattler carefully and positioned it over the vial, forcing the mouth open and watching the fangs penetrate the gauze-like sealer. Carefully, he pressed on the pit viper's head, expressing the gland and watching to see the clear drops of venom as they rolled down the sides of the glass jar.

Jeremy Myers headed antivenin production at the Carter Labs facility in Phoenix. The clinic supplied hospitals and poison control units all over the regional southwest through an LA distribution center. In addition to seventeen distinct species of rattlesnakes, Jeremy and his staff produced antivenin serum for treatment of bites from the western coral snake, scorpions, and black widows.

The mohave rattler moved under his hand in an attempt to free itself but the scientist kept it firmly under control until the milking process could be completed. The mohave is the most deadly of all the southwestern rattlers and Dr. Myers wanted nothing to do with the business end of this snake except to collect the venom and put the viper back in its cage.

"Is everything all right, Doctor?"

The voice belonged to Rachel Knight, his assistant. He did not turn or break his concentration as he spoke. "I'm almost through here,

Rachel," he said quietly. "Long Tom is getting tired of our intimate acquaintance and starting to show his displeasure."

"Be careful, Jeremy. That's a mean snake."

With his usual precision, Myers disengaged the serpent from the collector and moved over to the cage. He lowered the viper's body into the tank and executed the release with practiced skill. Even at that, Long Tom tried to strike, missing by inches.

"Take it easy, old fellow," said Jeremy quietly as he replaced the cover and secured it. "We're all done for now."

Only then did he turn and look at the technician.

Rachel Knight. *She's worth looking at,* he thought. Tall and raven-haired, the twenty-five year old woman could have been a successful model had she wished. Instead, the green eyed beauty had elected a career where she worked with the most deadly of creatures.

Dr. Myers had harbored reservations about hiring her two years before. Though unquestionably bright and academically qualified, he feared she would be too distracting in an environment where the ability to concentrate proved imperative. In his business, a moment of inattention or carelessness could mean death.

He hired her anyway.

In addition, she had drawn Dr. Myers out of his shell and shown him just how much fun life could be.

Rachel had a wide circle of friends and seemed unwilling to leave the doctor out of it. As a result, he found himself constantly being invited to one event or another in company with his pretty young assistant and others. He felt surprised at just how easily he had adapted to such a radical change in his own lifestyle.

Through much of his life until the present, Dr. Jeremy Myers had been reclusive, studious, and committed to his work—a classic academician. An attractive man of forty, he stood tall and muscular, with a fair complexion and sandy hair, but, nonetheless, was shy with people. He found it easier to deal with fellow scientists and re-searchers, even with the poisonous subjects of his work, than to grapple effectively with challenging social situations.

That, however, had changed now—thanks in a large part to Rachel. Though he would still not admit it, even to himself, he had developed a significant dependency on his colleague. In his own mind, he even acknowledged a little fear of it.

"Long Tom isn't mean, Miss Knight," he said, trying to keep his voice steady and level. "Imagine how you would feel if you were taken from your home, locked in a cage and only removed when someone wanted to force you to do something against your will."

Rachel smiled at him for a moment, then said impishly. "I suppose that would depend on who caught me and what he forced me to do. It sounds kinky enough that it might be fun."

Jeremy Myers turned beet red. His mouth moved as he tried to formulate some reply, but no sound came out. He stood there simply too shocked to speak.

Rachel's face, lit by laughter only a second before, suddenly became concerned and comforting. She moved up quickly and put her arms around him.

"Oh, Jeremy," she said quietly, "I'm so sorry. I didn't mean to tease you. I meant it as a joke. I'm not really that daring." She stepped back and looked into his eyes. "You must think I'm just awful."

The doctor got himself under control and said quickly, "Oh, no, Rachel. I'd never think badly of you. You're . . . well, uh, ..."

Whatever else he might have said, the desk intercom buzzed at that moment, forestalling it.

Relieved to have the diversion, he moved across the room and answered. "Yes, this is Dr. Myers."

"There's a shipment out here in the reception area, Doctor, and it calls for your signature only."

Jeremy looked up at Rachel and shrugged helplessly, then turned back to the intercom. "Who's it from?"

"Jake Roberts," came the reply. "The bill of lading says it contains a live specimen."

"I'll be right out," said the doctor. He turned to his assistant. "Prepare another examination cage, Rachel. Let's see what Mad Jake has sent us this time."

As he exited the lab, Rachel moved efficiently to set up the new cage. As she worked, under her breath, she said, "Almost, my dear Doctor. I'll get you to admit it yet."

Chapter Eight

Yuma, Arizona

James Bluesky of the Cocopah had left the Crawford ranch earlier in the afternoon, returning to the reservation just outside Yuma. He went to meet a visitor from Oklahoma, a Pawnee medicine man named Sharo, who had come west to hear the story of the defeat of the wind demon almost a year before.

The story of the Gathering had spread from tribe to tribe and been discussed in the councils of all the Indian nations from the Seminoles in Florida to the Eskimos in Alaska. Some, like the Pawnee, had sent representatives to the various members of the Great Gathering in order to hear the story first hand. James, who lived on a ranch just outside Yuma, had seen no visitors because Laloma of the Hopi and Smythe of the Navajo were much more accessible. Sharo had been the first to contact him in Yuma.

"What did it look like, this demon?" asked the Pawnee.

Bluesky shook his head, then spoke. "Invisible," he said. "Toward the end, we could see it because of what it did to the earth around it."

The Cocopah's eyes took on a haunted look. "It filled the air, like a huge building—a circular tower of force that dominated everything around it." He lowered his eyes and bowed his head. "I have never been so afraid," he said simply.

Sharo looked down as well, a sign of respect. "It must have been a difficult time," he acknowledged. "Did the creature truly come from the gods?"

Bluesky raised his eyes. He had no doubt. He looked at the Pawnee with confidence. "Yes," he said. "It could not have been otherwise."

Sharo nodded, as much to himself as in agreement with the Cocopah.

"I thought as much. I want you to understand that I believe," he said. "We Pawnee have lived with the close presence of the gods for all our lives. We too have seen their creatures."

James gave Sharo a searching look.

An awkward pause followed while Sharo cleared his throat, then the Pawnee continued. "Before the white man moved us to the reservation in Oklahoma, we ranged freely through Nebraska. There, long ago, our people encountered the Scaled One."

"The Scaled One?"

Sharo nodded. "He is an ancient being. It is said he is the father of all the snakes, including the one the Maya called Kulkucan."

"Kulkucan? Is that the same as the one the Azteca named Quet-zalcoatl?"

"The songs of the fathers say it is so," agreed the Pawnee. "The Scaled One is half man and half devil—a creature unpredictable and playful, yet sire of all the serpents of the world, including the feathered ones."

"Does this one still walk among you?"

"No. With rattle and drum, we drove it west many years ago. It has not troubled us since." Sharo hesitated. "Still, strange things are happening in the world. Your demon came from the past. It may be that old gods are stirring."

Bluesky spoke carefully. "Are you saying there is some connection?"

The Pawnee shook his head and shrugged. "I do not know, Bluesky. I have come to hear your tale and take it back to my people that they may decide."

"Our demon, so the songs tell us, came from the gods specifically to punish those who had strayed from the law," said James, "but it grew ambitious and sought godhood for itself."

"Had your people not defeated it before?" inquired the Pawnee.

Bluesky shrugged. "No," he said, "not defeated, but imprisoned. The first Great Gathering locked it beneath the earth. A white man, a professor at the university, unintentionally set it loose."

"The white men are good at that," agreed the Pawnee. "They are a most troublesome people."

The Cocopah refrained from nodding. "Perhaps," he agreed, "but they know many things about the modern world and some have become brothers to us." James thought about his friend, Kent Crawford. "And a white man destroyed the wind demon, the same one who originally set it free," he added, unwilling to ignore the contribution of Jack Foreman.

Sharo asked, "Did you doubt the outcome?"

Bluesky nodded. "The demon almost brought the end of all things, my brother. I have never seen so powerful a creature."

The Pawnee looked troubled. When he spoke, his voice remained quiet. "I return to my people after much traveling. I stopped here to learn of the wind demon. Just days ago, I stood in Alaska where I met with the angakok of the Tigara Eskimo tribe, a powerful shaman called Umigluk. He told of strange sightings in the sea—of large creatures, bigger than whales, that have been observed in the waters off the coast."

James shook his head. "There are many mysteries in the world."

"There have been reports at home of chixu, ghosts, disturbing the night," continued Sharo. "All tribes report unusual events."

The Cocopah smiled and shrugged. "All has been quiet here, my brother. The demon should have been the last of our troubles."

"Do not be too sure," cautioned the Pawnee. "Something is stirring in the world. There is a darkness coming. I feel your demon may have been only the first of many strange happenings."

The smile faded from Bluesky's face.

"I believe that all the original people will be tested," Sharo continued. "Legends are coming to life after many counts of fathers and sons thought them gone forever."

Bluesky nodded. He thought of the impending reunion of the gathering and came to a decision. "I will tell my brothers of these things when we assemble in Phoenix. We will pass the word to our tribes. We will watch for these happenings."

The Pawnee smiled, then said, "Now, tell me of your Great Gathering and the Wind Demon. Rumors abound. Your fame reaches from ocean to ocean. Many of the wise are curious. I have been sent in search of the truth from the mouth of one who saw it. My people are anxious to know how you defeated it."

"I will be happy to speak of what I saw and what we did, said the Cocopah. The tale is long."

For the next two hours, James Bluesky told the Pawnee the story of the demon and the charm. He told it simply and with humility. All the while, however, his mind dwelt on what he had heard from Sharo.

Chapter Nine

City of Phoenix

The wooden box containing the specimen sent by Jake Roberts had been transferred to Jeremy's lab and now sat next to the new cage set up by Rachel. The creature inside sounded unhappy. The box made thumping noises as whatever it contained thrashed about.

Dr. Myers did not like it. Normally, a specimen transported from the Roberts ranch arrived quiet and sedate, usually close to death. Everyone knew Jake abused snakes. In the past, Jeremy had to nurse them back to health and vigor before they could be of any real service. All the previously shipped Roberts vipers had arrived in a kind of stupor after the courier truck ride from Springerville.

Not this one.

As usual, Jake had put the catch in a custom wooden box of his own design and then wrapped it with brown butcher paper. The labeling on the outside read "Live Specimen—Poisonous—Handle with Care."

When Jeremy removed the brown paper, however, a further label appeared on the wood itself. It had been finger painted on the light blond pine in something that looked disturbingly like blood. In large letters, it said, "MANKILLER."

The air holes were very fine, drilled through the three quarter inch thick wood in a haphazard pattern at irregular intervals, too small to allow the specimen to escape, but also too small to permit looking in. Dr. Myers had tried to explain this to Jake several times, but it had been no use. Roberts did it his way.

Jeremy shook his head. "Reminds me of Robert Shaw in *Jaws*," he muttered to himself. "What the hell did Benchley name that character? Queeg? Queeg-queeg? No, that's Moby Dick. Queen? Quint?" He smiled in satisfaction. That's it. The crusty old sharkhunter in *Jaws* had been Quint. A tough and weird character that one. Well, Jake Roberts made Quint look normal. "Something about his eyes," he said in a low voice. "It's like he's looked at hell."

"Are you and the specimen having a chat?"

The question startled him for a second before he realized Rachel had come up behind him.

"No," he replied. "but this new arrival seems unusually active for a Roberts shipment."

"Be careful, Jeremy," cautioned the girl. "He may have hurt it."

"The box says it's a mankiller," he replied as he indicated the scrawled warning. "I'd say you've understated your case."

Rachel scowled. "Why do we accept shipments from that awful man?" she asked. "He's sick. He shouldn't be loose."

The doctor looked up from his perusal of the case and smiled at her. "Why, Rachel. Anyone overhearing a comment like that would think you didn't like our main supplier of specimens. He has delivered everything he said he would and more." He shook his head. "In the last twelve months, he has sent us at least a dozen of each of the major species in northern Arizona. We haven't had to go out and catch our own snakes for over a year. This guy is a natural at it."

"But when they get here," she replied defensively, "we have to nurse them back from the brink of death. The mortality rate is inexcusably high."

Myers sat back and ran a weary hand through his sandy hair. "They're snakes, Rachel. Poisonous snakes at that. We don't seem to be experiencing any shortage."

"If not," she retorted, "it's no thanks to Jake Roberts. If he had his way, they'd be extinct."

Jeremy paused. "Has he ever shown you his hand?" he asked.

"What?"

The doctor shrugged. "When he first came here, I interviewed him. I got curious, so I asked him about his hand." He leaned back in his chair as he remembered. "I asked him what happened and he looked at me with a strange fixed stare that, quite frankly, made me nervous."

"And?" she urged.

"So he took off his glove," answered Jeremy. "His hand is prosthetic, of course, but under the glove is what remains of the original. Not much really. He still has a rudimentary thumb but you can see the bone. His palm is half gone. Only the little finger remains of the digits."

"Snakebite?" She did not make it a question, more a request for confirmation.

"Yes," he said in a quiet voice. "He told me about it."

"About what?"

"About being bitten." He stared into the distance, remembering. "Jake appeared as rational at that moment as I've ever seen him. He sounded persuasive and logical as he explained to me how the snake struck twice." He shuddered. "It must have been incredibly terrifying."

"And then he killed it?"

The doctor laughed. "Killed it? No, he trashed it. He acted it out for me. He pulled his hand from the barbed wire and grabbed it. He broke it. He stomped on it. He . . ." Jeremy looked intent, searching for the words . . . "went insane and became a killing machine." He looked at Rachel again. "Jake Roberts became the personification of vengeance in that moment. He transformed into retribution. He punished that poor rattlesnake. I'll bet not enough remained when he finished with it to identify the species."

"So?" Rachel obviously thought this made her point.

"So then he walked to the hospital in town. Took him hours to do it. He checked himself in and then collapsed. They almost didn't save him."

"It might have been kinder if they hadn't," said Rachel.

"No, that's just it," insisted Myers. "Don't you see? He stayed hospitalized for weeks. He lost his hand. He had already lost so much." He shook his head. "Instead of giving up, he got out of the hospital and went out to learn about rattlers. He made himself an expert on their habits, their location preferences, their mating habits. He turned his pain into something else. He turned the ruin of his life into a mission."

"To kill snakes?" Rachel looked angry. "Are you lauding what he does?"

"No," answered Jeremy quietly, still seeing Roberts in his mind's eye. "But he chose to do something, Rachel. He acted on what he believed. Oh, I know he's not a well-balanced man, but he elected to do something. He doesn't just study these creatures." The doctor indicated the box before them. "He pursues them and conquers them. He changes the desert, and, incidentally protects those who might stumble into their world. I imagine that, if rodents could speak, they'd proclaim him their patron saint. He sends these specimens to us and contributes something tangible to science."

"I find him disgusting," said Rachel quietly.

"I find him quite remarkable," replied Jeremy. "I admire him for his unwillingness to surrender."

"But he's a killer," protested the girl.

"Are we better?" asked the doctor. "Old Long Tom, there. Is he going to live free again in the wild? No. He'll end up as a filler in dog food once we've milked him dry." He shrugged. "I really don't know that what we do makes us better than Jake."

Rachel stood still for once, at a loss for words. She had never seen Jeremy like this. It frightened her. "What we do is important, Dr. Myers," she said at last. "The antivenin saves lives. Without us, people would die."

Jeremy sighed. "You're right, of course, Rachel. We, too, contribute to the world around us."

The box on the table thumped again. The doctor moved toward it. "I think our specimen is getting impatient, my dear. I'd better see about getting it into its new home."

The process of transferring the snake to the new cage took five minutes. Jeremy removed the screws from the lid with caution. When he moved it aside and shook the occupant into the cage, he used heavy canvas gloves.

As the snake finally fell free, it tried to strike. The doctor's quickness and the glove averted disaster.

Then, however, another object fell from the box into the cage. It took a moment for the sight to register in Jeremy's mind. Rachel let out a choked cry.

On the floor of the cage lay a human hand and forearm—a right hand, the flesh already sloughing away from the action of repeated strikes by the rattlesnake.

"Call DPS!" ordered the doctor. "Get Dr. Sarno at ASU on the line!"

His assistant had already moved to the phone.

July 2nd

Chapter Ten

City of Phoenix

The McBurger on the corner of Cactus and Tatum in Phoenix had been built eighteen years before and included one of the playground/jungle gyms so popular in the late seventies. A maze of tunnels and boxes, the gym sat comfortably under an orange awning on the north side of the building. Openings in the box-like shapes grinned and leered, and the inclines, slides and ladders led through multiple pathways and turnabouts.

Heather Knealy, age seven, had been driving her mother, Janet, crazy all morning. The trip to McB's had seemed the only viable alternative to infanticide for Janet. The boundless energy of her sub-teen proved more than she could handle.

Janet's ex, Brian, offered no help. An attorney, he had left her for a topless dancer when Heather turned five. The child support and alimony were not enough to erase Janet's bitterness at the breakup of her marriage and the burdens of single parenthood.

As they entered the line, Heather immediately began tugging at Janet's sleeve.

"Can I go play on the climber, Mom?"

Janet sighed wearily.

"Can I, Mom? Can I go play on the slides?"

People packed the restaurant for lunch and Mrs. Knealy saw other Moms trying to deal with the exasperating demands of their children.

The tugging continued. "Mom! Can I go play on the jungle gym?"

Janet turned and knelt down next to her daughter. "No. You may not." She put a restraining hand on Heather's shoulder. "You will wait until we have gotten our food and eaten. Then, and only then, if you behave yourself, will I let you go outside."

"Aw, Mom."

"Never mind the aw Mom stuff. I raised you to be a young lady, not a little monkey."

Heather's lower lip trembled and her eyes brimmed with tears. "I don't like you," she said tightly.

"Hush," admonished Janet. "You watch what you say, young lady. We could just turn around right now and go back home."

Heather sat on the floor and sulked.

As Janet Knealy looked down on the cross-legged form of her daughter, she thought about what a miracle her child had been. Despite the hurried courtship and stormy marriage, Heather's birth had seemed to come just in time to save it. The first two years of the child's life had brought Brian and Janet closer together than ever before, bonding them in mutual wonder in spite of the drastic curtailment of their lifestyle.

But pregnancy had brought an unusual weight gain to the normally slim and athletic Mrs. Knealy and it had been impossible to lose all of it after the birth. Janet's legs had already begun to show varicose veins and cellulite had built up on the backs of her thighs. Stretch marks and the scar from her C-section hadn't helped either.

Brian appeared to gradually lose interest in sex, always claiming to be tired and evidencing little tolerance for Janet's needs. He had begun working late at the office and spending his spare time with the boys, leaving the care of his daughter to his wife. The result had been a deep rift between them.

Now, peering down at the girl-child who demonstrated the same stubbornness and determination she did, Janet could not keep a smile from her lips. Heather had grown up tough thus far. Good. She would need to be tough.

"What do you want, honey?" she asked as the line moved up and she found herself in front of the register.

Heather looked up from where she still sat on the floor. "I want a MaxBurger," she said.

Janet turned to the clerk. "Give us a McB. I'll have a chicken sandwich and a Coke."

She paid and accepted the tray.

"C'mon, Heather," said Janet. "Let's have lunch, honey."

They sat at a table next to the playground door and the little girl wolfed down her burger.

"Slow down. Chew your food." Janet scolded more out of habit than any hope of success.

Heather wiped her mouth on her sleeve and stood up. "Okay, Mommy, I'm finished. Can I go play now?"

"Go ahead, baby," said her mother, "but be careful out there."

At that moment, however, screams came from just outside the door.

A little girl tumbled out of one of the boxes on the jungle gym and the other children backed fearfully away. As the body fell, it trailed a long brown shape that seemed fastened like a necktie to its throat.

For Janet, the scene took forever. The little girl's mouth stretched open as she tried to scream, but no sound came out. Attached to her neck hung a large snake.

Suddenly, another serpent fell from the box and moved quickly toward the others.

Panic reigned.

Janet grabbed Heather and lifted her from the floor, turning at the same time and starting toward the door. They had to get out of there. Other parents reached the same conclusion.

Behind her, she heard other children screaming. She raced to the car, threw Heather into the front seat and climbed in after her. Crawling to the driver's side, she fumbled for her keys. It took a few moments, but she got the car started and squealed out of the parking lot, narrowly missing other people still rushing in panic from the restaurant.

At the traffic light, reaction began to set in and she could not keep her foot steady enough to work the brake. Heather cried hysterically in the seat next to her. The car bumped the one ahead gently.

The driver opened his door and began to get out. Janet had pulled too close behind him to pull around. The face of the stranger, a big man wearing a ball cap and overalls, glowered red with rage. However, he had taken only a step or two when he froze and looked off to his right.

On the pavement, just a few feet away from his foot, sat a rattlesnake, coiled and ready to strike.

The man turned and retreated to his car, slamming the door behind him. In seconds, he had raced away, running a red light in the process. Janet didn't wait to look again at the snake. She hit the gas and roared off as well.

The snake managed to avoid the first few cars, but had soon been flattened in the street. None of the other drivers seemed to notice. The sounds of ambulance and police sirens could already be heard in the distance.

Chapter Eleven

Barrio Libre, Tucson

Juan Mapoli of the Yaqui looked forward to the reunion of the Great Gathering with pleasure. He and his wife, Maria, had enjoyed a very affectionate reunion of their own when he returned the previous July. Both had doubted they would have the opportunity.

As usual with the Sabio, Juan had come home quietly and spoken to no one but Maria about the events that transpired in Phoenix. He sought no thanks or reward for what he had done. Though he represented his people, he had not acted with their knowledge. He had not consulted any elders or talked with council members. He had recognized what the gods required of him and acted on his own. To his way of thinking, his part in the Gathering's success could be attributed as much to divine intervention as to skill. He considered himself extremely fortunate.

He knew they had been lucky. He knew that the white man, Jack Foreman, had given much more than the rest. The archaeologist had been forced to accept the existence of powers beyond his experience, to evidence faith in people from outside his culture. He had been confronted with the ultimate choice and had risen to the challenge. Foreman had transcended himself, sacrificed his life for the good of all. He had been the hero.

The events of the defeat of the demon had changed Juan's view of white men. Until last July, he had viewed them as spoilers and exploiters, thieves whose superior technology and numbers had allowed them to defeat the rightful inhabitants of the North American continent. After meeting Foreman, his view had changed.

Juan had always been a loner, a wandering wolf, but now Juan Mapoli had a sense of community that stretched beyond the desert surrounding Barrio Libre. He felt himself to be part of something much larger than the Yaqui tribe. The threat of the demon had lifted his concerns above the merely local and reintroduced the old man to the wider world.

He looked at his wife, Maria. As old as he, her wrinkled face appeared to him a thing of beauty. Her substantial girth had resulted from bearing his children and working hard all her life. He felt a wave of tenderness sweep through him. "I want you to accompany me to Phoenix," he said.

"Why would I want to go there?" she asked in surprise.

Juan gave her a long steady look before replying. "Do you not wish to meet those I told you about?"

Maria turned away from him, wringing her hands. "What would I say to them? I am no sabio. I am only your wife."

Strong hands moved to her shoulders and turned her gently back toward him. His calm gaze met hers. "You are indeed my wife," he agreed in a kind tone. "You are the one who has made it possible for me to pursue my studies, to travel and to learn. Why should you not share with me the good times as well as the bad?"

Her eyes searched his. She saw no hint of mockery, only love and respect.

"Is it truly your wish that I come with you, husband?"

He nodded and spoke. "I have already said so."

She bowed her head. "Then I will do as you wish," she said.

Juan looked pleased. He embraced her and kissed her forehead.

"You will enjoy meeting Estelle Wonto," he said as he released her and moved toward the door. "And," he added over his shoulder, "you will meet the medicine woman, Lotus Farley."

"Ah yes," said Maria with a hint of humor in her voice, "that is the one who tempted both you and the Pima Witch." She moved up behind him, embracing him from the rear and resting her cheek on his back. "I want to see the young maiden that makes the witch Tom Bear want to be young again. And you too."

Her husband chuckled. "He said she almost made him want to be young again, Maria. The almost is important." Juan turned in her arms and held her tightly again. He bent his head and kissed her mouth. "I will always return to you while I live," he said.

They held each other for a long moment. Then Maria gently disengaged his arms and stepped back. "We are acting like young lovers," she said with a smile. "It has been a long time since we behaved that way."

"Perhaps too long," agreed her husband. "Maybe we should have another child."

"What?" Maria stepped back a pace and made a sweeping gesture with her hands. "Go on. Get out and go to your work. I am a sixty-five year old woman. I have born my children. You are getting senile."

Juan laughed aloud, his face like a crinkled tea-stained parchment. He winked at her and turned to the door.

"Be careful, my husband," she cautioned.

He turned the knob and pulled the door open, glancing over his shoulder at her. "I am always careful," he said still smiling. "But there may come a time when . . . ."

He trailed off as he watched Maria's face change. Her laughter gave way to a look of horror and she pointed down toward his feet.

He heard the warning rattle.

Everything seemed to move in slow motion from then on. It took an eternity for him to turn his head and look down. There were no sounds, no other movement. Coiled by the door sat a rattler fully five feet in length and as thick as Juan's forearm.

He saw no means of escape.

With agonizing slowness, Juan watched the snake open its mouth, baring the fangs. He saw as it moved backward slightly and then began the forward surge that ended as the fangs sank into the flesh of his calf.

Time returned to normal.

The sensation as the fangs penetrated his leg felt almost sensual. He experienced no pain to speak of. The creature bit and then withdrew, pulling away and coiling in case it proved necessary to strike again.

He became aware of Maria screaming and moving toward him at the same time. Her hand held a large cast iron frying skillet.

Juan tried to move to stop her, but his leg suddenly went dead, then felt as if it were on fire. Excruciating pain. For a moment, he feared he would fall toward the snake, but his wife pushed him aside and attacked it with the pan. He could not control his body. He hit the wood floor of the porch, using his forearms to cushion the impact, trying to look back at the battle between the rattler and Maria.

It ended quickly. The woman's face held a look of determination as she crushed the viper's head with the skillet. When she felt sure it was dead, she dropped the pan and turned immediately to Juan.

She held a knife in her other hand. Slitting the leg of his pants, she looked into his eyes for reassurance.

"Do it quickly," he said. "Be sure to cut deep enough."

With no further hesitation, Maria took the knife and slashed his leg starting just below the twin bite marks and all the way up to his knee.

When she would have bent her mouth to the cut, Juan stopped her. "No, don't suck on the wound. Express it. Push in on the sides and make it bleed."

His wife complied.

After the leg had bled cleanly for several minutes, Maria stood and spoke."I'm going to get the neighbor's truck. I'll be right back."

She ran next door, babbled something incoherent to Mrs. Smiley, grabbed the keys and jumped into the pickup.

She returned in minutes, but Juan had already lapsed into unconsciousness. Maria did not remember later how she got him into the vehicle.

July 3rd

Chapter Twelve

City of Scottsdale

The five snakes moved almost in unison toward the wide open door of the school. The leader slithered ahead of the others, very much like a point man on patrol. Classes had ended and the day moved quickly toward evening. Only the school secretary remained on the premises.

For the lead rattler, this represented a new experience. Used to working alone, to selecting its own prey, and usually unaware of the wide world around it, this mission stood as unique in all its life. In its head, another consciousness directed it.

It knew that the two-legs should not see it or the others. This must be carried out without any escaping. It had kept instinctively to the shadows, hiding from the sun. None of the serpents made a sound.

They crossed the threshold.

The leader slowed that the others might catch up; they, too, crossed over the tile and into the reception area. Tongue flicking out to sense the sudden diminution of its surroundings, the leader inched forward soundlessly. It had scented the food.

There! Just on the other side of the wall. The prey remained unaware and unguarded. It moved behind the wall without exuding any of the tell-tale fear enzymes. The sound of its regular breathing and even the soft thud of its heart became clear.

Suddenly, the viper felt vibrations.

"Marty James School of Real Estate. May I help you?"

Rhonda Wainwright had been the secretary in the Real Estate school for ten years. She thought of herself as underpaid and under-appreciated and often wondered why she put up with it. For two cents she'd drop the whole thing and go back to being a housewife. Though she would be paid no more if she did, her husband, Roger, would at least appreciate it. In the bonus category, her older daughter, Peggy, would have to stop playing Camille.

The voice on the phone sounded abrupt and rude. "How much are your classes?"

Rhonda exercised patience as she replied, "We offer a wide range of continuing education classes. If you wish, you can sign up for the full twenty four hours required and pay just a hundred dollars in advance."

It had been a particularly hectic day, a Saturday at the end of the month. Everyone who had waited until the last minute to meet their continuing education requirements for licensing had shown up for the marathon sessions. Between the three classrooms, over one hundred fifty students had attended the eight hours. It would be the same tomorrow.

"A hundred dollars?" The voice whined, "Isn't there a less expensive way to do it?"

The boss had gone out of town—usual these days—to Mexico where he and his family spent time building a vacation home. The result might be wonderful and hunky-dory for Marty James, but it left Rhonda with the burden of running the school and dealing with all the spoiled, cantankerous, inconsiderate clods she felt made up the bulk of the Real Estate profession.

"You are welcome to shop around, of course," said Rhonda. "I think you'll find our charges are very reasonable."

The Marty James School of Real Estate sat on the southern end of a plaza famous for hosting rock concerts. In the center, an amphitheater had been the site of literally hundreds of shows by the leading names in music. Though the concert hall had closed, the center still bore the name Rock Plaza.

"You guys are worse than utility companies," declared the caller. "You charge a fortune and those of us who work hard for our money have no choice but to pay what you demand."

Rhonda had too much to do. The phone had rung off the hook all day and every class required paperwork that had to be reproduced, collated and stacked. Every time she started to catch up, some clown like this one would call and ask idiot questions about a schedule printed clearly in their bulletin. Nonetheless, she forced herself to cheerfully respond.

"The Department of Real Estate sets the education requirements, ma'am. We provide classes that meet those requirements and help the professional become more expert."

She glanced at the clock and checked her watch. Time to program the phones and leave.

"May I send you one of our schedules for next month?"

She took a pen and registration card from under the counter and prepared to write down the address.

"No," said the voice on the phone. "I'll stop by one day this week and pick one up. I'd rather you didn't put me on any mailing lists." With that, the caller hung up.

Rhonda breathed a sigh of relief. *Time to go home.* She stood and turned.

The sigh caught in her throat. On the tile floor, a huge rattlesnake stared back at her.

"What the hell?" she said under her breath.

Without consciously thinking about it, she climbed up on the chair and then to the counter top.

She did not scream. Below, she saw four more snakes. She turned and looked out the door. The parking lot loomed empty but the setting sun made it seem bright. She saw no serpents there.

The largest snake had moved to the base of the counter and now rose, coiling to lift its head higher, its eyes never leaving Rhonda's face, its gaze hypnotic.

One of the others hissed, breaking the spell, allowing Rhonda to make a snap decision.

A glance told Rhonda that the closest snake lay a full yard from the door, inside the lobby. She hesitated no longer.

She turned and leapt off the edge of the counter, sailing through the doorway, landing on the sidewalk just outside. She ran up over the hood of her car, across the roof and down the back. She hit the tarmac in full stride and did not stop.

At the convenience store on the corner, she paused, heart thudding in her chest, breathing ragged, and looked in the door for help. She didn't see the clerk behind the counter. Where could he be?

Finally she spotted him. He lay sprawled on the floor by the shelves. A large rattlesnake struck at the body again and again.

Rhonda turned and headed for the street.

Traffic had grown heavy but she did not slow down. Holding out her hand with the authoritative gesture of a traffic cop, she ran into the street, dodging the cars that didn't stop.

Her luck held and she got across. At the filling station, on the corner of the intersection, a Scottsdale Police car sat, the cop inside watching the cars go past. She ran to the side, opened the passenger door and got in, slamming it behind her.

The officer, a hero sandwich before his mouth, bits of tomato and mayonnaise on his chin, looked up startled.

"Can I help you, ma'am?" he asked, wiping his face with a paper napkin and trying to swallow.

Rhonda sat there for a long moment, her mind wrestling with what to say, her stomach twisted in a knot.

Finally, she smiled and said in an efficient, matter-of-fact tone, "Yes, you can. There are rattlesnakes in the Real Estate school across the street and more in the convenience store on the corner there." She pointed and felt the sudden numbness in her arm.

"I believe," she continued, "that the proprietor in the store is dead. Also, I would be very grateful, officer, if you would please take me to Scottsdale Memorial Hospital right away. I think I'm having a heart attack."

Chapter Thirteen

Salt River Indian Reservation

Lotus Farley, medicine woman of the Tohono O'odham, struck a pose in the Theda Bara tradition and said "We simply must stop meeting like this."

Danny Webb, the only living Pima medicine man, looked up from the sofa and laughed softly.

The fact that Lotus looked beautiful and stood there naked made it difficult to appreciate the humor completely. She still, after almost a year, made him ache with wanting her every time they were together. They had made love only minutes before, but he felt himself stirring all over again.

"You're right," he said. "It's killing us. We live sixty miles apart, work long days with our people, and steal moments together whenever we can." He shrugged helplessly. "We've had less than four hours of sleep a night for the last two weeks."

She dropped her pose and turned to face him, her expression marked by concern. "Are you unhappy, Danny?"

He shook his head emphatically. "No!" He gestured at the room around them. "How could I be unhappy when I live in such richness?"

Danny's drab little one-room home on the Salt River Indian Reservation looked anything but rich. The stove and sink on the opposite wall sat next to a metal shower stall. Beside it in the partitioned corner, the toilet sat brooding.

Lotus cocked her head to one side and looked at him intently. "Is that what you want, Danny? Do you seek wealth?"

Again, he shrugged. "I don't know," he said honestly. "I have dreamed of many things. When my father lived, I kept those dreams to myself in order to survive. After his death, Tom Bear began to teach me that the old ways were worth keeping." He closed his eyes for a moment, then continued. "Now I have grown up a lot. I have attained one of those dreams . . ." he glanced up at the woman standing before him ". . . two of those dreams," he corrected himself, "but I still long for more." He looked confused as he concluded with, "Is that wrong, Lotus? Should I be content here?" He waved his hand, indicating the simplicity around him. "Am I wrong to want more?"

Lotus crossed the room in a rush and flung herself upon him, smothering him with kisses, speaking soothingly, reassuringly, between each of them. "No. Oh no, my love. It is a man's right to dream, to want to see his life improve with every passing day."

"But I feel guilty," he protested. "I look around me and see my brothers and sisters of the tribe, and few of them have as much as I have. What makes me think that I should have what they do not?"

Lotus drew back and looked at him, brushing his fine black hair out of his eyes. She shook her head, smiling. "You are becoming wise, Danny Webb. That is one of the hardest things a man can do." She leaned forward and kissed the tip of his nose. "A medicine man," she said, "must look at the needs of his people and strive each day to bring them more into harmony with those above. Only when we please the creator do we rightly achieve the material things of comfort that so many seek."

"But there are some who have achieved these things," he replied seriously. "Are they—simply because of material success—pleasing to the creator?"

Lotus shrugged. "Perhaps some are," she said quietly, "but the measure I spoke of meant harmony, not things."

Danny looked puzzled. "What do you mean?"

Lotus took his hands and placed them on her breasts. She trailed a finger down his chest, passing over his navel and gently brushing the top edges of his pubic hair. "Are you happy at this moment, Danny?"

His eyes took in the sight of the naked woman before him, he felt the pleasant weight of the breasts he cupped in his hands, the sensation of her fingers as they touched so near to his sex. "Yes," he replied with a smile. "I am."

"Yet you are still here in your humble house," she observed. "You have not attained all the things of which you dream."

"They do not matter at this moment," he said as he tried to draw her to him.

She pushed him gently away, resisting his embrace. "Listen to me, Danny Webb. Every moment of our lives is important. Each, as it arrives, is the most significant event that has ever happened to us. What we choose to do with this moment is the most challenging decision we have faced up to this point. The choices we make right now can change the pattern of the rest of our lives, dictate our success or failure."

"I understand the philosophy of now," he agreed, his voice husky with desire. "And at this moment, I want you."

Still, she resisted, her eyes intent on his. "And I want you," she said, "to understand. You can have the things you dream of. You can be whatever you want to be. If you work in harmony with those above to help your people, if you open Pima eyes to the importance of the moment, teach them to treat others with kindness and respect, reward cannot help but come to you."

"You are telling me to be patient," said Danny, trying now to control his desire.

"No, my love," said Lotus smiling sweetly. "I am telling you only to be. Be what you are, Danny Webb. Be as completely yourself as you can. If you do that, you are in harmony with the creator. If you do that, nothing you desire will be denied to you."

Danny broke immediately into a wide smile and hugged her to his chest. He found her ear, teased it with his tongue, and then whispered, "I knew that."

She moved against him in complete surrender now. Their bodies joining without hesitation. Even as they climbed toward release, she whispered back. "Of course you knew," she said, breathing hard as she met his thrusts with equal desire. "Everyone knows, but it is often necessary for us to be reminded."

An hour later, they began dressing. Lotus still had to make the journey to the Gila River Reservation where she kept her home. Both felt very relaxed and content.

The phone rang.

The telephone had been Danny's one modern acknowledgement of his new status as medicine man. It became necessary for him to be reached by those who sought to arrange for his services. It might be an inconvenience when he and Lotus spent time together, but it furnished the link to his clients and part of modern life.

With a resigned shrug, he answered. "Danny Webb. Can I help you?"

The caller, Maria Mapoli from Tucson, wasted no time. "Juan asked me to call, Danny. He has been bitten by a snake. He says you need to come down here. He says something important is going on."

"Is he all right, Maria?" Danny felt a cold knot forming in his stomach.

"We opened the wound right away," she said, "but Juan is very sick. The doctor called the snake unusually poisonous. They do not know if my husband will live."

"I will leave right away, Maria. Tell Juan I have gotten his message and will be there soon."

"He will wait for you, Danny Webb. He told me to tell you that."

Chapter Fourteen

City of Glendale

As is the case in most cities, zoning for certain types of business tends to clump competitors together in a single location. Glendale, a part of the Phoenix metropolitan area, but an incorporated city in its own right, is where the automobile dealers have their showrooms. Everyone is represented, from Audi to Volkswagen, and dealerships for over twenty makes of cars line Glendale Avenue where it crosses 45th, some spilling over onto Grand as well. You want a car, you go to Glendale.

Barbara Belasco had become a local personality. Tall and slim, she dressed her startling figure only in the finest and slinkiest apparel. Her black hair and dark eyes set off a face that, quite frankly, personified beauty. Her deep contralto voice and carefully cultivated hispanic accent made her a natural for the car business. Her television commercials had lifted "Bub" Rankin's dreary Buick dealership from second rate obscurity to genuine fame. It had been a true serendipity for Rankin. He had always been kind of a cheap sleaze, hung about with far too many gold chains, dressed in polyester leisure suits.

As Bub put it confidentially, "Barbie is wunnerful! The beaners come from as far away as Acapulco to buy my bombs now."

One might think that such a relationship would engender good will between the owner and the saleslady. That is certainly what Bub had in mind when he hired Barbara—good will and considerably more.

In fact, it had been that way for the first six weeks or so.

Bub had said, "Barbie treated me good, you know? I mean, shit wouldn't melt in her mouth, you know?"

So he spent freely to dress up his doll. His nights were an orgy of indulgence while Barbi-baby serviced his every whim. Each night brought another gift of jewelry, a new gown, bonus money.

Then, when Ms. Belasco had everything she wanted, she turned on him. Barbara turned out to be a gold-plated, grade-A certified, cold, cruel and calculating bitch.

"Ju wanted to play, leetle boy," she said with a twinkle in her eyes. "Well, we played. Now, no more games."

"Whattaya mean, Barbie?"

Saturday had arrived and Bub had been conducting a meeting of his staff at the time. This consisted of the lot manager, the new and used division supervisors and five of the salesmen. Barbara had not been invited.

The men sat in what Bub called his executive boardroom, a lounge with a big table and chairs, microwave and fridge, and a TV and VCR on which they watched porno movies.

Something about the set of Barbara's jaw warned even Bub Rankin that some serious shit was coming down. He looked nervously around the room and then decided to brave it through. "What can we do for you, sweetpea?" he said with an attempt at a smirk.

"Ju can see me in court," she replied seriously. Then another man, unseen but just outside the door, entered and crossed to Bub.

"It is my duty to serve you with these papers, Mr. Rankin," he said loudly, handing a sheaf of documents to the stunned Bub. "You are to report to Glendale Superior Court ten days from now at eight o'clock in the morning."

"What the hell?" Bub rose up out of his chair, his face beet red and his breathing ragged. "What the hell is this?" he bellowed.

"Eet ees called a Palimony Suit, leetle boy," she said in a calm and reasonable tone. "Eet ees exactly what you deserve."

For a long moment, Bub stood there, his mouth moving but no sound coming out, then he hurled the papers to the floor and advanced, his hands reaching for Barbara's neck.

She remained calm as she withdrew the little black box from her bag. Bub had not stopped advancing toward her when the stunner hit his outstretched hand. It dropped him in his tracks.

Barbara turned and looked at each of the other men in the room without making any effort to put the stungun away. "Anyone else want some?" she asked quietly.

No one moved.

"You were all weetnesses," she said. "The leetle sheet threatened me. I shock heem in self-defense." She turned and exited the room, smiling to herself as the commotion erupted behind her.

Barbara put the stunner back in her bag and crossed to the big keyboard on the hallway wall. She selected the keys for the Excalibur. She left the main building immediately and crossed the lot on foot. It seemed only fitting that she take it. The fire-red paint shone flawlessly, the chrome like a mirror.

She entered on the driver's side, seating herself on the padded plush leather. "My ass should get used to thees," she said under her breath. "Eet sure as hell got worked hard to earn it."

She turned the key and the engine roared to life.

The engine roared and disturbed the large rattler that had crawled in under the driver's seat.

The rattler saw the shapely leg just within reach.

The snake struck as Barbara put the car in gear and stepped on the gas.

The Excaliber sprang off the platform and roared out onto Glendale Avenue into fast moving oncoming traffic.

The noisy twelve car pile-up proved dramatic, but Barbara missed it.

The rattler escaped to the sewer and it would be some time before the coroner discovered that the woman had been bitten.

After he had time to assess his good fortune, Bub Rankin decided he did not miss Barbara.

He did miss the Excalibur, though.

Chapter Fifteen

Havasupai

Rattle, the Havasupai medicine man, sat with the setting sun to his back in his favorite Cataract Canyon location—under the ancient overhang on which his ancestors had carved and painted their sacred art. Here, almost a year before, the deer spirit had come to him and told him to go to the Great Gathering in Phoenix.

He called upon his totem. "Oh, spirit of my heart," he chanted. "Answer me, I pray."

He heard no reply. The Great Deer remained silent as it had all too often in the past year.

After the defeat of the demon, he had returned to his wikiup and his wife, Naomi. The exhilaration of his success as one of the upper world warriors still filled him with pride. The spirit had borne him on its own beloved back and enabled the old man to defy the beast, ultimately defeating it with his bow and a magic arrow. The arrow had been his friend Juan, transforming first into a crow and then into a serpent.

However, when the initial congratulations faded, Rattle found himself disregarded once again. Participation in the Peach Festival had been somewhat anticlimactic. Not many had heard about the demon—even among those who had, most understood nothing of what really occurred.

Oh, the children clapped and laughed joyfully when he told his story as they sat around the fire at the festival, but he felt a dreadful sameness to it, a blending of all the years stretching back into his youth when he had done exactly the same thing. Only the stories differed. Even the faces of the young grew cloudy in his vision, merging into the ghosts of other faces that had laughed, hands superimposed over the shades of other hands as they clapped, voices echoed by haunting whispers as they had cheered.

Rattle tried again to summon the spirit. "I seek your guidance," he sang. "Come to my side."

No reply.

The breeze that came across the river as the sun turned the western sky into a blazing canvas of orange and red and yellow and pink grew cool enough, even at the end of June, to cause the old man to gather his shirt at the throat with one hand and bow his head. The deeply incised image of the Great Serpent weaving its way along the surface of the overhang four feet above seemed somehow menacing. Rattle's head sank lower on his breast.

Perhaps he slept, though he could not be sure.

Once before, in this very spot, a tentative scrabbling sound had heralded the approach of the great deer. He had sat in wonder in the shadows as it moved forward to stand just before him, a four-legged figure, tall and majestic.

No sound came to him this time.

For what seemed only a moment, his eyes were closed and his head lowered. Then he looked up to see a horrible vision.

Standing motionless before him were two huge muscular legs, human in shape but covered with heavy reddish gold scales. Two large splayed feet gripped the rocks, their toes joined almost into paws. They, too, were scaled and hard. The legs extended upward to the limit of his vision from under the overhang and only hinted at the hinges of knees just above and out of sight.

The old man blinked twice and took a deep breath, hoping to banish the sight. When he looked again, the legs still stood before him, as thick as tree trunks, lumpy with cords of muscle that looped around heavy bones, all under a cover of scales.

Rattle tried not to breathe. Perhaps this nightmare would move on, leave him to call upon his great deer in peace.

It would not go away.

Something between a hiss and a sigh filled the air around the boulder. It penetrated the old man's senses like a deadly cold wind knifes through thin clothing. It assaulted his hearing, caused the very ground below him to vibrate in resonance, shook dust and small rock chips out of the stone above. Sand and pebbles rained down under the rock. Rattle covered his mouth and nose to keep from breathing the debris and choking.

Then, with agonizing slowness, the great form began to bend, coming into view as it squatted, then moved to a cross-legged, sitting position. The motion looked fluid and graceful, undulant, like the coiling of a serpent. The vast, anthropoid bulk of the creature filled the opening, bringing night under the overhang though light still shone outside. Even seated, it had to lower its massive head that it might look into his face.

Cold, black, reptilian eyes glittered in a huge snake's head that dominated an already immense frame. Wide scaly shoulders led off to massively muscled arms on either side of a broad armored chest where knotted sinew rippled and rolled with the movement.

The musty scent of the den wafted under the overhang, polluting the clean cool air and nearly choking the old man with the smell of decay. Though Rattle had smelled death before, this terrible odor spoke of something ancient, something alien. The old man's nose wanted to close, his throat constricted. For a split second, he feared he would gag. His lungs refused to expand to take in new air.

A long, black, forked tongue flicked out and then retreated. This repeated several times.

The old man continued to hold his breath.

The creature's huge head split two-thirds of the way down and the vast mouth opened to reveal large, vicious-looking fangs. The tongue flicked out again. When it spoke, the voice rumbled, vibrating through everything around. The rock, the ground, the very air seemed part of the deep penetrating sound.

"Sssss . . . you are the Havasupai called Rattle," it said. "You are the one linked to the deer. Sssss . . . is that truth?"

The old man could no longer hold his breath. He forced himself to breathe in, to expand his lungs, to open his throat. The heavy musk entered with the air. Strangely, he did not choke. In fact, like incense, the cloying smell almost overwhelmed Rattle's senses. He could breathe, though not without discomfort, but the odor was fetid and rank.

"What . . . that is, who are you?" Rattle asked at last. He did not know what this creature was, but he knew he didn't want to offend and anger it.

The creature looked up at the carved Serpent of the World and then back into the man's eyes.

"Sssss . . . Father to him," he replied in that earth shaking voice. "Father to all like him," he added.

"I do not understand," answered the old man truthfully. "What shall I call you?"

"Sssss . . . Call me Lord," said the figure before him.

Used to the missionaries on the reservation, Rattle balked at the term. With an inner, wry humor that he kept from his face, he thought that some of those missionaries were in for quite a shock in the near future if the strange being before him turned out to be the lord they spoke of.

"What do you want of me?" Rattle sidestepped the appellation.

"Sssss . . . Cooperation," came the one word reply.

"In what?" The old man felt honestly curious.

"You must tell the others to spare my children." The wide reptilian face proved difficult to read. It remained expressionless, a cold, blank, impossibility.

"How shall I do this? If I do, will you leave me in peace?" Rattle felt more than willing to walk all over the reservation telling people to spare snakes from harm if the monster would go away.

"All the two-legs," answered the creature. "You must go and tell them all. You must make them obey. Sssss . . . If you fail, I will destroy them."

Personally, the old Pai thought it a pretty tall order. He had just been directed, apparently, to tell every human being in the world not to harm snakes. If he failed to do this, or if anyone refused to take heed, man would be destroyed.

Finally, he asked, "Are you serious?"

A new voice entered the conversation, though the bulk of the snake thing kept its source from Rattle's view. Nonetheless, his heart grew lighter when he heard it.

"He does not understand, Scaled One. He is a simple man who has not even envisioned one such as you before."

The face of the creature disappeared from view as it turned to speak to the deer spirit.

"Sssss . . . It must be made to understand," it rumbled. "There is a new thing among my children, and an old thing." The deep voice sounded troubled and the hissing increased. "Sssss . . . I can gain control of them in time, but I cannot help if these men hunt and kill my own—will not help," it corrected itself. "I would lead the children if I must." The voice became menacing as the creature pointed at Rattle. "Sssss . . . I will make these over if there is no other choice. I have that power."

"You must give us time," said the spirit quietly. "This one and I must talk."

"Sssss . . . There is no time," said the creature. "It has already begun, the death."

Rattle, taking advantage of the creature's lack of attention on himself, crawled rapidly to the side and then out from under the overhang.

The great deer stood passively a few yards away and the old man moved up beside it, his heart beating rapidly. Looking through what seemed a shield of antlers, he saw the snake thing rise to its feet. Erect, it stood as tall as the boulder.

"We will do what we can," said the deer spirit. "This one and I will go to others and spread your word among them."

The monster's tongue flicked in and out nervously. "Be warned," it said. "I am not known for my patience. I am called the Relentless One, the Father, the Great." The huge cords of muscle under the scaly hide rippled like waves on a red-gold ocean. "If the killing begins in earnest, there will be no more time. There will be no mercy. There will be no men."

The silence that followed this statement lay thick and unbroken.

The snake thing turned and stalked away, disappearing into the canyon in moments.

Rattle embraced the spirit. "I have never been so glad to see you," he said.

The great deer did not answer, but gazed off to where the creature had disappeared.

"What is that?" asked the old man, trying to get his breathing under control. His lungs filled greedily with the suddenly fresh air now that the thing was gone.

"That is a god," answered the spirit quietly.

Rattle looked off in the direction of the spirit's gaze, his awe apparent. "I'm glad you are on my side, then," he said with gratitude. "You heard it. That thing threatened to destroy all the men in the world, said it would make them over or something. Can you imagine that?"

The spirit turned and looked full into the face of the old Pai, its eyes filled with sorrow. "It can," said the deer.

Chapter Sixteen

City of Phoenix

The US WEST crew was responsible for repair and maintenance of the underground phone lines that ran through the new utility system underlying much of downtown Phoenix. After the tremor, there had been numerous complaints of failed service. Big Jim Blanton, accompanied by Julio Rodriguez, Ed Millston, Paco Gutierrez and Paul Hart, had been busy for a week tracing understreet damage and repairing severed or displaced lines.

They had started at Central and Roosevelt and worked up, one intersection at a time, checking and effecting repairs on two or three a day for the past week. They currently worked under the street at Northern Avenue. The traffic cones were set, an officer from Phoenix PD had been assigned to control morning rush hour traffic, and the truck mounted compressor powered the air exchange system.

A huge block of residential and business development remained without any phone service whatsoever. Blanton expected to find serious trouble underground.

Julio and Paco had been the first ones down and reported several shifts in the leading edges of the huge concrete pipes that constituted the main passage of the tunnel. Where the fiber optic lines crossed those breaches, it had been stretched and, in some cases, broken.

Blanton scowled at the news. They would be able to splice the breaks, but the job of repairing the main passages under the pavement would fall to the city and require the street to be laid open once again.

Jim shook his head. Phone rates would go up as well in order to compensate for the costs of repair. For a small tremor, barely registering on the Richter Scale, the damage had been astounding. The taxpayers would not be pleased.

The radio squawked and Paco said they'd need additional help down below. Blanton turned to Millston and Hart.

"Better get down there and see what they need. I'll keep an eye on the machinery."

The two workers exchanged glances, then Paul spoke. "You just don't want to get your nice clean coveralls dirty, Big Jim."

Blanton couldn't help smiling. He nodded and replied, "That's why they pay me the big bucks, Hart. Now get your ass down there and help the others. Be sure you have all four radios on and set for the right channel."

"Right boss," Paul acknowledged. "C'mon Ed. Let's go help the wetbacks find the tunnel."

"Gonna be tough," said Millston. "It doesn't have hair around it."

All three men laughed as the two donned their gear.

The radio crackled again as Julio asked, "What's keepin' you guys?"

Blanton flicked the transmitter switch and replied, "Keep your pants on, Rodriguez. Hart and Millston are on their way."

As the two entered through the manhole, Paul lagged behind and helped Blanton hook the collar of the air tube over the opening.

"Go slow," Big Jim cautioned just before Hart disappeared into the tunnel. "Keep an eye on the gauges and stay in contact."

Blanton made the final connection and then moved back to the cab of their Ford. Breaking out his lunch, he turned the truck radio down and concentrated on his meal.

Below ground, Millston spoke over the radio. "Okay, Paco. We're down. Where are you?"

"North," came the the reply. "There's a lot of mud. Be careful."

Hart rolled his eyes before saying, "Great! I just got new boots."

The lights on the tunnel roof worked and the interior of the pipe appeared clearly visible for some ten yards, then apparently hit a breach. At that point, the lights had gone out except for a side-mounted battery-powered torch. Both Hart and Millston reached up and clicked on their helmet lights.

"Looks worse than what we've seen so far," said Paul to Ed as they moved up the tunnel. "Where the hell are Paco and Julio?"

As they reached the unlighted segment, the footing got soft and began to suck at their boots. Looking down, Ed's helmet torch revealed that his feet sank ankle deep in thick sludge.

"Christ!" he muttered. "They don't pay me enough for this."

"Just be glad we don't work for the city," said Paul. "All we have to do is patch the pulled connectors and splice a few lines. They'll have to dig all this shit up."

"Shit is right," agreed Ed. He touched the transmitter button on his mask. "All right. Where are you guys?"

He heard no reply for a long moment, then Julio's voice came over the channel. It sounded strange.

"Madre mio," he said. "What the hell is this?"

"Be careful," said the voice of Paco. "It looks deep."

"What is it, you guys?" asked Millston.

Millston and Hart continued to move forward in the tunnel and could soon hear sounds in the darkness before them.

"There they are," said Paul, putting his hand on Ed's shoulder and pointing. "What the hell are they doing?"

Ahead, the darkness had taken on a peculiar smoky quality and, in the pale glow of their helmet lamps, the view looked like a scene from Dante. The tunnel segment lay askew, turning at a weird angle and no longer level. The far end of the section rose up and the dim glow of lights—apparently the helmet lamps of Rodriguez and Gutierrez—shown unmoving above.

"Hey, you guys! What are you up to?" Ed moved forward and Paul followed a few paces behind.

No answer came from Paco and Julio.

As Hart began to ascend the steady incline toward the end of the tunnel, he heard a strange sound—a kind of hissing in the background.

"Careful," urged Millston. "Sounds like we may have some kind of electrical problem."

Paul slowed down, but continued to move toward Rodiguez and Gutierrez. Behind him, Ed came to a halt.

"There's something wrong with the walls and floor," he said in a small tight voice. "They're wavering."

"What?" Millston began looking to both sides, the beam of his helmet lamp jumping from one place to another.

Around them, the usually solid concrete walls of the main tunnel were undulating and blurring. The smoke obscured the true nature of what they were seeing until too late.

As Hart stepped off the edge of the pipe and began to fall, he cried out. In the pale light of the torch, the sudden emptiness stretched downward forever. The sides seemed to have a life of their own.

He came to rest in more mud, surprised to find himself unhurt. Next to him lay Paco. He reached over to see what had gone wrong, but the rapidly cooling flesh under his hand told him he had arrived too late. Paul sighed. He prepared to stand up, but thought he saw Paco's body move. As he looked directly, focussing the headlamp, he let out a choked cry. The body lay covered in snakes.

Above and behind him, Ed started to scream. "Noooooo . . . Oh God . . . ahhhhhhhhhhhhhhhhhhh!!!"

Hart reached up to hit the transmitter, but his arm felt heavy. He looked over his shoulder and saw his sleeve covered with a mass of snakes. They hung like fat ugly streamers in bands, like fringe. Then the pain started.

It lasted only seconds.

Chapter Seventeen

Shiprock, Navajo Nation

The destruction of the settlement at Chaco Canyon, New Mexico, had been traumatic to the Navajo people. There had been too much death. The manner of it, the vampiristic consumption by the demon only a year before, had made it impossible to tend the dead and give them proper burial. Many believed Chaco to be a place where thousands of ghosts roamed at night. Strange sounds were heard as the desert wind blew through the scattered stones that had once been the homes of three thousand people. In the dark of night, the emptiness seemed to cry with the voices of those who had lived there, wailing in fear and pain. None of the living would return to it or stay there.

The rubble that had once been the hogan of Archie Smythe remained most feared of all. The old man had been the most powerful medicine man—some said witch—in the Navajo Nation and his reputation continued to grow even after the demon took him. This could be credited to Gordon.

Young Gordon Smythe, Archie's great-great-grandson, returned after the defeat of the demon and raised the stones of the west wall, creating a monument of sorts. Gordie had sung of Archie's wisdom and told the tale of the Great Gathering whenever invited to sing. The young man's fame and reputation as a yataalii had also grown.

Gordie now lived nine miles east of Shiprock and worked part time in his cousin's bar. Bertram and Charlie Twoleaf had owned the place fourteen years. Charlie, however, had aspirations toward being a doctor and worked with a medical helicopter service, utilizing his experience as a medic in Vietnam. Since he often travelled, Bert had been trying to run it on his own. When Gordie's immediate family died, his cousin had offered him both a job and an apartment behind the bar.

The arrangement had been good for both of them. Bert had a girlfriend named Corlissa and had come close to losing her more than once because of the hours he worked in the bar. With Gordon to fill in for him, he paid much needed attention to his social life. It had improved things. The wedding date had been set for September 16th.

They had just closed up for the night, evicting the last customer and putting him in a cab. Now, the two men sat at the bar talking. The clock read 2:15 am.

"I wanted to remind you, Bert," said Gordie, "that I leave for the reunion in Phoenix the day after tomorrow. I'll be gone for six days."

"No problem," said Twoleaf with a smile. "Corry is gonna help out while you're gone. It's all set."

Gordon looked around at the little bar, the hardwood chairs and tables littered with the remains of another Friday night. He sighed.

"I guess I'd better get started cleaning up." He rose and went to the closet on the right, pulled out the mop and bucket, then went behind the bar for a wet rag.

Bert grabbed a second bar rag and starting to wipe down the tables.

"I hate to leave you just before the Fourth," said the younger man as he turned on the tap and filled the pail. "The timing could be better, but the demon got loose on July 8th last year and we're planning to hold a ceremony at what remains of the Kiva at sunrise that Monday morning."

"How're you gettin' down there?"

Gordon rolled the bucket out and began mopping the floor behind the bar.

"Charlie has arranged to take me by chopper to Springerville where George Buck is going to swing by and pick me up."

"That Apache?"

"Yeah, why?"

"Oh, no particular reason I guess," said Bert. "I just don't trust Apaches. They have a mean streak in'em."

"Not George," said Gordon. "He's a kind and gentle man. I've told you about him."

"Yeah," said his cousin with a wry smile. "He's the guy who thinks he used to be Geronimo."

"He was."

"So now he's a janitor for the local supermarket, isn't that what you said?" Bertram shook his head. "Doesn't make much sense to me." He went on wiping tables.

"Yes, he is a janitor," agreed Gordon as he wrung out the mop and went back behind the bar for fresh water. "He also used to be Geronimo. Why would what he does for a living matter?"

"I don't know about this reincarnation stuff, Gordie. Sounds too much like ghost business. I don't like you hangin' around with this guy."

"You aren't my dad and you aren't Archie," said Gordon with a sigh. "Don't start telling me what to do with my own time, Bert." He brought the filled bucket out and started on the main floor. "These men, and the Tohono O'odham woman, Lotus, are as much my family as you are. What we shared last summer . . ." he hesitated, searching for words, ". . . it may have been the most important thing to happen in five hundred years."

"Hey, don't get mad, Gordie," said his cousin. "I just sort of feel responsible for you now. I want you to know that, Charlie and me, we care about you."

"I know that, Bert. I care about both of you, too. But I also care about the men and the woman I'm going to see in Phoenix. We are the medicine people of the twelve tribes and the power of our combined strength and skill far outmatches anything any one of us can do separately." He shook his head. "Sometimes I feel so guilty that Archie isn't there with them instead of me. He would have loved it."

"He trained you, Fly," said Bert quietly. "He didn't do a bad job of it either, if you ask me."

"No, he didn't," agreed Gordon, "but I have an awful lot more to learn." He shrugged. "I traveled all over Arizona and New Mexico last year and the first half of this year, meeting with singers to learn their songs. I can do the Blessing Way, the Enemy Way, the Beauty Way and I am beginning to learn some of the Shooting Way chants. Still, there is so much to learn. I could travel like that all the time, spend all my days and nights memorizing the songs, and only scratch the surface if I live to be 100, let alone to 108 like Archie."

"You are still young, Fly," said Bertram. "You have plenty of time."

Gordon looked across the mop handle at his cousin, shaking his head again. "No, Bert. I need to know more now. I have a feeling. I can't explain it, but I have a feeling that something is happening—something important. I think there will be more strange things like the demon, more need for the Gathering. I can't tell you why I feel that, but I do."

"Well, there is little we can do if . . ."

Bert heard a frantic pounding on the door and muffled shouting outside.

"What the hell?" he muttered to himself and crossed to the door. "Yeah, who is it?" he shouted.

"Open the door, for God's sake," yelled a muffled voice outside. "Let me in, Oh, God. Oh please let me in!"

Bert signalled to Gordon who lifted the shotgun from beside the register and nodded. Twoleaf's Bar had been robbed only once successfully. The second time, Bert and Charlie had blown the armed robber halfway across the street. There had been no third attempt.

Crouching to the left of the doorframe, Bert slipped the bolt and turned the knob. Then, he opened the door with a sharp pull and dodged back further to the left.

Corlissa Berent half-fell, half-staggered through the door. She looked as pale as hospital laundry and her eyes were huge with fright. "Close it," she screamed, pointing back at the door. "Close it!"

Bert moved over to her and kicked the heavy door shut. It slammed with a satisfactory and solid thud. The girl threw her arms around him and buried her face in his neck.

"Oh, God. Bert, I've never been so frightened."

Over her shoulder, Twoleaf and Gordon exchanged raised-eyebrow glances. Neither of them had the faintest idea what could have scared Corry so badly.

"Take it easy, baby," said Bertram soothingly as he held her and stroked her hair. "It's okay. It's okay. You're safe here with me."

"Snakes," said the girl hugging Bert even more tightly. "Lots of them! They seemed to be playing with me, herding me." Her voice rose in pitch as the hysteria got a grip. "Rattlesnakes. I saw eight, maybe ten. Oh, God," she shuddered, "I hate snakes. I hate them."

"Snakes?" Bertram Twoleaf looked over at Gordon, beckoning with his eyes, still unable to break the grip of his fiancee. "They not like that, baby," he reassured her. "They're more scared of us than we are of them."

Gordon moved up behind them and put a comforting hand on Corry's shoulder. "It's okay, Corry. Bert and I will check it out. You can let go now."

"They chased me," she said in a small voice, her lips trembling. "They weren't at all afraid. I outran them, but you got the door open just in time."

"I'm sure you're . . ." began Bert.

"Look!" Gordon called out.

Corry turned with Bert and looked in the direction Gordon pointed. She did not scream. She fainted.

Squeezed between the door and the frame, just at floor level, three inches of rattlesnake head had been trapped and crushed when the door slammed. Its mouth hung open, fangs exposed, but the eyes were already clouding over.

Chapter Eighteen

City of Phoenix

The crew chief for US WEST went down the ladder immediately after losing contact with his men. Big Jim did not feel particularly courageous, but he did care about his job. One simply didn't lose an entire crew under a Phoenix street. He knew he should have been on the radio with them, but his lunch had been too tempting. Now, he needed to know what had happened so he could cover his ass.

As soon as he realized they were out of contact, he had called in reporting trouble. He pretended to be having radio difficulty so he wouldn't have to explain.

"Sorry base, I can't read you. You're breaking up. Must be batteries. I'll change them out and call back. Just get me some back up down here. I have no contact—I say again—no contact with my crew."

"What is the nature of the emergency?" It was the second time the dispatcher had asked.

Jim played with the transmit button, cutting in and out.

"It's . . . (squawk) . . . ful! I can't . . . (squawk) . . . plain, but . . . it . . .(click) . . . serious."

"Say again, Blanton. You're breaking up. What is the nature of the emergency?"

Big Jim did not reply.

The police would be on the way. He could not avoid bringing them in, but he still had a chance to salvage things. In five minutes, his job could be threatened, unless he got below and found out what happened to his crew. If he knew that much, he could concoct a story about why he had not tried to help them.

As Millston and Hart had reported, the area at the base of the ladder looked to be in good shape. The northern end of the tunnel led off at an odd angle, indicating a major breach. From that point on, the pipe appeared to be illuminated by only the single battery lamp one of the men had mounted on the wall.

Big Jim advanced cautiously, encountering the same break and soft mud as had the others. There he turned on his helmet lamp and saw the first rattlesnake.

"What the fuck?" he muttered to himself. "Why would rattlers be in the tunnel?"

Looking around, playing his helmet light over the surface before him, he made out other snakes. They seemed to be everywhere. He had counted five when he turned back and headed for the ladder. That had to be the answer, or at least a good enough guess to save his cojones from the fire.

As he reached the base, he heard the warning rattle. The big snake moved into striking position, coiling just to the left. Blanton leaped high and felt the impact when the viper hit the sole of his boot, but managed to cling to the ladder and climb out. He looked back down over his shoulder as he climbed. A second snake had joined the first. Jim's stomach felt filled with hot wire.

"Jesus," he said under his breath, "what a way to buy it. Those poor bastards."

The whole excursion had taken less than three minutes.

He went immediately to the truck and called in for additional help. "Base, this is Blanton. Nature of emergency is snakes. It looks like we've got a tunnel full of rattlesnakes. Better contact the proper authorities."

"Supervisor is on the way to your seventeen," responded the dispatcher. "Roger your report of snakes. We're calling poison control at ASU. Stay out of the tunnel. Await arrival of Cochran."

Jim took his finger off the transmitter and said, "Stay out of the tunnel. No fucking joke." Then he pushed it in again and replied, "I copy that, dispatch. Awaiting backup. Out."

He moved immediately to the truck and pulled a nearly dead radio battery out from under the seat. That would prove his claim to being unable to read base at first.

He sat in the truck and thought about the rattler that had struck his boot. Thank God the bastards couldn't get higher off the ground. His stomach now felt all tied up in knots. He perspired. The thought of the others down below with the rattlers gave him the heebie-jeebies.

Christ, what an awful day!

Chapter Nineteen

City of Phoenix

Department of Public Safety Lieutenant Ed Ramirez put his head in his hands and muttered his favorite descriptive expletive: "Fuck!"

He had been at the briefing just like everyone else. He had heard the reports about increased snake activity around the metropolitan area. The press buzz had just started. Ed felt the city would have a full scale panic on its hands before long.

Two kids at McBurger and a Circle-K clerk in Scottsdale had been killed by rattlesnakes within thirty-six hours. In a whole year, Arizona rarely had three deaths by snakebite. It looked bad. Those people had died quickly and horribly.

The expert at the briefing had said the conclusion could not be avoided. A new kind of rattlesnake had come to Arizona. Neither reclusive nor shy, it worked with others of its kind in what appeared to be hunting groups. Worst of all, it always proved deadly.

It bothered Ed even more that this represented only the tip of the iceberg. Probability said there were bound to be other incidents as yet undiscovered. Snakes did not always appear in front of witnesses.

"What's up, Ed? You look like a warmed over bowl of crap." The speaker, Lieutenant Rod Grimsley, shared the office.

"Thanks," said Ramirez in disgust. "That's just what I fucking needed to make my day."

"What's the matter?" Grimsley had just returned with fresh coffee and passed a mahogany stained cup to the other cop. "Something's eating you."

Ramirez shook his head. "I hope not anytime soon," he said with a shallow laugh. "It's these goddam snakes. The damned things keep showing up where they aren't supposed to . . . and I think it's been going on for a while. Remember when they had to stop play at the Tradition Golf Classic at fucking Desert Mountain three months ago? They had to let the sonsabitches slither across the fucking greens!"

Rod rocked back in his chair and put his feet on his desk. "Yeah, I remember. Didn't seem like any big deal at the time."

"You're right," admitted Ramirez, "but it proves this shit must've been going on for a while. Who the fuck pays any attention to snakes?"

"I think they're called herpetologists," said Grimsley.

Ramirez glanced sharply over at the other man. "Don't be a smartass. This is serious shit. Three deaths in two days . . . that we know of. How many fuckin' more are we going to find?"

"You really ought to try to clean up that language, buddy," said Grimsley. "You'll use it with Faye's mother someday if you aren't careful."

Ed looked sheepish, then sighed. "Last night at dinner, as a matter of fact," he admitted. "Faye got madder'n hell at me. Not just her Mom. The minister who's gonna perform the fucking ceremony was there too."

Rod threw back his head and brayed like a donkey. "There may be hope for me yet, buddy. Just you remember. If you lose that little lady of yours, I'm gonna be right there with a safety net . . . and Roddy is real good at consoling heartbroken ladies."

"Chill out, buddy. I'm not blowing this one. Faye's the woman of my dreams and we're getting married on August 15th. If I catch you within three blocks of her unless she's with me, I'll break every bone in your body."

Rod smiled knowingly. "Okay, buddy. Tell you what I'll do. I'll help you out. More than that, I'll make it worth your while. I'll bet you a week's pay you can't get through three days without saying fuck. In fact, I'll make it even easier. I'll bet you can't get through just the part of the day you spend here in the office with me."

Ed looked up, suspicious. "What's in it for you?"

Grimsley leaned forward. "If you lose, Faye and I go out to dinner . . . just the two of us . . . and you talk her into it and pay for us both."

"You're fu . . . uh, you're crazy," said Ramirez, shaking his head in the negative. "You'd risk a whole week's pay just to go out with my girl?"

Rod looked suddenly more serious. "Yes, I would, buddy. And no promises about being nice. If I win, I'm going to take my best shot."

Ed looked thoughtful for a long moment, then nodded. "Agreed."

"Put it in writing," insisted Rod, "and write Faye's home phone number on the top." He chuckled. "It'll save a few seconds when you lose."

Ramirez took a sheet of paper out of the top drawer and scrawled the agreement out, signing with a flourish. With some ceremony, he rose, folded the paper and put it in Grimsley's breast pocket. "We start today," he said. "I'm sure gonna enjoy spending your paycheck, Roddy."

Grimsley shook his head. "No, you're not. You're gonna spend more than that paying for Faye and me at Gregory's Penthouse."

"Fu . . . uh, no way. You've shown me the error of my ways. As of this moment, I'm a reformed man."

"Yeah, right," commented his partner.

Both men had just settled down at their desks when the phone rang. Rod picked it up first.

"Eighth floor, Lieutenant Grimsley." He listened for a moment, replied, "On our way," and slammed the receiver back into the cradle. He rose in one fluid motion, grabbed his gun from the rack next to the desk and said, "Let's go."

Ed followed suit and, as he slipped his own revolver into the holster, asked, "Where are we going?"

"Northern and Central." Rod answered as he moved into the hall.

"Why?"

Grimsley spoke over his shoulder, turning toward the stairs. "A US WEST crew chief just reported it and the dispatcher called it in. Trouble under the streets. A four man crew. They didn't come up out of a tunnel. The report says there are snakes."

"Aw, fu . . . uh . . . shoot," said Ramirez as he hurried along behind his partner. "It's gonna be one of those fu . . . uh . . . kinds of days."

Chapter Twenty

Tucson, Arizona

After cancelling their appointments for the day, Danny Webb and Lotus Farley drove in her Honda Prelude to Tucson. They had wasted little time in discussion. There could be no disagreement. If Juan Mapoli needed them, they would go immediately.

They did not exceed the speed limits by more than seven miles per hour the entire way down. Speeding only caused delays. Both knew about the Marana speed trap and others like it. When driving in the desert, it is easy to forget that the seemingly empty countryside contains little towns hard up for additional revenue. Speeding ticket fines pay for a goodly portion of the budget in some of them.

"It's hot," said Danny as he watched the heat rising from the pavement ahead. The air above the road literally waved. In only a few hours, the traffic would treble as thousands of people began their holiday weekend journeys. At 11 am, most had not yet started.

The road showed a pair of dark tracks ahead, from tires leaving rubber trails on the simmering asphalt. Arizona in the heat of summer is a baking oven, and even those acclimated to the temperatures retreat to the air-conditioned refuges the Zonies call resorts.

In July and August, humidity climbs higher and the temperature can reach a hundred-twenty degrees at mid-day. The nights are cooler—only a hundred-five or so.

"We'll be there soon," said Lotus, glancing away from the road for a moment. "They took him to County. Can you imagine that? County, for crying out loud. One of the great medicine men of the Yaqui tribe and he is sent to the charity facility."

"He hasn't got money, Lotus," Danny replied. "What did you expect?"

"They wouldn't have a state if it weren't for us," she retorted, her pretty face suffused with anger. "That wonderful old man made it possible to save their lives when the demon came." She stuck out her lower lip, a nervous mannerism that Danny had grown used to seeing. It usually indicated worry.

He shook his head. "They don't know that," he said. "The white men, except for Jack, Greg Johnson and Matt Sharp, thought it just a freak storm. They still do," he added.

"It makes me mad," she said as they took Speedway exit off I-10. "Juan is one of the kindest, gentlest, and most accomplished men I have ever known. He deserves better."

They proceeded to Tucson's Kino Community Hospital and parked in the large lot. Maria met them at the entrance, her seamed countenance breaking into a wide smile.

"He's out of danger," she said breathlessly, leading them to the elevator. "We got most of the venom out when I cut his leg."

"How did it happen, Maria?" Lotus had put her arm around the older woman.

"He opened the door and it struck," said the Yaqui. "It must have been right outside on the porch all night."

The elevator arrived at the fourth floor and they got out. Maria nodded to the nurse on duty and said, "These are the friends we've been waiting for."

"You still have two hours," replied the RN, "but try not to overtire him. Mr. Mapoli has had a rough time."

Maria led them down the hall and paused before a closed door.

"She's right," she said in a low voice. "We shouldn't stay long. My husband will never admit how tired he is."

"We won't be long," said Danny as he pushed the door inward. Maria and Lotus followed.

Juan Mapoli lay in the far corner of the ward on one of the big standard beds, his head turned to look outside. On the window ledge, a large crow sat staring in. As Danny and the women approached, the crow let out a cry and flew away. Lotus saw Juan's body jerk slightly under the covers, then he turned toward them, a weary smile on his face.

His voice barely croaked at first, as if he had forgotten how to use it. Lotus suspected she knew the reason. Juan could, as few Yaquis would ever admit, transfer his mind to the bodies of other animals. The sabio had done so at least once with the Tohono O'odham medicine woman at his side.

"Ah, my friends," he said. "Forgive me. My mind wanders. I should have seen you come in." His voice grew stronger as he continued. "I am glad you could come."

"You know all you have to do is ask," said Danny, moving to the side of the bed and taking the old man's hand. "We are brothers."

Light as a feather, or a dry parchment, Juan's arm lifted and the Pima felt a slight pressure. The old man winced as he tried to squeeze his hand in return.

"It is good to see you, my young friend," said Juan. "I did not think I would make it. That snake struck quickly and the venom raced through me." His troubled face broke into a weak smile. "It is Maria we must all thank for this meeting. Without her quick action, I would have died."

The old woman looked back at her husband and beamed with pride. "I only did what anyone would have done," she said quietly. "Even an old fool knows one must open the wound with a rattlesnake bite."

"Ah, but she first killed the snake," said Juan. "She did it with a frying pan."

Danny and Lotus exchanged looks and could not help responding to the glint of humor in the old man's eyes. They laughed and Juan joined them.

"Maria is not to be trifled with near her kitchen," said her husband, chuckling. "That poor snake never knew what hit him."

His wife turned red and bowed her head, embarrassed and yet too relieved to trust herself to speak. If the old man still had his ability to tease her and to laugh, then he would, indeed, be all right.

The patient in the next bed moaned and turned away from them so Danny pulled the curtain that surrounded Juan's bed to give him more privacy.

Lotus moved up and sat lightly on the edge of the bed. Her eyes searched the old man's and she leaned close. "Are you okay, Juan? Is there anything we can do?"

Releasing his hand from Danny's grasp, he placed it on her shoulder. "I am well, sister," he said. "I asked you to come for a reason."

"Tell us, Juan," she said. "We will do anything you ask."

"You must warn the others," said the old man seriously. "In the moment the snake struck, when the fangs entered my flesh, I sensed something. . . ." His gaze turned inward as he remembered. "It was a strange feeling . . . different than anything I have known before."

"What do you mean?" asked Lotus. "What did you feel?"

"A mind," replied Juan, "but a mind unlike any I have ever encountered. Powerful. I felt it almost like the force of a blow."

"What kind of mind?" Danny, too, had moved in closer and bent to hear the soft voice as it replied.

"I do not know." Juan shook his head slightly, his attention returning to his friends. "Nothing human."

Maria spoke from the foot of the bed. "Juan has told me he believes the snake sought him out. It meant to take his life."

Danny and Lotus looked full into each other's eyes. They shared the same thought.

"Did it have to do with the wind demon?" asked Danny.

The old man shook his head. "No," he said firmly. "The demon is gone for good. This is something entirely new."

"What could it be?" asked Lotus.

Juan's eyes met hers and, for just a moment, she saw fear there for the first time since she had known him.

"I don't know," he replied, "but it will want to kill us all. It must be confronted by the Gathering."

Chapter Twenty-One

City of Phoenix

Rush hour the day before the Fourth of July starts early and promises disaster. This 3rd of July would be one of the worst in Phoenix history.

DPS and the Phoenix PD descended on the intersection of Northern and Central in full force.

Big Jim Blanton had hoped to remain unnoticed in the melee, answering to his direct supervisor and then slinking off to get good and drunk. Such would not be the case.

The report of snakes and missing men had set off all the alarms Lieutenant Ramirez had feared. There were camera crews from Channels 3, 5, 10, and 12, reporters from the *Republic and Gazette, The Mesa Tribune, The Maryvale Star, Glendale Star*, and a half dozen radio station newshounds as well. The corner of Northern and Central looked like the stands at a mud bog event.

"Aw, Fu . . . uh, dammit!" Ed clenched his fists at his side and stamped his feet in frustration. "It looks like a fu. . . uh, a damned circus," he said.

Moving over to a black-and-white unit, he ordered them to move the people back and quiet them down. Around them, horns honked, people shouted to one another, traffic had already backed up for ten blocks in all four directions. The noise shattered thought.

A well-dressed man in a business suit approached, escorted over and introduced by Police Captain Ryan.

"Lieutenant Ramirez," he said, "this is Dr. Sarno from the ASU Zoology Department. He's here to advise you about the reported snakes in the tunnel."

"Are you prepared to go down in there, Doctor?" asked Ed.

The professor did a slight double-take before replying. "Uh, actually, Lieutenant, I understood you would go down after the men." He smiled nervously. "I fear I have not brought the proper equipment to join you." He looked over to the Captain. "You caught me on my way to a dinner party, I'm afraid. I had already left home when the university reached me on the cellular phone."

Ramirez controlled his rising desire to kick the supercilious little bastard in the balls. He turned instead to a sergeant next to him. "Who knows exactly what we're going to run into under there?"

"I have the crew chief for US WEST right over here, sir," said the cop. "He's been down there once already. Name is Blanton. He called in the report."

Ed moved briskly across the street with the sergeant and approached the man in the US WEST hardhat. "I'm Lieutenant Ramirez," he said. "Are you Blanton?"

"Big Jim," said the other offering his hand. "What do you need to know, Lieutenant?"

"Tell me what happened down there." He shook Blanton's hand and noted that the man trembled.

"We work in a five man crew," said Big Jim. "Paco and Julio went down first."

"What are their names?"

"Paco Gutierrez and Julio Rodriguez—that's with an ez."

Ed made a note and then said, "Then what?"

Blanton lifted the hardhat and scratched his head. "They'd been down about five minutes when Paco called in and said they'd need more help." He put his hat back on and continued. "I sent Ed Millston and Paul Hart down next."

"Anything unusual about that?" Ramirez noted the names on his pad.

"No," replied Blanton. "The tremor caused a lot of damage. Quite a few of our fiber optic lines were broken where they passed over seams when the pipes split."

"Okay," said Ed, "continue."

When Big Jim didn't speak up right away, Ramirez glanced at him sharply.

Blanton looked nervous.

"What happened next?" Ed studied the man's face.

"Well, . . . uh . . . I don't know exactly," said Big Jim. "I put the collar over the manhole and moved to the truck cab to listen on the radio, but the batteries were weak and the damned thing kept cutting out."

"Did they call for help?" asked Ramirez.

"Uh . . . no," said the crew chief, "I don't think so." He looked back at the officer. "Base checked in and I reported our progress. Then I discovered the weak batteries. I changed 'em then."

"So you were out of contact?"

Blanton perspired profusely now. "Uh, yeah, I guess so." He shook his head. "It couldn't have been more than a minute or so. When I tried to raise them on the radio, I got no reply. I didn't feel real worried or anything, but I decided to check it out."

"What did you do?"

"I moved the collar and went down inside," said the big man. "What else could I do?"

"And you found?" Ed had his pen poised above the pad.

"Nothing . . . at least nothing but snakes," replied Blanton. "It's really messed up down there. The city's gonna have a helluvah time straightening it out. It's kind of cloudy-like. I don't know what's causing it. I went down the ladder and stepped into the tunnel. The lights are mostly out, but there are a few emergency torches still burning along the tunnel wall. I started north to look for the guys, but I hadn't gone ten yards when I saw the the snakes."

"How many?"

"Christ! I don't know," said Blanton. "I counted five or six but there must've been more. One of 'em struck at my leg and I barely made it back to the ladder in time. I climbed right out and called in."

"No sign of your men?"

"No, sir. And nothing on the radio since then."

Ramirez turned to Grimsley, who had come closer and now stood by silently.

"If Sarno isn't going down there with us, who is?"

"We've got Dr. Jeremy Myers, the herpetologist from the Carter Antivenin Lab here in Phoenix." He pointed to where a group of men had clustered around the manhole in the northbound lane of Central. "He's waiting right over there, Ed."

Rod led his partner over to the group and introduced Ed to the sandy haired Dr. Myers.

The herpetologist stuck out his hand and gave them both a wide smile. "Hear you have a problem, Lieutenant," he said.

Ed accepted his hand and shook it. The grip felt firm and confident. This guy was an improvement over Sarno.

"The crew chief over there says he saw five or six rattlesnakes in the tunnel. He says one of them struck at him and he had to climb out." Ramirez looked at the manhole entrance. "There are four men missing down there, Dr. Myers. I need to know what happened to them."

Myers nodded. "That's what your people told me when they called. I've brought equipment and canvas suits for three men. Who is going down there with me?"

"I am," said Ramirez. "The sergeant will come with us." He indicated the silent officer who stood a few yards away. "Bowker there used to collect snakes for a hobby. He volunteered."

Jeremy moved over and shook hands with the sergeant. "What did you collect?" he asked.

"Managed to get most of the Arizona and New Mexico species of rattlesnakes," he said casually. "Gave 'em to the zoo and sold a few out of state when my wife and I split up and I had to sell the house."

"Good to have you with us," said the doctor. "The equipment is over there in my van."

Ed followed the two across the street to the vehicle and listened as the men discussed catching snakes in various impossible circumstances, Myers while training to be a herpetologist and the sergeant while pursuing his hobby. They talked about rooting vipers out of caves, from behind and under rocks, and under woodpiles. The Lieutenant looked back over his shoulder and thought these circumstances seemed about as undersirable as he could imagine.

Jeremy handed each man an outfit similar to overalls made out of a tough canvas material. Over this went a heavy jacket that buttoned snugly at the wrists. Each put on a pair of heavy leather boots that zipped up tightly along the calf and rose to just under the knee. For a final touch, each donned a pair of thick leather gloves.

"No viper in Arizona can penetrate this material with his fangs," said the doctor. "They can't get much more than a couple of feet up off the ground in any case. Striking range is really quite limited for rattlers. Just be careful about anything up at shoulder or head level they might be lying on."

Sergent Bowker stretched and turned, testing the freedom of movement available.

"Nice fit," he said.

"I designed the suit myself," said Myers with a grin. "My assistant said I should look more stylish and professional."

The doctor turned and picked up a wooden case as well as some yard-long metal poles with hooked ends. He handed the box to Ramirez and the other pole to Bowker.

"Since the sergent has had experience," he said quietly, "he'll be able to handle the hook better than you would. You can carry the specimen box and the torch. Just do what I tell you and you'll be all right."

"Okay," Ed replied. "Let's get at it though. Those men could still be alive and in need of medical help."

Jeremy looked at Ramirez and placed a comforting hand on his shoulder.

"Don't be nervous, Lieutenant. You'll be safe with us."

"Let's go." Ed did not sound happy.

"Right enough," said the doctor as he grabbed the other hook.

The three men moved to the manhole and the others stepped back to make room.

Ed had his gunbelt on over the suit and checked the safety strap on the holster before approaching to the ladder.

Jeremy stepped in and put a restraining hand on his arm. "I go first, Lieutenant," he said. "From here on, you just follow carefully and watch my back."

The three men moved, one by one, down the ladder and out of sight.

Chapter Twenty-Two

Springerville, Arizona

After the announcement of the discovery of the catacombs and Native American ruins in April, the Springerville area became a hot-spot for archaeologists, anthropologists and thieves.

Whenever a discovery of such importance comes to light, those who can profit by it flock to it like vultures.

Security for the site became a nightmare.

The hillside lay pitted and honeycombed with caves, tunnels and entrances to the complex. Most had been dug centuries before when the settlement was inhabited. Numerous others had been opened through the years by the pot hunters, gold miners and other thieves of time who lived, like destructive parasites, off the wealth the ancient ones had left behind.

Luke Morton worked as a rent-a-cop, a licensed guard, imported to the area from Phoenix by the firm that had contracted to handle site security. Technically, he and his partner, Vern Maxwell, were employees of Bonded Alert. Actually, they took orders from Professor Renard of the university.

By mid-afternoon, they had patrolled the mile long expanse on the west side at least ten times on foot. Neither had a very high opinion of the arrangement.

"My dogs are killing me," said Luke as he sat down in the shade and unlaced his right boot. The temperature stayed cooler than in Phoenix—ninety degrees. Luke's uniform shirt had soaked through with perspiration.

"If the professor comes by and finds you sittin' on your ass," cautioned Vern, "he'll see to it that we don't have to walk this beat ever again."

"Don't worry about the bone man," chuckled Morton. "He's my brother-in-law."

"What?" Maxwell looked incredulous. "Are you telling me that Patty is his sister?"

"Yep. My little Patty comes from good stock, Vern." He removed his sock and massaged his toes. "I knew when I married her she'd provide a ticket."

"A ticket to what?"

"A better life, imbecile," retorted Luke. "I ain't always gonna be a security guard."

"Yeah, right." Maxwell spat into the dirt. "They're just waiting until after the holiday weekend to put you in charge of the whole project, right?"

"Don't get smart with me, Vern," said Morton. "I got you this job, didn't I?"

"Yeah, you did," said the other man. "I don't reckon I can hardly thank you enough either." He paused. "I been trying to decide how to express my appreciation, Luke. I was thinking that staking you out for two hours on an anthill at high noon might at least start to convey exactly how I feel."

Morton pulled his canteen out and sprinkled a little water over his toes. He sighed. "Come on, Vern. Lighten up. This isn't such a bad job. It isn't like we really have to do anything. We just walk around, look important, and collect our checks." He put his sock back on and stuck his foot in the boot. "And," he added, grunting as he laced it up, "Renard has already told me this is just temporary. He thinks he can get me put in charge of the supply yard."

"Jesus!" Vern laughed aloud. "Talk about putting the fox in charge of the hen house. Doesn't the dumb bastard realize you'll empty the place out in a week?"

Morton looked up under angry brows.

"Not so loud. You want him to hear?" He finished and stood up, testing the boot. "Everybody knows that a big project like this uses lots of supplies. Who's to know if a small portion of the stuff finds its way to the Apaches?"

Vern chuckled. "Just you make sure I get my cut, Luke."

"I always have," said Morton. "No reason to change things now, unless," he added, "your big mouth screws things up."

The two men moved off again. They walked along the hillside, looking for any signs of intruders or souvenir hunters. They had been patrolling for about ten minutes when they heard something.

"What the hell is that?" Vern pulled his pistol free of the holster and scanned the rock behind them.

"Sounded like somebody calling," said Luke. He pulled his own piece and checked the chamber to see if there was a round in place. "I think it came from up there." He pointed to an outcropping of rocks about half way up the hill.

"Shit." Maxwell looked unhappy. "I don't want to climb up there. It's too damned hot for mountain climbing."

"Oh, come on, Vern. We signed on for the job. Maybe we've got us some pot hunters. The contract says we get a bonus if we catch pot hunters in the act."

"I haven't heard anything else," protested Maxwell. "Maybe an animal?" He sat on a rock. "You check it out and I'll wait here."

"I'll flip you for it," suggested Luke, digging in his pocket for a coin. "Two quarters. Even match and I go alone. Odd match and you do it."

"You're on," agreed Vern, rising and patting his pockets, then shrugging. He held out his hand. "Gimme a quarter."

Three minutes later, Vern Maxwell climbed up the steep slope while Luke sat comfortably below.

"How do I let myself get talked into shit like this?" he asked himself under his breath. The sun shone high in the sky and the hillside rose sharply. Even the rocks were hot. His uniform was thoroughly drenched by the time he reached the spot. Dense stands of manzanita tore at his trousers and the loose talus shifted under his feet until he finally found solid footing.

The rocks clustered in a fan-shape and, as he rounded the southern end of the formation, he saw a shadow behind it. Quickly he moved into it, leaning back against a large boulder and taking a kerchief from his pocket to mop his brow.

As he leaned back, he noticed khaki colored material just protruding into his line of sight from behind the cluster. He moved forward cautiously.

He recognized the brim of a hat—but not just any hat. It belonged to their boss, Dr. Renard. The archaeologist appeared to be crouched over a boulder, his jaunty bush hat pulled down over his eyes.

Vern approached cautiously, reaching out to grab the professor's shoulder. "Hey Renard," he asked, "what gives?"

The figure under his hand twitched, but said nothing.

Vern moved a step closer to get a better grip and felt himself falling. Hidden in the shadow was a deep crevice. The professor had not been crouched over the boulder but his legs and feet were in the hole and his body stretched upward in what must have been a desperate, last-minute attempt to escape.

Maxwell clutched frantically at Renard's clothing but fell the two feet into the cleft anyway.

Shrill rattling greeted him.

The three snakes struck him several times.

Shocked, he did not even cry out at first. Instead, he managed to say only, "Oh, Shit!" By the time he thought of Luke waiting below, his legs felt like they were on fire and his shout seemed to have no effect.

"Christ! Luke!" he yelled. "I'm a dead man."

In two minutes, long before Morton could reach him, he had become a martyred prophet.

Chapter Twenty-Three

City of Phoenix

As he moved down the ladder into the utility tunnel, Dr. Jeremy Myers wondered what the hell had happened. First, there had been the specimen from Mad Jake. That business with the hand and forearm had complicated his life. The FBI had actually come over and fingerprinted the damned thing before bagging it and taking it away. They asked a lot of questions about Roberts before leaving, keeping Myers for an unusually long time from his necessary business. Fortunately, Rachel had been able to do what needed doing so the only real loss could be chalked up to inconvenience and interrupted routine.

There had been no time as yet to conduct tests, but indications were that the venom sample would prove more potent than any Jeremy had ever encountered, and the snake had been exhibiting unusual behavior since its arrival.

The doctor had already, at the insistence of the police, been called in to test bodies at the morgue—including the two young victims from McBurger's and the Circle K clerk. No doubt remained. The fatal bites had been administered by rattlesnakes and the venom appeared unusually fast-acting and lethal.

Now there were snakes under the Phoenix streets. It just didn't make sense. What could have brought rattlesnakes into the Phoenix utility system? It had to be related to the tremor at the end of June, but what could have turned these normally reclusive creatures into aggressive killers?

"Better get your mind on your feet, doc," said Bowker from the top of the ladder. "You're about to step on a bunch of 'em."

Jeremy looked down and saw that the sergeant spoke wisely. The three big diamondback rattlers had already drawn up into the large, S-shaped loop that is the species trademark.

Why should they be ready to strike? He and his companions were still a good distance up the ladder. Given the dusky quality of the light and the still air, the snakes shouldn't even be aware of them as yet. And what the hell were diamondbacks doing down here anyway?

"Lieutenant," said Myers calmly, "please open the case and hand me one of the muslin sacks you'll find inside. These are beautiful specimens and I'll need one for testing."

Ramirez did not reply but, after a moment, the bag fluttered down and landed on Jeremy's head. The herpetologist took it and descended slowly to the floor level, stepping carefully so as to avoid injuring the vipers. All three struck at once, only to be thwarted by the heavy canvas safety suit.

Using the hook, he pinned the nearest rattler, ignoring the other two. He deftly grabbed it and firmly grasped the head. The snake began to thrash violently, as if it knew its fate, and Jeremy had to hold on with both hands.

Bowker quickly joined him at the base of the ladder and moved carefully up to the doctor's side. He took the bag from where it had fallen and opened it.

Using both hands, Myers inserted the snake and let go, effectively letting it drop into the sack. "Thank you, sergeant."

"Reminds me of childhood," he replied with a grin.

Within the bag, the snake exploded into a fury, lashing about and twisting around in a last desperate bid for freedom. Bowker tied off the bag and set it to the side.

"I've never seen a diamondback in the city," he commented as he used his hook to turn a second snake aside. It had struck four times at his leg, probably injuring its mouth. The third rattler had already turned and started moving north up the tunnel.

"Which direction are we heading, Lieutenant?" Meyers asked.

No immediate answer came back and both he and Bowker turned to look at Ramirez.

Ed had stopped about halfway down the ladder, white knuckles clutching the rungs, eyes screwed shut. He did not appear to be listening.

"Lieutenant Ramirez?" Jeremy spoke loudly enough to be heard, but his tone was understanding. "It's safe to come the rest of the way down now."

One eye opened and Ed looked around the base of the ladder. Bowker had hooked the second snake and lifted it away, depositing it three yards further on. It finally turned and followed the other up the tunnel.

With careful deliberation, the lieutenant eased his death grip on the ladder and took a deep breath, steeling himself. He came down slowly, every movement betraying his fear.

When he stood on the tunnel floor, he turned a pale face to the doctor and, struggling for control, said, "I've always been afraid of snakes, Dr. Myers. The fu . . . uh, the damned things give me the willies. I'll try to stay out of your way."

Jeremy put a comforting hand on his shoulder and said, "I understand entirely, Lieutenant. You're doing fine. Just don't pull out that gun and start shooting the place up, all right?"

In fact, Ed had been struggling against his impulse to draw the revolver since starting down the ladder. He knew better, but his fear argued powerfully with common sense.

Ramirez took another deep breath. It helped. He pushed the transmit button on his radio and said, "We're down at the base of the ladder. We've encountered at least three poisonous reptiles. Dr. Myers has captured a specimen. We're going to move on up the tunnel now. Ramirez out." He visibly took control of himself and pointed north.

"We go that way, according to the crew chief."

"I'll lead," said Myers. "You follow behind me Lieutenant. Sergeant, please bring up the rear."

"Yes sir," replied Bowker.

For the first time since entering the tunnel, Jeremy had a chance to actually look at it. The dim lighting was due to the infrequency of emergency torches mounted where each pipe section joined. The next one forward did not work and the one beyond lay nearly sixty feet ahead. The overhead strips were all out. He noticed something strange about the footing, too.

The entire length they could see ahead seemed suffused with a red and cloudy glow that came from somewhere beyond the range of their vision. It looked smoky, but nothing they could see indicated gas or fire.

"Check to make sure you have your masks," suggested Myers. "I don't think we'll need them, but each of you be sure you can put it on with a moment's notice."

The other two men checked their belts and patted the gas masks that hung there. The doctor did the same.

"We're ready, Doctor Myers," said Ramirez. Privately, he thought about how he would gladly sell his left testicle if he just didn't have to go any further into this damned tunnel.

"All right," said Jeremy. "We aren't out for a jog. I'll go very slowly and keep up a steady stream of chatter. Stay a few paces back and don't crowd me. The three snakes we saw on the way in may be all there were."

"Crew Chief reported sighting six, sir," said Bowker.

"Maybe he was wrong." Ed wanted very much for Blanton to have been mistaken.

"Let's go." Myers moved off at a leisurely pace and Ramirez matched it. Bowker came last. The reason the footing felt strange soon became apparent. The bottom of the tunnel was covered in a thin coating of mud. It sucked at their boots and made hollow squelching noises as they walked. It also made them extra careful. None of the three men liked the idea of slipping and falling.

The utility tunnels under Phoenix's city streets are not like subway tunnels. The reinforced concrete pipes are twelve feet in diameter, manufactured in thirty foot lengths. If facing north, a maintenance man would see the phone lines running along the right side about shoulder high and the power lines running along the left side starting at waist height. In the bottom is a recessed channel for runoff in case of flooding.

No one spoke.

The herpetologist saw many more snakes than the six reported. He counted a dozen as his eyes adjusted to the dim glow.

He saw diamondbacks (*crotalus atrox*), mohaves (*crotalus scutatus*), blacktails (*crotalus mollossus*), and rock rattlers (*crotalus lepidus*). None of them should have been there. Some shouldn't even have been in this part of the state. They were there, however, and the doctor noted that they were all moving north in a hurry, as if in flight.

The presence of four species in a twelve foot diameter pipe struck Jeremy as so unusual he could hardly accept the evidence of his own senses.

"Have you ever seen anything like this, Sergeant?" he asked without looking back.

The calm cool voice of Bowker replied without hesitation from a dozen feet behind. "Nope. Beats the hell out of me. Where could they have come from?"

Myers did not reply but quickened his pace. The snakes moved even more swiftly.

Entering the next segment of tunnel, the herpetologist felt his footing give slightly when he stepped on the place where the pipes should have joined. The gap looked small but noticeable. The next thirty feet of pipe had shifted and the far end had risen slightly. It probably did not amount to a foot of difference over the whole length, but it created an obvious incline and more mud. This segment showed no lights at all.

"Watch your step," he cautioned. "The pipe has separated and elevates gradually from here on." He turned on the bright flashlight he carried in his left hand. The hook remained in his right.

Ahead, the tunnel appeared to grow smaller. It took a moment to realize that the difference resulted from the rising level underfoot. It looked as if there had been a sudden surge of mud and water at the far end, filling the bottom part of the pipe with more than two feet of silt and mud.

"There must be a major breach up there," said the doctor. "There's too much debris."

Ed Ramirez struggled against freaking out. He could see two dozen serpents slithering along the floor of the tunnel. The fact that they were all moving away quickly brought no solace. The constant movement created strange, undulating shadows under the harsh glare of his flash. He felt his lunch rumbling as it threatened to rise into his throat. His hand shook as it rested constantly on the grip of his gun. The leather safety strap of the holster had been unhooked.

Again they moved forward. Myers walked at an easy pace, his body appearing deceptively relaxed. The lieutenant followed six paces back, his fear under control but insistent. The sergeant remained a bulwark at the rear, cool and competent.

Their passage through the unlighted segment went much more quickly. The snakes moved north ahead of them and none seemed inclined to stop.

"It's like they know," murmured Jeremy to himself.

"Atypical behavior," said Bowker from behind. "It's like they were following orders or something. None of my snakes ever did things like this. Hell, they would have been off in all directions. These are moving like an army in retreat."

As they approached the other end of the pipe, the next segment came into view. In addition to one emergency light at the far end, other lights could be seen in tight beams that crossed each other at weird angles.

"Flashlights," said Ramirez. "Or helmet lamps. Those have to be three of the torches used by the crew."

This part of the pipe lay wildly askew, turning sharply to the left and rising even more. Where it should have joined the darkened portion of the tunnel they just came through, the separation gaped four feet wide. Here lay the source of the mud. The wall of earth revealed when the pipe had been torn away wept a stinky gout of soil, sand and effluent.

Jeremy looked ahead but something even more wrong loomed at the other end. The tunnel opened into a red smoky mist. Nothing could be seen beyond.

"I don't like this," said the lieutenant quietly, amazed that his voice worked at all. The first flashlight shone just three yards ahead and the doctor, still in the lead, moved toward it. Before him, the floor of the tunnel rose steadily and the thick noxious mud made the footing hazardous at best.

Jeremy bent and retrieved the light. Then he saw the first body.

It lay in a crumpled heap, it's posture so unnatural that it looked like a carnival mirror reflection of a human being. When the doctor reached over to take the wrist and check for a pulse, the clothing moved. Withdrawing his hand and switching to the hook, Jeremy prodded the spot and saw the lumpy material shift again.

That upset the delicate balance that had held the body in position. It slid around in a slow, almost graceful, turn. What remained of the face became visible. Even Myers let out a gasp when he saw the ruin.

Ed Ramirez took one look and spun to the side, finally losing that lunch in a surprisingly dramatic arc of vomit.

Even the stolid Bowker sucked in his breath audibly.

As the body completed its shift in response to the prodding and gravity, a large diamondback glided smoothly out of the sleeve and moved off toward the red smokiness ahead. Almost immediately, another exited the corpse through a hole in the throat.

The face had become a swollen, putruscent mass that no longer bore any resemblance to human form. The fingers on both hands were missing. The body slumped in a particularly boneless way that made Ramirez turn away and try to empty his stomach again.

Bowker stepped up and carefully removed a wallet from the hip pocket. Flipping it open, he read the name on the driver's license.

"Millston," he intoned.

"Let's move on," said Myers. "There are three others unaccounted for. We'll collect Mr. Millston on our way back."

Ed wiped his mouth with a handkerchief, then thumbed the button on his radio. "This is Ramirez. We've found one body. We're moving ahead to search for the others." He released the button and turned. "Sorry," he said in a mumble. "I've seen worse—both in Nam and in the street—but to have it be snakes, it just makes me fu . . . uh, crazy."

"I've been working with snakes professionally damned near all my life," said Jeremy. "I've never seen anything like that either. It's just inconceivable to me that there could be so much deterioration in . . ." he glanced at his watch . . . "a little over two and a half hours since the first report." He looked over at their third companion. "What do you think Bowker? Have you ever encountered venom this destructive?"

The sergeant shook his head. "Nope," he said. "I've been bit twice and got treatment right away. I lost a little off my pinky finger here, but that's all." He held his gloved hand up and pointed to the spot. "I'd show it to you, but I'm not taking these covers off until we get out of here."

"Let's find the others," said the doctor. He turned and led the way toward the far end of the pipe, his light revealing still more snakes that slithered along the tunnel floor and then disappeared when they reached the limit of sight.

The reddish glow and the oddly crossed flashlight beams ahead gave no clue as to what lay beyond the lip of the pipe.

Ed Ramirez busied himself with a gut check. He felt embarrassed and angry at himself for appearing the least professional of the three. He took a few deep breaths and then followed after Myers.

"I don't understand why they're all running away," said Jeremy over his shoulder. "With these numbers, one would think there'd be a few overly aggressive individuals who'd turn and attack."

"It's like they learned after the first three tried it," said Bowker. Then he waved his hands in a negative gesture. "No, that's ridiculous. They aren't that smart. That's just my imagination talking. Forget I said it."

"No," said Ramirez, surprised to find his voice clear and strong. "You're right. It doesn't make sense, but they act as if they all learned from the first ones."

"They don't think that way," said Myers quietly. "They rarely work together. They're sensitive to smells, including fear enzymes and pheromones in the air—subtle things. They sense the chemicals our bodies exude when we're afraid, or angry, and they can get excited, but I've never heard of them passing on experience to others like that."

"Then explain what we're seeing, Dr. Myers," said Ramirez in a challenging tone. "I know you're the expert, but these fu . . . uh, bastards are doing just exactly what you said they can't be doing."

Jeremy had continued moving forward toward the far end of the segment. As he stepped up onto a small clump of mud, it suddenly shifted, revealing itself to be another diamondback that had been playing possum. The doctor flailed his arms for a second, trying to regain his balance, and then fell. The snake turned in an instant and tried to strike at Myers' face.

The shot echoed loudly in the close surroundings.

The snake flew back at the impact of a bullet that demolished its head.

Jeremy looked up to see Ed, pistol still smoking in his hand, frozen into classic shooting position—like the opening of a James Bond film. He partly crouched and turned slightly to the side, the revolver rock steady and still pointed at the target.

As he scrambled to his feet, the herpetologist could not help looking back at the twisted body that had been the Millston fellow. He nodded at the lieutenant.

"Thanks," he managed.

"Don't mention it," replied Ed, breaking into a grin. "I needed to know the fu . . . uh, the bastards can die."

The three men moved forward and found themselves at the end of the pipe. The reason they had not been able to see beyond it became clear immediately.

The ground dropped away sharply to reveal a huge cavern. They braced themselves as best they could and peered over the edge.

The reddish glow rose from mud-covered emergency lamps whose batteries had not yet died. At least two full sections of pipe had fallen inward, and lay twenty-five feet below like big, gray pasta noodles.

"Jesus Christ!" exclaimed the doctor.

"Son of a bitch!" said Bowker.

"Aw, fu . . . uh, shit!" added Ramirez.

"There are the other three," said the sargeant, pointing almost directly below.

"Do you suppose they could be . . . ?"

Ed didn't finish his question because he saw one of the bodies roll as dozens of snakes wriggled over or under it. The walls of the cavern writhed with squirming serpents.

"Are you seeing what I'm seeing?" asked Jeremy.

"I wouldn't have believed it possible," stated Bowker. "How could so many snakes gets down here in the first place?"

Ed looked from one to the other, unable to believe his ears, then shouted his frustration at them.

"For Christ's sake! You guys are the experts."

"Calm down, Lieutenant," said Myers in a quiet voice. "I'm an expert in handling and studying snakes. I've tracked them in their habitats and caught them under all sorts of conditions." He shook his head. "I have never seen so many individuals in one place. I have never seen so many different species together at one time, except in a lab or a zoo. This is as unique an experience for me as it is for you."

A fat mohave rattler chose that moment to make his break right between Ed's feet as the man crouched in the tunnel. It slithered over the edge without striking and quickly slid down the sharp incline.

Ramirez tried to stand but lost his balance and swayed forward. Only Bowker's quick grab of his belt saved Ed from tumbling over the lip of the pipe and falling to where the three bodies lay below.

"Easy," said the sergeant.

The Lieutenant swallowed audibly and moved carefully back from the edge. He had gone sickly pale. "Jesus!" he muttered. "Too close!"

Myers and Bowker both turned toward him.

"What do you want to do next, Lieutenant?" asked the doctor. "We can report that there are no survivors of the crew of four. Did you want to retrieve the bodies now?"

Ed couldn't believe his ears.

"Are you fu . . . uh, are you completely insane?" he asked in a much more shrill voice than he intended. "Are you suggesting we go down there?"

The sergeant's tone was eminently calm and reasonable. "Someone has to, Lieutenant," he said. "The next of kin aren't going to understand why we'd leave those poor bastards lying down there."

"But the place is crawling with snakes, Bowker!" Ed protested. He turned back to Myers. "Is there some way to exterminate them? Can we set the sonsabitches on fire or something?"

Jeremy turned back and looked down over the edge of the pipe.

"That may not be necessary," he remarked thoughtfully. "Look. They're moving off into that hole—all of them."

"What?" Ramirez momentarily forgot his fear and stepped back to the opening. A steady stream of snakes made its way toward a dark, unusually round hole that lay below on the right. "Where the hell does that lead?" he asked aloud.

"There's one way to find out," said Myers.

Ramirez stepped back from the opening and faced the doctor squarely. "There is no way in hell that I'm going down into that pit," he said, enunciating clearly. "Nor am I going to let you or the sergeant go down there until it is thoroughly cleared of those snakes." He stopped, waiting for a reply.

"I'm a volunteer," said Jeremy. "I am, as you so aptly put it, the expert here. I can go down there, tie lines around the bodies so we can haul them up, and, incidentally, check that opening below to see where it leads." He stood up and moved close to the lieutenant, his face directly before the other's.

Ramirez did not remember that Myers had been so tall. He hesitated a moment, then sighed loudly. "I gotta call it in," he said. "I don't want the responsibility."

"Do what you have to do, Lieutenant." Jeremy turned back to the tunnel mouth. "Bowker," he said, "give me that line we brought."

Ed called and spoke to the Captain.

"What's going on down there, Lieutenant?" asked Ryan.

Ed explained the situation, concluding with, "The doctor insists on going down there after the bodies. I've explained that we will not be responsible under the circumstances, but he is determined to go on anyway. I advise against it, Captain."

The pause lasted only a moment.

"Better let him go ahead," said Ryan. Then, in a more confidential tone, he added, "I don't like it either, Ed, but there're reporters all over the place up here. The crowd keeps getting bigger. We have no choice. We've got to pull them out."

The lieutenant sighed deeply, then shrugged. "Acknowledged," he replied. Releasing the transmit button, he looked at the doctor again. "Okay," he said, "it looks like my opinion doesn't count. You get it your way. The sergeant and I will brace up here and lower you down. For God's sake, be careful. I don't want to have to come after you. If you fall, the snakes will be all over you. Then we'd have to recover five bodies instead of four."

Myers grinned, his face lit by the reddish glow from below. "I have no intention of falling, Lieutenant," he said. "I know what needs to be done and I won't be long about it. I'll run lines to each of the three bodies and then slip over quietly to look at that hole." He looked over the edge, then shrugged, as if climbing down would be only a casual stroll. "It should take less than five minutes."

"I have a stop-watch function on this wristwatch," said Ramirez. "I'm going to time you. Bowker and me will start hauling you back up here on the tick whether you're ready or not."

"I understand," Jeremy answered. He turned and stepped to the lip.

"Myers," said Bowker. "Be careful down there."

The doctor grinned back. "Every inch of the way, brother. You can set that in stone."

Ed and the sergeant braced themselves in the tunnel mouth as Jeremy stepped off the edge onto the sharp muddy slope leading down.

Chapter Twenty-Four

Casa Malpais, Springerville

By the time Luke Morton reported the death of Professor Renard and his friend, Vern, the state of Arizona had been primed and readied to blow itself apart in real panic. His call to the police had been monitored by the press and exploded into the newspapers and over the air with all the subtlety of an atomic bomb.

The archaeological site called Casa Malpais, the Badland's House, had already been news, earning a front page story in the Arizona Republic on April 27th. The announcement of the expedition's discoveries at the conference in New Orleans had captured the public's imagination. These new developments made it even more mysterious and newsworthy. Now it had the equivalent of the Curse of the Pharaohs for added spice.

"SCIENTIST DIES AFTER DESECRATING TOMBS!"

The catacombs occupied a fifteen-acre stone pueblo on a rocky hillside. They contained ceremonial chambers built underground hundreds of years before. The Mogollons had lived in it for about a thousand years, abandoning the complex at least six hundred years before. The "Badlands House" is unique in the archaeology of the southwest.

The settlement features three-story masonry pueblos, stone staircases and sacred chambers. Carefully hidden entrances vary in size from large doorways to small crawlspaces.

Underground there are three to four acres of known catacombs ranging from small chambers to spaces fifty feet high and one hundred feet long.

The archaeologists who discovered and now explored the site predicted they would find something else underground, a major surprise. They had been enigmatic, however, in explaining what they expected to find.

The death of the head of the project along with a security guard—both due to snakebite—propelled the dig into the public eye and complicated the lives of all involved.

Luke Morton became an instant celebrity. He took his opportunity and ran with it, calling a press conference that lasted over an hour. He took a pool of reporters to the site and re-enacted his coin toss with Vern, his climb up the hillside to discover the bodies, the return to base and his call to the police.

Luke, shortly thereafter, became unemployed.

Dr. Margot Shayley, Renard's successor, expressed displeasure with the intrusion of so many outsiders into the quiet and academic atmosphere of the dig. She did not like, but understood, the delicate situation the project had blundered into. She cooperated like a cat— just barely—and then brought in double the normal security force and shut the site down.

All reports were required to pass across her desk and did. None of them made any progress from there.

She let it be known that Morton had been fired for opening his mouth to the wrong people. In the touchy, sensitive, paranoid world of academia, the subtle threat sufficed. No further interviews involved anyone connected to the project.

However, it took little time before the press put the deaths of Renard and Maxwell together with the children at McBurger's and the Circle K clerk. The ongoing story about the US WEST Crew and the rescue operation refocussed the attention on Phoenix. Shayley's silence and the unwillingness of anyone else connected to Casa Malpais to speak accomplished Margot's design. The press moved on.

"POLICE WARN PUBLIC—WATCH FOR SNAKES!"

Chapter Twenty-Five

City of Phoenix

Jeremy stepped off the edge of the pipe with a smile still playing on his lips. His expression lied.

This descent into the pit was the most foolish, stupid, senseless, dangerous thing he had ever done in his life. Worse, he knew it.

His heart thumped at twice its normal rate. He sweated profusely, though no one could have seen it through the heavy canvas suit. He fully expected to die.

The rope played out between his fingers, the leather gloves keeping a neat and firm grip on the line. The side of the cavern was coated in mud, but he found better footing than expected. The chamber had rock sides and the slime resulted from the breakage of pipes and what smelled suspiciously like effluent.

Below him, he could see literally hundreds of rattlesnakes streaking downward toward the darkness of the hole in the cavern floor. The opening looked remarkably symmetrical as he drew closer.

Mindful of his mission, he came to rest on the nearly level floor of the chamber next to the first of the bodies. One glance told him this particular victim was dead. The swollen features and completely boneless posture of the corpse left no doubt.

Privately, he hoped the man had not suffered. Death by snakebite is a particularly hideous way to die. The venom attacks the nervous system like a fire raging unchecked. The muscles dance as they are destroyed by the enzymes and consciousness does not flee immediately. Every excruciating moment is lived by the victim. Little can be done to ease the pain except to administer a nerve blocking agent—the same agent often used by obstetricians to ease the pain of delivery, a saddle block.

Jeremy had once been bitten by a rattler and walked a full two miles for transportation to the hospital. After his arrival, the outraged nerves had constricted the arteries in his right arm and cut off circulation. He almost lost the limb. Only the application of the block by an OB-GYN who happened to be there prevented on-the-spot amputation. The huge needle had been thrust into his armpit nine times before it found the nerve. He did not have to tell the doctor when the goal had been attained. His screams could be heard through the entire floor.

He would never forget.

The corpse had already begun to decay as the fast-acting venom broke down the flesh into an oozing, shapeless, ugly, open sore. As a human being, he felt horrified, but the herpetologist felt a terrible sadness well up inside him. The snakes would be hunted and killed for this. The strange and alien reptile minds would be stilled, crushed in anger. *There must be a reason.*

After tying one of the lines to the corpse's legs, he moved to the next. This man, too, was dead. The third proved no different.

When the retrieval lines had been hooked up, the doctor glanced at his watch. He still had a minute and thirty seconds before being hauled back himself.

He checked the ground around him and, surprisingly, saw no trace of the rattlers. Moving slowly and carefully, so as not to lose his footing, he crossed the muddy floor of the cavern and approached the gaping hole through which the serpents had apparently all disappeared.

He felt a sense of awe.

It led downward, sides cut with surgical precision—no curve or irregularity marred its perfection, as if something incredibly hot had melted it while passing through. It looked, in fact, as if the tunnel wall had been coated with glass and then instantly cooled.

As the doctor approached the edge, he heard . . . something. He found it impossible to describe. It might have been a hiss of serpents, or a distant throb, or even a tone created by air currents. It sounded eerie and strange and . . . disconcerting.

Then the first gentle tugs reminded him that he must return.

The ascent up the slope proved not nearly as difficult as the descent had been. No serpents could be seen, though Jeremy looked carefully every step of the way.

Once up and back into the pipe, Myers helped the others haul the bodies of the fallen out of the pit and laid them out on the tunnel floor.

A second crew had been sent down and soon reached them.

The new men saw no sign of snakes.

Bowker, however, remembered to retrieve the muslin sack with the diamondback specimen still inside.

The bodies were tied to stretchers and lifted, one at a time, through the manhole.

The police used extreme care in removing the remains. Some of the relatives had already gathered on the street above. The rest of the crowd closed in, hoping for a glimpse of gore.

When Jeremy finally climbed out into the light of the afternoon, he looked at his watch in disbelief.

The entire episode had taken less than ninety minutes from start to finish. It had seemed much longer than that.

Ramirez looked relieved. Bowker, as before, remained quiet and taciturn, a competent professional who had simply done his job.

Reporters fired questions at the doctor, but he shrugged them off and headed for his car, the specimen in the muslin bag held tightly at his side.

The police let him leave but prevented anyone from following. Captain Ryan asked him to call the station when his tests of the rattler had been completed.

Jeremy nodded, then started his vehicle and drove off.

July 4th

Chapter Twenty-Six

Cibeque, Apacheland

That holiday morning, George Buck had awakened early in his Cibeque apartment. Something felt different, but, at first, he did not know what. He lay there trying to sort it out. The feeling seemed familiar and his confusion lasted only a moment.

The voice in his head spoke clearly, "Good morning, Red Cloud."

Undisturbed by the experience, as many others might have been, he spoke aloud in a tone of welcome and respect. "Is that you, Goyathlay?"

"It is, my brother-self."

George took a deep breath, then looked suddenly alert. "You used my war name. Has something happened?"

"Yes, Red Cloud," said Geronimo. "I believe it is time for us to become Gerry again. We are needed."

Buck sat up in bed. "I started packing last night," he said, "getting ready for the reunion in Phoenix. I drive first to pick up Gordon Smythe in Springerville. His cousin will drop him there."

The inner voice answered with a certain amount of humor. "Did you think you were going to make the trip alone?"

"Of course," said George with a chuckle. "I am always alone . . . just you and I. It is only necessary that I remember not to speak to myself aloud when others are near. People grow extremely curious when that happens."

George Buck remembered being Geronimo in his previous life. Everyone knew he believed it. He had never heard his other persona as a separate voice, however, until the previous summer. Then the other had first spoken in his mind.

The great chief had been called forth by the release of the demon. George's physical body had passed over into the control of the medicine man, his consciousness relegated to the status of observer.

Later, necessity had dictated that the modern man reacquire control and, from then on, the two personalities had functioned as a team. "Gerry" had been the name they decided to use. It symbolized their dual personality.

The older self had remained always present since then, but this conversation brought forth the first words Goyathlay had spoken since the destruction of the beast.

"Another thing from the past has come into our world," said Geronimo in his mind. "It is not the wind demon, but something even more destructive."

"What is this thing?" asked George as he rose and moved toward the bathroom.

"I am not sure," answered his other self. "It is ancient beyond my experience, older by far than the beast."

"How do you know?" George felt frankly curious. He lifted the seat and relieved himself.

He sensed a moment of uncertainty, a hesitation very unlike the sure thoughts of the old soul that had been Geronimo.

"I have no clear image of the creature," said his other self. "It is ancient and powerful but somehow . . . innocent."

"Innocent?"

"Even more than the demon," said Geronimo. "At least the demon had dealt with men before."

"Of course it had," agreed George. "It had preyed on the villages of our people for close to a hundred years."

"But this is different," said his other self. "I sense that it . . . whatever it is . . . has no such experience of men . . . as if it has always been alone."

George looked into the mirror. He saw no indication in his face of the other personality's presence.

Geronimo's voice continued, lost in some inner seeing that his modern day self could not share. "This . . . creature . . . is consumed by loneliness, lost in a desolation I cannot identify . . . dark . . . "

"And you don't know what kind of creature it is?"

"I cannot see," replied the inner voice. "It is as if it has no image of itself."

"But you can hear its thoughts?"

Another hesitation. "No," came the reply. "I can sense the feelings but not the thoughts. It is difficult to explain. This thing appears to be without language as we know it."

George combed his hair and spoke easily, as if Geronimo were another person physically present. "Is it aware of you . . . uh, of us?" he asked.

"I do not think so," said his other self. "I think it is capable of communicating with us, but I do not sense that it even recognizes us as intelligent."

Buck returned to the bedroom and began to dress as he asked, "What should we do?"

This time he heard no hesitation at all.

"We must warn the others."

"Warn them of what?"

"This thing," said Geronimo, "seeks domination over the earth. It has already begun to do . . . something. I cannot see what."

"One of the others will know," said George. "I'd be willing to bet that there's nothing the gathering can't handle."

"Do not be so confident," replied his elder self. "We may not be so lucky this time."

Finished dressing, George picked up his bag and moved to the front of the apartment. "Is that everything?" he asked, as much of himself as . . .well, himself.

The inner voice did not answer.

George Buck shrugged and went out, securing the door behind him. Tossing the bag in the rear of the car he had rented for the trip, he started the engine and drove off, headed east toward Springerville.

Chapter Twenty-Seven

Phoenix, Arizona

The Fourth of July had been designated by President Bush as a special holiday for welcoming home the troops from the Gulf War. It offered a day of parades and celebration, a day of thanksgiving—a day where old wounds could be healed. Arizona had its own proud contingent of vets who showed up both to be honored and to enjoy the party.

That is what should have been. Instead, the populace awoke to panic.

The headlines in the *Arizona Republic* screamed, "SNAKES SLAY FOUR!" The *Phoenix Gazette* would follow later in the afternoon with "US WEST CREW LOST!"

There were articles about rattlesnakes, including a gruesome rehash of the McBurger's deaths and the Circle K killing. A feature article dealt with Dr. Renard and the security guard, Maxwell. Fully a third of each newspaper had been devoted to the sudden rise of incidents involving snakes.

The press could not be blamed. News, as they say, is news.

With relish akin to the lambasting of a former Arizona governor named Mecham, the newspapers waded into the fray with gusto and inventiveness.

The welcome home parade down Central had been planned to start at Northern Boulevard but the newly discovered cavern under the street forced it to move south. The designated replacement starting point became Missouri Avenue. This shortened the route—and the parade—and made the staging area a confused mess. It had been impossible for the city to reach all the participants and, despite radio and TV announcements, half the bands and floats still tried to reach Northern. Since the intersection had been closed, traffic backed up in all directions.

The closing would have been complicated enough with normal traffic. With the parade participants appearing on the scene as well, the strain quickly reached the breaking point. The headlines in the newspapers, far from keeping people away, drew the curious in even greater numbers.

Then the vipers came forth.

Every gutter along the street gave birth to wriggling serpents. Rattlesnakes of all kinds came out of the sewers and attempted to attack the onlookers without provocation.

Because they had listened to the warnings, many of the crowd were armed. Arizona is still a frontier state in many ways. One can carry an unconcealed holstered weapon in plain sight. The only time it can be used, however, is when life is threatened.

No one doubted lives were threatened.

The intersection of Northern and Central erupted into gunfire that sounded for all the world like . . . well, like the Fourth of July.

Incredibly, no people were hurt—other than old Beatrice Bonillie. She lost her great toe when Arnold Bonillie, her son, missed his first shot at the diamondback about to strike her. The second shot did not miss.

A count of the carcasses tallied one hundred seventy-three snakes killed on the street. The rest had apparently retreated back down into the sewers.

The police roundup report showed that six hundred armed men and women stood among those gathered at the intersection. Every one of them could proudly demonstrate how he or she had gotten at least one shot off. Half were military personnel.

No police charges were filed and not even one of the weapons was confiscated.

The Maricopa County Coroner reported late that afternoon that the death of Barbara Belasco had been due to snakebite, not the traffic accident first reported.

The next door neighbor of Agnes Littlebaum had smelled something peculiar while out in the yard. Entering the unlocked front door, she had encountered a huge rattlesnake that exited without attacking right after the door opened. Later, medical authorites theorized it simply had eaten its fill.

Exploring the house, she found the badly decomposed body of the old woman in the bathroom. With all the news coverage, she had no doubt about what happened. Though it would have been convenient to use the phone in the house, she could not remain there with the body and the stench. She called the police from her own phone after returning home.

Friday's headlines were assured.

Chapter Twenty-Eight

Phoenix

Arriving at Sky Harbor in Phoenix presented a new experience to Geraldo Vasquez. The Zuni Priest had no way to know, of course, but his sense of wonder at the white man and his works echoed those felt by his predecessor almost exactly a year before. The late Pasqual Quatero had taken the same flight.

For Geraldo, who had never flown before, it had been an ordeal he would not soon forget. The loud roaring of the engines, the force of motion pressing him back in his seat, the hum of machinery all around—it had set his nerves on edge like fingernails scraping across a blackboard.

The plane had been crowded, the people loud and rude. Not until a flight attendant noticed his white knuckles did anyone express concern or offer a kind word. Even that sounded perfunctory.

He debarked the plane with a deep feeling of relief—a feeling that lasted only seconds—then looked around. The sudden press of other human beings weighed on him like the walls of a small room. Geraldo had never been so close to so many other living creatures in his life. All through his youth and early manhood, he had stayed safely within the confines of Zuniland. This unique experience at once awed and terrified him.

Having no luggage but his single carry-on bag, he fled the terminal as if pursued. Once outside, he stood under the hot sun, waiting for the ride that had been promised.

A hand tapped him tentatively on the shoulder and it cost Geraldo no little effort to turn slowly and casually around instead of jumping into the air.

He saw a tall, older Indian with a calm face, dressed in a short-sleeved summer shirt and jeans.

"Pardon me," said the stranger. "My name is Kade Wonto of the Maricopa. If you are Geraldo Vasquez of the Zuni, I am your ride to the home of our host."

A small voice in the Zuni's head spoke quietly saying, "It has begun." Geraldo smiled. "I am that one," he replied. "I am here to represent my people at your gathering."

"Our gathering, my brother," corrected Kade gently. "You will see, as Pasqual did before you. We are all of the medicine way." He paused, then added, "Welcome to Phoenix."

Vasquez said nothing, but nodded.

"Have you any other luggage?" asked the Maricopa.

"No, this is enough," said Geraldo.

Kade shrugged, turned and pointed to a blue sedan parked a few yards down the drive. "My wife, Estelle, will drive," he explained, "otherwise we would be forever in getting out of here."

The Zuni followed Kade to the car, handed over his bag and watched the older man load it into the trunk. The Maricopa then opened the rear door and gestured for him to enter.

The car felt cool and the woman at the wheel turned and flashed a warm smile. "Welcome, Geraldo Vasquez," she said.

"Thank you," he replied.

Kade got in the other rear door and sat in the back with their guest. He sighed as he closed the door and relished the air-conditioning.

"Phoenix in July is like an oven," he commented. "I wish you could have been here in April and May when Spring blessed us like this every day."

Geraldo looked out the window. He could see the heat rising in waves off the pavement. Many wilted travelers had shucked their suitcoats and stood waiting for cabs.

"Thank you for meeting me," he said. "I have never been here before. It is all quite confusing."

"We will soon be at the home of Tom Bear," said Kade, as Estelle pulled away from the curb and wove expertly through the traffic. "We are fortunate that we do not have to cross the parade route. There has been considerable excitement there today."

Even with the windows closed, the noise from outside seemed loud to Geraldo's ears. Kade had spoken in his usual soft voice so the Zuni did not really hear. He elected not to ask the man to repeat himself.

Estelle sensed the awkward silence in the back and spoke over her shoulder. "How was your flight?"

"Fine," lied Vasquez. He wished the two of them would be quiet and leave him alone to look at the white man's city as they drove through.

Kade, ever the diplomat, spoke up immediately. "Geraldo must be tired after his journey, Estelle. Why don't we ride in silence and let him rest."

"Of course," she said. "I'm sorry."

"There is nothing to apologize for, Mrs. Wonto," said Geraldo with grace. "You have both already placed me in your debt. Thank you again."

She smiled gratefully back at him in the rear-view mirror and concentrated on her driving.

They exited directly onto the Hohokam Expressway and turned left, heading north to McDowell. There, they made a right and traveled east all the way to Pima road, then north again to Shea Boulevard.

As they drove up Pima Road, Geraldo could not help but contrast the barren reservation land on the right with the white men's homes on their left.

Kade watched the Zuni quietly and without staring. The Priest's eyes never stopped moving, taking it all in.

"The Salt River Reservation," said the Maricopa, gesturing to the side. "It stretches east from here to the Verde River and adjoins the Fort McDowell Reservation to the north. It is shared between the Pima and my people."

"How much land?" asked Geraldo.

"Nearly fifty thousand acres," said Kade with a smile. "We leased a lot of it to the white man, but the rest is used by the tribes for farming and cattle ranching."

The Zuni looked curiously at the other man. "Why would you lease it to outsiders?"

The Maricopa shrugged. "It is the tribe's only asset," he said. "It is the way we raise money for the people."

"And you think this is good?"

Kade pointed to the right as they passed a number of large modern buildings. "That is Scottsdale Community College," he said. "The lease is for ninety-nine years and will be renewed when it comes up. Because of this, our children attend good schools and many will go to college there as well."

"We do not share our land with the whites," said Geraldo. "Zuni became autonomous. We work very hard to keep them from interfering with our ways."

"Our people—both the Pima and the Maricopa—consider themselves modern," explained Kade. "They have embraced the ways of the larger community surrounding them."

"And yet you still hold to the medicine way," said Geraldo. "As does our host, this Pima witch named Bear."

"Yes," said the Maricopa. "And much of what we were has been preserved because of what Tom and I and the others have done."

The Zuni said nothing but returned to watching the reservation pass outside the window.

Estelle spoke for the first time in quite a while.

"Kade, we should have done our shopping earlier. There will be long lines at the check-out counters after the panic earlier today. The whole town will be on edge because of the snakes."

Geraldo turned sharply as he heard her words. "Snakes? What is this about snakes?"

Kade could not help but notice that their passenger, who had almost relaxed during the last ten minutes of their drive, had once again become tense.

"We had a small earthquake here several days ago," he said to Geraldo. "Apparently, it shook quite a large number of rattlesnakes out of their normal habitats and they've been showing up around the city. There is a lot of coverage in the news and there have been some deaths."

"From snakes? In the city?"

"Yes," said Estelle. "They had some kind of riot at the initial staging area for the parade. The crowd had guns and they killed a lot of rattlers."

Kade looked at the Zuni's face and saw a trace of . . . fear? "Is there something we should know, my brother?" he asked.

Geraldo shook his head in the negative. "No," he said, after a long pause. "Nothing . . . for now."

Chapter Twenty-Nine

Fort McDowell Indian Reservation

Cord Hames and Michael Coyoma had to fight through a group of holiday river-tubers in order to reach the road to the Salt River Reservation. The Fourth of July offered no good time for traveling. Fortunately, their destination lay only ten miles to the south. Driving in Cord's pick-up, they made better speed once they left the river behind.

The population on the Fort McDowell Reservation remained less than 400 people shared among the three tribes, Mohave, Chemehuevi and Apache. All three had lived in the region for many years by the time the government created the preserve in 1903. Michael, as medicine man of the Mohave, and Cord, medicine man of the Chemehuevi, had both become men of note since the advent and subsequent destruction of the demon.

Though they had been friends for many years, the attention paid to them after last July had bonded the two even closer together. The declaration of thanks from all twelve tribes had been read at a special village meeting and both men were now held somewhat in awe. Less fortunately, it affected business.

Michael had enjoyed a quiet practice, combining his studies of modern medicine with the ancient practices of his fathers. Cord, much more low-key, worked with his own people, presiding at ceremonies to mark attainment of puberty, coming to the age of responsibility, and initiation into ancient orders. Both had been busy and content prior to their involvement with the Great Gathering.

Now, many of their old clients had stepped back, made uncomfortable by the attention paid to the heroes. They felt—incorrectly—that the newly important shamans had better things to do than minister to their needs. This resulted in both men suffering economically because of their participation in the destruction of the beast.

"The tourists are like ants this year," said Cord as they drove south along Fort McDowell Road. "It gets worse every season."

"Don't be too quick to complain, my brother," replied Michael lying back on the passenger seat, his hat tipped over his eyes. "The revenue will do a lot of good later. The tribe needs it. Besides, they'll be gone by the end of September."

The day sizzled and the truck did not have air-conditioning. Both men were used to it, but each felt glad when they turned up the drive that led to the home of Tom Bear. There would be cool drinks, shade, and good talk. The Bear was always a fine host.

Here, too, they would see the others. Once part of the Gathering, all of the thirteen had discovered that to be away somehow made them feel less than whole.

The sense of homecoming became a tangible thing for both men as the old wooden house came into view. Tom's battered pickup sat off to the side and a modern sedan had been parked to the right of the porch.

"The others have begun to arrive," Michael commented softly. He glanced over at Cord. "I have missed them."

"I, too," said his friend smiling awkwardly. "We have not been together, except for the tribal ceremonies, since last summer."

"July 14th," agreed Michael. "The day Jack took the demon." He shook his head. "What a day."

The pulled up behind Tom's truck, parking their own vehicle beside the drive, that others would not be blocked, and got out.

As they climbed the five steps to the porch, Michael said, "This is just like then. I feel the same sense of something about to happen."

"The difference is that there's no demon this time," laughed Cord. "Today is the first day of a ten-day party."

"Do not be too sure," said a voice from the shadowed doorway before them.

The screen door opened and a stranger stood before them. They saw in him a man of power, his bearing and manner speaking of authority.

"I am Vasquez of the Zuni," said the man without warmth.

"Michael Coyoma of the Mohave," said Michael extending his hand.

"An honor," said the Zuni quietly without taking it. "Forgive me. I do not shake hands. It is a custom of the white men."

"Of course," said Michael, pulling his hand back to his side.

Cord did his best to cover the awkwardness of the moment. "I am Cord Hames of the Chemehuevi," he said, stepping past Vasquez and into the front room. "Is Tom here?"

The Zuni gestured with a turn of his head. "He is in the kitchen with the Maricopas."

"Kade and Estelle? Thanks," said Cord and, without a further glance, he moved through the doorway and into the other room.

Michael hung back, studying the Zuni who must be the one selected to replace Pasqual Quatero as Chief Priest of the Gray Wolf Clan. "Welcome to Phoenix," he said. May I know your first name?"

"I am Geraldo," said the Priest.

"Is anyone else here yet?"

"No," replied the Zuni. "We are the first. A young man named Danny called from Tucson a while ago. He and the woman named Farley are returning tomorrow with the Yaqui named Mapoli."

"It will be good to see Juan again," said Michael. "He is a very wise elder."

Geraldo did not smile. "If you mean the Yaqui, I am afraid he will not be very good company for a couple of days."

"Why not?" asked Michael.

"Rattlesnake bite. The Pima and Tohono O'odham maiden are bringing him here to nurse him."

"Welcome Michael."

The Mohave medicine man looked up to see the Pima witch, Tom Bear, standing in the kitchen doorway, framed by Kade and Estelle Wonto.

"Ho, Bear," said Michael. "Hello Kade, Estelle. Geraldo just told me about Juan. How did it happen? Is he all right?"

The old man walked over to a large and worn chair, taking his seat with a sigh. "I know very little, my friend," he said. "Apparently, he opened the front door and the snake was on the other side."

Cord came out of the kitchen and joined them. Soon, all five had taken seats in the living room facing Tom.

"It is good that Lotus and Danny were able to go down there on such short notice," said Estelle. "If anyone can be of help to Juan, it is Lotus."

"I spoke with Danny," said Tom with a shrug. "He says Juan will be all right now. The danger is passed."

"No," said Vasquez from where he sat to the side. "The danger is only beginning."

"What do you mean, Geraldo?" asked Kade.

The Zuni looked at the Maricopa and his face looked as hard and unyielding as stone. "There is something this Gathering must do. I know that now. But," he added, "I do not have to like it."

He looked at Tom Bear and his face softened only a little. "I would not have come had it been left up to me, but the council at home ordered me to be here."

"How could you have stayed away?" Estelle hardly believed what she heard.

Geraldo turned and looked at the plump woman in her expensive clothes and did not try to disguise his disapproval. "It is easy for you, Mrs. Wonto, to drive your fancy car here from your comfortable home just down the road. You Maricopas and Pimas have left your heritage behind and accepted the dominance of the white men." He looked down and closed his eyes. "The Zuni do not have such fancy cars or houses. We still live in our pueblos much as our ancestors did. We have not turned from the creator. "We observe the laws."

"And you think we do not, is that it?"

Geraldo looked up, his eyes blazing with anger. "I think you are as white as the wider world surrounding you," he said simply.

Tom nodded. "So you do not like us," he said. "Then why are you here? Do not tell me you could not have successfully argued with your council. Your status would have given you the right."

"I would have," said the Priest, "but then I thought about the report that Ahaiyuta and Matselema had appeared to Quatero and others during your last gathering. I could not take the risk of deciding what their will might be. Then, too, I had a vision."

"What kind of vision?" Kade asked.

"I saw a great serpent rise from a rock and it threatened me," said Vasquez.

"What did you do?" asked Cord.

Geraldo shrugged. "I did nothing," he said after a moment. "The Terrible Two rescued me." He sighed. "I knew then that I must come here. I knew it for the will of the gods."

All six were silent for a long moment.

Finally, Michael spoke. "Well, we know it has something to do with snakes," he said. "Juan bitten, Geraldo's vision, the stuff that has been in the news—it couldn't be much more clear."

"Does anyone know anything more?" asked Kade.

Each of the men shook his head, but Estelle spoke up. "Regardless of what you may think, Geraldo, my husband and I have not given up our heritage, nor have we somehow tried to become white men." Her voice grew quieter as the anger she felt came forth. "We—all of us—have done what we can to preserve the old ways, the truths taught to us by our fathers and their fathers before them. We have obeyed the laws. We have sung our praises from the hilltops as the creator commanded that we do."

Vasquez looked at her and then at each of the other faces in the circle. Finally, his eyes returned to Estelle. "I have learned many things in my life," he said. "One of the most important is that even a Priest of the Gray Wolf Clan can sometimes be wrong." He gave her a sad half-smile. "We shall see."

"Of that I believe we can be sure," said Estelle, calming a little. "I have had troubling dreams." She looked at Michael. "You are right. It has to do with snakes, but this new sudden plague of attacks is only part of it. There is something much bigger here than we suspect right now."

"Perhaps one of the others will know more. We must await their arrival," said Tom. "For now, it is time to eat. Come into the kitchen, all of you, and let us see what Estelle has prepared for us." He rose and led them into the other room

Geraldo Vasquez lingered at the door before finally entering to join them.

Chapter Thirty

Oraibi, Third Mesa, Hopiland

Harold Laloma, Coyote Clan Priest, limped from the kiva and returned to his rooms in the pueblo. Though only one of many priests, he possessed unequalled status among them. To Harold, Taknok-wunu, the Spirit Who Controls the Weather, and Yaponcha, the Wind God, had appeared and spoken. With him they had stood against the wind demon.

The limp had been the price he paid—that and a streak of almost white hair that no herb or dye had thus far been able to hide. It ran from forehead to neck and developed in the weeks after his return from Phoenix. Despite these reminders, Harold knew joy. After the formal ceremony of thanks before the whole tribe, his prestige rose high among the People of Peace. After all, the Gathering had saved the world.

When it became generally known that there would be an annual reunion, the first to come to Harold had been William Concha. He had been the one who drove the priest to Phoenix the previous July, taking Harold to the hospital that his broken leg might be set and put in a cast.

"I would like to take you to Phoenix again," he had said. "I am proud to have been the one who did so the first time."

Since he did not own an automobile, Harold had been pleased to accept. It eliminated one more detail and, as the Fourth of July approached, he felt glad to have it arranged.

Now, his bags were packed. One contained gifts for the others that made up the gathering, including a drum with a snakeskin head that he intended to give to Tom Bear. It had been made by Harold's grandfather, a great medicine man in his own right. Old Bear, who had drummed them to the Palace of the Phoenix, would understand and appreciate it. Another bag contained his personal gear and the clothing he would wear for the ceremony. A third contained his paraphernalia, a sack of corn meal and bundles of pahos he had made in anticipation of the reunion. This time, blessed with a clear mind and time to plan ahead, he would go to the white man's city prepared.

Harold lit his clay pipe and smoked reverently, collecting his thoughts and opening his heart to the gods. It had been his honor in March to lead the delegation of priests to the great black rock where Yaponcha lived and to help seal the cracks with corn meal that the wind god might be restrained in his power when his breath passed over the mesas. All in all, it had been a good year for Harold Laloma but he felt, deep inside, that new tasks lay just ahead.

A voice spoke from above, recalling Harold from his reverie. "Harold, my brother, may we enter?"

"Come in Joseph," he said breaking into a smile. "You are welcome in my house."

Joseph Lansa came down the ladder, followed by John Lakona. These two, more than any others, had become close to Harold during the adventure a year before. They had witnessed his emergence from the kiva with a compound fracture of his right leg—had, in fact, set the leg for him and helped him on his way to Phoenix.

"We came to wish you a pleasant journey," said John. "May it be less exciting than the last."

Harold laughed with them, something he had done little of in the recent past.

"Have the gods spoken to you, my brother?" Joseph inquired.

Harold heard this question often these days, but shook his head. "When they are ready, they will say what they wish. Until then, I have no reason to think they will single me out."

The other two priests took out their pipes and lit them. The three men smoked quietly together.

After a few minutes, Joseph cleared his throat. Harold looked at the other man attentively.

"There is a matter to be spoken of," said Lansa.

Lakona nodded. "It is the snakes," he said.

Their host looked from one to another of them but said nothing. They would go on when they were ready.

Finally, Joseph continued. "This is the year of the dance and it lies little more than a month away. Already the young men have gone out and begun gathering the serpents."

"But, already," said John in his most serious tone, "there have been problems."

"Three bitten," commented Lansa. "One of them died."

"Is this so?" asked Harold. "But why have I not heard before this?"

"It is being kept a secret lest the people grow upset and consider it an ill omen," said Lakona. "The Chief Priest kept it from you because of your impending journey. He did not wish you troubled before you meet with the others."

The two visiting priests exchanged a glance.

Joseph spoke. "John and I have come to you on our own. If the elders knew we were here speaking of this matter, they would be displeased."

"We felt you should know," added Lakona. "It may be that one or more of your gathering knows something of what is happening."

"We wanted you to know," put in Lansa, "so that you could get word to us if that is true."

"We are worried," said John. "This equals the worst season in our past, but comes a month early. If this trend continues, we will have more incidents before the dance. This could be the most destructive and frightening time of our people's history."

"Could it be that the bitten were ill prepared?" asked Harold.

His fellow priests exchanged glances.

"No," said Joseph. "One I trained myself. The other two received their training from the Chief Priest." He shook his head decisively. "No, it is not for lack of preparation."

"What is it then?" Harold did not hesitate to ask.

"It is the snakes," said John. "They are unusual."

"How so?" asked Laloma.

"They do not take to the ceremonies," said Joseph. "The serpents act as if they were under some other influence." He sighed. "It is as if they are told to attack their captors."

"But this is not normal," said Harold. "Each year we observe the courtesies. We bathe them and stroke them and make them comfortable in their captivity. Why should they suddenly act in such a strange manner?"

Both priests shrugged.

Joseph said, "I do not know, my brother. But they do not respond as they have in the past. It is as if some evil spirit possesses them."

Harold thought for a moment and then looked at the others. "I will ask those who attend the gathering," he said. "Perhaps one of the others will know what we must do."

Lansa and Lokona looked at each other.

"That is all we can ask of you, my brother," said Joseph. "We thank you for whatever you are able to learn."

Harold bowed his head humbly. "I will do what I can," he said quietly. "This must not be allowed to become an omen."

"We know you will do your best," said John. "May those above speed you on your journey."

After an awkward pause, both men rose.

"We did not mean to delay you," said Joseph. "Concha awaits you outside." He smiled. "It may be nothing, Harold," he said. "Or it may be something of great import." He looked his fellow Coyote Priest apologetically. "I simply do not know."

"I will ask," said Harold. "That is all we can do."

Lakona and Lansa nodded.

"That is what we hoped, my brother," said John.

An hour later, Harold Laloma rode toward Phoenix. He had much to consider on the journey.

Though curiosity plagued William Concha, he dared not disturb the famous priest while they drove south. It would be many miles before he had the courage to ask. It would be many miles later before Harold answered. Even then, the words he used gave no clue to Concha what occupied his mind

"We shall see, William," he said. "We shall see."

Chapter Thirty-One

Underground, Deep Under Casa Malpais

She had ruled before the coming of man, before the fiery Eye of God struck the earth. In the time before speech, her will had been the law for all creatures of the land. Her strength and cunning were the stuff of legend even before the living learned to report the past.

She had been born a serpent—not any serpent, but queen of all. Her body stretched seventy feet in length, nearly six-and-a-half feet in girth at her widest point. Her brain rivaled man's in size, though it worked differently. Her children had ruled for centuries. One of her descendants had been the mighty Quetzalecoatl, the feathered one. Another had swum the ocean and stirred the hearts of all who saw, giving rise to tales of sea serpents.

She could only be called magnificent.

The lesser creatures learned quickly. She used no subtlety in what she taught. Either they served her, or death would follow. They did homage by driving their culls—the weak and lame—into her underground lair that She might be fed and leave the upper world alone. Only thus could there be peace on the surface.

It had taken years for her to teach the lesson. If they did not provide the food, She came forth from the dark to sate her hunger, moving among the beasts of the earth in the night, an undulant shadow that took their young, strangled their leaders, and left the rest in panic. Even the great mammoth learned to fear her. Though intelligence is a strange word to apply to that time of life on earth, the creatures living on the surface recognized necessity—could see what She required. They knew what the end must be if she continued to roam the night.

What She might have made of her kingdom if left unchecked would never be known, however, for—on the day the great Eye of God struck the earth—the burrows beneath the hill came crashing down, imprisoning her within her den.

Ensuing months brought drastic change to the surface world. The swampy conditions lessened, the temperature dropped. Beasts that could not find shelter and food died.

She did not die.

On impact, the meteorite penetrated six hundred feet below the surface of the earth, compressing and fusing the rocks, flattening itself as it pierced the ground. The shock waves had been tremendous and debris rose into the sky in ballistic trajectories.

A natural spring and reservoir running through the rocks adjacent to her den broke through, flooding the chamber from floor to roof in moments. She had no warning.

One moment, She lay coiled in the snug warmth of her cavern, and the next, water engulfed her. Natural gasses trapped within the rocks combined—in particular, a sudden chance union of carbon, chlorine and other free gases. She never knew what happened. The water froze instantly, suspending her bodily processes.

The impact of the meteorite threw hundreds of tons of debris into the atmosphere, banishing the sun for weeks. The temperature on the surface dropped. Snow fell and blanketed the plain.

In the chamber beneath the earth, the temperature settled at ten degrees Fahrenheit and remained there.

She remained, suspended between life and death in dreamless slumber, entombed in the ice, unaware of time itself.

When the 1991 tremor struck Arizona, the airtight chamber breached and air filtered in. The fractured ice began to melt, exposing her frozen body to the temporal world after twenty-five thousand years of suspended animation. A particularly severe aftershock stimulated her heart. It began to beat.

When, some days later, She awakened, She picked up the thread of life exactly where She had left off. Her body still responded to the surprise of the impact. She sensed, shortly thereafter, that everything around her lay still. The darkness in her chamber did not diminish.

She tried to move, but her body would not respond. Slowly, pain made its way along the nerves and screamed in her brain. She tried to make a sound. Nothing.

Weakness overcame her. She attempted to raise her head, but the effort returned her to unconsciousness. She slept another three days.

When She awakened again, She felt better. Hunger burned like a flame in her middle. She knew She must eat to grow strong. She reached out with her mind and demanded that She be fed.

Nothing stirred.

Where were her servants? Why had they not herded sacrifices to her lair? Why had She awakened alone in the dark?

Her mind, without speech, stretched out toward the familiar and encountered only silence. It shocked her. No response. None who had tended her needs, who served through fear or the promise of reward, answered the call. She knew only the silence of the dark, the burning hunger, and a feeling of incredible loneliness. She managed a weak hiss.

She would not have understood the term "telepathic." She did not know how She could reach out with her mind and touch others. She could not have conceived the concept of mind control. She knew only that what She desired came to be. This must be. She possessed the greatest strength. She ruled.

She expanded her awareness, stretching in all directions, seeking life that would serve.

Nothing.

Frustration and rage surged through her. Lesser creatures miles away writhed suddenly in pain. Dogs howled. Birds rose in startled flight.

Only as the echoes of her soundless cry faded did She become aware of a pitiful response. It came so faintly to her that She could not, at first, discern its nature.

Then, slowly, She realized She had been answered.

That which responded mirrored her very self, yet must be far less. Her mind reached out eagerly and touched it. The creature surrendered instantly. Suddenly, She lay on the surface, her mind in the body of another snake.

That had been some time ago.

During those first hours, She learned much of her situation. She could control any other serpents She chose. The little minds, similar in every way, folded immediately before her greater will. She could direct them, use them, inhabit them. They obeyed as slaves.

She summoned them to her lair.

It took hours more for the first wriggling sacrifice to enter her chamber beneath the earth. By this time, ravenous hunger ruled her every thought. It made not even a mouthful.

She called more. They responded. It took a hundred to abate her hunger.

Temporarily satisfied, She experimented with her power. It took another day to realize she could control limitless numbers of the little ones. She tried greater distances and found her powers virtually boundless. She might be trapped beneath the earth, but she possessed both a kind of mobility and a means of satisfying her hunger.

Only then did She become aware of the two-legged creatures above.

She reached out in an attempt to control their minds, but they were foreign and strange.

After trying for hours, rage and frustration boiled over and She struck at one of the creatures while possessing the body of a little one. She watched the two-legs die. She took control of more servants and killed another of the creatures.

Joy surged through her.

She had discovered the means by which She could act.

Over the next period of awakening, She experimented further—sending out her little ones, possessing them, individually and in groups, directing them to kill when She wished. Everything went as She planned. Her will among the lesser creatures once again became law.

The abortive assault on the city of the two-legs on that particular day, however, taught her a new caution and respect for the creatures with incomprehensible minds.

She experienced shock when so many of her little ones died so quickly. No real harm resulted, of course, but She withdrew the rest of her minions and conducted her experiments elsewhere. She would stay away from the two-legs' cities for now. The conquest of the surface would require a more sophisticated plan of attack.

She hissed quietly in the dark and then slept.

Chapter Thirty-Two

The Roberts Ranch, Springerville

It had been five days since Jake caught the specimen and sent it along with his special gift to the herpetologist. He laughed as he pictured Jeremy's face when he opened the shipping crate.

"Bet Doc pissed his pants," he cackled.

He had known, of course, that the law would come looking for him. What else could they do when he sent Myers the hand? With almost a full week for his preparations, the FBI could not have surprised him.

He found it child's play to hide and watch the black cars drive up and disgorge their cargo of dark-suited men. His place of concealment lay in sight of the house, but absolutely undetectable.

"Fuckin' FBI," he muttered under his breath in disgust.

They looked funny, all with their sunglasses and suits, entering his home like an assault team.

Jake chuckled as they kicked in the door. They would find some surprises awaiting them in there.

Gunfire and the yells of startled agents erupted and he grunted in satisfaction. They would be roiling about like a disturbed anthill out there. Step one, his carefully planned ambush, had been accomplished. The time had come to proceed with step two.

He raised the hinged door and climbed down the narrow wooden ladder, closing the lid over him and banishing the light. The surface above would look like what it used to be, an old well cover properly secured, surrounded by junk and likely unused for a hundred years.

He descended into the darkness and stepped lightly to the floor of the shelter. He and Dad had built it in the late fifties when the world seemed even crazier than today and the cold war raged.

He turned on the light switch and five battery powered ceiling lamps came on, illuminating even the farthest recesses of the chamber.

Jake liked it bright when under the surface. A small and enclosed space like this could all too likely harbor one of the serpents he spent his time hunting. As usual, he did a quick tour of the facility to make sure.

Everything ran off batteries. In addition to the solid bank of stored charge just behind the north wall, he had sixty more batteries hooked up and sitting in a pile amidst the chaos above. Who would look twice at a pile of old car batteries in a junk pile?

He had all the conveniences. In many ways, the shelter made a nicer home than his trailers. The big freezer gleamed in the corner, almost new. He had purchased it from a private party and trucked it in at night. The fridge had been stocked with beer and water lay stacked in the first storage locker next to the batteries.

The furniture had been handmade. The bed, table and chairs were well-crafted, and cases of reference books lined one wall. Jake felt proud of what he had accomplished.

A small regular door at the far end opened up on an underground stream that emptied itself into a wash two miles away. His sanitary facilities were built right over it, eliminating the need for piping in water or handling usual plumbing. The water tested out as a little too alkaline for drinking, but it served for bathing and cleaning.

As revealed by the discovery of Casa Malpais, the entire area around Springerville was honeycombed with caverns and volcanic flumes. Tests revealed that the network of faults, caves and tunnels extended for miles in all directions. The Mogollons had merely enlarged the spaces provided by nature.

Even Jake would have admitted his insanity. It took no education in psychology or psychiatry to see his behavior as different than the norm. His actions sometimes went out of control, his ability to consciously direct himself swept away by rages that took over and ran their course before reality returned. Jake didn't care.

He chuckled. "Sonsabitches entered my house without knocking," he muttered to himself. "Shouldn't have done that. It was rattler exercising time."

He sat in the padded easy chair and put his feet up. "Guess it would be wise to stay down here a few days," he said as laughter bubbled forth again. "Bet there's some pissed off law up there."

He busied himself with the usual solitary activities, reading, preparing a simple meal, napping. In that way, the day passed swiftly into evening and finally darkness came.

Moving back up the ladder after extinguishing the lights, he silently opened the trap and crawled out. The desert sky looked like black velvet studded with silver sequins.

Even Jake was awed by the desert night sky. Springerville, unlike Phoenix, had no blazing city lights to disturb the awesome splendor of stars, planets and moon. Cloudless and warm, the night rustled with a gentle breeze.

He crawled noiselessly along a pre-planned route toward the house, taking extreme care because he expected it to be under surveilance. Jake wanted to know how many watchers and where they lay concealed.

As his night vision adjusted, the clear starry sky made the desert look bright. The shadows were a warm familiarity, friendly and welcoming.

Reaching a point just yards away from the trailer, he propped himself comfortably up against a concrete-filled oil barrel.

The vehicles had departed now and the place looked deserted.

He knew better than that.

When in control of his faculties, Jake possessed a skilled tracker's stealth and keen powers of observation. He knew how to look at a landscape. He did not search the shadows for figures. Imagination would have provided dozens in moments. He turned toward the building and waited for something to catch his attention.

Thirty minutes passed before he saw the glow of a cigarette off to the left of the house, in a stack of crates that somehow looked different to his practiced eye than they had before.

One man, there.

Jake waited, not moving, his body disciplined through years of such enforced immobility.

Ten minutes later, he heard a cough from the right. It came from the old tool shed.

Two men.

Still, he waited. After two hours, he turned and moved back along the route, returning at last to the trap. It opened noiselessly and he entered, closing it behind.

His mind wrestled with possibilities. Two men. That seemed about right. Chances were good that they believed he had fled.

How iong would they keep two men on site? Probably not long. If he laid low, Jake would be assumed to have skipped and the observation of his house would become periodic.

How long should he stay below? He decided that three days ought to do it. By then, the men would be needed elsewhere. Little could be gained by stationing two agents in an empty desert. Besides, they could not be sure what had killed the man whose hand had been found with the specimen. They might suspect that Jake had something to do with it, but it had obviously been removed after death. Bitten and chewed as it had been, they could determine nothing of what happened without interviewing the man who sent it.

Whether others had died or been hurt in the assault on his home remained another question. If they had rushed in and encountered all twelve loose rattlers in the trailer, there might have been some deaths. In that case, there would be more motivation for the bureau and they might be more dedicated about their search for him.

"Better make it five days," he mumbled as he switched on the light. He glanced around. Nothing had been disturbed.

He sniffed. A trace of something floated in the air, a musty smell, but faint.

Jake felt tired. Taking a bottle of whiskey off the shelf, he went to the bed, undressed and climbed in. He drank a third of the booze, feeling it burn his throat as it went down, then put it carefully on the floor and turned out the lights.

Sleep came swiftly.

Chapter Thirty-Three

Phoenix

Jeremy and Rachel stood by the cages and observed the snakes. In one was the Diamondback he had brought from the tunnel. In the space next to it coiled the Mohave that Roberts had sent with the hand. The second snake, though smaller than Long Tom, proved otherwise a good specimen. Both the doctor and his assistant watched in fascination as both snakes exhibited the damndest behavior. The two vipers seemed to move in their separate cages in tandem, as if their bodies shared one mind.

"I've never seen anything like it," said Myers. "What could be causing it?"

Rachel just shook her head and shrugged.

Suddenly, Jeremy had an idea. He turned and lifted the cover off Long Tom's cage as well. Inside, behind the glass, the Mohave moved exactly as did the others.

"Son of a bitch," he exclaimed to himself. "Rachel, get all the covers off!"

He started to the cages on the left and his assistant took those on the right. Each cloth lifted away revealed that the snake inside moved in unison with all the others.

It looked so weird that neither of the humans could think of anything to say.

Rachel laughed, a nervous, high pitched and unsettled sound.

"What is it?" The doctor did not turn to look at her, but watched the cages in fascination.

"It reminds me of a water ballet," she said after a moment's hesitation. "Like an old Esther Williams movie, you know? Look at them. They move together, precise and machine-like." She had difficulty keeping her voice under control. "It suddenly struck me as funny—only then it didn't."

Jeremy looked at her. She appeared pale and her eyes showed fright for the first time since he had known her. He wondered briefly if he looked any better or more in control.

Moving to a cabinet set off to the left, he opened a panel above the main display area and took out a bottle of brandy. He poured two glasses, watching to see if his hands shook. They remained steady, but he did not know why. Turning, he passed a glass to Rachel. She took it, grasping it firmly with both hands.

"Doctor's orders," he said, lifting his glass and taking a heavy swig. She followed suit and both turned back to watch the activity in the cages.

The snakes moved in a strange pattern, crossing the bottom to the right, then nosing into the corner as if trying to dig out through the glass. After a few moments of wriggling and striving, they would turn quickly and move to the left and perform the same digging action in the opposite corner. One snake alone, trying to escape, might move exactly in that way, but twenty moving in perfect unison stretched beyond rational explanation.

The doctor moved over to the telephone and dialed Sarno's number at ASU. It rang a half dozen times before he realized the university lab would be closed for the holiday.

He hung up in disgust.

He reached for his rolodex and began thumbing through, trying to remember if he had the professor's home number, but Rachel suddenly called to him.

"They've stopped," she said. "They're all acting normally again."

Jeremy returned to her side. Sure enough, the snakes lay still or moved about individually. No two acted alike.

Rachel looked at the doctor with doubt on her face.

"We weren't just imagining it, were we? I mean, you saw them all moving together just like I did, didn't you?"

He nodded wordlessly.

"Don't just stand there, Jeremy Myers," shouted Rachel, a touch of hysteria in her voice. "Tell me I'm not going crazy."

"You aren't going crazy," he said, then added as an afterthought, "unless we're doing it together."

He sat heavily on a lab stool and shook his head. "I've been chasing snakes for twenty years here in the southwest," he said. "I've found them lying in the open in broad daylight so fast asleep that you could pick them up and put them in a specimen bag without even waking them. I've see them hunting, eating, mating, hiding, threatening and in just about every other state you can imagine a snake might be in." He shook his head. "I've never seen them acting like these did or, for that matter, even like those in the tunnel earlier today."

"There has to be an explanation," suggested Rachel. "We're trained observers. We're professionals. These are living creatures. They act in certain ways. There has to be a reason."

The doctor turned to her and smiled. "And then again, maybe there isn't," he said lightly. "I have been around long enough to know that there are still mysteries in the world, even the world of nature. We aren't so wise that we know all the answers yet."

"Jeremy," said his assistant, "I know what I saw."

He nodded. "And I saw it too," he agreed. "That doesn't mean we can explain it or even that it has ever been seen before. We'll watch and see if it occurs again. We'll study this lab to see if there is some kind of equipment—air conditioning, electronics, maybe something automatic—that turns on when this atypical behavior begins."

"Now you're talking," said Rachel. "I was afraid you'd tell me to forget it." She paused and looked frightened again. "I don't think I could do that. I'm not sure I'll ever be able to do that."

Jeremy moved toward the equipment locker. "I'm going to set up the camcorder and set it to watch the diamondback and the Roberts mohave. The tapes last six hours. You'll be responsible for replacing them. Okay?"

"No problem," said his assistant becoming more confident now that she had something to do. "I'm going to stay right here and watch.

That was the damnedest thing I ever saw and I intend to be right here and ready if it happens again."

"Good." Jeremy mounted the camcorder on a tripod and used the view-finder to focus on both specimen cages. Running the cable to the VCR, he made the connections, popped in a new tape and set it to record at Extended Play speed.

Once he had checked to make sure everything worked properly, he hung his lab coat on the rack and took his suit coat down.

"Where are you going?" asked Rachel.

"I'm going to drive over to Dr. Sarno's house and see if he's home. If he is, I'm going to suggest he set up monitoring equipment at the university specimen lab as well. I want to know if this is something that happens just here or in both places."

He stopped just as he was about to go out the door.

"Be careful, Rachel," he said, turning back to face her. "Whatever you do, don't go trying to handle any of the specimens until I get back. I wouldn't want anything to happen to you."

"Don't worry, doctor," she said looking warily at the rows of cages. They seemed threatening to her for the first time in her professional career. "I'm just going to watch." She turned and gave him a half-smile. "Don't be too long, will you? I'd feel better with you here."

Jeremy looked like he wanted to add something more, then sighed and shrugged. "I'll be back as soon as I can," he said, then left, his mind already trying to frame the words he would say to Dr. Sarno.

Chapter Thirty-Four

Springerville

At noon Gerry pulled his rental car up in front of the bus stop on Highway 60 in Springerville and found Gordon waiting, his bags resting against a hitching post.

"George," called the Navajo, his face breaking into a grin. "I had just begun to worry. It is good to see you, my friend."

"Gerry," said the driver, returning the smile. "There is something going on and my elder self has come forward again."

Gordon nodded respectfully. "Welcome Goyathlay," he said, "and welcome George. May whatever it is be yet another reason to bind our friendship closer."

The Apache stopped the engine and got out, moving swiftly to the rear and opening the trunk. He and Gordon quickly loaded the bags and then both got into the car. They wasted little time heading toward Phoenix.

"It has been too long," said Gerry to his companion. "And yet it seems that we were together only yesterday."

"I cannot imagine what it must be like," said Gordon, slouching back in his seat and resting his head on the back. "How do the two of you manage to function in one body?"

"At first, as you may remember, it could be only one at a time," replied the Apache. "George is the modern man who has skills like

driving a car. Geronimo is the medicine man who knows the desert."
He shrugged. "In very little time, however, the two began to integrate.
Neither of us has an ego problem so we are able to find compromise
and take action as quickly as most people think normally."

"Yet you remain separate personalities." The Navajo could not
keep awe from his voice."

"It might be easier to think of us as simply schizophrenic and let
it go at that," laughed Gerry. "I think there are many doctors in the
white world who would lock us away for good."

The two rode in silence for thirty minutes or so and then Gordon
spoke. "You said that something is happening in the world. What is
it that caused you to become Gerry again?"

"Something has awakened that should have died lifetimes ago,"
replied the Apache. "We do not yet know what it is, but it threatens
us as the demon did."

"Could it have something to do with rattlesnakes?" asked Gordon.

Gerry turned to him and gave him a strange look. "What makes
you ask that?"

The younger man shook his head. "We had a scare last night. A
number of rattlesnakes showed up at the bar. Bert's girlfriend swore
that a bunch of them followed her trying to attack her."

"Maybe she only imagined it," suggested the other.

"That's what we thought at first," said Gordon, "but when we let
her in and slammed the door, we trapped one in the jam."

Gerry did not immediately reply. Instead, he began to hum a
strange and haunting little chant. Gordon, ever the yataalii, committed it to memory even as he heard it.

Finally, the Apache spoke. "I am not sure," he said, and, after a
moment's hesitation, continued, "but that would explain some things.
It will have to wait until we are all together on the Reservation. When
the gathering is assembled again, it may be that we will be able to
understand the task before us."

"So you, too, think there is something that must be done," said
Gordon, relief showing in his voice.

"Oh yes, Fly," said Gerry, smiling grimly. "There is another quest
for the medicine men of the twelve tribes. I do not yet know what it
is that is expected of us, but we have been called again."

"That is what I think too," said Gordon. "I have been studying and learning all I can over this last year. I've been driven by a feeling deep inside that there is some urgency about it."

"This is a time of change and of choice," said Gerry. "The world is rapidly rushing toward some cataclysmic change and man must choose a direction. It must be that we are the instruments of some force that would direct man toward selection of the path that leads to good, which brings hope for the future."

"What is so special about now?" asked the Navajo. "Why should all this come about and make us players in the game?"

"Nothing happens by chance," replied the Apache. "Everything is part of a master plan, call it the will of the gods if you wish."

"But why us?"

"Because we are here," answered Gerry. "Because we will serve."

"But why choose medicine men?" Gordon seemed unwilling to let go of the topic until he understood. "There are so many wise men in the wider world. Why choose those of us who come from among the poor and isolated?"

"Because we were the first, Fly," answered his companion. "The gods have not forgotten that they chose us." The Apache turned toward the younger man and smiled. "It has been sung through the ages, Gordi. The children of the gods are the hope of the world. Only we can show the white man, the black man, and our own people, that we are all just people and that we live on a fragile planet that requires our respect and care."

"Do you really believe there is hope of that?"

"Of course," replied Gerry. "That is why we are here. That is why we will be shown what must be done and then try to do it. If we fail, the worst that can happen is that we will die. If we succeed, perhaps the world will take one step closer toward the harmony we seek."

"I hope you're right," said Gordon.

"We are," replied the Apache.

July 5th

Chapter Thirty-Five

Salt River Indian Reservation

The Volkswagen camper pulled into the drive before Tom Bear's house and James Bluesky got out, thanking the Pima driver who had given him a ride from the information center. The VW pulled away as he turned toward the house. For just a moment, the morning sun hid behind a high cloud. It cast a long and serpentine shadow that led from where he stood to the front porch. A chill ran through him despite the July heat.

"Ho, Bluesky," called a voice from the side of the house. "Come join us. It is good to see you."

James looked over and saw Tom Bear sitting under the shade of an arrow-weed shelter supported by mesquite posts. With him were Kade and Estelle, Michael and Cord, and an Indian James did not know.

He moved over to them and smiled. "It is good to be back, Tom Bear. Greetings to all of you." He took a seat, expanding the circle and waited for the introduction he knew would come.

"This one is Geraldo Vasquez, Chief Priest of the Gray Wolf Clan of the Zuni," said Tom formally. "He is the one selected by their elders to replace Quatero. He has come to us with a disturbing tale."

James nodded to the Zuni Priest and received one in return. "Welcome to the Gathering," said James respectfully. "Your brother, Pasqual, held our greatest regard."

"I have come to understand that," said Geraldo.

Bluesky expressed surprise at what he heard. Quatero had been rough of speech, unaccustomed to using English. This Vasquez spoke with the diction of one long familiar with the language. Given the Zuni resistance to the way of the white man, it seemed unusual and surprising.

"Did you have a good journey here from Yuma?" Kade's tone indicated more than polite interest.

"Uneventful," answered the Cocopah. "But I had an interesting visitor a few days ago."

"Who?" asked Geraldo.

"A Pawnee medicine man who has been flying around the country looking into unusual events."

"He came to learn of the demon?" asked Estelle.

"Among other things," replied James. "He told me that there have been many strange happenings of late. He told me to warn the gathering."

"What could compare with the wind demon?" asked Cord.

"He spoke of large creatures in the sea, reported by our Eskimo brothers. He spoke of a scaled one, Father of All Serpents, that his people drove west earlier in this century. He spoke of ghosts troubling the living back in his native Oklahoma."

"Indeed," said Tom thoughtfully, "there is a wider world than the one we know here in the Southwest."

"There is more for us to do," said Kade.

Tom looked at his friend and chuckled. "Kade, my brother," he said in a kindly tone. "Did you think we meet again—the medicine people of the twelve tribes—merely to celebrate the spirits of our fallen?" He shook his head. "No. We are here to do a thing. By the time the others arrive, we will begin to learn what it is."

"It has to do with the serpents," said Geraldo quietly. "Of this I am certain. There is something ancient that threatens our world."

"The Pawnee says the old gods are stirring," said Bluesky.

"I have felt that something important is going to happen," put in Estelle.

Tom looked from one of them to another, his seamed face grave and serious.

"Then we may not spend the week reverently honoring the past," he said. "Perhaps it would be wise to organize what we have here and see what we need. It may be that we will find ourselves with a reason to travel."

They were interrupted by the sound of another car coming up the drive. Tom watched as the vehicle came into view and their host broke out into a big smile.

"It's Danny, Lotus and Juan," he said, rising and moving toward them. Seeing the fourth passenger, he turned and added over his shoulder, "And Juan has brought his wife, Maria."

The other rose as well, rushing to join Tom in greeting old friends and to see what could be done for the Yaqui.

By the time Lotus brought the vehicle to a halt, the others were all crowded around. Tom opened the door in the rear to welcome Maria Mapoli and greet Juan.

"Can you walk, my brother?" he asked.

"I have crutches," said the old man, "but I can go anywhere."

"Don't listen to him, Bear," said Danny. "He's supposed to stay off that leg for at least a week. The venom is mostly gone but the knife cut deep."

"And in that way saved my life," said the old Yaqui. "I will be fine. Make way. Let me show you how I can walk."

Indeed, Juan climbed out of the car unaided and demonstrated his proficiency with crutches. He moved easily and without obvious pain, swinging the wounded leg as if it bothered him not in the least. "You see?" he crowed. "I can go anywhere."

Maria, however, moved to his side and spoke sternly. "Then it is to bed that you will go, husband," she said. "I promised the doctors you would rest and rest you shall or I will find another use for my frying pan than serpent slaying."

The old man looked at her affectionately and laughed. "The queen has spoken," he said. "I must take a nap or she will never let me be." He turned to their host. "Tom, my friend, lead me to my room and I will tell you of the snake and my warrior woman."

When Maria moved to help, Estelle took her by the arm.

"Let the men talk, Maria," she said quietly. "Tom will see that he goes right to bed. When the Bear comes out, you can go in."

The old Yaqui woman nodded, but her eyes watched with concern as they helped her husband up the steps and into the house, Tom on one side and Danny on the other.

"It is all bravado," she said confidentially to Estelle. "He is as weak as a newborn."

"Tom knows," assured the Maricopa woman. "It is essential that they talk. This way, they will take less time and Juan can rest all the sooner."

Lotus had gotten out of the car and now greeted Cord, Michael, James and the silent Geraldo Vasquez. Kade and Estelle introduced Maria all around and soon they had moved into the house, that Maria might not be alone nor too far from her husband.

Ten minutes later, Tom and Danny came out of Juan's room and signalled the others to return outside. Maria went in to see the old man while everyone else exited.

Chapter Thirty-Six

City of Phoenix

Lieutenant Ramirez tried to maintain a sense of order in a world that had suddenly gone insane. He also sought to win his bet with Rod Grimsley. It would not be easy.

The coroner had confirmed that the death of the old woman, Agnes Littlebaum, had been due to the bites of a rattlesnake. That made . . . well, the Circle K clerk, the two children, the dealership lady, the professor and the security guard at Casa Malpais, the four U.S. West crew members and whoever belonged to the arm sent to Jeremy Myers by the madman, Roberts . . . twelve. There were probably more but they hadn't been reported yet.

"What the fu . . . , uh, what do they expect us to do?" he asked no one in particular. "How the hell do you police snakes?"

Rod had just come into the office with the coffee and caught the tail end of it. "Seems to me the citizens at the parade had the right idea," he commented dryly as he set the steaming mug down.

"Great!" exploded Ramirez. "That's all we fu . . . uh, that's all we need! Vigilantes. Citizens with guns blasting at everything that wriggles!"

Grimsley burst into laughter. "Listen to yourself, Ed," he said when he could control himself. "You sound like the poor little vipers need protecting."

Ramirez glared at his partner. "You know how much I hate those fu . . . uh, how much I hate snakes. I wish they'd all go somewhere else. But I don't want the public running around shooting them on sight. People are going to get hurt, Rod. We have enough trouble with armed civilians as it is. Have you checked the lists from the gun stores?"

Grimsley suddenly turned more serious. "A lot of activity?"

"Up almost two thousand percent!" Ed replied vehemently. "Everybody suddenly wants to own a gun."

"Christ!" said Rod, all traces of humor gone from his face now. "That's all we fuckin' need, to be out on the street with thousands of armed yahoos."

"Watch your language, Grimsley," said Ramirez with a grin. "That's a word we're avoiding, remember?"

Rod looked at his friend and said, "I'm proud of you, Ed. You're into the second day and you've been doing great."

"Yeah," acknowledged Ramirez. "It isn't easy, but I'm going to beat the fu . . . uh, the damned thing."

Grimsley smiled. "Maybe," he said. "You still have to get through today and most of tomorrow. We'll see."

"Just don't make any plans for that paycheck," replied Ed. "Me and Faye are going to like spending it."

He stood and shrugged on his holster, following it with his jacket.

Rod glanced from the steaming coffee to his partner, obviously preparing to leave. "Where are you going?"

"I'm going to pay a call on Dr. Myers at his lab. I tried to reach him last night, but he had taken off somewhere to meet with that Dr. Sarno from ASU. I want to see what he's found out about the snake from the tunnel."

"Want me to come along?"

"No," said Ramirez. "Check the reports and see if there have been any more deaths. If there were, you chase them down. I'd also like you to call the city engineer and see what he can tell you about that weird hole we found leading out from the collapsed tunnel."

"Right."

"I should be back in a couple of hours. We may have to go up north and see Dr. Shayley at that dig up in Springerville. I'm not completely happy with the local report. It seems the lady doctor put a lid on everything and information on what happened is sketchy." He sighed. "I have a hunch this may all be tied into that archaeological dig, but it's just a hunch."

"How could that be?" asked Rod.

Ed shrugged. "I don't know," he said simply. "That's where Roberts disappeared according to the FBI, and it's where the security guard and the other professor died. It has to be linked in some way."

"Any problem with jurisdiction?"

Ed smiled. "No, I cleared it with the Captain this morning. He checked with the Feds and they said it was okay. We're expected. Dr. Shayley has agreed to see us. If Myers is free, I may even ask him to join us. I hope this doesn't take too long. Traffic is murder right now."

Ramirez arrived at the Phoenix address and parked in the lot. Entering the building, he encountered a receptionist that would not let him pass until she had cleared his visit with her boss.

Ed thought wistfully about how much he would like to have her at the department. He would see less nut cases and more material witnesses. Still, she made him wait and he hated the bitch even while admiring her efficiency. She kept him cooling his heels for twenty minutes. Finally, Dr. Myers finally appeared.

"Lieutenant Ramirez," Jeremy greeted his visitor. "Good of you to come by." He shook his hand. "I have quite a number of things to show you." He led the way back into the lab. "Here is where we test the vipers, extract the venom and begin the process of creating the anti-venin." He indicated the cages. "This is the diamondback we took from the tunnel. There's nothing unusual about it except for some observed behavior I'm not ready yet to report." He pointed to a second cage. "This is a Mohave rattler we call Long Tom. He's been with us a while and his days of usefulness are almost at an end. Still, there is nothing particularly noteworthy about him."

He paused, then stepped up and put his right hand on a third cage.

"This," he said, "is the specimen sent to us by Jake Roberts, the one accompanied by the hand and forearm. The FBI is digging into that."

"So what's unusual about this one?" asked Ed.

"Well, nothing," said the doctor, "unless you know its venom is three times stronger than the other samples we've collected."

"Three times?"

"Exactly," said Jeremy, leading the officer over to the lab table. "This snake is a mutation. I'm not certain yet what caused it, but I believe it has to do with exposure to some organic chemical. It is a medium I haven't encountered before. It has accelerated the snake's metabolism, and it seems to have affected the potency of the venom."

"What do you mean?" asked the lieutenant.

"Well, venom functions in two ways. It's a nerve agent, acting to paralyze the victim, and it contains enzymes that break down the structure and make it digestable."

"How does that work?"

"When a snake strikes at a small animal, usually a rodent of some kind, the venom paralyzes the victim and renders it helpless."

Ed took a seat on a lab stool and listened.

"When it begins to swallow the creature, the venom works at breaking down the cellular structure in order to make it easier to digest. The result is that the body breaks down swiftly."

"And this works three times faster than the others?"

"That's it," said Jeremy, warming to his subject. "This snake," he indicated the Mohave that Roberts had sent, "is three times more efficient a killer than the others. The venom breaks down the flesh and this mutation feeds on it even after the victim is dead." He looked at the specimen in fascination. "I don't understand how it works yet, but this is really exciting. It's new. If it were to breed true, we might really have a problem on our hands here in Arizona and, in fact, in all the Southwest."

"You say that as if it isn't going to happen," said Ramirez.

"I don't think it will," said Myers. "I've watched it now for two days. It may be suited to mating with others of its mutated kind, but not with normal snakes."

"You mean it won't breed true?" Ed felt interested in spite of himself.

"It lives too fast," said the doctor. "This snake is only months old, but it's already exhibiting traces of extreme age. It probably won't last the week."

"You mean we can figure they'll just die out?"

Jeremy shook his head. "No," he said sadly. "We'll have to find their location and exterminate them. If they're left to breed among themselves, they'll flood the area with mutations." He looked worried. "The problem is that mutations don't stay like they are. It may be that these vipers will change again. The compound that affected them seems to be highly unstable. They may mutate into something more able to co-exist with other snakes. Then we would be in trouble."

"But if we find them now, we might be able to stop them?" Ed sounded hopeful for the first time.

"Maybe," said the doctor. "But there's something else."

"What?"

"The unusual behavior," said Jeremy. "I think something is controlling them. I don't know what it is yet, but they're acting like an army, not like individuals." He turned to Ramirez and shrugged helplessly. "I can't explain it. Nothing like this has ever happened before in all my years as a scientist." A look of genuine fear crossed his face, the first Ed had seen there. "There's some other influence at work here and it is inimical to man."

Chapter Thirty-Seven

Salt River Indian Reservation

This journey from the Havasupai habitat to the Salt River Reservation proved considerably less exciting than the first. Rattle felt grateful. He caught a ride with the ranger all the way to Tom Bear's door and arrived to find many of his friends waiting.

After the usual greetings and introductions, he learned about Juan and the rattler. His first question came out in a rush. "Did he kill the snake?"

When Estelle answered that Maria had done it, he did not look relieved, but even more concerned.

"We must be careful about killing the serpents," he said, his face reflecting his deep conviction. "I have been told to warn you."

They sat on the front porch—Rattle, Tom, Kade, Estelle, Cord, Michael, James, Geraldo, Danny and Lotus. Juan remained inside asleep and healing under the watchful eyes of Maria.

Tom looked around and spoke, his suggestion tentative but well thought out. "Perhaps we should await the arrival of George, Gordon and Harold before we begin our talk," he said. "The Gathering is not yet complete."

Rattle nodded in acknowledgement, but still looked worried. Upon seeing this, Tom and Kade exchanged a glance heavy with foreboding.

After an awkward silence, Michael said, "Are we still planning to hold a ceremony on Monday?"

Tom spoke, his voice a clear confirmation of the intent. "Yes, we will gather at sunrise and honor the memory of our brothers, Jack Foreman and Pasqual Quatero." He sighed, feeling the pain again as if the loss had occurred only yesterday. "It is the least we can do."

"What about the detectives, Johnson and Twohats?" asked Cord. "Will we see them and the weatherman called Sharp?"

Lotus shook her head and spoke. "No, Twohats will not be here. He called and told us," she glanced at Danny for agreement, "that he would join us in spirit, but that his father had need of him in a case of murder back on the reservation. Matt Sharp moved to New York City and has probably forgotten us. Johnson is now the police Captain in Tempe. We have not heard from him."

"But that means there will be but twelve," said James. "We were thirteen when we faced the demon."

"He's right," said Danny. "We represented the twelve tribes but Jack embodied the thirteenth, the white man."

"Do not be impatient," said Rattle, his thoughts still with the scaled creature that had threatened him. "There may be more to this than you know."

Geraldo snorted in disgust. "Do you mean to tell me that you would ally yourselves with the white men?" he asked, his voice heavy with derision. "Have you not learned enough about their ways by now to know that they are despoilers, bent on subjugating our people and ending our traditions forever?"

Tom held out his hands, a gesture calling for patience. "You forget," he said, "that a white man saved us all. He gave himself to the darkness that the demon might be destroyed utterly."

"Strange talk," said Lotus, "from a people who have exercised their autonomy so strongly. Has the white man not given you what you sought? Do the Zuni not make their own laws, speak their own language, live under their own rule?"

Geraldo fixed her with a piercing gaze. "We do," he said. "But we do not do it by the grace of the whites. We do so because we are strong, reverent and still in harmony with those above."

Danny Webb could not sit still any longer. He spoke, his anger evident in every word. "Why is it," he asked, "that those who are given the most complain the loudest?" He pointed a finger at Vasquez. "You and your people are among the strongest and most steeped in tradition because the white men were willing to let you be." He spat to the side. "Are you so ungrateful that you cannot acknowledge the debt you owe? Do you not see that the Zuni are strong and reverent and in harmony because the white man agreed that you are the best judges of your own destiny?"

"How dare you?" asked Geraldo, his voice a clear and clarion challenge. "You are Pima and younger than all of us. How dare you accuse a priest of the Zuni?"

Tom broke in, his voice level and firm. "He dares, Geraldo, because he is your equal, a full medicine man of my tribe, an honor to our people. He dares because he is right." The old man slumped in his place, angry with himself for allowing things to get beyond his control. He needed to act the host.

Lotus spoke, a voice of compromise amidst the emotion of the moment.

"Do not quarrel, my brothers," she cautioned. "We are a fragile union of the old blood. We can ill afford to let our tribal pride step between us and the importance of what we do here."

Geraldo spat. "We are gathered to revel in past glory and honor fools," he said. "The white man and my predecessor were nothing less. I have made a mistake. I should not have come here. The gods would never sanction such a meeting of children, useless women and old men."

"Stop!" The commanding voice belonged to Juan Mapoli who stood, framed in the doorway, supported by Maria.

"How dare you disrupt the peace of this gathering with petty jealousy and complaints?" The old Yaqui looked around the group, his eyes piercing and his frail body trembling with effort. "I am sabio and the representative of my people, as all of you are representatives of yours. It is a disservice to them if we sully the gathering with squabbling and dissention. We are the best our people have to offer. We have a higher debt. We cannot permit ourselves to forget why we are here." He looked directly at Geraldo. "You are here, Priest, upon the command of your council. You are the newcomer, the stranger, the outsider. Are you so wrapped up in your own petty dissatisfactions that you cannot see what we represent?"

Vasquez lowered his gaze, embarrassed.

Leaning on Maria, the old man came out of the doorway and Tom made a place for him on the legless sofa.

Sitting heavily, Juan looked at the others, his eyes burning in sunken sockets. "I am an old man." He spoke in a weak but passionate voice, and all ears strained to hear. "I do not lightly travel from my home, especially not after having been bitten by a viper." His lower lip trembled as he wrestled for strength within. "I am Yaqui, descended directly from the great medicine man Mapoli, who lived when our history began. I do not join groups or go to meetings. I do not give my loyalty to those of other tribes. I am the last, perhaps, of an ancient line. Do you think I would be here if it were not of importance? Do you imagine for a moment that I would jeopardize my wife and my own health if it were not to a purpose?"

Lotus leaned toward the old man filled with concern. She could not remain quiet. "Please, Juan. Remember, we need you."

The Yaqui took a deep breath and visibly brought himself under control. He closed his eyes and he breathed heavily as he centered his being.

When he opened them again, he appeared calm. "Forgive me," he said to all. Addressing himself to the Zuni, he continued. "We are here, Geraldo, my brother, to find those things that unite us and strengthen them, not to find those which separate us." He shook his head, his weariness evident.

Tom laid a friendly hand on Juan's good leg. "We had already agreed not to talk of these matters until all are present. We still lack the Apache, the Navajo and the Hopi. They should arrive soon. Why don't you return to bed. I promise I will call you when they get here."

The sabio looked around the porch, his eyes meeting those of the others and lingering for a long moment on each. Finally, he bowed his head. "You are right, of course," he agreed. "I must rest if I am to be of any use to us." He beckoned to Maria who moved quickly to his side and helped him rise. "Ah, my beautiful maiden," he said to her. "All these years I have leaned on you. Come, let me do so yet again and we will go back to the healing dreams of sleep."

Slowly and with difficulty, the two moved back into the house.

Those remaining on the porch were not quick to break the silence Juan left behind. Each thought of his or her part in what had transpired.

Tom stood. "It may not be the proper thing for a host to do," he said, "but I am going to take a walk in the ravine." He caught Danny's eye and said, "Call me when the others arrive."

As soon as he stepped down from the porch, Useless, who had been hiding during the shouting, came out to join him.

"Ah, there you are," said Tom, bending and stroking the cat from crown to tail. "I wondered where you had gotten to. Come, my friend. Let us walk together."

The two moved off, the cat weaving between the old man's legs whenever he took a step. They had soon passed out of sight.

Geraldo rose and spoke, his voice indicating nothing of what he might be feeling. "Perhaps silence will aid us all in regaining our inner peace. I will go into the house and pray."

He turned stiffly and left the rest sitting there.

"He is right," said Lotus, moving to Danny's side. "It may be that we all have things to consider, things to think through." She smiled. "You all look so glum. Don't be. We have important work to do."

Cord and Michael got up and went down the steps, turning toward the leaf shelters. After a moment, James joined them.

Rattle nodded to the others, then rose and started out in the same direction as Tom Bear.

Kade and Estelle remained with Danny and Lotus on the porch, one couple on each couch. They had no need of words between them. They sat in silence, each lost in his or her own thoughts.

Chapter Thirty-Eight

Casa Malpais

After the death of Dr. Paul Renard, the dig at Casa Malpais stayed leaderless for approximately twenty hours. By the end of that time, his assistant, Dr. Margot Shayley had taken control. No one else possessed the necessary qualifications. She told herself she had no choice. The dig had become the most important single event in her professional career and in her life.

"You understand why I had to step in when I did, don't you Roger?" She spoke to the man she had chosen to move up into the number two spot.

Roger Brogan had worked with Shayley on three sites in the past fifteen years. This, however, stood head and shoulders above the previous two. A major find, this could prove to be the archaeological discovery of the decade.

Neither Margot nor Roger had wanted Paul to go public. They wanted to keep a lid on the project until they had ascertained whether or not they had found it all. They were scientists first and publicity hounds second. Unfortunately, Renard insisted on the opposite course. Paul went public at the April conference in New Orleans.

"Yes, I understand," said Roger in a patient tone. "The unfortunate announcement at the New Orleans Conference, the lurid publicity after Paul's death, the natural curiosity of the public—all of it would have turned this site into a carnival. I think you did the right thing by clamping the lid back down. Stone-walling isn't the heinous crime most people think it is." He looked into her large brown eyes and smiled. "I think you handled it perfectly," he said, "but I don't think it's wise to proceed until the authorities have finished their investigation."

"That could take months," replied Margot. "We're so close. We can't let this delay us."

"We're not even sure the lower chamber exists," insisted Brogan. "It may just be wishful thinking."

"No," shouted the woman. "The seismic echo, the smoke tests, the overall layout convince me." Her own vehemence startled Dr. Shayley. She took a deep breath, counted mentally to ten and then spoke again in a more controlled manner. "There is another level beneath those we've discovered so far. It may date back to as far as thirty thousand years ago."

"But that predates the arrival of man," protested Roger. "If you think it was man-made, who did it?"

"My studies show man migrated across the Bering land bridge from Asia anywhere from 15,000 to 35,000 years ago. That's when I think this lowest chamber was created."

"The Folsom and Clovis samples were carbon dated at no more than 10,500 to 13,000 years ago," insisted Roger. "The rest is all speculation."

"Speculation!" Margot nearly exploded. "How can you say that? The Bering land bridge appears to have been exposed at least twice. The first time probably 50,000 years ago, but, most likely, 25,000. That fits all the data so far. It brought the end of the ice age. Animals and primitive humans were driven out of northeast Asia by the glaciation and crossed to North America."

"How could they have survived?" Roger remained stubborn. "At the end of the ice age, what did your human or near-human migrants eat?"

"Woolly mammoth, steppe bison, wild horse and caribou were among those that had already crossed the bridge," retorted Margot. "My hunters simply lived off them during the hard crossing."

"Okay," agreed Brogan, willing to speculate on the theory. "If you're right, that took them into Alaska. How do you get them this far south?"

Margot paced, scratching her chin and thinking out loud. "The land bridge disappeared then. The water levels rose and it forced my hunters to retreat from the coast and go deeper in. At the same time, the ice barrier between Alaska and Southern Canada melted." She turned and looked triumphant. "Rivalry. Competition," she said. "Tribes were forced to turn south because the fauna had spread too thinly to support all the migrants."

Roger looked at Margot with undisguised admiration. "It sounds plausible," he said, "but we'll have a long way to go if we want to prove it."

"Not necessarily," said his boss. "That's close enough to the time that the meteorite hit and created Meteor Crater. Maybe that's when the tunnels and caverns were created."

"And our Mogollons came along later and just enlarged what already existed?"

"That's what I think," Dr. Shayley said positively. "At least that's what I think we're going to prove."

"Then you believe this lowest chamber predates the settlement?"

"I think it may predate the impact," she said unable to keep the awe from her voice. "More than that, I think our Mogollons knew it."

She moved over to a cross-cut map on the large work table. Beckoning Roger to join her, she pointed out the features that seemed to bear our her theory.

"See? They carved out their prayer rooms on this level all around the area where the lower chamber should be. They apparently made no attempt to break through."

"What stopped them?"

Margot shook her head. "I don't know, but I'll bet we can find out if we just go ahead and break through ourselves."

"What about the visit from the FBI and that pair of Phoenix DPS officers?"

"I'll handle that," said Margot. "But I want you to press ahead with the excavation. Sweep the chambers that surround the central area. Find a place where we can cut through without disturbing anything of importance."

"You're the boss, Doctor," said Roger, and rose in preparation for leaving.

Dr. Shayley stood and took off her glasses. "Don't hurry. Now that the planning is done, it might be fun to, uh . . . well, you know."

He chuckled and moved up to her, taking her face in his hands and placing a firm kiss on her upturned lips. "I still don't know how you managed to keep it from Paul all these years," he said.

"I did what I had to do, and managed to have both of you," she replied simply. "It got me where I wanted to be." She looked up into his eyes with a wicked smile. "You aren't complaining, are you?"

Chapter Thirty-Nine

Salt River Reservation

Gerry and Gordon did not hurry on their journey to Phoenix. Their rental car had air-conditioning and riding felt wonderful. It would not be wise to arrive in the valley before sunset when the temperature began to drop. Accordingly, they stopped to look at scenic views, had a late lunch at a truckstop and even pulled off the road in the mountains just to enjoy the clear, clean air before descending into the Salt River valley and its pollution.

They spoke about Gordon's continuing education, his growing fame as a singer and his sense of urgency about this reunion.

"I can't explain it," said Gordi as they passed Apache Lake and made ready to turn west toward Apache Junction. "I felt a compulsion. I studied with seven different yataalii this past year. Even I'm surprised I could to retain it all."

"Archie would be proud of you," said Gerry. "You have become everything he wished you to be, Fly."

The Navajo smiled. No one called him Fly anymore, except Bert when they were alone. Archie had named him that as a child when his persistent questions reminded the old man of the buzzing of an insect.

It would be good to return to his brothers of the Gathering and to Lotus as well. A frown crossed his face as he remembered that she and Danny were as close to married as they could get. He sighed.

Gerry missed nothing. "What is it?"

Gordon gave him a wry smile. "My thoughts were about Lotus Farley," he admitted. "But then I remembered that she's hooked up with Danny, so I sighed."

"You won't be the last to sigh over that one," said Gerry, remembering the pretty Tohono O'odham medicine woman. "She is all the more remarkable since most of their women do not suit my tasts."

"She came to me at a time when my heart fared little better than an open, raw wound," said Gordon. "I don't think I could have done what had to be done, despite Archie's wishes, if it hadn't been for her."

"She is quite a woman," said Gerry. He gave his companion an understanding look and added, "But we already knew that, didn't we."

Gordon nodded.

They turned south and entered on the north side of the reservation. Less than five minutes later they pulled up at Tom's house.

The old man met them, beaming a welcoming smile and embracing each in turn.

The usual greetings followed. Nine medicine men, one medicine woman, one witch, two wives, all hugged or shook hands or spoke in their usual manner—all except the tenth shaman, Geraldo, who only nodded and said, "An honor to meet you."

Both Gerry and Gordon sensed the tension with the Zuni, but knew enough to wait until a better time to ask Tom.

Gerry did a quick head count. "Who are we missing?" he asked.

Tom said, "We lack the Hopi."

"Harold?" Gordon felt surprise. "Has he sent word?"

Tom shook his head. "Nothing, but I expect he will be along soon enough. Meanwhile, everyone else is here and, this time, the only one hurt is Juan."

"What happened?" asked Gerry, turning to look at the Yaqui, his face indicating concern.

"A rattlesnake bit him two days ago," replied Maria.

Juan raised his hands and made a gesture of dismissal. His face looked much more rested than before. "Do not worry," he said lightly. "I am recovering well and should be ready to resume normal activity tomorrow." He chuckled and pointed to his bandaged leg, adding, "Except for foot races, of course."

Their host looked around at the faces of his friends and smiled. "You are all welcome here," said Tom. "I am especially grateful that our brothers, the Zuni, sent Geraldo to us. The gathering would not be the same without their wisdom."

Vasquez looked uncomfortable, but nodded graciously.

"There is much to speak of," continued Tom, "but we have agreed to wait until all are here so let us hope that Harold arrives soon."

"What have you planned for us?" asked Gordon.

The witch looked over at Estelle. "Mrs. Wonto and Kade have been kind enough to help me in preparing for our reunion," he said. "I will let her tell you what we had in mind."

Estelle stood and faced the others, her nervousness apparent. "You convened the gathering last summer on the 12th of July. This is only the evening of the 5th, so we have some time before any of the formal ceremonies begin." She relaxed as she warmed to her subject. "We thought it would be fun to spend tonight here. We have arranged a barbecue and felt it would be interesting to share stories around a campfire. We'll quit whenever we feel like it and retire for the night."

"What kinds of stories?" asked Rattle.

Kade spoke up. "We thought we'd wait until we actually begin. We can pick a particular subject, if we want, or just tell anything that comes to mind."

"And tomorrow?" asked Gerry.

"If Harold has arrived by then," said Tom, "we will go together with Cord and Michael and do what most tourists seem to like at this time of year. We'll float down the river on inner tubes."

"Tubing?" Geraldo looked shocked. "Is this appropriate for men and women of our stature?"

Danny laughed. "No," he said. "It is decidedly inappropriate. That's why we thought it would be fun. It will make the heat less oppressive and show us one of the ways we have learned to deal with the white community that surrounds us."

Geraldo scowled. "I do not think this tubing is a thing I would enjoy."

"Have you ever done it before?" asked Lotus.

"No."

"Then try it," she urged. "We are all men and women of responsibilities, too often caught up in the serious nature of our work. Why not do something inappropriate just this once and forget the work for a day."

"Not all our activities over this week will be fun," put in Kade. "We do plan some serious things as well. Join us, Geraldo. Be a tourist for one day."

"Please, Geraldo," said Estelle. "You'll enjoy it, I promise."

Looking trapped, the Zuni scanned the other faces. All seemed to be urging him to accept and participate. Then, he noticed Juan. "What of Mapoli?" he asked. "He cannot swim with that leg. Who will stay with him?"

Cord spoke up. "We have arranged a canoe for those who do not swim," he said. "Juan has already agreed to try it."

The Zuni had been outmaneuvered. If he refused now, it would be antisocial and he did not want to widen the gap between himself and the others. "Very well," he said as graciously as he could.

"Good, then that's settled," said Tom. He rose and looked up at the sky. "The sun is setting," he said. "It is time to make ready for our meal. You all know where the showers are and where you can change if you wish to. We will gather here in an hour."

Michael took Gerry and Gordon to the hut they would share with Cord and him. The rest had already settled in.

Danny and Lotus remained on the porch with Tom Bear.

The older man looked worried. "It is all very fine to make plans," he said quietly. "But I have talked with Geraldo, Rattle and James. They each brought disturbing news. Our gathering may turn out to be considerably more than a mere reunion."

"We will talk when Harold arrives," said Lotus. "Whatever it is we must do will be clearer once we have discussed it together."

The old man sighed. "I had so wanted everything to go simply."

Chapter Forty

Deep under Casa Malpais

She had heard the sounds above her, the digging that spoke of others trying to work through the rock and reach her lair. By possessing the bodies of the little ones, She had seen the two-legs working in teams, hammering, chipping, sweeping, bustling with activity. They seemed to want to dig further into the hill. Perfect.

She wanted her freedom. Her mind had searched and sifted through the creatures of the world above and found nothing that presented a threat to her supremacy.

The two-legs remained incomprehensible to her, but they were not a threat—at least not, apparently, until they gathered in large numbers. Then they seemed capable of acting together. She had seen such things before. During the time of her reign, She had watched the insects that ate wood as they strove and built. Perhaps these two-legs were insect-like and acted with a colony consciousness. That, at least, She would be able to understand.

She moved in the absolute dark, her tongue sampling the air, her long form stretched to its full seventy feet of length. She longed for freedom of movement. Her lair extended one hundred-twenty feet long, a dozen feet high and twenty feet wide. She did not think of it in these terms, of course. She knew that She could turn with great difficulty within the chamber and all the distances were relative to her own girth.

The thrice-daily feedings had begun to restore her strength, though She had grown tired of the taste of her own kind. She longed to wrap herself around a mammoth and squeeze it until shapeless, then open her maw and take it within, feeling the bulk slide down her gullet. She remembered the variety that once had been available to her.

She still did not understand what had happened. She had no idea how much time had passed. Her ability to possess the little ones and observe the upper world had shown her a very different place than She remembered. Like a spoiled child, She knew only desire and gratification. Anticipation always involved food or a test of physical strength. Relationships had, even before the change, involved only her dominance of the other species and life forms. She had been alone for decades before her imprisonment began.

She did not think as humans did. She did not have philosophy. She knew only the exercise of power and the pleasure of feeding.

She had never envisioned a time more sophisticated or complex than when She had a full belly. Everything She did and every thought that passed through her mind connected to that mental picture of satisfaction. The rest—the night pilgrimages to the surface to teach her lessons, the development of her ability to compel other creatures by thought—had been a by-product of this instant gratification of need.

But now, trapped below the surface, able only to observe the creatures above and to attack in rage when frustrated, She began to think.

Thinking was something new. She had searched her lair and could discover no exit. She had called the little ones to her. She had satisfied her hunger. She had even found a way to vicariously reach the surface. Still, She could not leave the darkness of her chamber.

She began to build images in her mind.

The concept of "what if?" is the gap that separates lower and higher minds. The degree to which this question is answered is the difference between a moron and a genius. When a creature develops the ability to create that which it can imagine, it has made the leap and bridged that gap.

Many other life forms on the surface of the earth have made the first tentative steps in this direction. Beavers build dams. When did the first envision a way to stop the water from flowing? The hive mind creates structures, uses component parts to fulfill a plan. When did the first hive consciousness develop? To a lesser degree, nest building and the production of young are primitive steps toward this new state of consciousness. To a greater degree, a pride of lions hunting a herd of gazelle exercise imagination, cooperation and planning.

But in most cases, these actions are still related to the sating of hunger and the protection of the young. They are still by-products of the image of satisfaction, the memory of what it is like to be full and safe.

Her enforced imprisonment, the darkness, the loneliness, created a need to bridge that gap stronger than She had ever faced before. Her brain had the capacity; it had simply never been used. Now, for the first time, She used it.

Her observations through the eyes of the little ones of the world above began to create a need for analysis. The lesser creatures were similar enough to those in her past that they presented no mystery, but the two-legs were, indeed, different.

She recognized it in the structures they created, something symmetrical and unnatural in their appearance.

In her experience of the world before what She began to think of as "the change," rivers did not run in angled troughs under the ground. Openings to the surface were not uniform in appearance. Rocks did not grow out of the earth in ordered rows.

She saw the changes and began to wonder how they came about. She saw the two-legs and observed them, discovering that much of what She saw had to be their work. She searched for, but could not find, a hive mind that directed them.

She tried to think what else could bring such things into being.

She struggled with the concept. Enforced hours and days of inactivity in the darkness deprived her of sensory input and left her only with her mind.

She had no choice. She had to think it through.

Chapter Forty-One

Salt River Reservation

The barbecue was well under way when Joseph Concha and Harold Laloma pulled up at Tom's house. The greetings took even longer this time, but Concha finally pulled away, leaving the gathering complete.

When told of the plan for the evening, the Hopi priest agreed enthusiastically to the story telling and soon took his seat with the others, munching a burger and catching up on old times.

He met the Zuni, Vasquez. He had heard much of the priest since Geraldo's selection as head of Gray Wolf Clan. He knew Vasquez possessed an education and refined ways, and could be considered a conservative traditionalist. He had wondered several times if such a man would attend the gathering.

With the meal finished, the shamans smoked tobacco together to set the mood, then Kade stood and asked what they would like to talk about.

"Snakes," said Geraldo.

"Yes," agreed Rattle.

"Good," said Juan.

Kade looked at the rest of those in the circle and saw that all nodded. "Snakes it shall be then." He looked from one to the other all around. "And who will be first?"

"Juan," suggested Lotus. "He must tell us all about the rattlesnake that bit him."

Again all agreed.

So Juan retold the story of the rattler on his porch, of Maria's quick thinking and even swifter action. He made them laugh when he described her dispatching of the viper with the skillet and then shudder as he graphically told them of the wound she put in his leg in order to save his life.

Publicly thanked by all for her quick thinking and loyalty, Maria felt very proud.

Juan finished his tale by speaking of the mind he had sensed just before the snake struck. "I sensed fear and a kind of cold hatred," he said. "Whatever this force is—I think it fears this Gathering."

Rattle, however, spoke next and he told them of his meeting with the Scaled One. As impressed as most of them were, no one felt more surprise than James, who became convinced it must be the same being as that described by the Pawnee, Sharo.

The old Pai told of the stench and the reptilian eyes, the huge bulk of the creature and the human form covered in scales. He related the conversation between them, including the obvious distress of the Scaled One and the threat it conveyed about destroying all the two-legs by making them over.

"When I asked the deer spirit," said Rattle, "it told me the threat is real." He looked over at Maria. "We must be careful not to kill any more serpents."

James Bluesky then told his story of Sharo's visit and about the Scaled One the Pawnee said had been driven west with rattle and drum. He said, "The Pawnee told me to pass on the warning that ancient evils seem to be stirring everywhere in the world. Our encounter with the wind demon may not be the last such meeting for the Gathering."

Gordon, when his turn came, told about Bert's girlfriend and the rattlesnake killed by the slamming door. "Corry said the snakes chased her," he reported, "and we almost didn't believe her. Then when we saw the rattler in the door . . . well, it changed things."

Gerry spoke next. He explained that he had awakened once again as the integrated dual personality that somehow encompassed both George Buck and Geronimo. He said, "Another thing from the past has come into the world—ancient but somehow innocent. I sensed its loneliness but also grave danger."

Geraldo came to his turn and looked around the circle, his face grim and hard. He told of his vision, describing the rock shape that became a living snake. He spoke quietly of his own fear and the feeling of helplessness. He told them how the serpent had prepared to strike, how he had closed his eyes and prayed, and how his prayer had been answered by the Terrible Two, Ahaiyuta and Matselema.

"I knew then that I had to come here," he concluded, "but it is not easy for me. Forgive me if I have seemed unfriendly. All this is very strange to one who has lived all his life in Zuniland."

When the others looked next to Cord Hames, he shook his head and pointed to Michael.

"Neither of us has sensed a thing," he said. "We have only heard the news reports about the deaths."

"That is the truth," said Coyoma. "We have not been visited by gods or visions."

"Nor have we," said Danny, indicating Lotus beside him. "We have spoken with Juan and Maria so we knew this might come up, but we have had no special contact with supernatural beings or even live snakes."

"Nor have I," said Tom, his tone of voice indicating the same puzzlement as his face.

"Nor I," said Kade, "but Estelle has been having dreams of late that seem to be more like what the rest of you have experienced."

"Nothing specific," protested Estelle. "Simply that something momentous was going to happen soon."

"It seems I am to be the last," said Harold from where he had been sitting quietly in the circle. His face looked strange in the firelight, as if what he must say would prove somehow distasteful.

"Did you have a vision, Harold?" asked Lotus.

The Hopi shook his head. "No," he replied, "but just before I left, my two fellow priests, John Lakona and Joseph Lansa, visited me. You have heard me speak of them before. They set my leg last year."

"And what did they say, Harold?" asked Kade.

"They told me very serious news," said the Hopi. "They told me that the snake harvest in preparation for the great dance has been going badly—that there have been deaths."

"But the Hopi are the best snake handlers anywhere," protested Danny. "I have seen them. How can this be?"

The Coyote Priest shook his head. "I do not know, Danny. It is already worse than at any time in our history and the dance lies more than a month away. It is a very bad sign."

Gerry spoke. "It would seem that we do not yet have enough information to act. One of our number has already been attacked, two have been warned. Two of us have had premonitions and one, Geraldo, had a full vision including participation of the gods."

"And there have been many deaths from snakes this year—more than at any time in the state's history," put in Cord.

"What does it mean?" asked Tom.

"Something is still missing," replied Gerry, his brow creased with thought. "I wish Jack could be here. He could think."

"That's it," said Danny. "That's what we lack. We represent the twelve tribes, but we lack the white man."

"The thirteenth tribe," said Kade. "Perhaps you are right."

"But who would that be?" asked Michael. "The archaeologist is dead. The weatherman has gone away. The detective has been promoted to greater responsibilities."

"It would not be the same men," said Tom. "We need someone who knows science in the white world. We need an expert on snakes."

Juan laughed. "They are called herpetologists," he said, "and I know which one we want."

"Who is that?" asked Gordon.

"His name is Myers," replied the Yaqui. "You will go to the river tomorrow without me. Maria and I will pay a call on this man."

"Perhaps we should cancel our plans," suggested Lotus. "It does not seem proper that we spend the day floating on the river when there is work we might do."

"I agree," said Geraldo.

Juan laughed even more and the strain of his injury washed away in genuine mirth. "You won't get out of it that easily, my Zuni brother. The rest of you continue as Estelle and Tom planned." His laughter faded slowly and he added, "The task will begin soon enough."

July 6th

Chapter Forty-Two

Casa Malpais

At 8:30 am the next morning, Lieutenants Ramirez and Grimsley arrived at the site of the excavation of Casa Malpais accompanied by Jeremy Myers.

Dr. Margot Shayley and her assistant, Roger Brogan, greeted them at the site office and the five of them sat down over coffee to discuss the purpose of the visit.

"We believe the deaths that occurred here are related to the increased snake activity throughout the state," Ed began. "We'd like to know exactly what you're doing here and Dr. Myers would like to collect some specimens for testing."

Dr. Shayley, an attractive woman in her forties, smiled. "We'll be happy to cooperate, Lieutenant, as we have been doing with Agent Pierce of the FBI and the local authorities." She turned her attention to Jeremy. "I've heard of you, of course, Dr. Myers," she said. "Roger will be more than happy to show you where you can find all the rattlesnakes you wish. We'd be delighted to have you remove as many as you like."

"Have they been a problem?" Jeremy didn't like the woman. She seemed too smooth.

"They're everywhere," put in Roger. "The entrances are labyrinthine, as you may have read, and require that we pass through some tight and extremely narrow openings. Unfortunately, the snakes seem to favor these spots and ledges beside them as resting places."

"But no one else has been hurt?" Rod was curious.

"Other than Dr. Renard and that guard, no," replied Dr. Shayley. "We are professionals and conduct our activities with considerable care. We employ two herpetology students from the university to handle any snakes we encounter."

"What exactly are you doing here, Dr. Shayley?" asked Rod.

"We're exploring and mapping an ancient Mogollon habitat," replied Margot. "They lived here about 700 years ago and were in residence for at least a century. The population probably never exceeded 800 individuals, but they did a great deal of work in digging out the natural chambers and creating a series of catacombs."

"Is that it?" asked Ed. "I mean, is it just mapping out the passages and chambers?"

"Well," said Brogan, sitting back in his chair, "we think there may be something more to discover here, if that's what you mean."

"We aren't prepared yet to discuss our expectations in detail," added Margot, "but the news story did say we hope for more."

Ed Ramirez knew they condescended. He didn't like it, but tried to keep the irritation from his face and voice. "What is the purpose of the excavation?" he asked.

Dr. Shaley answered. "This area has some unique characteristics that make it a fruitful site for study." She ticked them off on her fingers. "First we have Meteor Crater. Second we have a plethora of underground faults, fissures and caves—probably the result of tectonics and the impact. Third we have an ancient ruin that contradicts much of what we thought we knew about the people who lived here."

Brogan picked it up. "Dr. Shayley and I believe that there may be a sealed chamber from much earlier—say 25,000 years ago—before the impact of the meteorite."

"Containing?" Jeremy could not disguise his fascination.

"Probably only fossils," admitted Roger, "but there is the possibility that humans were here by then, at least primitive humans."

"So you're looking for anything they may have left behind, is that it?" asked the herpetologist.

Margot smiled. "Fossils, tools or weapons, fragments of cloth-ing—anything that can help us ascertain the time period when the lowest chambers were first used would do the trick."

"You actually think you might find things that old?" Jeremy understood something about prehistory and was skeptical.

Margot's eyes sparkled as she spoke. "We haven't yet, Dr. Myers, but it is a distinct possibility. Unfortunately, this is all speculation at present and archaeology doesn't deal in wishful thinking. We have to have hard evidence."

"If you did find artifacts that old underground, what would it really prove?" asked Lieutenant Grimsley.

"If it only helped us more closely pinpoint the date of the impact of the meteorite," offered Roger with a shrug, "it would be valuable. On the other hand, it might give us something really spectacular— some article or fragment from the first people to colonize this area of the continent."

Dr. Shayley laughed. "You're an incurable romantic, Roger." She looked at the three visitors. "We may find nothing more than what we already have. Even if we do discover something, it might take years even to recognize it as significant. In our business the answers come slowly when they come at all."

"Could I speak to the herpetology students you employ?" Jeremy wanted to confirm that there had been no unusual or anomalous activity among the vipers.

Margot nodded. "Roger will be happy to round them up for you," she said. "Would all of you like to take a tour of what we've found so far?"

Ed Ramirez felt that queasy sensation starting in the pit of his stomach and working its way up. The thought of entering another tunnel or series of tunnels filled with poisonous snakes set his teeth on edge, but he nodded, not trusting himself to speak.

Strangely, Rod looked reluctant. "Maybe we should split up, Ed. I'll look at the place Renard and the guard died. We can cover more ground that way. Besides, maybe we can get to town early."

The look Ed turned on his partner could have been used as a study of human expression. It encompassed fear, anger, resignation and courage all at the same time.

When he finally spoke, he said, "You're probably right, Rod. Dr. Myers and I will take the herpetology students with us in case we run into snakes. You can climb the hill and look at where the fatalities occurred."

Jeremy felt mixed emotions. He wanted to see the dig, but he wanted much more to interview the students away from their bosses. "I think it would be better, Lieutenant Ramirez, if you take the tour while I meet with the two who have been handling the snakes. They probably have specimens in a lab and we'll want to talk shop."

Ed's look of betrayal almost made Jeremy regret suggesting anything of the sort, but it passed quickly from his face as he steeled himself for the ordeal.

"Fine," Ramirez agreed shortly. "That's the way it'll be then." He stood and looked at Dr. Shayley. "Is there someone who can show me around this place?"

Margot's face expressed dismay at all three men wanting to head off in different directions. She made an instant decision. "I'll take Lieutenant Ramirez on a tour of the site," she said. "Roger, why don't you accompany Lieutenant Grimsley to the hill where Paul died. On the way, you can drop Dr. Myers off at the field lab and introduce him to James and Pamela."

Roger could also see what had happened, and moved quickly to comply. It wouldn't matter. After all, what harm could a herpetologist do? "If you gentlemen will accompany me," he said to Rod and Jeremy, "I'll arrange our transportation."

"Okay," said Rod. "We'll see you back here in a couple hours, Ed."

"Yeah, right," muttered Ramirez.

When the other three had exited, Ed turned to find Dr. Shayley studying him.

"You don't seem eager to see the archaeological find of the decade," she teased.

"Oh, yeah, I am," he replied. "I can't fu . . . 'scuse me," he covered it with a sort of fake sneeze, "can't wait."

Chapter Forty-Three

The Mesas, Hopiland

Elmer Smith handled snakes. For thirteen years he had presided at the ceremonies, teaching the young ones to capture and tame the vipers, the snake brothers. For all of those years he had been the master of his craft, never letting a mundane thought intrude on the purity of mind or the concentration required to do what he did. He understood the vipers, he had lived in their scaly little heads, had felt their cold hearts beating, knew them as only one of their own might know them.

From the first day of the harvest, he had kept them in their places—dangerous rattlesnakes in a confined area, yet serpents of beauty who would serve to show the brotherhood between man and snake. No one possessed as much skill as Elmer.

He had studied with Abner Youngman, the legendary handler, who, even thirty years after his death, lived on in the annals of the Hopi. The old snake master had taught him well. Elmer had become the most famous student of the most prestigious teacher.

But this year, things were different.

Normally, when one of the snakes moved from the area designated for it, Elmer simply fanned at it with his eagle wand and it retreated. The snakes remembered the feathered predator as their natural enemy. The feathers were usually enough. If the serpent persisted, Smith picked it up and placed it back where it belonged, in the knot of vipers that always formed in the corner of the pen. Normally, the serpents accepted their lot, moving within the designated area as obedient and calm as sleepy children.

This year, they moved restlessly, hissed at each other and shook their rattles in continuous pandemonium. They seemed never to be at rest, constantly seeking release from the pen. They acted as if they were under some compulsion to escape.

Elmer did not know what to do. He sensed the difference, knew that the pen verged on the edge of control. He knew he could not continue to act as shepherd for this flock. He felt perspiration on his face, under his armpits and even creeping in rivulets down his thighs. He felt fear.

Fear and snakes are anathema.

The big mohave rattler from the pink cliffs had been the pride of his captor. The young man, called George Smiley, had been true to his name when he presented the viper for acceptance as one of the sacred snakes. The largest ever brought out of the desert, it measured eight feet, two inches and almost six inches across at its thickest point.

In accordance with tradition, the snake had been bathed and scented. It had been stroked and comforted, fed and praised. It had been lulled into sleep and carried gently, reverently, to the holding pen. There it had been placed with the others, but there the similarities ended.

From that moment on, the Mohave acted strangely, behaving as if it and the other snakes were of a different species altogether. It moved more quickly, fed more voraciously, existed on a plane totally unlike that of the other snakes.

For the past hour, it had been testing Elmer. It would provoke the others, hissing and rattling like a sideshow pitchman, then move unobtrusively out of the the way. When one of the handlers responded to the activity, it would slither quickly toward the weakest point of the pen and attempt to escape.

Smith had been the only one able to control it. The serpent seemed unaffected by the eagle wand, ignoring the gentle brushing. Since it would not respond to this herding technique, Elmer would grab it firmly behind the head and lift the heavy body, moving it efficiently back to the far side of the pen. Every time he set it loose, it struck at him, but he was too quick for it. It had become a contest of sorts.

To an observer, it might have seemed the serpent put on a well-rehearsed performance. The agitation, attempted escape and capture might, after a while, even have appeared normal.

In his heart, however, the handler knew the Mohave intended to kill him.

He held his eagle wand before him like a shield.

The kiva remained silent except for the hissing of the snakes. Other men and the boys came and went on missions of their own, but Elmer spoke to none. He had been tasked with controlling the serpents.

He focussed all his concentration on his job.

But then the pattern broke down.

The Mohave started forward once again, intent on leaving the pen, but this time four other vipers followed. The five snakes moved almost as one, quickly toward the place where Elmer reclined. As they moved away from the wall, they spread out, forming a fan-shaped skirmish line.

Smith rose to his feet. He stood alone in the chamber, the other men momentarily absent.

The snakes did not hesitate, but moved swiftly toward him, closing in from all sides and forcing the handler to back up toward the wall.

Elmer's heart beat wildly.

He turned toward the Mohave, instinctively side-stepping the strike of one of the smaller rattlers that had moved up from the left side.

The bigger snake, which remained at the center of the line, coiled, its larger body blocking any retreat.

Smith brushed with his wand at the next viper to advance, this time from the right. It had no effect. The rattler struck, actually hitting the wood inches from his hand.

All the while, two emotions warred within the mind of the handler.

First came utter disbelief, incredulity. In thirteen years, no snake brothers had ever done such a thing. A coordinated attack defied possibility.

Second came raw, panic-driven fear.

As another, even smaller snake, tried to strike, Elmer gauged the distance, gathering his strength to leap over the serpents in his bid for freedom. His body almost bursting with adrenaline, he leaped up and outward in a soaring arc, only to be met at the apex of flight by the fangs of the Mohave.

It struck him on the calf of his trailing leg and he felt the penetration and sudden added weight.

He crashed to the floor of the kiva, breath gushing out from the force of his fall.

He next sensed the rattler's fangs expelling venom into the wound, immediately followed by a raging pain that moved quickly up his leg. He tried to rise, to reach down and remove the Mohave from where it clung, but then felt the multiple strikes as the other snakes reached him.

He fell unconscious in seconds, died in minutes.

Chapter Forty-Four

The Roberts Ranch, Springerville

Time passed slowly for Mad Jake Roberts. He felt the walls of the shelter closing in—a crushing, suffocating feeling— and it grew in intensity as his third day under the surface dragged by. He climbed the ladder four times during the afternoon, but didn't dare to open the trap.

The watchers were still there. He had ventured forth the night before to verify it, taking the same route through the junk piles. He had prowled much of the night, a silent shadow blending into the darkness, approaching within feet of the agents in their concealment. In the night, it seemed a game. He knew the ground, they did not. He considered killing both men, but that would only bring others and might start an even more thorough search of the area. He doubted they would be able to locate his hidden entrance, but the risk was too great. Though confined during the day, the nights brought freedom of sorts. Why chance it?

So he chafed and fretted under the ground as the hours passed, waiting for the night to set him free.

Because stayed awake much of the night, he slept most of the morning. Noon until sunset proved most difficult. He read and drank, ate, and lay in his bed, and planned what he would do once the surveillance was lifted and he could go resume his normal—if anything about Jake could be considered normal—life.

Then, two hours before the dark, he had an idea. He could kill at least one of the agents and get away with it. He could strike in the darkness and never be suspected. He would use a snake.

All he had to do was catch a rattler and throw it into the agent's lap. With luck, the bite would be fatal, but even if not, the watcher would go to the other for help and both would probably leave in search of medical assistance. That would give him time to get back into his house, something he wanted but didn't quite have courage to try.

He chuckled to himself. "Perfect. I'll get a couple of the scaly little bastards so I have something to amuse myself."

The next two hours were filled with things to do.

He gathered his telescoping rod and hook, two muslin bags for the specimens, packed a sandwich and changed into his hunting gear. He made a list of things he would take from the house after the departure of the agents. He prepared a cage and dissection table for the specimen he planned to keep, all the while humming little songs to himself, his spirits high now that he had a plan of action.

Just before dark, he opened the door in the rear of the shelter and crawled through the opening in the rock, intending to follow the course of the spring out into the wash. The way ran narrow and twisted, but no one would spot him using it.

When he had made it partway through, however, he couldn't get over the feeling that the passage had somehow gotten larger. Using his flashlight, he illuminated the rock walls. They even looked different. He saw considerable dust and crumbled stone along the edges of the watercourse. The natural tunnel seemed wider.

"Must be my imagination," he said to himself. "I've got to lay off the booze a little. It's distorting my sense of perspective."

He shrugged and continued on his way. The usually difficult journey went swiftly and smoothly. The walls did seem farther apart, the rock roof higher.

"Memory loss," he whispered in the dark. "I just don't remember it right."

Eventually, he came out of the hillside into the wash. He moved quickly in search of the specimens.

His quest proved difficult. He had hunted this area so thoroughly in the past that most of the reptiles were gone. In addition, hunting snakes by flashlight increased the danger.

He checked crevasses and fissures that once supported large numbers of rattlers, but now lay empty under the harsh beam of his lamp.

"Shit!" He cursed to himself as he had to range further and further from the spring outlet. Though still early, he had a great deal to do this night. He did not want to postpone his plans. Anything might happen to change them. The agents might move their observation posts, the weather might turn sour.

The desert was cloaked in beauty and mystery. Not occluded by light from the cities, the night sky glowed with breathtaking clarity.

Unhindered by moonlight, Jake's night vision revealed the desert in all its glory. Like a crab in a strange dry sea, he scuttled quietly up and down the hillsides, searching.

He hunted for over two hours before he finally heard a warning rattle. He turned the light on the crevass and saw a group of Western Diamondback Rattlesnakes, two adults and three babies.

Perfect!

Using the hook, Jake lifted the male and bagged it quickly. The other adult, obviously the female, lay coiled protectively around her young, rattling viciously. He drew his machete and cut off its head. Why waste time?

The remaining vipers were barely mature. He scooped them up into the second bag.

Jake took a few moments to hack up the body of the female. It felt good to hear the satisfactory chunking sound as the machete chopped through the meat, severing bones and dicing the snake into pieces. His face broke into a wide smile and his eyes got glassy as he pursued the task. God, he loved his work.

Finally, he retrieved his specimen bags and started back. He checked his watch. It lacked some minutes of midnight so he could proceed as planned. He circled the ranch and returned to the trap by crawling through the junk tunnel.

When he went to open it, however, he discovered it remained secured from inside.

"Fuck," he muttered. He had forgotten to release the catch. Since he exited through the spring tunnel, he hadn't remembered to open the door.

Well, he had no choice. He piled his equipment and the second bag next to the entrance, took the adult diamondback in its sack and crawled toward the house. He would deal with the agent, then double back to the wash and return through the spring tunnel to the shelter. Then he would release the trap, reach out and drag his equipment and remaining specimens inside.

The agent in the tool shed provided the best opportunity. Jake made his way patiently to the back of the structure. Once there, he sat quietly and listened.

A scrape of movement alerted him and he watched as the man walked out into the open, just four yards away. The cool, moisture laden air clung to him.

The agent shivered in discomfort. He had donned his jacket and still looked miserable.

The man moved back inside and tried to close the window, but it was stuck. Jake held his breath, but the agent didn't see him couched just outside and below the sill.

Further scraping indicated the movement of furniture. After that came silence.

After a minute had passed, Jake rose without a sound and peered within.

The agent sat in a chair, one leg propped up on a crate, and hunched up as if trying to sleep. Best of all, he had his back to the window and the chair tilted back against the sill. The man could not have been more cooperative. Jake hardly believed his luck.

Fortunate or not, however, he wasted no time. He felt through the muslin until he had identified the business end of his diamondback. Trapping the head, he slowly removed the bag from the rest of the snake. When he had it completely out, he changed his grip, firmly holding the serpent just behind the head and by the tail to keep it silent.

Jake wanted to call to the man, to taunt him and then throw the snake at him, but he knew better. Even if bitten, chances were good that the agent would get help and be saved. It would not do for him to remember seeing Roberts. The Fibbies were already pissed enough. No, it had to be a quick drop and hasty retreat without being observed.

He held the snake out at arm's length, let it fall over the man's neck, then stepped quickly out of sight.

As he moved away from the window, he heard the snake hiss and the agent scream. He tried hard to keep his laughter soundless as he quietly ran toward the wash.

Chapter Forty-Five

Casa Malpais

Ed Ramirez followed Margot Shayley, rappelling down steep slopes to enter the twisting labyrinth that comprised the entrance to the catacombs of Casa Malpais, the Badlands House. Though he expected to, he saw no rattlesnakes.

When asked about them, the archaeologist replied, "Our herpetology students have caught and removed all the snakes that were in here when we first opened it up. They have quite a collection of them over in the field lab. I'm sure your Dr. Myers will find all the specimens he could want." She looked back at the white-faced cop, her eyes twinkling. "There were snakes in all those fissures we just passed."

Ed tried not to let his discomfort show. He kept his face blank and concentrated on the path. "The department appreciates your cooperation, Dr. Shayley."

The woman moved with the practiced surety of a veteran, finding the next step down or angled turn without hesitation.

Despite the treacherous footing, a part of Ed's mind attempted to analyze how the woman did it. He knew she had travelled this route hundreds of times, but could not help admiring her smooth, seemingly effortless, progress. His awkward movements marked him as a blundering novice, slipping and sliding whenever he missed a step.

The carefully hidden entrances varied in size from doorways to small crawl spaces.

"These catacombs and chambers constitute an area about four acres in size," said Margot as she dropped to her hands and knees and moved through a low opening in the rock.

"Wonderful," said Ramirez to no one in particular. Shed snakeskins still dotted the fissured walls above. "Just wonderful," he muttered again as he crouched to follow the doctor through the passage.

The tunnel was only five feet long, and Ed emerged into darkness. When he moved forward to get clear of the overhang and stand up, a hand shot out and grabbed his shoulder, jerking him back to the wall.

"What the fu . . . uh, what is it?" he asked with vehemence.

"You almost went off a ledge," said Margot's voice. "We turn to the right here." She shifted her flashlight and the lieutenant saw that, had he taken another step, he would have fallen twenty feet to the jagged rock shelf below.

"Uh, thanks," he managed to say.

"Don't mention it," said the doctor. "We can't have our important visitors dying here, Lieutenant. What kind of press coverage would we get then?"

"Yeah, well, uh . . . I never thought of it that way," Ed mumbled.

He became aware of the sound of machinery.

They turned a corner and entered a chamber lighted by a generator powered lamp. Several other people were already present.

"How is it going?" Margot asked, raising her voice to be heard over the generator, though the engine did not seem exceptionally loud.

A man wearing a blue hardhat entered at that moment. His face lit with pleasure when he saw her.

"Doctor. I had just decided to go hunt for you. You never seem to have time to visit us down here any more."

Margot returned the smile. "You're right, Richard. Administration is an alligator that consumes time."

The man looked curiously at Ramirez.

"Oh, forgive me," said Margot with a sigh. "This gentleman is a visitor, Lieutenant Ramirez from the Arizona Department of Public

Safety. Lieutenant, this is Richard Ames, one of our archaeology students."

"How do you do, Lieutenant?" Ames offered his hand and Ed took it. The grip felt firm and friendly.

"I'm really glad you came down, Dr. Shayley," said the student. "We've found something on the lower level. I know you'll want to see it."

Margot's demeanor changed instantly. The excitement she obviously felt flushed her face and her eyes grew brighter. "What is it?" she asked.

The student smiled. "There's a carving or a painting on a rock wall. It forms an arch. The forward team is cleaning it right now. Come see it."

"Lead me to it," she said, turning the younger man around and literally pushing him ahead.

Ignoring Ed, she followed the student through another door-sized opening and disappeared from view.

The lieutenant hesitated only a moment before following. He caught up with them in a few seconds, but stayed back and asked no questions. The doctor seemed completely unaware of his presence.

"When did you find it?" Margot asked as she hurried the younger man along.

"Just fifteen minutes ago, Doctor," replied Ames. "We were following the new orders from Dr. Brogan, sweeping and using the steamer to clean the walls, when the painting started to show up. We immediately switched to brushes and, when I saw the image, I left to get you."

Ramirez followed them down a series of rough steps into another, smaller chamber.

Three others, all wearing the blue hardhats, were working on the far side with brushes.

The chamber appeared to be about twenty feet high and had been carved out of the natural rock. Ed surmised that the room had once been an irregularly-shaped cave or tunnel, but it had been expanded into a large rectangle by the ancient Mogollons.

The wall on which the others worked looked flat and smooth, except that it had an arch carved at the top, almost gothic in style.

The intricate incising showed the heads of serpents on each side, fully two feet high, mouths opened and fangs exposed. Between them, creating the arch, hung the undulant, scaled body of a great snake, a dozen feet from snout to tail, represented realistically.

The wall below had been about three quarters washed and cleaned and on it appeared a painting, worn and splotched in places, of the same snake coiled in a huge circle.

Upon seeing it, Margot stopped dead in her tracks and stared.

Ed hung back by the entrance.

The others, seeing the administrator enter, had stepped back and waited respectfully for her reaction. Every face wore the same bright-eyed excitement, the same look of anticipation.

The doctor walked forward and ran her hand over the head of the serpent that stared out from the center of the wall. She caressed it almost lovingly. "Magnificent," she whispered.

The chamber grew silent as all held their collective breath. The room glowed with battery powered lamps.

Margot stepped back and turned to Ames. "This is a great discovery," she said quietly, her voice tinged with awe. She rewarded each of the others with a warm smile of congratulations. "You may have found what I wanted," she said. "Casa Malpais may be about to surrender it's last secret."

Suddenly, she seemed to snap out of her reverie and turned to look back across the chamber.

Ed Ramirez became the focus of five sets of staring eyes.

The moment seemed to stretch out.

Finally, the doctor laughed and walked toward the policeman. "Congratulations, Lieutenant," she said. "You are witnessing a very exciting new discovery."

"It's very impressive," replied Ed.

She turned and gazed up at the wall, the arch, the painting. "Yes, it is, isn't it?"

"What do you think it means?" asked Ramirez.

A guarded look came over the doctor's face for a moment, then she smiled again. "We won't know for a while, Lieutenant, but it may be something bigger than you imagine."

She turned back to Ames. "Call Dr. Brogan," she said quietly. "Tell him to meet me in my office after he's inspected this."

"Yes, ma'am."

She backed away from the wall, obviously reluctant to take her eyes from the painting, then took Ed's arm and firmly led him out.

"I'm afraid I'll have to cut our tour short, Lieutenant. This is a major find and I'll have to consult with Dr. Brogan before we know how to proceed. I'd appreciate it if you and the others would leave us for today. You can come back in a week or so if you feel it is absolutely necessary."

"I understand, doctor," replied Ed graciously. "We've probably seen all we need to for today." He thought privately that he would be glad to get out of this place deep in the earth.

They did not speak again as they made their way out of the catacombs, saving their breath for the exertions required to negotiate the difficult path.

Margot appeared to be completely preoccupied with her own thoughts.

Emerging once again into the bright sunshine, Ed blinked and rubbed his eyes. "I'll collect Lieutenant Grimsley and Dr. Myers," he said. "We'll get back to town and leave you to your work."

"I appreciate that, Lieutenant," said Dr. Shayley. She offered her hand, her grasp perfunctory.

"Goodbye, Doctor," he said. "You'll be seeing us again."

He did not know whether she heard and understood him. She seemed already lost in speculation about the painting and the arch in the chamber.

"No doubt, no doubt," she said, turning away and walking briskly back to her office.

Ed watched her go. What a strange woman. A practical down-to-earth type or she wouldn't be in charge here, yet somehow vulnerable and . . . he shook his head. He knew better than to try to analyze women.

The lieutenant made his way down the hill to where his companions waited.

Five minutes later, back on the road, they headed for Phoenix.

Chapter Forty-Six

Fort McDowell Indian Reservation

Geraldo Vasquez eyed the inner tube with suspicion. He still did not think it appropriate for one of his station to go floating on the river with the tourists. He hated the idea of ignoring the serious business of life merely to have fun. It would be something he had never done before.

They had all arisen at dawn, donning bathing suits and loading into the pickup trucks. Cord and Michael had arranged for rental tubes. They arrived at the river to find a delegation of some twenty Chemehuevi and Mohave who had come to pay their respects to the visitors.

The serious and ceremonial nature of the meeting became somewhat affected by the sight of Lotus in a skimpy string bikini. The men, regardless of age, crowded around her while ignoring the others. The female members of the delegation waited only a few moments before corralling their men, some with very unsubtle epithets and even a swat or two.

Through it all, a village elder named Peter tried to express thanks to the Gathering for its service the previous summer in ridding the world of the wind demon. Only Gordon and Tom were able to maintain the dignified expressions required of them for such a serious occasion. The rest hung back with the crowd, giggling like school-children—all except Geraldo.

He did not own a bathing suit and had been forced to accept the loan of one from Tom Bear. Since Tom was taller and weighed more, the suit looked huge on the slight frame of the Zuni. The wiry little priest stood far off from the crowd, wishing fervently he could be any place but there. He feared he did not look dignified.

He did not.

But dignity had not been ordained as the order of the day for the shamans. They had come to the river to have fun and shared a spirit of bravado and excitement. The work would remain. Today they would play like children.

Rattle, at first, had planned to simply doff his clothing and go naked on the river.

Danny and Lotus had been forced to speak sternly to him until he understood the propriety required when among the tourists.

The Pai expressed amazement at the idea of bathing costumes. "Why would one dress to bathe?" he asked.

Lotus and Danny exchanged a glance at once amused and help-less. They both agreed that wearing a suit to swim was like getting dressed for sex. Nonetheless, they patiently explained there were laws about nudity in public places and they would all have to obey.

"White men are crazy," muttered the old man, shaking his head.

Danny and Lotus persisted, trying to keep from laughing aloud, but finally got the old man to agree to leave his khaki shorts on.

"Besides," suggested Danny, suddenly inspired, "you wouldn't want to expose yourself to too much sun. A burn down there is extremely painful."

Rattle looked up at the cloudless sky and the bright sun and nodded slowly. "Perhaps you are right," he agreed. "That is a reason for obeying these rules."

The Verde ran swift and cold. As Cord and Michael tied the tubes into a raft-like affair, the others entered the water.

James Bluesky, who bathed in the river every day, dove in and surfaced again, only to complain. "Too warm," he said.

Kade and Estelle, looking plump and old fashioned in archaic 1950's swimsuits, entered the water stoically, as if it were nothing to plunge into the cold.

Rattle jumped in and splashed about like a child, his age seeming to melt away.

Danny and Lotus dove in together and came up tickling each other and laughing.

Gerry and Gordon both walked into the river and immediately ducked under the surface only to appear many yards further upstream, gasping claims of victory after their contest.

Tom and Harold launched the canoe which, despite the absence of Juan and Maria, they had elected to bring anyway.

Geraldo stood on the river bank, dressed in his baggy trunks, holding an oversized truck tube, looking for all the world like a lost little boy.

Danny approached him, took the tube and tied it with the others. He indicated the Zuni should sit in the center. When Vasquez complied, he found the cool water felt good. He decided this might not be such a bad thing to try after all.

When all had been prepared, they cast off from the shore and let the current take them downstream.

The Salt River is only a river during certain periods of time each year. Further south, fed by the Verde, it runs through Phoenix and tourists are often surprised to see the signs for *The Great Salt River* while below them the bridge spans only a wide expanse of dry earth.

As the snow melts on the mountains in Northern Arizona, the run-off can add vast amounts of water to the lake and dam system that serves the state. Then the authorities are forced to release water from the dams to relieve pressure. The rivers can become dangerous. In 1979, every major bridge between Phoenix, Tempe and Scottsdale was washed away by the raging water.

But not this summer. The weather stayed hot, the river cold, and companionship soon thawed even the stern Geraldo Vasquez. In no time, they were laughing and dunking each other, swimming underwater and leaping at those who could be taken unaware, ultimately just relaxing lazily as the current took them down. Since they started north of the Highway 87 bridge, the river was uncrowded until later in the adventure.

There were others. Most were white tourists or locals, but the shamans were impressed with the courtesy they encountered.

People having fun are just that—people. And people can be nice if given the chance.

Part of the good behavior resulted from the order established by the tribal rangers who collect the fees and police the river. Those who failed to obey the rules were escorted from the reservation and banned for a number of years.

Tom and Harold took charge of the canoe, the center point of their flotilla, and changed off with Michael and Cord from time to time when they wished to cool off in the water. They spoke of nothing important, discussed no business, and seemed to enjoy just getting to know one another.

Harold spent much of his time preoccupied with thoughts of Hopiland and the deaths he had come to report. He knew in his heart that something important transpired at home, but still had no idea what could be done about it. From time to time, he resented this outing on the river for he was anxious to see Juan and learn what had happened at the offices of the herpetologist.

Tom, during one of his shifts paddling the canoe, spotted a rattlesnake sunning itself atop some rocks on the riverside. Perhaps he imagined it, but the snake seemed to watch them as they glided past, almost like a sentinel.

Once he had seen the first, he noticed other rattlers as they made their way down the river. There never seemed any active threat of danger, and he never saw them when there were tourists nearby, but he counted at least six different snakes, all watching from vantage points along the bank until the shamans drifted by.

He mentioned it to Gordon and Danny, who also kept watch.

Gradually, the carefree nature of their outing changed from fun and frolic to a kind of half-hearted play mixed with anxious watch-fulness.

Everyone caught on. Lotus and Kade spotted snakes as did Estelle and James. Gordon saw three and even Geraldo saw two.

When they reached the end-point and got out of the river, the subdued group made its way quickly to the trucks and headed home.

Chapter Forty-Seven

City of Phoenix

Juan Mapoli sat impatiently in the waiting room of the lab. Jeremy Myers had called ahead and announced his imminent arrival so the old man and his wife agreed to wait.

If he had been asked to explain why he knew that he, and ultimately all the Gathering, must speak to the herpetologist, Juan would have found it difficult. It manifested viscerally, a part of the old man's connection to nature, an undeniable element of the matrix that made up this unique and aware human being. Regardless of reason, Mapoli knew that he must stay and wait, so he took a mushroom from his pouch, popped it into his mouth, and chewed thoughtfully while Maria read the magazines that littered the table.

He knew why he had come. Myers had been the man consulted by the police regarding all the deaths. Myers had been the scientist whose opinions were highly regarded. The herpetologist represented the authority upon which the white world relied—as had the archaeologist, Jack Foreman.

The similarities between the two were too great for Juan to ignore. The Gathering had proved the worth of the white man in the adventure of the wind demon. The Yaqui had seen how the forces of the universe worked without effort, meshing the elements of the Native American world with those of the modern white world. He knew that the power came not to one group alone but to the combination of those who represented the spirit of man—and that they could not ignore the brothers whose skin happened to be of a lighter shade.

So, despite the pain of his leg, he waited and thought about the potentials of this new liaison with the world so foreign to his southwestern desert.

The wait seemed long.

Myers did not arrive until three in the afternoon. When he did, he hurried in, bearing specimen cases from the dig at Casa Malpais.

Juan guessed the last thing the doctor wanted would be to have his valuable time taken by a Yaqui medicine man wanting to talk to him about snakes.

Nonetheless, Jeremy proved to be a good human being, a kind man. He showed no rudeness, even though pressed for time. Instead, he invited the old man and the woman into his office to speak their minds.

"There is a reason for all these deaths," said Juan as an opening. "I think you must have realized by now that something controls the serpents."

Jeremy did not know how to reply. Though he resisted the idea, he had been thinking exactly the same thing. It made sense. It explained what otherwise could not be reconciled with the knowledge he had accumulated in a lifetime of study. Unfortunately, he was in no mood to discuss it.

He sighed. "Mr. Mapoli," he said, his voice expressing weariness, "I don't wish to be rude, but I have spent all morning traveling to and from the ruins of Casa Malpais. I have brought back three specimens that I must test. If there is something in particular that I can do for you, please tell me what it is. Otherwise, I fear I must ask you to leave and let me get on with my work."

The old man looked at the younger scientist and nodded. "Fair enough. I believe there is a way that I can help you to determine exactly what is going on."

Myers sat back in his chair and looked at his visitor with genuine interest. "Okay," he said. "Talk to me."

"I have an ability," began the old man, then paused and laughed. "No, that is not the way to start. Forgive me, I spend much of my time alone in the desert. I forget that the wider world requires proof."

Jeremy was intrigued. "What can I do for you?"

The Yaqui looked at him, his deep-set brown eyes like windows on another dimension. "Would you be willing to take fifteen minutes for a simple experiment?"

"What kind of experiment?" Myers' curiousity had been piqued.

"I would like for you to select a specimen of snake, any one you wish from among your stock, and let me try to communicate with it."

"What?" The doctor could not hide his disbelief.

"It will cost you only fifteen minutes," suggested the old man. "If at the the end of that time you feel your time has been wasted, I will leave willingly."

The doctor thought for only a moment, then agreed. "Tell me what it is you want to do and perhaps I can cooperate."

"That is the problem, Dr. Myers," Juan replied. "I cannot explain it." He paused as he considered how much he could safely tell. "I represent a group of men and women who are the shamans of their respective tribes. We represent the tribes of the southwest. We are meeting here in the Phoenix area because, last year, we worked with the police and solved an important puzzle."

"Some kind of conference?" The doctor tried to get it straight in his mind.

"We call ourselves the Gathering," replied the old man. "I know that what I have to tell you will be hard to believe. For this reason, I had in mind a simple demonstration of what I can do. It should not be dramatic, but it should prove conclusively to you that I am who and what I say I am. If it accomplishes that much, we can go on from there."

"What kind of demonstration?"

"Have you ever read Castaneda?" asked Juan.

The doctor nodded. "I have," he said.

Juan smiled. "Then you will understand, even if you do not believe," he replied. "I am a medicine man of the Yaqui. I can transfer my consciousness into the body of another creature, essentially giving it my body and taking control of the one it inhabits."

Jeremy shook his head. "Mr. Mapuli, Castaneda is fiction."

The old man smiled back. "Give me fifteen minutes to prove it. What have you got to lose?"

"Okay, what do we have to do?"

Juan said, "Select any specimen you have, Doctor. Put me in the room with it." He turned and indicated Maria with his chin. "Allow my wife to accompany me and to do what she deems necessary for my protection. Then all you have to do is observe. If, at the end of fifteen minutes, you are not convinced that I have transferred my mind to the body of the snake, I will leave without a further word."

"Very well. I agree."

Rachel entered the lab. "Jeremy, where have you been? I've been worried sick."

"Miss Knight," said Jeremy, "I'd like you meet Mr. and Mrs. Mapoli. They are Yaquis from Tucson."

Rachel looked quizzically at the doctor but greeted the man and woman. "Pleased to meet you. I'm Rachel Knight. I assist Dr. Myers."

"I will need a chair," said Juan in a quiet but commanding voice.

Rachel looked at Jeremy, who nodded his approval, and went to the far end of the lab and got a desk chair on rollers.

The old man's face split into a wide smile. "That will be perfect."

He sat and Maria reached into her bag and brought forth some ropes.

"What is all this about?" asked the assistant.

"An experiment," said Jeremy. "Never mind. Just bear with us for a few minutes and we'll see whether or not some old folk lore is truth or fiction."

Maria secured her husband to the chair, making certain the bonds were tight but not painful.

The doctor inspected them and then turned to Rachel. "Please cover all the cages except the Roberts specimen. I would like it to be directly in front of Mr. Mapoli."

Rachel looked at the doctor as if he were crazy, but moved to comply.

In a few minutes, Juan's chair had been placed in front of the cage and he looked at the mohave rattler within.

"This will do quite nicely," he said. "Maria, please give me two more mushrooms."

The older woman moved to his side, fumbled in the pouch at his belt, and put two in the old man's mouth.

Juan chewed thoughtfully, staring at the specimen for a few moments before closing his eyes.

Jeremy and Rachel watched.

Maria stood by.

Suddenly, the Mohave Rattlesnake in the cage became agitated. It began to circle the cage as if being herded or pursued, abruptly turning back and trying to coil up defensively, then moving on again.

"What are you doing?" asked the doctor.

"Shhhhhh." Maria turned and placed a finger to her lips. "No questions now. Ask later."

The specimen began to move toward the center of the cage. It still appeared distressed, but each turn around the area brought it closer to the middle.

After a few more minutes, it sat coiled and staring back out at the old man in the chair opposite.

"Now you can ask, Doctor," said Maria, "but do not ask this," she indicated the old man's body on the chair. "Ask Juan," and she pointed to the snake that now sat motionless in the cage.

Jeremy and Rachel exchanged glances, raised eyebrows figuring prominently in their expressions.

"You can ask any yes or no question," said the old woman patiently, as if explaining a game to children. "My husband will answer."

"Are you telling me that he has changed places with the snake?" Myers could not keep the incredulity out of his voice.

Again the old woman pointed to the snake. "Ask him," she repeated.

Jeremy stood before the cage and looked in. "Have you switched bodies with the snake?" he asked, feeling foolish.

The coiled serpent moved slowly, extending its head and upper body to the right and lowering its nose gracefully to the cage floor.

"To your right means yes," said the woman. "To the left will mean no."

"Is it hard to control?" asked the doctor.

The viper lifted it's head and then lowered it to the opposite side. No.

"Is this some kind of trick?" Jeremy turned to the old man and looked into his face. It was a mistake.

The eyes in the human face were coal black and filled with fear. Maria pointed again to the snake in the cage.

Once more, the head had moved and lay extended to the right.

The doctor spoke to his assistant without turning to look at her, bending to peer directly at the specimen before him.

"Set up the cameras, Rachel. Do it now."

"Yes, doctor," she replied.

Chapter Forty-Eight

The Roberts Ranch

Jake moved quietly and quickly away from the trap and headed toward the ravine leading to the wash. He could hear commotion behind him as the agent in the shed called out for help.

Scuttling over the edge, the snake hunter lost his balance and half slid, half fell down the side. He landed with a muffled thud that knocked the wind out of him for several moments.

When he could rise again, he moved with a lurching gait up the wash until he came to the spring outlet.

The opening looked even larger than before, as if the rocks that formed it had been literally ripped away.

Winded, dizzy, hurting from his fall, the man entered the darkness and stopped to rest. After a few moments, he began making his way through the passage.

He had gone twenty paces or so when the stench hit him.

Then he heard a noise, a buzzing and rustling sound that came from all quarters at once—almost like singing.

He stopped and turned. In the half-light of the tunnel behind him, he saw movement.

The buzzing became recognizable as the rapid movement of rattles, hundreds, maybe thousands of them. The starlit desert offered just enough illumination as he peered back toward the entrance for him to see that the walls and floor of the tunnel behind were undulating.

He let out a sobbing cry of fear and turned, plunging deeper into the rocks, frantically making his way toward the solid comfort of his shelter. If he could get there, he could secure it and then, fuck'em, he'd be safe.

The buzzing and rattling and rustling continued behind, echoing all around in the narrow rock passage. He wanted to light his lamp, but some inner warning cautioned against this action. He did not want to attract attention. A greater part of him shivered in fear of what light might reveal.

In his haste, he stepped and felt a serpentine form under his boot, wriggling and lashing at him. The knee high boots protected him from the strike and, though he stumbled, he regained his balance without falling and continued headlong up the passage.

The smell continued to grow more oppressive, a foul, dank and nauseous odor that continually threatened to choke him as he gasped and ran.

The song of the snakes grew in volume, louder with each yard gained, and it rang like nothing Jake had ever heard before.

"Must be millions of 'em," he muttered as he ran. The din increased until it was an ear-splitting whine and buzz, a cacophany of movement and rustling.

Finally, however, he made the last turn and found the entrance to his shelter. The door remained closed, but opened when he turned the knob, admitting him to the dark safety of his hideout. Crying with relief, he squeezed in and slammed the door behind him, throwing the safety bolts into place with a satisfactory thunk. Inside, the sound was muted. He moved over and reached for the light switch, turning it on and breathing a deep sigh as the darkness gave way to the sure and steady glow of his battery powered lamps.

He inspected the interior of the shelter as always. If the damned vipers had come in through the spring outlet, they might have found a way into the room, but, no. His sanctum retained integrity. He felt secure.

Jake tuned off the lights and went quickly up the ladder to the trap. He opened the hatch and reached out, finding the specimen bag and his equipment just where he had left them. He dragged them into the opening. After securing the door, he climbed back down and turned on the light again.

"I'm safe," he said to himself. "I'm safe now."

He moved again to the rear entrance and put his ear to the door. He could just hear the irritating buzz that told him the vipers remained locked outside.

He went to the cupboard where he kept the whiskey. Lifting down a fresh bottle, he took off the cap and drank deeply, feeling the fiery blend burn his throat as it went down. Holding the bottle under his nose, he inhaled deeply, banishing the lingering stench of the passage outside.

He sweated and stank from his panicked flight so he removed his shirt and grabbed a towel to dry off. Flinging the soiled garment across the room, he heard a rustling sound and turned quickly in his fear. He saw the specimen bag with the three young rattlers.

"Ah," he said to himself. "I'm forgetting my guests."

He reached for the bag and grabbed it but did not notice that the closure at the neck had come loose. One of the young snakes, no more than a foot long, got its head out and bit his finger. It got his good hand so he felt it right away.

With a cry of rage, he grabbed the snake's head in his prosthetic hand and crushed it to a pulp.

Tying off the bag again, he hurled it against the wall. It hit with a satisfactory whack, then fell right onto the dissection table. He grunted his approval even as he bent to examine the wound on his index finger.

Small, but he could see that venom already reddened the area. He pulled out his knife and made two cross cuts, one over each bite mark and expressed the sides of the wound. It bled cleanly.

He poured whiskey from the bottle directly onto the area, gritting his teeth as the pain lanced through his hand.

Not too bad, he thought, reexamining the bites.

A wave of dizziness came over him.

"Small wonder," he said aloud. "Running from the FBI, pursued by half the rattlesnakes in the world, bitten by a little bitty bastard. No question. I'm allowed to be shaky."

He took another deep swig of the whiskey and sat heavily on the edge of his bed. "I'll just lie back and rest a spell," he said. He noticed that the lights were still on. "Ought to turn'em off and save the batteries," he muttered, but he could not rise.

Jake Roberts closed his eyes and slept.

He awakened to complete darkness. He lay there for a long moment trying to discover what had brought him out of his slumber. Then he heard the buzzing humming, singing sound of the serpents.

"The lights," he whispered. "How long have I been asleep?" He reached out toward the bedside table only to discover that his hand had been secured somehow.

"What the fuck?"

As his eyes became accustomed to the dark, he saw a faint source of illumination behind his head. He tried to rise and turn but could not. He was bound to the bed.

He struggled to no avail.

He lifted his head. His eyes searched the dark and the faint luminescence either got brighter or his eyes adjusted.

The room around him seemed a speckled, wriggling sea of snakes. They writhed and slithered over everything, a carpet of undulant horror that hissed and sang so loudly it hurt his ears.

Every variety imaginable, in uncountable hundreds, moved in the small shelter, rattling and singing as if they were some kind of reptile chorus.

Eyes nearly popping from their sockets, he realized he had no hope of escape. Jake screamed—he screamed until his voice grew ragged.

At any second, he expected them to swarm up over the bedside and smother him beneath their disgusting, wriggling bodies. He saw their eyes reflected in the glow, gleaming in the dark like pinpoints of hatred. He heard their hissing, a steady whooshing sound like a rain squall. Above all, the very air trembled with their rattling.

The moments passed and he remained unharmed.

Just as he had begun starting to hope, when some little part of his mind latched onto the possibility of escape, the glow behind him grew brighter and a living nightmare moved into his range of vision.

It walked as a man and glowed a hazy red, black eyes glinting like obsidian. It loomed anthropomorphic and huge, having to half-crouch to fit into the room. It hissed and the voices of all the serpents answered, almost as if they were singing to their god.

Jake watched the huge head move closer, a snake's head but imbued with horrible intelligence. The man struggled frantically with his bonds, burning the flesh from his ankles and wrists as he lunged and twisted trying to get free.

The great reptile face above him split into a wide smile.

The creature leaned forward and spat onto Jake's shoulder. When the wetness hit his flesh, it burned and frothed and ate the tissue like acid, but—like cauterizing flame—it sealed the wound as well.

The pain seered, excruciating like red hot coals. It did not abate.

The monster lifted a huge scaled hand holding a shiny sliver of metal. Jake's dissection knife was dwarfed by the long taloned fingers. It held the knife where the man could see it, seemed to reconsider, then shook its head. The blade dropped to the floor.

Using a razor sharp claw, it made an incision on Jake's shoulder.

The smile broadened as Jake's eyes widened.

He screamed. He tore his throat raw with shrill screaming. His ragged voice ranged and filled the night for endless hours as the giant creature worked. Jake's voice reached levels of agony unknown to human ears and ripped through the buzzing song of the snakes like explosions on a battlefield. He screamed until his larynx burst, and even after that the tortured, bubbling moaning sounds continued.

Chapter Forty-Nine

Phoenix

Juan Mapoli moved with difficulty into the mind of the serpent and acclimated himself to the change in perspective. What he saw before him appeared a blurred and incomprehensible combination of light and shadow. Still, he knew what lay outside the cage, so he felt comfortable.

The snake had tried to keep him out. In fact, the struggle had been harder than he could ever recall with one of the scaled brothers. In addition, there he sensed something different about the body of this viper.

Juan could feel the heart beating. It ran several times faster than usual. More, the body responded to every impulse as if it were a coiled spring ready to lash out in a new direction with the speed of thought. This snake was not normal.

With calm and patience born of long practice, the old Yaqui medicine man took control and brought the body to rest, coiled, and then faced out toward the room beyond the glass.

Now, if Maria could remember her instructions, he would be able to show the scientist more of the wide world than Myers anticipated.

At first, he feared he would not be able to hear, but the questing tongue, so sensitive to vibrations, tasted and heard the sound of the doctor's voice.

He moved to his left, stretching the neck and laying the head passively on the floor of the cage.

With the second question, he moved it to the right.

Over the next five minutes, he became aware that the doctor and his assistant had set up a camera to videotape the demonstration. This did not please Juan Mapoli, but better this man knew what he could do than dismiss the Gathering as an assemblage of cranks and fools.

Without warning, another mind touched his. Juan found himself paralyzed, unable to direct the snake, unable to move.

He felt the probing of an intelligence—a foreign and alien thing, but a thinking being.

The old man reached out to make contact.

The other mind recoiled, snapping away like a whip, but then it returned even more strongly, and it posed a question.

Juan could feel it, knew it for a request, but it took no form he could identify. It felt too different to be communication.

An image formed in his head. It appeared to be a snake, but he sensed something strange about it, a feeling of age and massiveness that made it all the more difficult to understand.

Juan visualized the image of a man. He picked Myers. Carefully, he added detail until he saw the doctor as if the figure stood there in his head with him.

He heard clearly, as if it had been actual sound, a hiss that reverberated through the scaled reptile body like thunder.

The shaman envisioned the projected human figure sitting cross-legged and speaking.

"What are you?"

Again, there came a sense of rapid retreat, then a return with even more force.

"WWWWhhhhaaaat?" It was a clumsy attempt, but the sense of it rang clear.

"The sounds are language," said the image of Jeremy Myers, like a lecturer before an assembly. "We communicate by sounds."

"SSSSSoooouunds?"

"That's right," the image nodded to its unseen student. "We speak in sounds."

"MMMiiinnnddd." Not a question. It came forth as a statement.

A rapid and bewildering flood of feelings and images followed, incomprehensible to the old man.

"Slow down," he said through the Myers image. "Slower and perhaps I can follow."

The feelings that came next expressed disdain, dismissal, even contempt.

The huge snake image turned and swallowed the Myers image, then glared at Juan, coiled and towering far above him.

"You are impatient," said the old man.

"Ssssslow," hissed the snake. "I am bigger."

The mind must have been absorbing Juan's thoughts as fast as they formed. Every new concept taught it words, ideas, terms to use.

"SSSSbetter."

"Who are you?" asked the Yaqui.

"SSSSnaake."

"Is that all?" Juan could not believe it. No reptile had that kind of intelligence.

"SSSSnaake." Only this time there was an image of other creatures—strange, ancient animals—all in submissive positions before a great serpent.

"I don't understand," said the man.

The image changed. Into the picture walked Jeremy Myers, exactly as Juan's imagination had drawn him. The figure, dwarfed by the huge reptile, fell down and prostrated itself in an attitude of worship.

Juan would have laughed if he had the vocal equipment. "You want us to worship you?"

Rage, cold and final, assaulted his senses. He felt as if he were being beaten into submission. It reminded him of his battle with the wind demon in the upper world.

"Worship." It was a command.

Juan sent his denial as swiftly as an arrow and felt the other mind recoil.

The attack doubled and the old man wilted under the psychic blows.

"Never." He sent his final refusal.

The consciousness withdrew, as if it sought some meditative answer to such blatant recalcitrance

Juan made ready to return to his own body. The time had come to leave. However, when he reached out, he found nothing. He encountered a vague, formless, gray nothingness. He tried again.

Again, he failed.

In rising panic, Juan realized he was trapped in the body of the snake.

Chapter Fifty

Deep under Casa Malpais

She had awakened with great excitement. Certain noises beyond the wall indicated heightened activity among the two-legs. It might be that her imprisonment and loneliness would soon be at an end.

She wondered what kind of servants the bipeds would make. She promised herself She would be disciplined and consume no more of them than one a day, in order to make the supply last. There would, after all, be other food. Meanwhile, She called her little ones to her and fed.

Passage of time in the deep chamber registered on an inner clock not subject to regulation by light and dark. Her sense of hours or even days passing could not be explained. It broke down into periods of sleep and wakefulness, to hunger and feeding. Even before the chamber had been closed, this had been the case.

She lay there listening.

The world waited for her. She knew her destiny. She would soon return to claim her rightful place.

Ah, what a day that would be, when She would no longer be held in her prison alone—when She would venture forth into the wide world and hold dominion over all the creatures that walked or crawled on the land or swam the oceans or flew in the air.

And then, many miles away, Juan Mapoli took possession of the body of the Mohave Rattlesnake in Jeremy Myers' laboratory.

That particular little one had been the first She contacted upon awakening. It had already taught her much about the two-legs and, to it, her telepathic link had grown strong.

She sensed the change and reached out to check but encountered something entirely new. A steady stream of chaotic thought, filled with strange symbols, surrounded her mind as She probed for the source.

At first, it frightened her. None of the living things in her past had possessed noisy minds. She withdrew but then found herself compelled to return in fascination.

What could this mean?

Suddenly, it all started to make a terrifying kind of sense. These creatures represented a higher order—like herself. She asked, "What are you?"

The chaos remained untranslatable.

She projected an image of herself, regal and glorious.

Immediately, the jumble of thoughts organized into a return image—the image of a two-legs. As her mind watched, the image became more and more familiar.

She hissed. She knew him now, the one who caged the little ones.

The next thought that formed in her mind demanded from the image. "What are you?"

The thought came as powerfully and imperiously as her own. She withdrew and then realized that in withdrawing, She had already given an advantage. Immediately, she returned with more force.

"What?"

The projected image of the two-legs made noises with its mouth. These were confusing, but the other mind—the one she had actually contacted—also explained in thought.

"The sounds are language. We communicate by sounds."

Another new concept.

All the creatures on or beneath the surface in her time had spoken through chemical signals, actions and reactions. There had been no language. The idea of communicating by sounds seemed so foreign to her that it took a few moments for the implication to sink in.

"Sounds?" She formed the response in her mind carefully, trying to reproduce the same pattern.

"That's right." The sense of approval. "We speak in sounds." A tone of condescension, an air of superiority.

How dare it! How could this frail two-leg image even think of itself as an equal to her!

Anger and frustration drove her into a frenzy and the great body lashed about in the dark.

She sent the image of herself again, but this time it devoured the two-leg projection. She meant to frighten the being she confronted.

"You are impatient," replied the mind.

Though She could hardly believe it, this being remained unaffected by her obvious power.

However, as the contact continued, the images became more clear and she began to understand how the sounds delivered the thoughts. She knew this must be mastered completely. Not only were these creatures of a higher order, but they might ultimately pose a threat. That could not be allowed to occur.

She sent her demand that the two-legs join all others in worshipping her, providing food and doing service.

The incredulity of the other mind's response, the disdainful dismissal of her demand, created an anger greater than She had ever known. She seethed with the need to punish this impudence.

She used her power to assault this creature who did not yet know its place. She felt the resistance, doubled her effort, and finally sensed a gradual weakening of the opposing mind.

Triumphantly, her consciousness surrounded the other, cutting it off from everything else, isolating it as She had been isolated. Then, she waited silently observing to see what it would do.

She sensed a moment of indecision—then it changed. The creature stopped viewing itself as trapped, hopelessly and forever, and found freedom. It did not contend or resist, but accepted imprisonment, granting forgiveness to the one that imprisoned it.

Such a thing could not be tolerated.

She screamed silently.

Chapter Fifty-One

Salt River Reservation

The Shamans returned to Tom's home exhausted from too much sun and troubled by the ominous appearance of the snakes on the river banks. They found William Concha waiting on the front porch.

"What are you doing here, William?" asked Harold.

"I have been sent to bring you home," replied the man.

"But I have not finished here," said the priest.

"The council has sent you this," answered Concha, placing an envelope in Harold's hand.

With an apologetic look to the others, the Hopi priest opened the letter and read through its contents. It took only a minute, but, when he finished, he folded it carefully and the look on the old man's face had changed.

"What is it, Harold?" asked Tom.

"I have been ordered to return. There is priest business I must attend to at home."

The others exchanged looks of dismay. Good manners and their respect for Laloma kept anyone from prying, but every expression said this could only be a setback for the gathering.

Tom spoke for all of them. "When do you think you will return?"

Harold shook his head. "I do not know, my brother," he replied. "There has been another death."

"From snakes?" Lotus voiced what all feared.

The Hopi nodded. "One who held great importance to our people," he said in a quiet tone. "A friend."

After an awkward silence, Rattle stepped forward and placed a hand on Harold's shoulder. "Is there anything we can do?" he asked.

"No." The Hopi turned to Concha. "I will gather my things and join you at the car."

William nodded, then went down the steps, leaving the shamans together.

Harold turned back to Rattle. "Thank you, my friend," he said, "but the journey back must begin immediately. I do not know when the need for my presence there will end."

The old Pai stepped back.

Harold spoke to all of them. "I am sorry," he said. "I would not leave you now were it not that I am summoned. If I cannot return by Monday, please pay my respects in the ceremony for Jack and Pasqual." He turned to Tom. "I thank you for your hospitality, Tom Bear. I must hurry, for William takes me to those who are not patient men."

"I understand," answered the Pima.

"Come back as soon as you can," said Kade. "We will be waiting here for you."

The Hopi priest went inside and emerged only moments later with his bags. He handed one to Geraldo. "Will you give these for me when you go with the others to honor the dead?" he asked. "Here are pahos and cornmeal."

The Zuni agreed. "I will."

"Thank you, Geraldo," said Harold formally.

With no further words, the Hopi moved down the steps, got into Concha's car and waved to the others from the passenger seat as it started and pulled away.

The shamans stood in silence as their companion departed. The sense of loss was tangible, an ache that would not heal. Each of them felt they had lost a brother.

They had.

Harold traveled north with William but they did not speak. Being summoned by the council meant something momentous had happened. To call their priest back after he had come so far meant a change of heart. It must be, thought Harold, that his cooperation with the gathering no longer met with the approval of his superiors. This caused considerable inner conflict.

As a Hopi Priest, Harold had a duty to his people second only to his duty to the gods. But that duty to the gods had been exercised when he attended the first gathering and helped them defeat the demon. Now, he did not know what he must do. The great conflict of the priesthood had come home to roost directly and heavily on his shoulders.

If the gods wanted him to stay and the council wanted him to go, what should he do?

He could not talk this over with Concha. Though the man had become a friend, he had no right to knowledge of the decisions or motivations of those who decided for the clan. The man did not have the training to offer intelligent advice and did not share the secrets.

Harold prayed for guidance.

William seemed sensitive to the old man's need for time to think. He did not speak. He knew, and Harold knew as well, that there could be no disobedience of the council. If such occurred, it would be a sign in their minds of Harold placing his will above the will of the gods. This would be unforgiveable.

Harold felt torn between his loyalty to the Gathering, his friends with whom he had shared a great adventure, and loyalty to his people. He worried over it. There seemed no solution that did not involve betraying one or the other. He desperately sought an answer.

What would he do if asked to withdraw irrevocably from the Gathering? Unthinkable! Such a loss would handicap his friends, remove a necessary member from the circle of power and dilute the strength of all. He could not allow such a thing to happen.

He thought of the other priests. Perhaps he could speak with Joseph and John. They had already indicated a small amount of rebellion against the will of the elders. Maybe, in one case or another, he could fan that spark into flame. It would be dangerous. If he did not move carefully, it would mean censure or worse for all of them. Angering the council could bring only disaster. But what else could he do? The Gathering must be complete. Someone from the Hopi had to be a part of it.

Elmer's death came as a heavy blow. The handler had been a close friend and associate, one of the trusted and uniquely trained individuals within a small band which comprised the hierarchy of the tribe. His loss struck hard.

More than that, the summons from the council indicated that forces inimical to the Gathering must be at work, though how that could be still eluded Harold's imagination. He resolved to listen with care when he confronted his superiors. Perhaps understanding would come in time.

Meanwhile, the journey dragged on and left far too much time for soul searching. Harold worried. The snakes were already in captivity in large numbers throughout the villages of the mesas. If Elmer had been killed, he could expect that others would die as well. How could a mere priest stop an army of snakes?

Chapter Fifty-Two

Phoenix

At Carter Labs, Jeremy Myers observed in stunned silence. Either the old Indian had been able to take over the body of the snake as he said he would, or the Yaqui was one hell of a hypnotists. His mind rebelled against the evidence provided by his own eyes.

Suddenly, in the space of seconds, both subjects changed their demeanor and movements. The doctor saw at once that Juan had run into difficulty. The human form, which had appeared to be in a trance or even asleep since the demonstration began, started to evidence signs of awakening and consciousness. The serpent had ceased moving and appeared paralyzed in the cage.

Maria looked frightened and moved quickly away from her husband's form where it sat strapped to the chair.

"What is it, Maria?" he asked.

The old woman turned wide eyes to the doctor. "Something is wrong, senor," she replied in a quavering voice. "The snake is awakening, but it is in Juan's body."

Though he had begun as a doubter, Jeremy now believed. The human form of the old man remained secured to the office chair, but the muscles of the frame were bunched in effort. It crouched—nearly coiled—in the seat and opened its eyelids.

Slowly, it turned and looked directly at the doctor. The eyes were inhuman—black, reptilian and cold.

Juan's body hissed and the tongue flicked out.

Jeremy moved back quickly and turned once again to the cage. In it, the snake sat frozen nearly upright, The Mohave twitched and tried to move, but it could not. The tight coil that lay beneath it hardly seemed enough alone to hold it so high in the air. Fully two and a half feet of the serpent rose straight up, like a pillar or a statue. The snake's eyes were fixed as if it were asleep, but it quivered as if it were terrified.

The doctor turned toward the woman again and asked, "What should we do?"

Maria shook her head. Her lower lip trembled. "I do not know. This has never happened before. Juan has always been free to come and go as he pleases."

"Should I do something or do we wait?"

The body of Juan looked from one of them to another, then began to speak. The words were halting and awkward, as if language had never been used before. "Wwwhhhooo are you?" The voice rasped, a grinding sound, totally inhuman.

Jeremy felt his throat tighten up in sympathy. "I am Dr. Myers," he replied, watching the at once familiar and alien face for reaction. "Who are you?"

The mouth worked itself into a hideous grin, but Myers saw no humor there.

"You are the one who sssssstudiessss sssnakesss?"

"That is part of what I do," answered Jeremy.

The creature in the chair—definitely not Juan—spoke again. "You will kneel before me."

"Why?" The doctor's face wore an expression of interest. He did not take offense.

"Because I am superior." It handled the voice more effectively now, sounding more natural.

"In what way?"

"I am bigger."

The doctor laughed. "No, you are not."

The creature hissed. "Not what you see, human Myers, but what I truly am." The face wore a look of arrogance.

"And what is that?"

Jeremy had backed up to the dispensary cabinet and reached for a hypo kept for emergencies. It contained a fast acting sedative.

The eyes—those inhuman black obsidian eyes—followed his movements without fear. The smug look remained. "Sssssnnnaaak-kkeee." The reply came clearly.

He almost dropped the syringe. "You are a snake?" he asked.

"THE Sssnnnaaakkkeee." The creature emphasized the first syllable.

Jeremy's eyes moved unwillingly to the Mohave in the cage. "That snake?" He could not keep the incredulity from his voice.

The creature's laughter erupted as a frightening sound, not at all human—unless one considered the hooting and screeching of the insane to be human.

"No," it said gasping after its expression of mirth as Juan's body labored for air. "That is only a tool I can use."

"Where are you then?"

The creature ignored Jeremy's question as the frail body in the chair suddenly convulsed, the old man's muscles rippling and bunching, the cords binding the arms cutting deeply into the flesh.

Maria screamed and the doctor lunged forward, stabbing the needle into the neck just as it began to rise.

He pushed the plunger home as the bonds broke and the effect was instantaneous. The eyes clouded over and it fell back.

"Whaaat?" The one word question trailed off as it dropped heavily back into the chair.

Suddenly, movement could be seen within the cage. The Mohave began to thrash about, twisting and turning as if engaged in a violent struggle. Then, without warning, it struck at the glass wall before it—not once, but a dozen times.

Jeremy could do nothing. The serpent struck the glass again and again in rapid succession until the head became a crushed pulp. It fell to the bottom of the cage, twitched once, and then lay still.

Maria had moved up to the cage at the first strike, screaming out her husband's name. "Juan!" she cried. "Juan, stop!" Her hands pressed against the glass as if she would cushion the fatal impacts, but she could not halt the destruction.

Afterwards, she still knelt before the cage, her hands upraised, tears streaming down her face.

The doctor turned to issue instructions to Rachel but found her passed out on the floor.

Slowly, Jeremy sank into the chair that Maria had left unoccupied, shocked and trying to comprehend the events of the last hour.

Could he believe the evidence of his own eyes? Had he really seen what he thought he had seen or had it been some kind of hallucination brought about by the Yaqui medicine man?

A violent spasm of coughing issued from the chair next to his. Turning, he saw the eyelids of the old man open. They appeared human again, obviously suffering pain.

The Yaqui looked at him and spoke, his voice croaking out the words deliberately. "Interesting, don't you think doctor?"

Sunday, July 7th

Chapter Fifty-Three

The Roberts Ranch

Agent Matt Pierce of the FBI wanted nothing more than to locate the bastard Roberts. He and the others had gone so far as to establish a betting pool to reward the lucky man that found him. They all hoped fervently that he would resist arrest.

Glen Thomas, the unfortunate agent in the shed, had died despite the heroic efforts of his fellows, but not before reporting clearly that the snake appeared to have been dropped on him. The conclusion seemed inescapable, that Jake Roberts still hid close by . . . and now he had definitely committed a murder.

The ranch teemed with suits. Working in groups of three, they started from the house and combed every square inch of the grounds. The piles of junk, up until now considered harmless, were being systematically dismantled and nothing larger than a machine screw went uninventoried. Still, it took a while for them to find the battery hook-ups.

"Hey Matt," called agent Farah when he discovered the wiring, "come look at this!"

"What is it?" Pierce's weapon found its way hopefully into his hand. He and several others joined the man who had called.

"He's got a whole fuckin' series of batteries hooked up here," said Farah. "Must be emergency power for the house."

"Is that all?" Matt frowned. He looked at the thick cables wound together like snakes and felt his temper rising again. There were too many snakes out here in the desert. The only good thing about Roberts was that he killed the bastards.

He knelt down and tugged on the insulated pack and was surprised when it pulled part way out of the sand and led off in a totally unexpected direction. "Wait a minute," he said. "This leads away from the house, not toward it."

He stood there for a long moment, then exchanged a look of pure pleasure with Farah.

Matt rose and spoke to one of the others. "Go back up and order us several sets of insulated gloves and get them dropped in here ASAP. The rest of you stand by. Don't touch those batteries or the cables. We wouldn't want to tip him off if this is what I think it is."

Waiting an hour an a half for the gloves seemed one of the hardest things Pierce had ever done. His fingers itched to find their way around Roberts' throat. He took out his weapon three times, checked the loads, even cleaned it again to make sure it wouldn't misfire at a crucial moment. Finally, the chopper arrived.

A team of five agents donned gloves and began walking the length of the cable. Five more used shovels and picks to clear the debris. All were careful not to break it. No one spoke. All were intent on following the wire as it led off from the pile of batteries. They began to look eager as it took them toward a last major pile of junk at the edge of a ravine.

"Careful now," said Matt in a low voice to the others. "We don't want to alert him until we have to."

The cable disappeared into the ground next to the secured lid on an apparently abandoned well.

"Power for the pump?" Farah spoke sotto voiced, scratching his head.

"No," whispered Matt. "This has to be it." He reached down carefully and tried to lift the well-cap. It didn't budge.

"Who has the pry bars?"

Three men stepped forward, each one carrying a large, long-handled metal bar.

"Careful, now," cautioned Pierce. "He's probably armed and we're about to let him know we're at the door."

The rest of the team drew their weapons and clicked off the safeties.

At Matt's signal, the men with the large pry bars attacked the outer edge of the cap. It resisted, but they were determined. Most of them had been friends of Thomas.

With a wrenching of metal and wood, the lid popped up and lifted on hinges.

"Bingo," said Farah.

Then the stench reached them.

A terrible odor rose up, foul, gut-wrenching, stomach-emptying, like the smell of gangrenous flesh. More than one agent lost his lunch.

"Christ! What the hell is that?" asked Farah, covering his mouth and nose with a handkerchief.

"He'd better not have gone and died down there," said Matt, gritting his teeth. Covering his own face with another hanky, he peered down into the dark. "There's a ladder," he said, his voice muffled. "I'm going down."

"I'll be right behind you, buddy," said Farah. "The rest of you cover us."

It took considerable courage for him to lead the way down into the dark, but Pierce wanted to be the one to find Roberts.

He broke out his flashlight just after he got inside and went down the ladder as quickly as safety would allow. At the bottom, he found the light switch.

Just as his fingers touched it, he heard a hiss and a low keening sound, mixed with a curious thumping and sliding. He snatched his fingers back and held onto the ladder, suddenly unwilling to step down the final foot and a half to the floor.

"Did you hear that?" Matt whispered to Farah.

"Yes," answered the other, "and I don't like the sound of it."

The horrible odor hovered even stronger here, making both agent's eyes water and forcing them to break the silence by clearing their throats again and again.

Pierce played his flash around the area but the entrance at the foot of the ladder proved to be a narrow box and most of the room beyond remained concealed. The light explored every inch visible before Matt took the final step to the floor.

"Ready?" he asked as he crouched at the base of the ladder.

"Whenever you are," replied his companion.

He rose silently and hit the switch.

The room flooded with light.

Matt edged around that final wall, gun at the ready, hammer back. Farah crouched to the floor behind him. On a silent three count, both men entered the chamber and moved to opposite sides of the door.

At first, they thought the room empty, but soon discovered they were mistaken—horribly, indescribably mistaken.

The room itself was in chaos, furniture upended, cabinets overturned, doors ripped off their hinges. Supplies meant to last for years were scattered about and torn open so that everything had been covered with a lumpy layer of debris.

That is why they didn't see it at first.

It had burrowed into a junk-filled corner of the room and struggled frantically to butt through the wall.

"Jesus Christ!" exclaimed Farah.

"Holy Mother," said Matt, backing away and crossing himself. "What the fuck is that?"

It made a mewling sound as it found it could no longer hide. With much thumping and sliding it managed to turn so the men could see it clearly. It hissed.

The squirming thing looked vaguely reminiscent of a human body, but horribly altered.

It lay naked, covered with bubbling sores that wept serum and glistened remarkably like scales. The hide—it did not look like skin—had blackened in places and seemed to form a speckled pattern, not unlike the markings of a rattlesnake.

It had no arms, but what remained of shoulders tapered down unnaturally to a long body, and the bones of two legs were barely visible under a single sheath of flesh, as if they had been melted together and then shaped anew by an inhuman sculptor.

The bare head was curiously flattened. It had nothing where ears should have been, and a wide crushed bump that might once have been a nose now appeared to be composed of two sucking apertures that must be nostrils. A wide lipless mouth leered toothlessly as it used what had apparently been its chin to start the crawling, wriggling progress that brought it toward them.

Worst were the eyes—blood red windows into hell that appeared, nonetheless, undeniably human and reflected the creature's total loss of reason. It hissed and mewed and crawled toward the two agents, a look of insane hope on its sickening face.

Both men gasped and exchanged a glance in which mixed equal parts of loathing and compassion.

They emptied their revolvers into it but it still did not die. They had to reload and fire several times before they finally put it out of its misery.

Later, they found the arms and feet, neatly stacked on the dissection table. Fingerprints identified it as Roberts.

Farah and Pierce split the pool.

Chapter Fifty-Four

Salt River Reservation

The shamans had been upset the day before at the departure of Harold Laloma, and Juan's failure to return had cast a pall over what remained of their spirits. With a rekindling of that spirit, therefore, they greeted the old Yaqui and his wife when they returned that Sunday morning accompanied by Jeremy Myers.

Jeremy had insisted that Juan and Maria spend the night at his home after the ordeal in the lab. He had been eager to talk with the old man about the body exchange and wanted to know if Juan had learned any more about the being that addressed them. He had already made a tentative connection between it and Casa Malpais in his mind.

When the Yaqui invited him to meet with representatives of the twelve tribes, he jumped at the chance.

Almost all the shamans seemed happy to see him.

Cord felt sure that the presence of the white man, representing the thirteenth tribe, made the final piece of the puzzle, but the departure of the Hopi had left the Gathering still short one crucial member.

Gordon spent much of the morning telling Jeremy about the Gathering the year before and how they had defeated the demon.

Rattle quizzed the white man at length about anthropomorphic snake gods but found the doctor's lack of knowledge disturbing.

Geraldo, alone, did not welcome the doctor and his assistant. He instinctively mistrusted whites and, as a result, remained cold and rude.

Each of the shamans told of their experiences with snakes and Jeremy became fascinated with the variety, from bite to visions.

Juan became distressed when he learned of Harold's departure. Though weak from the ordeal with the snake, he made quite energetic complaints about the recall of the Hopi by his council. "You should not have let him leave," he said. "We need the Hopi more than any other member of the Gathering. He is the one most qualified to deal with the serpent."

"How could we have stopped him?" asked Cord. "He was recalled by the leaders of his clan."

"I do not know," answered Juan truthfully, "but you should have stopped him nonetheless. Without him, we do not have the power. The Gathering is incomplete."

"We must respect the wishes of the elder of his tribe," said Tom. "It is not for any of us to criticize and interfere in the governing of a people by their own authorities. We must honor each other and our separate ways."

"But what we do here is not separate, Bear," said Juan. "We must act as the Gathering, not as members of different tribes."

"Juan is right," added Lotus. "The Gathering is something much more important than our tribal interests."

"But, Lotus," protested Danny, "Harold knew that. If he felt he had to return, the reasons for his recall must have outweighed his participation here with us. We must trust that he will come back when he is able."

Geraldo shook his head. He had heard enough. "What makes you think any of you know what is so and what is not? Being one of the wise is not so simple. Since I first arrived I have waited for some sign that you are, indeed, worthy of the honors heaped upon you by our peoples. I have waited for some ceremony, some reverence to the gods, some statement of purpose for this Gathering. Instead, we have barbecued, been to the river like a group of white tourists, told stories." He looked around at the faces of the others. "Does anyone know what it is we must do? Do any of you know what my vision meant? Does anyone even have a guess as to why we have come together?" The Zuni glared at them, his stare a challenge.

An awkward silence followed for most of them did not.

Finally Gerry spoke, breaking into the awkwardness of the moment with clarity and perception. "We know," he said. "We have not put the pieces of the puzzle together yet, but we know the answers to your questions, Geraldo, and to many more."

The priest turned to say something derisive, but his words were stilled when he saw the Apache's face.

It may simply have been a trick of the light, but Gerry had grown very pale, his visage so white that he looked like a marble bust. Even more disconcerting, Geraldo and the others saw two images, super-imposed over each other like a double-exposed negative. One of Gerry, looking as George Buck had looked all his life. The other, however, distinctly resembled the countenance of Geronimo. There could be no doubt. The mouth turned down in a striking crescent, the dark eyes peered fiercely out of the rugged face of the legendary old war chief and shaman.

Even the brash Zuni priest could not speak.

"I see a great beast with scales," said the dual image, its voice also two voices at once, a horrible, echoing, penetrating sound.

"Eiyeee," exclaimed Rattle, envisioning the scaled one.

The countenance of the Apache seemed paler yet and at the same time continued to glow. It turned burning eyes on the Havasupai.

"The Father of All Serpents," said Rattle in a hushed tone.

"We are in opposition to a god?" asked Geraldo in a weak voice.

"No," replied Juan steadily from across the circle. "There is another."

The ghostly double image of the Apache turned to the Yaqui and the eyes burned with curiosity. "Speak," he commanded.

As Maria gripped his arm with reassuring strength, Juan told of the experiment in the clinic and how he nearly lost his life to the wiles of the ancient serpent.

"It is at once evil and innocent," concluded the Yaqui. "It wants only what it once had by right of power many centuries ago. It wants to be worshipped and fed."

"It can be tricked," said Jeremy, suddenly leaning forward, his face intent. "It is strong and intelligent, but it does not understand men."

"Where is this thing?" asked Lotus.

"Casa Malpais," replied Juan, Jeremy and Gerry all at once."

"Where? What?" A confused chorus of questions came from the others. No one knew what they meant.

"It claimed to be bigger," explained Jeremy.

"It is a snake," said Juan, "and it appeared to me while I possessed the body of the Mohave."

"The archaeologist at Casa Malpais said they still had a major discovery to make," added Jeremy.

There were some seconds of awkward silence before Juan spoke again. "I told you we would need Harold," he said in a resigned tone. "He is the one to lead us this summer. It must be him. The Hopi are the masters of the serpents."

Chapter Fifty-Five

Casa Malpais

Excavations began the same day as the departure of Ramirez, Grimsley and Myers and continued for twenty-four hours. At that time, the lead digger broke through the wall into the chamber beyond. A runner immediately fetched Dr. Shayley while they enlarged the opening. None of the diggers entered the chamber, however. Those had been specific and emphatic instructions.

As she had planned, Margot entered the large cave at the head of the others.

They first encountered a dank, decaying odor that seemed to well out of the darkness and overpower them.

"God! What the hell is that?" asked Brogan.

Margot had a strange look on her face. Her eyes were bright but she seemed distracted, as if a million tiny voices were quietly competing for her attention. "It's cold," she said in a dreamy tone. "We may be the first to have walked here in more than twenty thousand years."

A bank of ice lined one wall, but the entire chamber felt damp and muggy, indicating that the melting process had been going on for some time.

"We'll need lights," said Roger.

"Just be careful what you touch," warned the doctor. "It's entirely possible this chamber will furnish the proof that unlocks a major secret in man's past."

Brogan had been shining his flash in an ever-increasing arc when he let out an exclamation of surprise. The beam focussed steadily on a gleaming pile of whiteness off to their left. "I'll be damned!" he said.

The torch revealed a pile of bones large enough to fill an area twenty feet by thirty feet. Massive skulls stared back at them from eyeless sockets.

"Woolly mammoths!" Margot could barely control her emotion. "This is it, then," she said in a hushed tone. She turned and hugged Brogan, her enthusiasm unrestrained. "We've found it, Roger. We've found an untouched link to the past!"

Brogan shook his head. "I don't know about the untouched part," he said slowly. He played his light on the wall. "That barrier appears man-made. Our Mogollons must be the ones that sealed it off. Why?"

"Sacred remains," said Margot, "or reverance for the gods." She added, "Who knows?"

"No one," said Roger quietly. "but I think we ought to go slow here, Margot. There's something strange about all this."

"Slow?" Dr. Shayley laughed out loud. "I want everything else stopped while we map and catalog this chamber. I want every man and woman on site right here in twenty minutes. Work is to go on twenty-four hours a day until we've uncovered every bit of information this discovery has to offer."

"Is that wise, Margot?" Brogan felt uncomfortable with the idea. "The other work is just as important. Do you really want to halt everything in order to comb through this? Think, Doctor. Wouldn't a smaller, more trustworthy crew be better? If too many people get in here we risk damage to critical artifacts, destruction of vital data. A more careful and patient examination might completely validate your theory." He paused, then added, "Besides, we don't want any leaks to the media."

That finally hit home. She reacted as if she had been slapped in the face.

"No news leaks," she said, anger rising. "I want all of Casa Malpais sealed off immediately. If anyone—and I mean anyone—

breathes a word of this before I release the information, they'll never work in the field again."

"Take it easy, Margot. That's why I think a smaller crew would be better."

She considered it for a minute, then shook her head. "No. I want everyone down here and I want you to supervise directly. We go on twelve hour shifts commencing immediately and one of us will be here at all times until I say differently. Is that clear?"

Roger nodded. "You're the boss, Doctor. Do you want to tell the others or shall I?"

"You go," she said. "I'm going to see how far back this stretches. I'll be here when you get back."

Brogan looked worried. "That isn't smart, Margot. We should go over this in teams. We've no idea what we'll run into down here."

She turned on him, an expression of scorn twisting her features. "Don't be such a wuss, Roger. Where did you pack your balls? What could be dangerous in a place that's been sealed for twenty thousand years?"

"There could be deadfalls, cave-ins, gas or even something alive and dangerous," said Brogan. "Don't take any unnecessary risks."

"What do you think I am?" she demanded. "Some star-struck first year arch student who can't find her ass with both hands? I'll be careful. You just get moving. This is my discovery and I want to look it over alone before the work starts."

"You promise you'll be careful?"

She sighed. "Yes, I promise. Just get those cute buns moving, okay?"

"All right," he agreed, "I'll hurry. Just go slow and easy, Margot. I don't want anything to happen to you."

"Move," she said, raising her voice and sounding sharper than she'd intended.

He went.

Doctor Shayley didn't wait to watch him leave. She turned and moved forward, her flash picking a path through the ice, rock and bones. The light vibrated slightly because of the tremor in her hands, a tremor born of excitement.

"I'm the first," she whispered to the dark, "the first in twenty thousand years."

Chapter Fifty-Six

Salt River Reservation

Danny awakened with a start. He had been dreaming, but the images were strange and terrifying. He had seen a giant serpent, coiled amidst a cave filled with bones. He had seen a huge snake man, a giant that seemed to beckon him. He felt a tremendous urgency about leaving.

Crazy. He couldn't leave the Gathering. They needed him—he needed them. Yet he felt a compulsion that left him dissatisfied unless he thought of moving.

He paced.

Irrational. It was past midnight. He and Lotus had retired at ten and both had been exhausted. Why awaken only two hours later, and walk the floor?

Danny moved to the window. The moon made a crescent that glowered down like a lopsided leer. The cloudless sky glittered with stars and the air hung thick with humidity. Even this late, the temperature remained ninety-six degrees and his skin felt moist.

"What is it, Danny?" Lotus sat up in bed, rubbing sleep from her eyes, peering through the dim light at her lover across the room.

"I don't know," he replied. "I know it doesn't make sense, but I feel I have to go somewhere . . . do something . . . only I don't know what."

"Did you dream?" She seemed hesitant, unusual with Lotus.

"Yes, but the dreams were weird."

"A giant snake? The snake man?"

Danny turned from the window, his eyes glittering in the darkness. He took a deep and audible breath before he spoke. "You, too?"

She nodded, then realized he might not be able to see. "Yes," she said. "We are called."

"Where?"

"North."

"By who?"

She hesitated, then the words spilled out. "I think by the being that Rattle called The Scaled One, the Father of All Serpents."

"Why?" Danny did not move from where he stood, his voice sounded petulant and resentful.

Lotus rose, letting the sheets fall away from her perfect body. She crossed the room and took him in her arms, pressing herself against him, intentionally stirring his passions to buttress his confidence.

"The deer man told us the god warned him. Perhaps it only wishes to talk."

A sigh came from the other side of the wall to their right, from the room of their host, Tom.

Danny at once placed a gentle hand over her mouth and whispered in her ear. "Let's go outside. We shouldn't awaken the others."

She nodded and moved to the foot of the bed, grabbing a robe and slipping it on.

Danny pulled on his jeans and the two moved carefully to the door. Opening it quietly, they crept through the large front room where Jerry, Cord, Rattle, Michael and the other bachelors slept on mats. Once they reached the porch, they moved down the steps and over to one of the vatos Tom had built behind the house.

Here, still speaking in hushed tones, they continued their conversation.

"I do not know, Lotus, how I feel about being summoned through my dreams by a snake god." Danny sat in the darkness and looked up at her, his face lit by the stars.

"I do not think mortals have much choice when gods speak," she replied,

"But what if it means to harm us, as did the demon a year ago? To answer this summons might be to destroy the Gathering."

"To ignore it might be to lose a great ally," said another voice from the shadows.

Both Danny and Lotus jumped. They had not heard anyone approach.

"Forgive me," said Rattle, stepping out of the darkness, "I did not mean to startle you."

"What are you doing awake?" asked Danny, rising to his feet.

"I, too, dreamed of the Scaled One," said the old Pai. "He wants us to come to him."

"All three of us?" Lotus was not about to be left out.

"Four," said a voice from the shadows.

They turned and saw Juan standing under a tree nearby. He smiled when he saw their expressions.

"Did you think I would miss an opportunity to meet one of the gods?" he asked.

Danny looked concerned. "But what about the others? Everyone will want to go. Are we all summoned?"

Rattle frowned. "I do not think all of us going together would be wise. Remember, I have met this creature. This is not a game."

"The others will have different task," said Juan in a low voice. "It is they who must prevail upon Harold to return to us."

"So we just split up and go our separate ways, huh?" Danny sounded unhappy. He kept remembering how hard it had been to assemble the Gathering the first time. It seemed something always came up to pry them apart.

"No," said Juan. "We will travel almost all the way together. The Scaled One is very near to Casa Malpais. Myers, the herpetologist, reports that there was a strange occurrence outside Springerville. One of his FBI contacts phoned him just this evening. In fact, he must go to view the result tomorrow."

"And the rest will go to the mesas to get Harold?" Lotus felt excitement rising within her. At last, the waiting would come to an end.

"What is it we must do?" asked Danny. Despite his dream and everything he had heard so far, he still did not know what adventure the Gathering embarked on.

"No one knows," said Rattle, holding up his hand and urging caution. "We gotta meet with the god. Then we'll understand."

The first order of business in the morning would be the ceremony at the ruined kiva for Jack and Pasqual. After that, they would depart for the north. Even those still sleeping within the house would have troubled dreams this night.

"Despite this need to go," said Danny, "we owe our respect to the memory of our friends. Do you suppose the Scaled One will understand?"

"It does not matter," replied Juan. "Nothing will prevent me from attending the ceremony tomorrow."

"Being called by a god may be a good excuse," said Rattle quietly.

Danny shook his head. "No, my brother. We made this appointment long ago. It will be taken care of first."

The Havasupai nodded, but he did not look happy. "We must hope this is a just god, then," he said more clearly. "If it is not, there will be payment for our loyalty."

Chapter Fifty-Seven

Casa Malpais

When Roger Brogan returned to the dark and silent chamber, he became increasingly apprehensive. He called out. "Margot! Margot! Where are you?"

No response.

The others would start arriving any moment, but Roger feared Dr. Shayley might be upset if he let them go in without her approval. As a result, he decided to find her first and confirm his orders. Besides, she might have run into trouble. Deathly quiet reigned in there.

As he entered the dark chamber, his torch illuminated a path by the pile of bones, revealing ice-shrouded walls. The sharp stillness almost took his breath away. Like Margot before, he felt he must be the first in thousands of years to walk in these corridors deep under the earth. With a feeling of awe, he moved more deeply into the yawning chamber.

"Dr. Shayley! Are you all right?"

Still no answer.

As he moved on, Roger began to feel a building pressure in his inner ear, as if he were flying or driving up into the mountains.

"Margot. Answer me!" His voice echoed hollowly in the dark.

He turned a corner and came to an abrupt halt.

Margot Shayley sat on a stone tower elevated almost twelve feet above the floor of the room. Around its base twined the form of a huge serpent, so realistically portrayed that Brogan almost cried out. Then he noticed the missing scales, surfaces that looked so ancient they must have been crumbling for centuries. Over all, it appeared to be a dusty gray color, portrayed exquisitely in every detail yet covered with decay and debris. He saw rudimentary wings—frail looking membraneous representations.

He spoke, his face breaking into a smile. "I'll be damned. You did it, Margot. You've found irrefutable evidence of pre-human work older than any before. Congratulations!"

The doctor did not move or speak. She sat regally atop the stone.

Alarmed, Brogan asked, "Are you all right?"

The giant serpent raised its head and opened its eyes. They were white and blind.

Roger felt the scream building deep inside, but it never made it to his throat. A powerful force closed on his mind, shattering thought and reducing him to a living statue.

He did not struggle. He did not fear. He did not think.

Roger Brogan had been shut down like a car when the ignition is turned off. His body waited.

Slowly, the great serpent uncoiled from the base of the stone and moved to where the male human stood. Without pause, it struck and hungrily devoured him.

When the first of the workers arrived at the entrance to the chamber, Margot Shayley greeted them—a strange and different Margot. She moved like a sleepwalker, awkward and clumsy. When she spoke, her icy voice sounded hollow, echoing in the otherwise silent chamber. "No one enters without my say so."

Looks of confusion passed from one to another of the group. Why had they been brought here if they could not enter to work?

She moved closer to them, eyes unblinking and gait disjointed, like a puppet on strings.

"I will select three teams," she said. "Each will work in a different area of the chamber. No one is to enter the quadrant assigned to another team. Is that clear?"

Though obviously puzzled, each nodded. They had already heard the warning about leaks and ruined careers. No one wanted to cross Shayley. She could be a bitch on wheels.

For some, feelings of excitement started to build. This must be an extraordinary find to require such secrecy. They looked at each other with shining and eager eyes.

The doctor stood before each of them in turn, looking at them as if she had never seen them before. She assigned the first team to work just inside the door cataloging the bones in the pile.

The second team received instructions to enlarge the entrance and set up lights. The third, consisting of the larger and stronger men, would accompany Margot behind the barrier of ice and work in the deeper recesses of the cave.

Though all had been summoned, only twelve had been selected for the three teams. The rest were told to go back to their work above but be prepared to return on a moment's notice.

Disappointment reigned but no one dared argue or question. They turned and slowly filtered out, not daring to speak until they were well away from the boss's range of hearing.

The three teams of four stood together, proud to be the select few who would share this great discovery. Dr. Shayley warned the team leaders once again about entering a work area other than their own.

"I will make life a nightmare for any of you who do not obey me," said Margot in a flat and powerful voice. "Do not test me in this."

"How do we report to you when we find things?" asked Janet Bryce, a third year archaeology student.

The doctor turned a lifeless stare on the woman and replied in the same tone of voice. "You don't. I will check in with you every couple of hours. Catalogue it and wait for me."

"Yes, ma'am," replied Janet, her eyes indicating she thought all of this just too weird.

Margot turned to the four strong men she had selected as team three. "You follow me. No lights. I have something I want to show you. I guarantee it will be the biggest surprise of your lives."

Without another word, she turned and walked into the dark. The four, led by young Richard Ames, followed in single file.

Monday, July 8th

Chapter Fifty-Eight

Phoenix

At sunrise the next morning, the shamans and Jeremy gathered at the ruined kiva where the adventure with the wind demon had climaxed exactly a year before. On this spot, Jack Foreman and his student had loosed the beast from its centuries old imprisonment and begun the process that would result in both their deaths, the student first and Jack later.

Despite their feelings of pride at what had been accomplished here, a general tone of sadness affected each of the shamans. Jack and Pasqual, who had both died in the confrontation with the demon, had become true friends. The white man had touched the hearts of all and the Zuni had brought them wisdom and kindness. Even now, after a year, they were missed and loved.

The pile of rocks which had once been a tower in the desert now lay in rubble. The beltway road passed only a few hundred yards away. The roar of traffic disturbed the very air.

A marker had been placed over the site by then-Lieutenant Greg Johnson and weatherman Matt Sharp—a simple stone, cut in the shape of a pyramid. The inscription on the side read, "Here, in the summer of 1990, white man and red man saved the world."

Though they were only eleven, twelve places had been marked in the sand, Harold's place occupied by the bag containing pahos—

prayer sticks—marked with bleached cornmeal. Geraldo had seen to this himself, even before he moved to his own segment of the circle.

The Zuni's place was marked by two interlocking circles, in one of which rested Pasqual's pipe. Vasquez sat next to it in the other.

Jeremy Myers had insisted on participating, representing the white world as had Foreman. He took his place next to the pyramid, where Jack had stood in the ceremony whose anniversary remained a week away.

Gordon Smythe, the Navajo yataalii, stood nervously in his place. Ceremonies for the dead caused great discomfort for his people. To address the spirits of those departed might invite the mischief of ghosts. Still, he presided in hopes this would lay to rest the souls of his friends.

"I am called Fly," he said. "None of us witnessed Jack and his student move the stone aside, but all of our peoples share responsibility nonetheless. Today is a day for remembering and reverence. Let us not forget how we came together because of what happened here a year ago today."

Juan passed among them, moving counterclockwise, giving out herbal tea—not Rivea Corymbosa—Morning Glory, but a bitter sweet blend that suited the occasion. Each prayed in his or her own way and then drank.

Gordon uttered no other formal words. The mute evidence of the rubble and a corner of the original boulder, still showing the wind demon symbols, was eloquent enough.

All the shamans smoked quietly and remembered their friends. All took time to think of the thousands who had died before the terror ended. All gave thanks to the gods that they had been successful.

After an hour of such meditation and rumination, the day began to warm up and they stood, each in their places, for a final farewell.

Geraldo sprinkled cornmeal on the marker and stacked the pahos at its base. Gerry helped by digging a small hole under the edge of the pyramid and then filled it in after the Zuni had placed Pasqual's pipe reverently within. Each of them, in turn, sat quietly by the marker and spoke his or her message for their friends.

Juan remembered his first discovery of the demon, drinking beer with the white archaeologist, and how frail the old Zuni had been when he came to them.

Lotus recalled her discussion of the kiva and the painting with Jack, and how Pasqual had shared the adventure in the spirit world, where they had been saved by the gods themselves.

Danny recalled his farewell to Foreman just before he helped roll the rock over to seal the kiva, and the bravery of the old Zuni when the demon attacked them in the underworld.

Tom Bear lived again in memory the trip to the hospital with the Zuni after Pasqual's second heart attack, and the kindness of the white man, the professor who understood little of what had occurred but developed perfect faith.

Cord and Michael remembered the first true meeting of the gathering when Jack brought them the charm. They remembered the dignity of the Zuni Priest.

James Bluesky, the Cocopah, recalled the rescue of Rattle and realized that Jack had, even then, begun planning to dynamite the kiva. He thought of Pasqual, the representative of the craftsmen who had made the exquisite charm.

Geronimo/George spoke to the stone of his friendship for both the Priest and the archaeologist.

Gordon sang quietly to the marker of the wisdom of the white man and the courage of the Zuni. Each had given him strength when his weaknesses might otherwise have brought about their defeat.

Kade Wonto, the Maricopa, remembered the Zuni's kindness to his wife, and the effort put forth by Jack to elicit the help of the authorities.

Rattle sat quietly and saw in his mind the white man struggling in the kiva with the demon possessed Navajo. He saw the Zuni fall even as he made his own way up the ladder to safety.

Geraldo sprinkled more cornmeal over the marker and tried to understand how one not of the people could sacrifice his life for the others. He thought differently now about Quatero as well. Perhaps the old man had not been such a fool after all.

Finally, however, time came to depart.

They had taken all the vehicles and loaded up their gear, each according to destination. Lotus, Jeremy, Juan, Danny and Rattle rode in Lotus' car. The rest were in Tom's truck, Gerry's rental and the Wonto's car.

They planned to meet in the desert, a mile from the dig at Casa Malpais in twenty-four hours.

Satisfaction filled them as they left Phoenix together, enroute to their adventure at last. They knew a strange confidence in the future—though none of them could have said what it might hold.

Chapter Fifty-Nine

Casa Malpais

She had her servants now. The two-legs—they called themselves humans—were perfect. They worked industriously and tasted delicious.

Despite her resolve to limit herself to one a day, the need to regain lost strength and bulk required that her intake be increased at first. The four large men had been most satisfying.

The work of opening Casa Malpai so that She could regain the outside world progressed nicely. By controlling the female called Margot Shayley, She held them all.

These creatures posed no threat—their minds were capable but malleable. Once She had reached in and severed the personality from the other processes, they behaved like ants doing the bidding of the queen. One by one, She had been doing exactly that.

Those who had not been summoned below had to suspect something unusual going on, but they did not know what. She had touched all of them enough to allay their fears. Each had been seeded with a dream of riches and fame. Each had been manipulated into thinking he or she would benefit from the news of this startling new discovery.

Those who went below never came up again. Only the doctor, her strange lurching walk now the subject of some jest among those above, moved freely back and forth among them. Margot looked pale and fanatical, but most attributed it to the zeal she felt about the great discovery.

She looked through Margot's eyes and selected those who would serve, either as laborers or sustenance.

Knowing they too must eat in order to maintain strength, She sat those already under her control down in groups and brought her little ones to them. The humans ate the flesh raw, their faces expressionless, their jaws moving rhythmically, their throats swallowing bone, scale, blood and flesh as if they were the same.

Some of her captives—those who had eaten the parts containing venom—died. She had these stacked by the others like cordwood in the ice for her pleasure later.

She exhibited no cruelty. Those She took did not suffer. Their minds were quickly and effortlessly snuffed out, and the bodies became soldiers for the queen, just as it had been destined. She would have been horrified at the idea of protracted suffering.

But culls and the wounded remained, after all, food.

Starting with the entrance to her chamber, She had them open a path twenty-five feet wide to the surface. This task would take some time, of course, but they worked tirelessly once they had been relieved of the burdensome handicap of individuality. They hammered and chopped and cut away the rock at an admirable rate.

Meanwhile, She continued to explore the workings of the minds of those as yet unchanged.

Mary Swenson, a sophomore who had signed up for a summer job, had just recently been accepted to the archaeological degree program and it had so far been the most exciting time of her life.

Not only had she been selected to work on the dig at Casa Malpais, but she had met Jim Minter on the site and fallen deeply in love.

No one did much bed checking on site. Perhaps because Margot believed in her own sexual freedom, she had pointedly not interfered in the after-hours lives of her crew. As a result, Mary and Jim had been living together for weeks.

Neither had as yet been summoned to help out on the new excavation on the lowest level, but both eagerly anticipated the opportunity. Having just finished a shift working in one of the upper galleries, they had returned to their quarters and bathed. Now they lay on their camp bed entwined in each other's arms.

Jim had a body like a gladiator, all hard muscle and masculine beauty. Four years older, he had considerably more experience than the willowy blonde. He couldn't believe his luck in connecting with her.

Mary's beauty took his breath away. Her natural blond hair shone almost platinum, both above and below. She had medium-sized breasts, a slim waist and flaring hips that led to long, perfectly formed legs.

When they made love, Jim continually marvelled at what a turn-on she could be, her every move and gesture graceful. Her young body and firm muscles responded exquisitely—more than any woman he had encountered before. She felt and tasted like silk and honey.

Mary found Jim to be the ultimate lover, everything her romantic upbringing had promised. His strong arms holding her turned her to jelly in moments. The feel of him inside her caused her to reach the heights of ecstasy again and again.

Now, as they moved together in the ancient rhythm of love, she closed her eyes and let herself go, completely happy.

Suddenly, he stopped moving and his legs began to quiver.

Opening her eyes in alarm, Mary looked up to find an expression of pain on Jim's face. It stayed there only a moment before his features grew blank and cold. He began to move again, but his violent thrusts seemed passionless pistoning that began to hurt immediately. Though large, he had always before been careful and gentle.

"Do you like this?" His mouth barely moved.

"What?" She looked into his eyes and found them empty. The jabbing pain continued and his voice had been the voice of a stranger.

"Do you like this mating?" Drool began to ooze out of the corners of his lips and fall in drops onto her breasts.

"Jim," she tried to push him away, "stop this. You're frightening me."

The tempo of his movements increased.

"Ah," said the voice, "I see how it works. Not really very different at all, is it?"

The pain had begun to grow severe. Mary bit her lip and continued to try to push Jim's heavy body away but the arms held her like steel bands pinned to the camp bed.

"I feel it rising now," said the voice in her ear, and then it hissed with pleasure.

The thrusting became frantic and powerful and Mary cried out without pleasure even as she felt him explode inside her.

Finally, he stopped moving. His body covered hers and his weight crushed her beneath him.

"Interesting," said the voice.

Mary whimpered, her insides throbbing from the abuse, her stomach cramping.

The arms moved and finally levered his bulk off of her. She looked up through tear-filled eyes and began to scream.

His face had lost all semblance of personality and intelligence. Vacuous and slack, his drooling mouth moved toward her, his eyes showing only whites.

"I will remember," said the voice, now thick and slurred. "This may be a thing to be used."

His mouth moved to her nose and neatly bit it off. "You will be prettier like this," said the voice. "You will be more like me."

By the time the nearest of those who heard the screams could respond, Jim had chewed up the nose and swallowed it. Mary screamed and continued screaming. Her face bled profusely.

Nothing anyone did could elicit a response from Minter. He lay on the camp bed, naked, comatose and brain dead.

When they tried to get permission from Shayley to call an ambulance, she denied it. Mary and Jim were carried to the infirmary where a nurse and doctor took them back behind closed doors. The screaming stopped soon thereafter.

Chapter Sixty

The Roberts Ranch

Lotus pulled in at the Roberts ranch at 8:45 am. FBI agent Matt Pierce greeted Jeremy.

The agent looked at the Native Americans in the car and then turned questioningly to Myers. "Friends of yours, Doc?"

"Allow me to introduce Lotus Farley of the Tohono O'odham, Danny Webb of the Pima, Juan Mapoli of the Yaqui, and Rattle of the Havasupai. They are medicine people and should see whatever it is you have to show me."

Matt looked skeptical. "Forgive me, Doc, but what we have for you isn't very pretty. It fell short of pretty before we filled it full of holes. It's even less attractive now."

Lotus got out of the car. "Don't worry about me, Agent Pierce. I can handle it."

Both Farah and Hernandez, who had come up unannounced, gave a whistle of appreciation.

"Knock it off," said Pierce. Turning back, he nodded to himself. "Okay. We put the remains on ice until you got here, Doc."

He led them into the shed where a large wooden crate sat propped on sawhorses in the rear. It had been packed with ice and empty Circle-K convenience store bags littered the floor near it.

The corpse lay on its back, or so Jeremy supposed. He found it difficult to be certain. Only when he checked the features could he be sure. He saw a six-foot oblong of scabby flesh. The face looked only vaguely humanoid. He would have been hard-pressed to guess this had once been a person until he found the arms and feet tucked into the ice beside it. That it could have been Mad Jake seemed incredible.

Both arms had been ripped off at the shoulders and the ball sockets had been taken with them. The prosthetic hand remained still strapped to the arm.

How could such trauma have been sustained?

The feet had been neatly severed at the ankle but an examination of the corpse showed that the remaining leg bones tapered to a tail-like affair.

With a cold, sinking sensation in the pit of his stomach, Jeremy realized that the stumps must have been shaved to near points before being fused together. "How did this happen?" he asked Pierce.

"Damned if I know," replied the agent. The coronor says he's never seen anything like it. All this apparently got done to him the day before yesterday. The wounds are cauterized and there are no signs of infection."

"Who are we looking for, a surgeon?"

"Coroner says it isn't that simple." said Matt. "Some unknown substance melted and reformed the skin at every step, some kind of acid is his guess. Whoever cut the fucker up, sealed it off as he did it."

"He must have been unconscious through most of it," said Jeremy looking with pity at the body.

"No," said Pierce, "his larynx burst from screaming. You want my guess? The fiend brought him back around every time."

"But no mind could stand up under that kind of pain," protested Myers. "Unstable in the first place, Jake would have snapped, lost it completely."

"He did," said Farah. "You should have seen it when we found it—a crawling, mewling, pitiful, mindless . . ."

"That will be enough, Paul," said Pierce.

"Oh, yeah, sorry," Farah apologized.

"A sorry sight," said Matt quietly. "We couldn't make out much in the dark and it seemed menacing. Not until we had finished firing did we realized it couldn't have harmed us. I, for one, will always feel terrible about it."

"Yeah, me too," added Farah. "It was pretty ugly down there."

Jeremy looked again at the creature in the crate. "Who do you think did it?" he asked.

"No suspects," said Matt. "In addition to the fact that we had the entire ranch staked out, no one has any idea how it could have been done in the first place. Roberts had a back door through the rocks into a wash. It had been recently enlarged. Our best guess is the butcher entered that way." He looked unhappy. "We didn't know where the fucker had hidden out. Both Roberts and whoever did this fooled us completely."

Jeremy, after two days of conversation with the medicine men and Lotus, thought he knew who or what had done it, but wisely kept silent. Even though he called Matt Pierce a friend, he knew better than to talk about the vengeance of the gods.

Lotus, Danny, Juan and Rattle looked at the body but said nothing. The Havasupai seemed the most affected by it. He went back and sat in the car.

An hour later, the five had returned to the road and the Roberts place disappeared in the rearview mirror. No one spoke for a while.

Finally, Jeremy could stand it no longer. "Do we actually want to meet with the thing that did that?"

Danny answered, "It has summoned us."

Rattle added, "It is a god, doctor. What we want has nothing to do with it. It punished that man for killing it's children."

They were a good ten minutes away from the ranch, heading toward Springerville, when Lotus pulled over to the side of the road without warning.

"Why are we stopping?" asked Jeremy.

She gestured but did not speak.

On the hillside right next to the pavement they saw freshly dug earth and it formed the undulant shape of a snake that pointed off into the desert.

"I think we go that way," said Danny.

The idea of meeting the thing that had metamorphosed Mad Jake did not give wings to Jeremy Myers' feet. He had been thinking. The god had supposedly punished Roberts for serpent slaying.

The doctor ran an anti-venin lab.

A small voice in his head kept asking him if this meeting could possibly prove a good career move.

The five of them got out of the car and walked slowly away from the road. Lotus took the lead.

Chapter Sixty-One

Hopiland

The two pickups and the sedan drove as close as they could before parking and spilling their occupants forth. It would still be a long walk up third mesa and into Oraibi. The shamans knew that Harold would be found in his village. It could be no other way.

Cord, Kade, Michael, James, Gordon, Gerry, Tom and Geraldo did not linger by the vehicles but began to climb silently. All but Geraldo had visited Hopiland within the past year because they had gone there to accept the thanks of the People of Peace for their part in the destruction of the demon.

This time no welcoming ceremony awaited them. Though their friend might have guessed they would come calling, their visit would not please some others. They did not know what kind of reception to expect, but had an urgent need for Harold to complete the Gathering.

On their previous visit, the climb had taken hours, the pace set by a Hopi guide. Now they set their own.

Tom, who had visited Harold many times before, led the way.

"What if he won't come?" asked Cord.

"He will," replied Michael. "He has to."

"It isn't Harold I'm worried about," muttered Tom. "It's the elders. What if they won't let him?"

"Our presence must account for something," said Kade. "We were honored here not very long ago. They can not have forgotten."

They stayed silent after that exchange, except for heavy breathing, because the climb up the slope taxed their strength.

When the shamans were in sight of the mesas' crest, they stopped and rested in the shade of an overhang.

Gordon broke the silence. "What of this Scaled One the others are meeting? The description Rattle gave us is enough for me. I wouldn't want to cross him."

"The Scaled One," said Tom, "is a god, the Father of All Serpents. It is important that we understand what He seeks before we act. It would not do to anger him."

Gerry, who had heard nothing of this god in either incarnation, felt curious. "Why?" he asked. "What is it about this being that makes him so terrible?"

Geraldo answered, "He has great power."

"What power?" asked Michael.

"The power to transform," said Kade. "I have heard of this creature before. He wreaks vengeance on those who slay the serpents."

"But why?" Cord asked.

"The protection of his children," said Tom. "This one is the father of all the snake brothers. It is his world into which we intrude."

"Is there no reason to kill the vipers?" asked James.

"Only in self-defense," answered Tom. "He will forgive a necessary killing, but punishes those who wantonly seek out his own."

"Is that what happened to the snake hunter, Roberts?" asked Cord.

"I do not know," said Tom. "Roberts died when the agents watching the ranch found him. No doubt the others will tell us when we meet them tomorrow. This Roberts took pride in being a serpent slayer. He hunted the snake brother for the pleasure of killing."

The comment brought an uncomfortable silence.

After resting for ten minutes, Tom stood and looked at his fellow shamans. "Let's go." He led them the rest of the way to the top.

Children spotted them first. Some ran ahead to spread word of their arrival, others laughed and began to pace them.

The medicine men moved as a group into the village.

They had not gone far when a familiar figure waved from amidst a small cluster of people coming toward them.

"It is Harold," said Tom quietly, "and he is accompanied by other priests."

"Ho, Tom Bear," called Laloma. The Hopi appeared nervous and only three of the priests smiled. The remainder looked suspicious and unfriendly. "I am surprised to see you here my brothers."

"We had to come," answered Tom. "The gathering needs you, Harold. The source of our problem has come to light and we must move quickly if we are to stop it."

Interest warred with caution on the Hopi's face. He turned to his fellow priests and said, "Let me walk with my brothers that they may tell me of these things and then I will return."

Tom and the other members of the gathering hung back a respectful distance while the priests talked. It took only a moment to see that they were clearly divided. Harold, John Lakona and Joseph Lansa appeared to be in favor of letting Harold go. The other five argued against it. Minutes passed and the talk continued without resolution.

Finally, Geraldo stepped out of the group and spoke in a loud voice. "Is this the hospitality of the People of Peace?" He spoke to Tom, but the Hopis heard and turned back to watch as he continued. "Is this the way our Hopi brothers greet the medicine men of the tribes? I, for one, will see that my people learn of this. I have travelled far and made the climb from below. I am the Chief Priest of the Gray Wolf Clan of Zuni." At the sound of his voice, others came forward to see what all the commotion was about.

"We must be patient," answered Tom in a placating tone. He understood what Vasquez intended and thought it might work. "After all, we visited unannounced. They have not had time to prepare."

"Even the children of my people understand honor," retorted Geraldo. "The smallest of them would not keep us standing unwelcomed in the hot sun."

That seemed to do it.

Laloma and the other priests came to them as a group with soothing words of welcome.

The witch, the Zuni Priest and Harold exchanged a glance in which twinkling eyes, twitching lips and stifled mirth were common.

They were led to a shaded place and served beverages. There were numerous apologies and protestations that surprise had been responsible for the confusion.

"Good thinking, Geraldo," whispered Harold when he had the chance.

"*S'nada*," replied Vasquez. "I was hot and thirsty. Besides," he added with a chuckle, "you were losing the argument."

"Tell me what you have learned," said Laloma, when all had been served and the general conversation died down.

"We know what is affecting the snakes," answered Tom.

The excitement this simple statement produced exceeded even the Pima's expectations.

"What?" asked Harold.

"Tell us," urged John Lakona.

"You have no idea what this means to us," added Lansa.

All leaned forward avidly, awaiting an explanation.

"There is an ancient snake buried in the earth near Springerville," said Tom. "Somehow it has been awakened."

"It has powers of mind," added Gerry, "that let it control the lesser snakes. That is why they have been acting so strange."

"An ancient snake?" Joseph, ever the conservative, looked skeptical. "How do you know?"

"The Yaqui has confronted it," said Gordon from off to the side. "He has spoken with it."

Lakona asked, "Where in Springerville?"

"The excavation site at the Badlands House," answered Tom.

Harold shook his head. "Why is it always the archaeologists who loose these monsters on us? Why can't they leave the past buried where it lies?"

Gordon smiled as he replied, "It is too easy for us to blame the white men. All of us here are involved in preserving the past—the songs, the traditions, the magic. Why should we wonder that those who have mastered technology should use it for the same purposes?"

"Where is the Yaqui?" asked Harold, looking around, "and Lotus and Danny? Rattle?"

"They had another task," said Gerry. "The giant serpent is not the only thing with which we contend. There is something even older now walking the world."

"And what is that?" asked Lansa.

"The Father of Serpents," replied Cord.

"The Scaled One," added Michael.

There was a moment of silence before Joseph spoke. "You mean a god?" he asked.

Tom and the others nodded.

"And that is where the others are?" asked Harold. "They have gone to meet this god?"

"They must ask what we are permitted to do," explained Gerry. "The Scaled One does not forgive the killing of its children. We must find out how we can stop this ancient serpent without offending the god."

"There must be a way," said Harold. "The snake brothers are quickly getting out of control. We have had to postpone the collection of serpents for the dance. There have already been too many deaths."

"We hoped," said Geraldo, "that you would have some ideas, Harold. The Hopi are the masters of the snake brothers. That is why we need your help."

Harold exchanged looks with John and Joseph and the other priests in the group, then rose.

"We will go and talk," he said to Tom. "Please rest and refresh yourselves. We will see that you are tended to." He left and the other priests followed.

When they were alone, Kade said, "I hope they come up with something."

"Perhaps Rattle and the others will learn what can be done," suggested Gordon.

"What about us?" asked Tom. "Perhaps we should be talking about what we can do instead of counting on the others to come up with a solution."

"You're right," agreed Gerry. He turned to Gordon. "You led us last time, Fly. What do you suggest?"

"I have been thinking," replied the Navajo. "I do not believe songs and ceremonies will help this time. I am not Archie Smythe."

"Archie is gone," said Gerry. "You are the yataalii now. We all look to you for guidance."

Gordon shrugged. "I think another must lead us."

"You did well before, my friend," said Tom.

"But I had been taught what to do," he answered. "This is different. I am not even sure I understand what it is we face, let alone what can be done to stop it."

"We have to go to Casa Malpais," said Tom. "We must take Harold and whatever the Hopis can offer and we must join forces with the herpetologist and the others. We have no choice but to go and confront this ancient thing."

"And pray the gods will show us the way to defeat it," said Geraldo.

Chapter Sixty-Two

Casa Malpais

By afternoon, the passage from her chamber had been widened enough. She considered the cost in terms of human lives to be negligible. Oh, it had meant the irrevocable destruction of the personalities of every human being at the site, but She had an army now—a mindless colony of automatons that served like ants to do her bidding. They worked until they dropped. She simply ate those that died.

She made her way slowly to the entrance and slithered into the outer room for the first time in twenty-five thousand years. Her slaves did not even notice. The hammering and pounding did not abate.

Even the simple act of exiting her chamber taxed her strength. She stopped to rest and chided herself for being sluggish. Though she finally had enough food, skin hung on her massive frame like loose cloth. It would take time to regain her former glory. It still required enormous effort to move any distance at all.

She was blind. She had realized that soon after awakening. Fortunately She could use the eyes of any living creature She possessed, so it did not mater. Those of her new slaves were better than hers had been even in youth.

After she had rested, She coiled her massive body and turned back toward her former prison.

She called the Shayley human to her side. Even seen through human eyes, the doorway looked very small.

She thought about sending the Shayley thing to work at the rock with the others. All the humans here had been neutralized. There seemed no need to keep up the appearance of normalcy, but, once the way to the outside lay open, that might change. Better to keep this one away from the digging. Humans listened to it and obeyed. To waste such a valuable asset would be foolish.

Controlling human minds in large numbers proved easier than She expected—unless She left the independent thoughts intact. In that case, control proved very difficult indeed. For this reason, She had decided to erase those functions from all those within the dig. She watched the work progress through the human's eyes.

The quickest way to the surface would be a tunnel directly through the hillside. This could eliminate the twisting and turning progress now required to gain access to the lowest level.

Instead of following the labyrinthine passages hollowed out by the Mogollons, She directed her workers to cut across them. The result would be less effort for her and the digging should take them to the surface in another day. The limestone could be easily broken up and hauled away.

The humans could lift large blocks in their stick-like arms with very little damage.

She had learned from exploring the minds around her about the power of dynamite but feared an explosion would bring the hill down on top of her. She had no desire to be buried alive again. She chose instead to expend her human tools. They were hardy enough to give her hours of labor before collapsing and required little rest before being called on to do it again.

These had all been healthy and well-fed to begin with so their ability to work would not deteriorate for some time. A good thing, for She had not been able to draw any new humans to her so far.

She knew a plentiful supply waited out there in the wider world. She had seen them in large numbers through the eyes of her little ones. Influencing them at great distances, however, proved difficult. Her effective range for controlling humans appeared to be limited. It angered her to be so weak. She promised herself that such a thing would never be allowed to happen again. She must secure enough servants that her needs would always be met.

She brought the Shayley human up and stood it in front of her face so that her perspective through its eyes would be as normal as possible.

"How long?" She demanded.

"Twenty-four hours," the flat reply came quickly. "The work goes well."

She felt pleased now that She had not erased this one. The female had an interesting personality, almost snake-like herself. It would be nice to have someone to communicate with. She had never been able to do such a thing before.

For the first time in her long life, She felt lonely.

The mind of Margot Shayley had been only partially shattered and enough remained that she understood what had happened to her. She found it at once terrifying and wonderful.

As the serpent manipulated her, different parts of her brain were stimulated and odd images presented themselves for her perusal. Though she had no volition of her own, static moments actually permitted her to think . . . even to dream.

Her communicative functions were related to serving the queen. The queen? What an odd thought . . . yet that described exactly what the great serpent meant—a queen to be served, a ruling force that must not be questioned.

Still, a part of Margot wanted to flee, screaming in panic at what she had witnessed, especially when Roger had been devoured and she could do nothing. The snake had begun at his feet and, as more of him disappeared into the huge maw, his head and torso got redder and mishapen. The queen, in the process of swallowing, crushed the man's bones with audible pops. Though he never made a sound, Margot could not forget the pain and fear in his eyes as he died.

Little of the higher functions of her mind—only memories and logic—remained, but she possessed enough to know despair. Trapped within, she wailed and gibbered in a prison of endless night.

Chapter Sixty-Three

Outside Springerville

Lotus Farley led them along the wash. Their journey to the Roberts Ranch had taken them a little north and west of Springerville into the Coyote Hills. The White Mountains and Mount Ord rose majestically to the southwest.

The day could not have been more beautiful, the sky cloudless and the temperature cool. They saw no one else around, not even traffic on the road.

The men followed in a line, Jeremy a few paces behind Lotus, followed by Juan, Danny and Rattle. They had gone only a quarter mile or so when they began to hear a strange sound ahead, a buzzing or humming that grew in volume as they moved toward it. Circling a small knoll, they came upon a stunning sight.

As they passed between two large boulders, they came upon a place where the water had carved a wide path between the hills. At the far end stood a rock wall where debris of all kinds had been trapped whenever the monsoon storms caused the wash to run.

For hundreds of yards, the ground lay buried under a carpet of snakes, all of them making noise according to their kind—as if they were singing.

Diamondbacks, Mohaves, Leafnoses, Shovelnoses, Sidewinders, Blacktails, Twin-spotteds, Kingsnakes—all manner of serpents lined up in ranks like troops in review.

"What in the hell?" Jeremy couldn't believe it.

Juan placed a restraining hand on the doctor's arm and spoke in a low voice. "I believe this is the place we seek."

"I've never seen so many at once," said the herpetologist. His excitement could not be contained.

"Be careful, Jeremy," said Lotus. "Remember that we are here to meet the father of all these creatures, the father of the first serpent. He will know what is in your heart. He will know everything you have done."

The din increased as more snakes appeared on the hillsides above.

"Incredible," said Myers. "No one back in the city will believe me. I wish I had a camera."

Suddenly, the noise came to an abrupt halt.

"Look," said Rattle, pointing to the rocks. "He comes."

The huge form of the Scaled One had begun a slow and majestic walk toward the little group of humans. The serpents moved to make way for the giant, a living sea that parted before him.

Jeremy could not accept the evidence of his own eyes. The anthropomorphic shape advanced, sunlight glinting off red scales. Huge, fully fifteen feet tall, and muscled like a weight lifter, yet it moved fluidly and with grace.

Strangely, none of the shamans felt fear.

Rattle, who had spoken with the creature before, stepped forward and stood with his arms folded across his chest. "We have come, lord," he said, "as you asked."

The black eyes in the snake head atop the massive shoulders and neck looked back passively. The creature squatted and then sat in a single, smooth motion. Even then, it towered over them.

The heavy, ancient, musty odor of the thing smelled strong but, here in the open, it did not overpower Rattle as it had when the Havasupai sat under the overhang.

The huge mouth opened and the dark, forked tongue flicked out. "Ssssss . . . Rattle," it said, its voice a rumble, "I know now what has returned from the dark past to trouble my children."

"It is a serpent," said Juan from his position to the right. "It has attacked humans using your children as weapon."

"Sssss . . . it is my daughter," said the giant. "She passed into sleep long ago."

"We must stop her," said Lotus. "She has caused great harm with her attacks and many deaths."

The massive head turned to look at the young Tohono O'odham woman, a suggestion of humor on its scaled face. "Ssss . . . you, woman? You will stop her? How?"

Danny moved to her side, then spoke. "Not Lotus alone," he said. "We are many and we will do what we must to protect our people."

The tongue flicked out again. The humor vanished to be replaced by sadness. "Sssss . . . She has always been willful," it said. "I sired her when you and those like you were only lesser animals in the world. She does not understand how you have mastered the earth, populated it and tamed it to your own purposes."

"She must be stopped," said Jeremy, "or there will be a great dying, both of my kind and yours."

"Sssss . . . you are the scientist," said the creature leaning forward to peer at the white man. "You are the one who cages my children."

Jeremy wondered if he would leave this place alive. "I do not kill them," he said in his own defense. "I capture and study them. I create antivenin that my people will not die when they are bitten."

"Sssss . . . I know all about you Dr. Myers," it said. "I have watched you through the eyes of the one you call Long Tom. I have seen that you are not unnecessarily cruel. You need not fear me."

This pronouncement brought a feeling of relief that ran visibly through the small group of humans. The herpetologist had been a risk.

"Sssss . . . I will help you," said the creature. "But you must not kill her."

"But how can we promise that?" asked Rattle. "She threatens our world. How can we stop her without ending her life?"

The scaled monster before them sighed. "Sssss . . . you must return her to her sleep," it said. "She slept through the ages under the earth until your kind awakened her."

"Hibernation?" Jeremy asked. "How long?"

"Sssss . . . twenty-five thousand of your years," rumbled the voice. "She slept in the ice until your people breached the chamber."

"Twenty-five thousand years!" Myers exclaimed.

"Why can't you stop her?" asked Rattle.

The creature shrugged. "Sssss . . . even a god has limitations," it replied. "I have tried to reach her mind, but she will not hear me. She is the last of the great serpents I made in the time before your kind. I once promised never to interfere with her. I am still bound by that promise. If I confronted her awake in her domain, I would have to destroy her. This I will not do."

"But how can we put her back to sleep?" asked Lotus.

"Sssss . . . you claim to be the dominant species on this world," said the scaled being. "You have the thing you call science. Use it to stop her but not kill her."

"You said you would help us," said Juan. "How?"

"Sssss . . . I will protect your minds," said the creature. "She has learned a new trick, my daughter. I will keep her from using it on you."

"Is that all?" asked Jeremy. "Is that the help we came all this way to seek?" He sounded bitter.

The giant stirred and rose to its feet. "Sssss . . . you may go now," it said, then turned and stalked away.

They watched in silence until it had passed over the rock wall and out of sight.

"What the hell are we supposed to do now?" asked Myers, anger in his voice.

"We've got to figure out a way to freeze a snake, doc," said Juan.

Chapter Sixty-Four

Oraibi, Hopiland

When Harold returned, he sat among the others and sighed. "There have been easier things," he said to no one in particular. "The elders are still divided about what we should do. Half want to cancel the ceremonies and the dance this year and wait for the problem to go away. The other half want us to go to Springerville and stop this at its source."

"And who prevailed?" asked Gordon.

Harold smiled. "We did, of course. I have been talking with Joseph and John for the last hour. We will all come with you to do what we can."

"And what is that?" asked Geraldo. "Do the Hopi have some magic that will aid us?"

"We shall see," replied Harold. "The three of us will begin at sunrise tomorrow morning in the desert near the Badland's House."

It took an hour to gather all the gear the three priests would need and everyone had to help carrying it back down to the vehicles.

Joseph Lansa and John Lakona were excited to be joining the gathering in such an important venture. They tried to appear dignified and reserved, but their happiness could not be disguised.

Leaving the mesas behind, they drove south until they hit Highway 40 near Holbrook, then drove southeast on Highway 180 to

Springerville, arriving just at sundown. They made camp at the agreed upon place—a full mile away from Casa Malpais—and waited for the others to join them.

Harold and the other two Hopis immediately set about unpacking their gear and were soon working on a sandpainting. The others, having been informed they could not help at present, sat a respectful distance away and talked.

An hour later, they were joined by Lotus, Danny, Juan and Rattle, but Dr. Myers did not stay. He took Lotus' car and headed back toward Phoenix, promising to return as quickly as possible with help and equipment.

The four new arrivals told of their meeting with the Scaled One and the prohibition against killing the serpent. When they said that the only help offered was that the god would protect their minds, the others were equally disappointed.

Harold left his two fellow priests working and joined the others. He did not say anything when he heard about the meeting with the god but his face grew thoughtful and he soon returned to the painting.

One by one, the shamans rolled out in their blankets and slept. It was a beautiful night under the stars and the air stayed cool. They agreed to keep a watch until morning and Gerry volunteered to be first. He watched the Hopis work with professional curiosity.

They had cleared an space some twelve feet in diameter and laid down a large disk of white sand. The whole area was illuminated by camping lanterns hung from poles. Each man worked on a different portion, moving carefully and stopping only long enough to mix new colors when needed.

Depicted in the painting sat the ruin of Casa Malpai, but under it were heavy black lines and pockets where figures took shape. At the bottom was a large dark oval within which Harold built a large, coiled serpent. Around the outer edge of the disk, evenly spaced, were thirteen symbols, one for each of the twelve tribes and one for the white man.

As he worked, using his hands deftly to bring startling images to life in the sand, Joseph stood by his side and chanted, brushing at the air with an eagle feather wand.

Gerry eventually awakened Rattle who took the next shift and spent it wandering restlessly around the perimeter of their camp. Several times, he came upon snakes—who come out often at night in the desert after the heat of the day—but they were easily turned away.

After awakening Juan, Rattle did not return to sleep but walked out into the desert until he was out of sight of the camp. Here he sat on the ground and focussed his mind. He intended to summon the great deer spirit, his totem.

The words of the god had troubled the Havasupai. He did not trust the science of the white men. His world connected to the earth through links of spirit between men and gods. The Scaled One should have done more if it was indeed his daughter that threatened them.

Rattle chanted and prayed.

In very little time, he heard the tentative steps of the spirit approaching.

Juan did not return to sleep either. After his watch, he moved into the darkness, finding a rock upon which to sit. He had difficulty summoning birds at night. They slept and calling one forth took a great deal of effort. Nearly an hour passed before he heard the soft flutter of wings.

Minutes later, the crow took wing and flew directly toward the site of the dig. It would not return until first light.

Gordon Smythe dreamed. The ghost voice of his great-great-grandfather whispered to him.

The night passed in silence, meteorites occasionally flaring for a moment in the sky. The land seemed to hold its breath.

To each of the shamans came the things in which they believed. Whispers and visions and ghosts and totems rose in their minds to instruct, to guide, to enlighten.

With the first lightening of the sky, they all awoke and greeted each other with clear eyes and a new confidence.

Tuesday, July 9th

Chapter Sixty-Five

Casa Malpais

The morning did not arrive cloaked in sunshine. A gray pall lay over the area, as if the gods had turned their faces away. Within the ruins that had been the Badland's House, the creatures that stirred were no longer human. Many had worked through the night with torn and bloody hands at clearing the path to the outer wall. No chatter sounded. A dismal cloud of silence hung in the air.

The two-legs moved about with a heavy, awkward stride—in a parody of human gait. Faces remained blank or—had any normal man been there to observe—moronic. No one noticed or cared. Only one intelligence flourished in Casa Malpais. It had never been human and thus did not know the difference.

She thrummed with excitement, felt more alive and younger than ever before. Anticipation filled her with purpose.

Her servants had made good progress. A breach in the outer wall could now be only hours away and enlarging the opening would take no time at all. She would be free today.

The Shayley thing stood by her side.

"What is it like in the wider world?" She asked.

The former human drooled, tongue lolling. When it spoke, the speech was slurred. "There are many," it replied.

"Many humans?"

"Many. Like grains of sand in a desert," said the slave. "The earth teems with them. They have conquered the air and the sea and the land. They have even reached the moon."

She used the mind of the Shayley thing like a reference file, following the thought back through its process until the image came into focus.

"The orb in the sky, the one that grows and shrinks like a mouth—from gaping round to closed," She thought. "You call it moon?"

"Yes." The reply came flatly, disinterested.

"There are humans tall enough to touch the sky?" The thought disturbed her. Perhaps She should know more before venturing forth from her lair.

Unable to cope with the complexity of the question, the slave stayed silent.

Again, She regretted erasing all the humans. She needed information and these servants lacked the ability to furnish it. The raw data remained there, but it proved tedious to discover and nearly impossible to understand. She reminded herself to capture new ones as quickly as possible.

The time had come for her to plan what She would do once free of her prison. She had searched the minds of those who served and accumulated a vast store of knowledge, but everything seemed so foreign to her that little of it made sense.

These humans were a remarkable species. Images of war and battle had been common in their thoughts. There were things called machines, for example. She had a rudimentary idea of what machines were. There were generators and motorized carts within the complex. She had seen these through the eyes of the Shayley thing, but understanding still escaped her. The scenes She had taken from memory showed huge birds that spit flame and traveled across the sky at incredible speed. There were great vessels that floated on the sea, vessels containing hundreds of these humans. There were sticks that they could carry that, when pointed at something, destroyed it in an explosion of flame and smoke.

Obviously, the two-legs could be dangerous unless they were controlled.

Having learned of a nearby place called Springerville, where many of them nested, She planned to test her strength. She could sense the nearness of their busy minds but they remained too far away for her to control them.

Several of her little ones had been sent out to serve as eyes. She would know her enemy before putting herself at risk.

She had sent one of the human slaves out in company with them. The broken bones in both of its arms made it of limited use, but its eyes would offer her a better picture of the wider world than those of the serpents.

Meanwhile, the work continued. Some of the slaves were failing. She had those that stopped functioning carried below and stored in the ice. She must not eat today. Mobility and speed would be required for her plans. Feasting and celebration would come later.

The three Mohave Rattlesnakes moved in perfect unison, making good progress toward the town. Their tongues flicked in and out, testing the air for the vibrations of life. She controlled them—a single thought motivated them—and all of their senses fed directly into her.

The slave stumbled along behind. It continued to grow weaker. Despite her elimination of its pain, the two-legs body deteriorated rapidly. Still, it could serve until it dropped.

She felt wonderful.

Sight, She decided, mattered most. After the blackness of the underworld, the variety of shades of light and dark, the textures of sand, dirt, trees and grasses were overwhelming. Only when the hillside had been opened and She could move her real physical body out, would She know more joy.

The process of controlling her servants, even at a distance, posed no challenge. Her mind dominated what remained of those who served and She controlled all of them at once. It required no effort at all to keep those who remained behind at their digging while directing her outside scouts. She grew more confident. There seemed no important limits to her power.

Chapter Sixty-Six

City of Phoenix

Jeremy had wasted no time in returning to the city. He made his first call at precisely 8 am—to Ramirez. "Ed? This is Myers. I need your help."

"What's up, doc?" Ramirez chuckled into the phone. "I've always wanted to say that."

"I found out what's going on," replied Jeremy, "but it's too complicated to go into over the phone. How fast can you get to my office?"

"I'll have to find Rod. He's in the building someplace. We can be there in thirty minutes."

"Good. That'll give me time to make a few more calls." Myers hung up the phone without further explanation and took out a scrap of paper Juan had given him. He dialed and waited for an answer.

"Tempe Police. How can we help you?"

"I need to speak to Captain Greg Johnson," said Jeremy. "Tell him it concerns the Gathering."

A moment later another voice came on the line. "Greg Johnson."

"Captain, this is Doctor Jeremy Myers. I'm a herpetologist with Carter Labs in Phoenix. I was asked to call you by a Yaqui medicine man named Juan Mapoli. He seemed to think you'd be willing to believe what I have to tell you."

"I'm listening," came the reply.

Myers tried to organize his thoughts. "There's been an increase in poisonous snake activity throughout the state," he said. "Juan and the others have discovered the reason for it. It's more than a little fantastic and I'll have to convince a lot of important people that I'm not crazy. He told me to call you and ask for your help."

"What kind of help?"

Jeremy could hear reluctance in the Captain's voice. "I'm about to meet with Lieutenants Ramirez and Grimsley from DPS. I'll need some specialized equipment in a hurry to take up to Springerville."

"What would you like me to do?"

"I'd like you to be here when I meet the Lieutenants. As I understand it, you know these medicine men and have had some experience with them and the . . . uh . . . supernatural."

A heavy sigh came from the other end of the line. "Christ!" said Johnson. "What have they gotten into now?"

"I won't try to tell you over the phone," said the doctor. "I don't even like thinking about it. Please come."

"Give me the address." The Captain's tone was resigned. "I guess I knew counting on a pension would be a longshot."

Jeremy next called Professor Sarno at ASU, and then there were others.

An hour later, Jeremy stood before a diverse group of men. Displeasure at the disruption of their accustomed routine showed on their faces.

"You all know me," he began. "I'm a scientist. I've worked with most of you at one time or another. I'm not given to flights of fancy or imaginings."

"We're willing to concede," said Ramirez from his place at the table, "that you are a reasonable man, Dr. Myers. Just what is all this about?"

Jeremy had rehearsed it to himself a hundred times this morning, but he still did not know if he would have believed it coming from another person.

"A team of archaeologists made an important discovery at Casa Malpais," he said. "They found a lower chamber that had apparently been sealed for thousands of years. In that chamber, probably at the

264 The Serpent Slayers

time of the impact at Meteor Crater, a giant serpent had been frozen alive."

Sarno sputtered his incredulity. "Why haven't we been told? How could they keep something so significant a secret?"

"The serpent apparently awakened before they broke through to its lair. It has prevented them from telling anyone."

"Alive? After thousands of years? Impossible!" The professor's face showed his indignation.

Rod Grimsley, however, had heard the rest of what Jeremy said. "Uh . . . what do you mean by prevented, doctor?"

"The creature seems to be telepathic to an extraordinary degree. It is able to control minds."

Ed Ramirez spoke, his voice harsh and cutting—the three days had passed and his bet with Grimsley was over. "Fuck! Is that what all this is about? Are you telling me some fucking giant snake is controlling all the others?"

"I'm afraid that is exactly what I'm telling you, Ed. And we have reason to believe it has taken control of the humans in Casa Malpais as well."

"Come on, Myers," shouted Sarno, his fury finally breaking free. "Are you crazy? A giant telepathic snake? Controlling an army of poisonous snakes? Enslaved humans? Have you lost it all, man?"

Jeremy looked at the professor and shrugged. "Whether you choose to believe me or not, I'm telling you the truth."

"Have you seen this giant serpent?" asked Sarno.

"No."

"Did someone at the dig tell you about it?"

"No."

"Then how do you know?"

The doctor sat back in his chair and sighed. "A group of Native American medicine men told me. I accompanied them north to Springerville and saw what I consider to be irrefutable proof."

"Medicine men," exploded the professor.

Jeremy shrugged.

"What proof?" asked Grimsley.

"I can't tell you," said Myers.

Everyone began to speak at once, but the man in the police uniform who threw back his head and laughed soon captured their attention. Captain Greg Johnson took a moment to regain control.

"Forgive me," he said, wiping his eyes and trying to catch his breath. He looked at the doctor with genuine sympathy on his face. "It's just that I know exactly how you feel. When I met those medicine people I found myself in exactly the same position. You can't talk about it because it's crazy, nuts." He looked around at the others and his face grew serious. His eyes touched Sarno's and froze the professor before he could speak. "That doesn't mean it isn't true. That group of twelve men and one woman taught me there is more to the world than we imagine."

"What do you mean?" asked Ed.

"A year ago, as a new detective, I received a missing persons report. The victim turned out to be a student at ASU. With almost no explanation, I got assigned TDY to DPS."

"Why out of your area?" Grimsley had professional curiosity.

"Do you remember the killer storm?"

"Who could forget it?" Ramirez looked around at the others. "It wiped out half of Cave Creek."

"Turned out not to be a storm," said Johnson, "but . . . something else."

"A damned peculiar storm," said Rod. "It wiped out a town north of Phoenix. Then it hit New Mexico. Then it came back to hit Cave Creek and Carefree. It just blew out when it got to Phoenix."

"Doesn't that tell you something?" asked Captain Johnson. "It was more than a storm or tornado. It was an ancient evil, an intelligence like nothing we've seen before." He paused and looked around the table. "And it didn't just blow out when it got to Phoenix. Those medicine men killed it."

"Aren't you letting your imagination lead you astray, Captain?" asked Sarno. "I remember that storm well. I recall nothing supernatural about it."

Johnson turned to face the professor. "I ran that investigation, Dr. Sarno. Are you telling me how it went?" He turned to the others. "We kept the truth from the public. We had to."

"What did it turn out to be?" Grimsley could not have remained silent if his life depended on it.

"A demon—a creature made up of wind. The Native Americans had imprisoned it hundreds of years ago. The archaeologist, Jack Foreman, set it free. The shamans destroyed it with his help."

"And this new thing, this serpent?" Ramirez asked.

"I know nothing about it," admitted the captain, "but I'd be inclined to believe the doctor and ask the difficult questions later."

Ed leaned over and whispered something to Rod, who rose and left the office.

"Well I, for one, will not accept such nonsense," said Professor Sarno. "This is ridiculous." He stood and moved to the door, turning to face the others. "You may be willing to listen to this hogwash, but I am not. This talk of giant serpents and human slaves is crazy. If you come to your senses and need the services of a scientist, call me. Otherwise, count me out."

"Did you know Jack Foreman, the archaeology professor?" asked Greg.

"Yes," replied Sarno, "I did. So what?"

"Do you know how he died, professor?"

"It had something to do with an accidental explosion at a Native American site, didn't it?"

The Captain nodded. "That's right. And it explains when and why the so-called storm ended."

The professor sat back down.

Ed spoke aloud, ticking off each point on his fingers. "Okay let's see. We've seen a sudden increase in snake activity, including too many deaths. We have visited the site at Casa Malpais where the archaeologist in charge hinted at a new major find. Now Captain Johnson says the medicine people may well be telling the truth."

Grimsley re-entered and caught his partner's eye. Rod shook his head.

"And no one seems to be home at the site. We just tried to call."

"If what I have been told is true," commented Jeremy, "there's no one left at the dig to answer—at least nothing human."

Ed made up his mind. "What do you need from me, doctor?"

"I want DPS to authorize my contacting this group of individuals and back me up if I don't get cooperation." He passed a list to the Lieutenant. "And we have to arrange for choppers to deliver them and their equipment to Casa Malpais. Finally, I'll need a group of men—something akin to a SWAT team would do—to meet us and go in with me when we're ready."

"What about these medicine people?" asked Grimsley.

"They are waiting for us now just outside the dig—doing what they can to contain it pending our arrival." He looked at his watch. "I'm afraid, gentlemen, that we have very little time."

Chapter Sixty-Seven

Springerville

"What shall we do, Harold?" Gordon asked.

The Hopi glanced up from his preparations. He looked thoughtful for a moment before he replied, "We must go into the underworld."

Lansa and Lakona did not acknowledge the others. Their eyes were tightly shut, their lips moving as they prayed. They held cornmeal in their right hands and pahos in their left.

"Who?" asked Geraldo.

Laloma smiled as he stood up. "Why all of us, of course," he said. "How could it be otherwise for brothers? Only John and Joseph will remain here."

The shamans looked at each other and their eyes conveyed the sense of harmony they had all awakened with that morning.

"The white scientist has not yet returned," observed Rattle.

"No, but he will," answered Juan. "The Gathering will be complete when we are tested. For now, all is as it should be. The wise of the twelve tribes must confront this creature and return it to the darkness from which it came."

Lotus put an arm around Danny and the other around Cord. "We have work to do," she said simply. "The others will join us when the time is right."

They turned toward the Badland's House and their eyes shone like steel, each unflinching and unafraid. With no visible signal, they started toward the site. They walked toward their goal with purpose, free of fear.

Tom brought up the rear, beating the drum with a steady rhythm. He began to sing under his breath—not a song with words, but a chant that kept time with his heart. One by one, the others joined in. No one attempted to sing exactly with the Pima witch. Each sang his or her own song and the blend became a mix of power and confidence.

The desert passed beneath their feet like a rolling carpet. They stayed just to the side of the road, which had been widened months before because of the equipment required at the archaeological site.

Juan, sharp-eyed and alert, first saw the scarecrow-like figure weaving drunkenly on the road ahead.

"One comes," he observed.

It took little power of discernment to see that the person who walked toward them suffered some malady. It appeared human—or at least in the form of a hominid—but moved in a reeling, swaying gait that bore little resemblance to the healthy stride of a man.

The loose-jointed, awkward, precarious steps were like those of a marionette with a few broken strings. It lurched and stumbled and then recovered, as if driven by an unseen tormentor.

Gerry said, "Watch for snakes," just as Michael saw the first of the vipers moving with the approaching man.

"One," he said quietly.

"Two," added Kade, pointing.

"Three and four," said Danny from where he walked at Lotus' side.

The shamans came to a halt. Slowly, they fanned out, careful of where they stepped.

The stranger continued to approach, accompanied by his serpent escorts. As he drew nearer, even Tom's old eyes could see he was not alive in the normal sense.

The creature's arms were broken—compound fractures of both with white slivers of bone showing through. They bounced at impossible angles and the face gave no sign of what should have been excruciating agony. Instead, it wore the vacant and mindless look of an idiot. The slack jaw appeared badly bruised, lips swollen, tongue lolling and purple. Blackened eyes stared emptily from sunken sockets.

When the figure had approached within ten yards, it came to a sudden stop and the eyes seemed suddenly to come alive. The face split into a wide grin, made all the more horrible because the left side of the mouth was gashed—broken teeth and a steady trickle of blood adding to the garishness of the scene.

The cold, dark, unblinking eyes swept over the thirteen and the tongue moved sensuously over the cracked and bleeding lips. When it spoke, the voice sounded as horrible as the vision, a croaking, ragged sound that made Danny swallow uncomfortably.

"Ahhhh . . . the shamans," it said. "You have come to visit. How nice."

Harold stepped forward, still holding cornmeal and pahos. He looked at the figure before him with anger forming a knot in his stomach. "What have you done?" he demanded.

The eyes turned on him and glared back. "Your tone lacks respect," it observed. "I will teach you better manners before we are done."

"Answer his question," demanded Lotus stepping forward.

The ruined face turned toward her, the mouth curving into something that imitated a smile. The eyes widened slightly as they took in her shape.

"A female. How interesting. And another without any understanding of who you face."

"But we do know," said Juan quietly. "You are the worm that slept beneath the hill. You are the one who, unprovoked, has attacked our kind."

"Of course," said the creature. "Do you expect me to deny it? You are inferior. It is my privilege—no—it is my obligation to assume my rightful place, to conquer and use you."

"But look what you have done!" exploded Kade, his compassion for the human form the monster inhabited moving him deeply.

The creature actually seemed surprised. It raised the mutilated arms and looked at them for the first time. The splintered bones protruded from angry purple wounds. Blood and serum ran from the flesh and dripped from the fingertips.

The voice sounded puzzled as it said, "Do you mean this?" The eyes rolled up so that only the whites showed. "This is nothing. It is only a vehicle from which I can greet you until my true form is free."

"It is a human being," cried the Maricopa.

"It is a shell," corrected the figure. "The pitiful thing that lived in it is gone. So are the others. It cannot suffer for it has no mind of its own."

"You did this to all of them?" Gordon was aghast.

"I regret it," said the creature. "That is why I have come out. I need more." It looked at Gordon, eyes appraising. "Perhaps I will choose you when the time arrives. Would you like that?"

The Navajo shuddered at the thought.

Suddenly, Danny called a warning. "More snakes!" he yelled.

Indeed, four more rattlers had come up to the group and lay coiled only a few feet away. That made eight. Five more slithered up on the other side and James called the alarm.

Thirteen. One for each.

The figure before them began to make a strange huffing, sobbing sound. It took a moment for Harold to recognize it. "Laughter?" he asked.

"I know I do not do it right," said the creature still wheezing. "I have only seen it once. Still, it provides a most exhilarating sensation." It tried to clap its hands before it, but the ruined appendages bent back at an impossible angle and began bleeding began.

It continued as if uninterrupted. "Are you afraid of my little ones? I have brought only one for each of you. Do not resist and it will go quickly for you."

Harold carefully bent and set the pahos on the ground, releasing the cornmeal from his other hand at the same time. As he spoke, he moved among the snakes, picking them up one by one and putting them in a burlap sack he had taken from his belt. "No," he said, without breaking rhythm, "I am not afraid. I have handled these since I was eleven years of age."

After he bagged the fifth, the vipers tried to strike, but the Hopi moved too quickly. His hands were a blur until they were locked safely behind the head of a snake. As soon as it disappeared into the bag, he moved on to the next.

"You cannot be in all places at once," he added with scarcely a pause for breath. "These brothers are not like you. They must obey the god." He had captured the eleventh by this time.

"I will not hurt them. I will set them free when this is done." He captured the last and turned with the bag held before him to face the creature yet again.

It looked at him through narrowed lids. The smile had all but disappeared. "It will not be so easy for you when next we meet," it snarled. "Come and see, shamans. Come and join me in the dark."

The figure before them suddenly gasped and pitched forward on its face. It twitched once and lay still.

Lotus moved forward quickly and knelt beside it. She placed a small hand on the back of the neck. "It's dead," she said.

"Thank the gods," exclaimed Kade.

"End round one," said Gerry.

Chapter Sixty-Eight

Casa Malpais

She knew rage.

Her mighty tail lashed out and smashed five of the workers against the rock wall they had been struggling to break down.

Humans. Pathetic little grubby creatures she could crush with no effort at all—they dared to threaten her dream of conquest!

Worse. She had tried to reach into their minds and take them, only to find She could not.

Again, her weakness rankled and drove her into a frenzy. It must be the distance. If they came closer, She would have them.

And they were coming. They had said so. She had only to prepare for them. It could be no real contest. As the queen, her will would triumph in the end.

She sent one of the former humans to watch from the hill above the main entrance, waiting impatiently as it climbed to the top and positioned itself. Once there, She could use its eyes. A glance told her the Shamans continued to approach.

Good.

She remembered watching some of the humans play a game before they were changed. She had observed for hours in the guise of Dr. Shayley. Now the intricacies of the contest might be of use. It had taken what seemed forever to understand, but comprehension had finally come.

She called the Shayley thing to her. "Tell me again of the game called chess," she commanded.

The slave balked. It surprised her. She had thought all will had been destroyed. It took precious minutes to search out and neutralize the last vestiges of resistance. She battered down the final barrier.

The mind of her slave opened to her as if it had been a manual of the rules.

"The object is to capture your opponent's king," it said. "The way to capture an opponent is by using strategy. Employing diversionary actions, you trick the opponent into moving as you wish and then spring a well-prepared trap."

She understood. She used to do that with the food provided by the servants before the darkness came. The sacrifices had been driven into her lair, confused and frightened. She would play with them— blocking their escape, allowing them to hide and then surprising them, driving them from place to place until She tired of the game and fed.

The game of chess, as She had observed it, worked the same way only there were many pieces. Some were sacrificed to lure the opponent to his doom. Each piece had a specialized purpose. The least of these were called pawns.

Excitement surged up within her.

She had many pieces to play.

There were more than enough pawns.

She watched as the group of humans approached. The question had nothing to do with the number of pieces, but how to gain time needed to set an effective trap. What should she do?

Feint. These humans used the term to describe a move that took place across the board from the place of intended action, to distract the opponent.

She summoned twelve of the slaves and armed them with picks, axes and shovels. This time She took care to select undamaged ones. They must not fail because of already existing wounds.

She must anticipate the shamans' moves. They would have to enter the site by the front. They could not know of the almost prepared direct access through the hillside. If She timed it right, She might even be able to get behind them and drive them into her trap.

She set others to work around the entrance, moving rocks up the sharp slopes and bracing them where they could be rolled down on any who tried to enter. These humans were not very hardy when rocks fell on them. They squashed easily.

The rest, nearly a dozen, were put to work breaking through the outer wall. It would not take long. The hard part had been completed. There were already three places where daylight shone through. Creating a wide enough access would be the work of minutes.

She walked the Shayley thing around one more time, eyeing the preparations. The slaves worked well, but even the strongest would not last much longer. She would need more soon.

She summoned more little ones. The thirteen vipers had proven valueless with her scout, but now she brought a hundred into the entrance and had them hide everywhere. Let the humans try to catch a hundred at once.

Through the lookout's eyes, She saw that the shamans had arrived at the bottom of the hill. They stood there looking up but making no effort to climb.

She waited. Would they make the first move or leave it to her? The hillside rose steeply and there would be a distinct advantage for those in the higher positions. Though the game might be new, She felt She would be good at this. The time had certainly arrived for finding out.

Excitement built within her. The contest would soon begin at last. Oh yes! This chess might prove to be entertaining.

She sent the first wave out through the opening armed with their picks and shovels. The dozen slaves moved easily into positions around the entrance. She posed them in plain view.

The shamans saw them and it engendered agitated discussion among them. They did not appear to agree.

She tried again to reach out and simply take over their thoughts but the barrier remained. This disconcerted her. Her powers of mind had never deserted her before. Still, they were only humans. It would not matter much in the long run.

When She addressed them, a dozen voices spoke in unison.

"Welcome," She said. "Will you come up or shall I come down?"

Chapter Sixty-Nine

Casa Malpais

The shamans had crossed a mile of desert under a brooding sky by the time they arrived at the foot of the hill that contained the catacombs of Casa Malpais. They had spoken little since the death of the human and the capture of the snakes.

Harold led them. As the Hopi, the master of serpents, he could do no less.

John Lakona and Joseph Lansa remained behind at the first camp, bent over their sandpainting, praying to the gods, using every bit of influence they might have to aid their brothers.

The Gathering stood united. Twelve shamans representing the twelve tribes strode forth as warriors to face a terrible evil of elder times. Their hearts and minds were united in purpose. Tom Bear, the thirteenth, beat the drum for them as he had once before.

As they came finally to a stop and looked up toward the entrance, the ruins seemed to glower back—dark and lifeless, yet threatening.

Juan's sharp eyes picked out the pathethic creature that perched atop the hill. It watched them with an unblinking stare and the Yaqui knew it could no longer be called human. He signalled its presence to his companions.

"Okay, we're here," said Michael. "Now what?"

"The thing we must confront readies itself to come out of the hill," said Harold. "We must drive it back below."

"Then what?" asked Gordon.

"By that time," said Danny lightly, "the cavalry will have arrived."

"Myers?" asked Geraldo. He scowled. "Why involve the white men? Why not settle this ourselves?"

"And how would you do that?" asked Juan in a mild voice.

"We kill the snake, of course," said Geraldo. "We kill it and bury it again."

"But what of the Father of Serpents?" asked Rattle. "Did he not say we were forbidden to kill his daughter? Dare we disobey?"

"What can he do?" asked the Zuni. "How is he to know?"

Lotus stepped up and put a hand on Vasquez's shoulder, her voice low but intent. "We have seen what he can do," she replied. "You do not want to anger that one. His vengeance is just but terrible."

"You mean he'll turn me into a snake?" Geraldo's said. "I am not a child to believe such tales."

"We saw," said Danny. "The snakehunter Roberts had been transformed. He was . . . " the Pima shook his head and swallowed, ". . . this is nothing to scoff at. The god had cut off his arms and feet and changed him into a human serpent. He suffered greatly in becoming so. The agent told us his vocal chords had burst from screaming."

The Zuni looked from one face to another, searching for refutation of this claim, but Lotus, Juan and Rattle all nodded in affirmation.

"He speaks the truth," said Rattle. "The Father of All Serpents had no mercy."

"And he has ordered us not to kill his daughter," said Lotus looking into Geraldo's eyes. "I, for one, will not."

"Nor I," added Rattle.

"No way," said Danny.

"It might be the last thing any of us ever did," cautioned Juan. "The father said we could put it to sleep again. He hinted that he has need of it at some time in the future."

The Zuni pursed his lips and finally nodded in acquiescence. "How, then, do we stop it?" he asked.

"The task of driving it below is ours," replied Harold. "Once it is back in the chamber it came from, the white man will use his science to put it to sleep. Then it can be buried again until the Father has need of it."

At that moment, the dozen ragged figures streamed from the entrance above and arrayed themselves in a skirmish line. They were a frightening sight. They were whole—that is, not broken of limb as had been the one met in the desert—but obviously not normal either.

They moved in unison in a peculiar and disturbing manner, like puppets on a string, their eyes wide open but unblinking. The men were bearded for they had not shaved since being taken. All were filthy and wore rags. Like a row of scarecrows, hair sticking out in mottled clumps, limbs skinny and bruised, they carried picks, axes and shovels, brandished awkwardly in bloody hands.

All twelve came to a halt in the same instant and all eyes turned down to focus on the shamans below. "Welcome," they said in unison. "Will you come up or shall I come down?"

Harold answered for them. "Come down," he called to them. "We will await you here." Then he turned to his companions. "You must not hesitate to kill them," he said in a loud whisper. "There is nothing human left here. These are like the dead already. All we can do is set them free."

The shamans exchanged looks of discomfort.

"Are you sure?" asked Michael. His medical training made it difficult for him to consider the taking of life.

"It is true," said Juan, taking a knife from the sheath on his hip. "I came here during the night and walked through the entire complex. These are the dead. They are animated only by the spirit of the one we have come to stop."

Danny took his war club from the bag at his feet and then the shield that Tom had given him.

Each of them took weapons from their gear and donned them. They had no guns. Each chose something traditional—tomahawk, bow and arrow, knife, club. They were grim and determined as they looked once more up the side of the hill.

"Come down," yelled Harold at the creatures above. "We await you."

As one, the twelve clustered by the entrance began to move. The eerie sight chilled the shamans, for the dead did not act like humans would. Soundlessly, without any exchange of words or glances from one to the other, they moved as one being over the lip and started down the slope.

Several stumbled and fell right away, impeding the movements of the rest. The snake must be finding it difficult to control so many. Instead of a headlong charge, the creatures lurched down the slope in ragged disarray.

The first to reach the bottom was far ahead of its companions. Danny smashed it once with his club. It fell to the ground and lay still.

The next two fared no better. Juan dispatched one and Rattle the other. Both used knives.

Following those, however, three came down at once and immediately attacked Lotus. Though she dispatched the first with a quick jab of her own knife, the second landed a solid shovel blade on her back. Only the fact that she twisted away at the last moment saved her from the pick wielded by the third.

By this time, Gerry had leapt to her assistance and clubbed the second one to the ground with his own shovel. Cord shot the third with an arrow from his bow.

Tom and Geraldo struggled with the next while the others closed with the remainder. The outcome never seemed in doubt, but Kade took a blow on the shoulder from the flat of an ax and crumpled under the force of it. James and Gordon sprang to his defense and sheltered the inert form until the others had been stopped.

The servants of the snake died without uttering any sound at all. All twelve fell to the onslaught of the shamans. The attack over, their bodies lay—at last at peace—at the rocky foot of the hill.

No feeling of elation came to the victors. Kade regained his feet and stood swaying, still trying to recover from the axe blow. Lotus felt his shoulder and pronounced it dislocated. Danny and Gerry held him while Gordon popped it back into place with an audible snap. The Maricopa fainted but came around again. He refused to stay down and, instead, stood and swung the arm to keep it from swelling. Use, he said, would keep it mobile. Fortunately, no bones were broken and it had gone back into place easily. Still, Wonto no longer possessed youth. He knew he would pay later for this bravado. Just now, however, he felt needed.

No other figures appeared at the entrance. No secondary attack manifested itself. All was silent.

Harold realized that all the others had turned to look at him. He answered their unspoken question. "I guess we climb up and look around," he said.

Chapter Seventy

Phoenix

Jeremy made the phone call he hoped would provide the help required. Even with the cooperation of DPS, Sarno and the considerable resources of ASU, he knew the task was too big without government help.

The business card said SITON MANAGEMENT, an in joke Matt had told him—one of the many cover names used by the agency.

"Management," said the cool and impersonal female voice. "How can I direct your call?"

"Uh . . . yes . . . I'd like to speak to Matt Pierce. This is Dr. Jeremy Myers."

"One moment, please." There followed a series of beeps and clicks and then the electronic sound of ringing. After the second ring, the familiar voice sounded clearly on the line. "This is Matt Pierce."

"This is Jeremy. I could use some help."

Matt sounded genuinely pleased. "Hi, Doc. I was wondering if I'd hear from you. I just got back from the Roberts place an hour ago. What can I do to make your life easier?"

Jeremy had a list already made out. "I need a specialist in cryonics, a lot of liquid nitrogen, some glycerol and access to something that can be adapted to serve as a seventy-foot-long cryogenic cylinder, and a way to transport it all to Springerville. I also need it yesterday."

Matt whistled quietly into the phone. "You don't want much, do you? Okay, tell me about it."

Jeremy did just that. He explained about the dig at Casa Malpais, what he had been told happened there and what he expected to find. He didn't know what to expect from Pierce. They had been friends for years, but the agent had always been hard-headed and practical minded. Would he believe?

Pierce, however, had been present at the discovery and death of Jake Roberts. He seemed prepared to believe a lot these days. "But, my God, Doctor," exclaimed Matt, "that's fantastic. Are you telling me there's a twenty-five thousand year old prehistoric snake alive under the archaeological site?"

"That's right, Matt, and I need your help quickly or my friends are going to get killed."

"I'll see what I can do. Give me your number and stand by there."

Jeremy did so and the agent hung up. For twenty minutes he fidgeted, wondering if he had done the right thing. The shamans were depending on him because he represented science, but he knew himself to be little more than a dairyman. He collected stock, milked it and then packaged the result. He might be of some help when they actually reached the serpent, but he knew very little of cryogenics or cryonics or whatever.

Twenty minutes later the phone shrilled and he answered on the first ring. "Myers," he said.

"Okay Jeremy," said Matt. "You're a very lucky herpetologist. It seems there's a lab in southern California set up for something just like this. Don't ask for details. It's all classified. I can tell you this much. It was created in the mid-seventies to deal with the possibility of retrieving extraterrestrial life forms that might crash on earth. In the eighties, the White House had them look into cryonics in case of assassination."

"That's wonderful," said Myers as he felt relief flood over him. "What can you get for me?"

"Everything you asked for and considerably more," said Matt with a chuckle. In about five minutes, you and the others should be waiting outside your office in the street. Choppers are on the way to pick you up. The specialists and equipment are already enroute directly to the site from California."

"So fast?" Jeremy was surprised.

"They originally designed this as a crisis response situation, remember?" said Matt. "The staff at the lab is on alert twenty-four hours a day in case of assassination. The extra equipment you asked for has been assembled there."

Myers worried. Sarno had gone back to the university to pick up whatever supply of Succinyl Choline was on hand. Experimental in nature, this Curareform drug was an anti-cholinergic that had been shown to paralyze reptiles without killing them. It interfered with muscular transmission by inhibiting the release of necessary chemicals to the body. Jeremy had a small supply on hand but, even if supplemented by the stock at ASU, he doubted it would be enough.

The mass of things goes up by the cube of their linear dimensions. A seventy-foot serpent would weigh something like six-thousand pounds. It would take a huge quantity of the drug to be effective.

"I need something else," he said to Matt. "We're rounding up all the Succinyl Choline we can find but it may not be enough. Can you locate some for me and get it to the site?"

"What is it?"

"A tranquilizer and muscle relaxant based on curare, the poison. It works on reptiles. We keep small amounts on hand but this creature will require a large dosage."

"I'll take care of it," said the agent. "Listen. You better get moving. I'll see you at the dig when you get there."

"Thanks, Matt," said Jeremy. He meant it. The agent had just solved seventy-five percent of his problems.

After hanging up, he glanced out the window. Much to his relief, Dr. Sarno returned clutching a package, probably containing the drug from ASU. The DPS officers and the Tempe Captain were there as well, accompanied by a number of officers.

Rachel had packed his equipment and had it ready by the door. He kissed her on the way out.

"Be careful," she urged. "I don't want anything to happen to you."

"I'll be all right." He squeezed her hand reassuringly. "And when I get back, you and I are going to talk about some changes around here."

Once outside, Ed Ramirez joined him, along with Rod Grimsley and Greg Johnson. He told them about his conversation with Matt Pierce and the help being provided by the government.

The police looked less than enthusiastic.

"I hope you know what you're doing, doctor," said the Captain. "Once the Feds get in on a project, it has an unfortunate habit of getting out of hand."

"I trust Matt Pierce," said Jeremy. "He'll keep it under control."

Ramirez hurrumphed, "Maybe."

The sound of arriving helicopters could now be heard and the police stopped traffic while they landed in the street in front of Dr. Myer's office. It took only minutes to load up and they were soon headed northeast toward Casa Malpais.

Jeremy watched the city recede behind him and hoped they were doing the right thing.

Chapter Seventy-One

Casa Malpais

The work of clearing the way through the outer wall to freedom continued, complicated by the need to keep the sounds of digging muffled. She didn't want the shamans to learn of the back door to the site. The slaves battered at the wall with huge rams of rock wrapped in heavy canvas and suspended from chains. The opening was four feet wide.

Even as the medicine people were defeating the last of the armed contingent sent against them, one of the teams brought a whole section of the outer wall crumbling down. Now, save for some clean-up and trimming, the breach gaped ten feet wide and nearly twelve high. Enough.

The slaves fell back as She moved up to the opening, her tongue sampling clean fresh air for the first time in more than twenty-five thousand years. It filled her with a sense of power. Strength flowed through her like current through a wire. She felt alive and confident.

She called the Shayley thing to her and surveyed the outside world through its eyes. The overcast sky did not prevent her seeing that the earth had changed greatly since the coming of the eye of god. Some of the surface was dry and cracked. Prior to the impact, this land had been greener and cooler. Though She had learned of her long sleep through the mind of Doctor Shayley, it had been an intellectual perception. Now, seeing the reality before her, it hit home.

For just a moment, bitterness overwhelmed her. Her life had been as near perfect as She could conceive until the great change. To have that time of leisure and comfort so far behind felt unfair. However, She had always been one to rise to the challenges of the moment. If that time had passed, her new time had arrived. She would face this new world with all the cunning and power that had been hers in the elder times. These humans would not defeat her. She would conquer them, make them her servants and once again know a life of contentment.

On the opposite side of the hill, Harold and the others were about to begin their climb when a low rumble caught Geraldo's attention.

"Wait," he said. "Something just happened behind the hill."

Juan agreed. "I heard it. Perhaps the creature seeks a way to come up behind us." He squinted up at the entrance above. "Do not think it has given up. More than a hundred people worked on this site according to Dr. Myers. We have seen only thirteen so far. More are probably lying in wait for us above."

"While others open a back door and come around," said Kade, his shoulder still throbbing. "Yes, that would be a way to trap us. Perhaps we should circle the site one time. There's no hurry about going in, is there?"

"No," said Harold. "Our task is to keep the creature contained until Myers arrives. Some of us must stay here and watch, but the others can scout the rest of the hill."

"Then Kade should stay," said Danny. "His shoulder is still painful."

"And I will remain with him," Lotus volunteered.

"Very well," said the Hopi. "Tom, would you stay with them? If you see anything suspicious, all you need to do is beat the drum and we will come back."

The Pima witch nodded.

"Good," said Harold. "Cord, Michael, Danny and Rattle will come with me." He turned to the Apache. "Gerry, you take James, Gordon, Juan and Geraldo with you. We'll go to the right. You take the left. All will meet on the far side."

Each group moved off at a trot. The distance around the hill measured roughly three miles. Surprisingly, Rattle, the eldest, took the lead. Despite the danger, a spirit of friendly competition started among them and soon Cord, Michael and Danny were pushing for the lead. Harold, limping a little because of his leg, fell rapidly behind. Rattle finally stopped to wait for the Hopi. When he did, the others turned and came back.

Under the hill, She had been preoccupied with the opening of her door to freedom. When She returned her attention to the shamans, looking through the eyes of her watchman atop the hill, only three of them remained visible.

Where were the rest? She moved her lookout along the top until he could see the slopes. Five ran in full view along the foot to the left, and the last five were visible moving to the right much more slowly.

They would find the new opening before She could use it. Again, rage overwhelmed her. Every time She thought to outmaneuver these troublesome humans, they acted to thwart her desire. She had no choice but to heave herself out through the back door and bolt for freedom.

She summoned the rest of the slaves from the site and lined them up, ready to lead the way outside. It took too long. While She tried to organize her army, the shamans continued their circuit and soon came in sight of her position. The opening would be obvious from there. It could not be disguised.

She gathered her slaves and marched them out. Along with them, She sent her little ones. These were composed mostly of Mohave rattlers for they had proven the most deadly and easily controlled.

She followed in all her magnificence. The Shayley thing walked beside her, eyes for her mind.

Seventy feet of serpent came forth from the hill and even the shamans stood by in breathless wonder.

She reared up, coiling her body beneath her, lifting her head high, small stubs of wings flared. She rose above the coil fully twenty feet in the air and opened her mouth and hissed.

The sound reverberated on the air like a storm wind in the leaves of forest trees.

And then an answer came from the desert directly opposite. Up into view rose the Father of All Serpents, the Scaled One, towering fifteen feet and moving toward her.

She knew who approached even before she really saw him. She stopped. For no other living thing would She have given ground, but the Father of all instilled fear even in her.

For just a moment, She considered resistance. It lasted no longer than that. The Father ruled everything she held dear. The Scaled One remained her Lord.

She turned, with a sigh that might have been surrender, and slunk back into the hill. At least there, He would not follow. He had promised never to invade her domain while she ruled.

The Father of All Serpents had come to her at the height of her power and told her that this place would be her kingdom. He had granted her sway over the creatures around her, agreed not to interfere, as long as She remained.

She had argued. Why should She confine herself to this insignificant place? Why should She not rule everywhere? Why would her creator want her to remain so?

He had answered that, in a future time, She would be needed. He had told her he would one day summon her. For now, She must stay.

Though rebellious by nature, she found that her lair under the hill provided for all her needs. She never had to venture far from it. Food and servants had been plentiful. Over the years She allowed herself to become complacent, to settle into the routine of satiation and content.

Now, She chose to return to her prison rather than confront the Father alone.

As She moved back through the entrance, her tongue sensed a new vibration—a steady whump, whump, whump that betokened the arrival of yet other players in the game.

Chapter Seventy-Two

Casa Malpais

From the sky, looking down, the hill housing the site of the dig looked insignificant. Though he had been there before, Jeremy could not believe this place could really be the center of earth-shaking events. Nonetheless, it had become one. As they drew closer, he saw movement on the ground. Figures waved to him. The shamans were clustered on the back side and gestured for them to land there.

For just a moment, he thought he saw a large reddish figure hurrying away into the shadows, but it disappeared before he could focus his full attention. No one else seemed to notice.

The helicopters came in to land in a cloud of dust. They had barely touched down when several more roared down out of the western sky to join them. Jeremy told the police to wait in the choppers, grabbed his fatigue jacket and went out to greet his friends. Before exiting, however, he took a tranquilizer gun from the rack of his equipment and loaded it with succinyl cohline. He pocketed an addititonal dozen darts.

Harold greeted him and spoke urgently. "We are happy to see you," he said. "The serpent has retreated into the hill."

"For a minute there," said the doctor, "I thought I saw the Scaled One."

"You did. The Father of Serpents appeared and drove her back within. We must be careful. She has not been defeated. There are still humans and snakes under her control."

Ed Ramirez had come up when the conversation started. He looked at Jeremy with impatience.

"You'd better keep everyone aboard the choppers, Ed," said Myers. "This creature has a powerful mind. The shamans and I don't seem to be affected, but I don't know about the rest."

"If any of the humans come out from under the hill, you must kill them," urged Harold.

"Are you telling me to kill innocent civilians?" Ramirez asked with surprise.

"There are none living within the hill," said Harold. "I don't know what the creature has done, but it has destroyed that which was human in them. What remains may look like a man, but it is not. We have already killed thirteen of them. They are horrible."

"Look, Ed," the doctor took his arm and walked him back toward the helicopter, "you guys can come in after I tranquilize the snake. I don't know what distance is required, but it can control minds."

"I'm going in," said the lieutenant stubbornly.

"If you did, and it turned you against us, we might fail," said Jeremy. "I don't want to risk that, do you?"

"There is no returning from what it does," said Harold. "The humans it has taken do not suddenly awaken to a normal life. Whatever it does is permanent."

Warring emotions showed on Ed's face, but he finally agreed. "Where do you want us?" he asked.

"Get back in the choppers and away from the site—a couple of miles at least. Leave an outpost with a radio link where they can watch the entrance. I'll signal when I've tranquilized the snake."

Matt Pierce came up just then and beckoned Jeremy aside. "I want to apologize, doctor," he said. "It seems there are those within the government who have an interest in your creature. I'm afraid it isn't going to go as you've planned."

"What do you mean?" asked Myers.

Matt looked uncomfortable. "I'm afraid this operation is now out of your hands and mine," he answered.

"But they don't realize the danger," protested Harold.

Matt turned and looked at the Hopi for the first time. "I don't believe we've met," he said pleasantly enough. "I'm Matt Pierce, FBI."

"Laloma of the Hopi," replied Harold. "We were just explaining to the policeman that the creature seems able to take control of human minds. You've just brought it a hundred more servants if it decides to act."

"What about you?" Pierce turned intelligent eyes on the medicine man. "Are you somehow immune?"

Jeremy looked uncomfortable. "We're supposed to be protected," he said.

"Are protected," assured Harold. "We've been here for hours and we're all right. We've even seen the serpent face to face."

"You have?" Myers was excited. "How big is it?"

"Over sixty feet long. We didn't take time to measure carefully," answered the Hopi dryly. "It will impress you, Dr. Myers. I can guarantee that."

While they spoke, a squad of soldiers debarked from one of the choppers and took positions just outside the entrance. Suddenly, they all stood as one and began to march into it.

Juan had seen it and came rushing up. "It has them," he shouted. "If you can't stop them, they'll be turned against us."

Pierce and Ramirez both looked indecisive.

Jeremy turned to Ed.

"Get back on your choppers and get out of here. Do exactly what I told you. If you don't, a lot of people are going to die."

The lieutenant hesitated for just a moment longer, then made up his mind. "On our way," he said as he turned and sprinted back to the waiting helicopter.

"Where's he going?" asked Pierce.

"He's taking his men out of here until I've put the snake back to sleep," said Jeremy. "Unless you want to lose more men, you'd better do the same."

Another squad of soldiers unloaded from one of the choppers and headed toward the hill. Suddenly, they fell, moving awkwardly for a moment on the ground before rising. When they stood, all did so with identical movements and in unison.

Matt took one look and ran for the chopper. "Radio the other teams," he shouted at the pilot as he leapt through the open door. "Get everybody up and away now!"

The rhythm of the rotors changed, sped up, and all but two of the helicopters rose and flew out. The two that remained disgorged a diverse group. There were white-coated scientists, gray-suited agents and military personnel. They shared common blank, inhuman faces and the same peculiar lurching gait the shamans had observed in those from under the hill.

Harold tapped Jeremy on the shoulder and beckoned to the others. "Move," he said, and led the way toward the entrance. "This is probably our best opportunity. The creature will be struggling to control all the new minds."

Jeremy held his air rifle across his chest. He had loaded it with two darts and the others remained in his pocket.

The shamans drew up beside them and they passed in a tight group through the opening into the hill.

Chapter Seventy-Three

Casa Malpais

She felt panic rising. Seeing the Father had shaken her. Now, as She returned to the darkness of her lair, the oppressive weight of the hill above stifled her, made her feel old for the first time.

She ignored the activity around her and headed for the depths. Only when She had reached her own chamber did She calm down enough to be aware of her servants.

The mohaves and other snakes were fleeing, no doubt under a compulsion planted in their minds by the Scaled One. The humans under the hill lay in mindless exhaustion throughout the complex. Without her to animate them, they were capable of little more than lying still and breathing.

Outside, new two-legs arrived in huge numbers. Looking through the eyes of the one She had left on the hill top, She saw their strange machines land and begin to disgorge their occupants.

The shamans stood in a cluster off to the side except for the one who seemed to be their leader. He had approached a smaller group that contained . . . *ah, Myers.*

She reached out and tried to touch his mind, but the barrier remained. Her tail shook in rage and frustration.

Another group of humans ran from their machine and She reached for them. To her surprise, their minds lay open and unprotected. Hope rekindled within her.

She turned them all, snuffing out their individuality, and marched them toward the entrance. Once they started on their way, she reached for another group.

Trying to control all of them became difficult. Her second capture turned sloppy. The two-legs suffered horribly as She extinguished their personalities. She regretted it, briefly.

During this, however, the humans seemed to become aware of her actions and they fled to their machines. Though She struggled to touch them all, She took only two of the machines before the others flew away and passed out of range.

She brought her new slaves out of the flying things and turned them toward the hill.

These warriors would be used against the others and then they would know her power. Wait! Where were the shamans and Myers? In her effort to control the others, She had lost sight of them again.

Her sentinel atop the hill scrambled from side to side, but his eyes provided no clue to their whereabouts. Frantically, She moved from consciousness to consciousness within the hill, trying each servant's vision for a glimpse of them. Precious minutes passed.

Suddenly, She saw them. They rushed toward her chamber, here under the hill, and most of her slaves already lay behind them.

She tried to move the remainder into the shamans path, but those in position to help had reached the limits their bodies could endure. Only three staggered to their feet and those were overwhelmed when the medicine people came upon them.

Fresh slaves had entered the complex with the last batch, but they were minutes behind and might be too late. She started them toward the chamber at a dead run.

The Shayley thing had followed her below. She positioned herself by the pillar with what had once been Margot between her and the door, and waited.

This would be the final test. She could not imagine that it would be the end.

Jeremy led them into the hill. The humans they encountered were like the others they had seen, mindless and broken. Most of them lay in some kind of stupor. The shamans encountered no resistance in the first few precious minutes of their advance. Jeremy knew the creature would flee to the security of its own nest, so he continually led them down.

He had no difficulty predicting where to go. The path had been hewn out of the rock like a jagged wound. It ran straight and deep, a decline illuminated by generator-powered lights.

The stench was overpowering, causing his eyes to water. The foul smell of decomposing bodies and the unwashed that could still move combined with the cloying mustiness of the tomb. Added to that came the powerful odor of the serpent, ancient, dank and alien.

Rattle and a few of the others pulled out bandannas and held them over their faces as they ran. None, however, slowed for even a moment.

A half-hearted attempt at resistance manifested as they entered one of the lower chambers, but the creatures that tried to stop them were little more than living skeletons and had only to be pushed aside.

Dr. Myers carried the weapon they needed. Finally, they came upon the remains of a wall. Beyond it lay stygian blackness. Jeremy held up his hand signalling a halt.

"This is it," he said. "This must be the entrance to the lowest level. It will be here."

They moved forward together into the dark.

The chamber was silent save for their own ragged breathing. It had been quite a run—nearly a quarter mile, even if it was all downhill.

They had taken only a few hesitant steps when a strange, female voice spoke from the shadows. It came to them weakly but still held a sharp tone of command.. "Halt! Come no further."

Harold stepped forward immediately and answered, "Who are you?"

"I am the queen," answered the voice. "Why have you intruded on my rest?"

"It is your unrest that has troubled us. You have disturbed the land above," answered the Hopi. "We have been sent to help you find peace again."

A hiss sounded in the darkness. "You would dare to kill me?"

"No," answered Laloma. "We have spoken to the Father and will only usher you once again into a long sleep."

"What if I choose to fight you?" The voice sounded petulant.

"We will prevail," said Harold. "It is not only our desire, but the wish of the Scaled One as well."

Lotus and Danny had found flashlights by the door. They chose that moment to light them.

In the dim glow, as their eyes adjusted, the shamans were confronted with the sight of Margot Shayley.

Jeremy, who had seen her before, let out an involuntary cry of pity and dismay.

The once beautiful woman stood mercilessly revealed in the light, her hair matted and tangled. One side of her face was covered with scabs that wept pus and serum. Her clothing had become a haphazard collection of rags that covered nothing. The once alluring body showed through the threadbare fabric like a caricature of a human being. Her right shoulder and clavicle had been broken and her arm hung at an unnatural angle. Deep lacerations covered her stomach, hips, groin and legs. She appeared to be coated with a layer of filth and muck and more blood. Curiously, one perfect breast—the right—remained virtually unmarked.

All of them recoiled from the sight.

"What have you done?" asked Geraldo, much as Kade had asked out on the desert, his tone outraged and demanding.

"What do you mean?" Margot's mouth moved awkwardly, bloody drool cascading over her lips and dripping from her chin.

"What have you done to this woman?" asked Gerry, his voice ragged with emotion.

"This?" The voice sounded puzzled. The twisted grimy hands gestured. "This is merely a servant."

Despite their horror at the condition of the figure before them, the medicine people had begun to move forward. With each step, the light revealed more of what the chamber contained.

At least fifty bodies had been stacked on the ice.

As the shamans advanced, Margot retreated. It was a horrible spectacle to watch. Her body moved in spasms with each step. If anything could have brought home the fact that what confronted them no longer remained human, this did.

When Dr. Shayley disappeared around a boulder, Jeremy and the others hesitated to follow, waiting a few moments before doing so. They moved cautiously up, thrusting their flashlight around the edge and peering carefully about before advancing again.

This part of the cave looked huge and the light from the two small lights did not reach to the walls. The shamans and Jeremy stayed within this island of light.

Margot sat on a pillar of stone.

"Come forward," she commanded.

Carefully, looking all about, eyes trying to pierce the darkness that surrounded them, the shamans approached her.

"I had never seen humans until recently," said Dr. Shayley in a conversational tone. "You are really quite remarkable."

"From the way you have treated those you came in contact with, I would have thought you held us in little regard," said Gerry.

"But that is not true," said Margot. "I have learned a great deal from all of you." Burning eyes turned toward Jeremy. "Especially from you, Dr. Myers."

"You remember, then?" asked the doctor.

"Of course," she replied. "You and the Yaqui, Juan, taught me about humans. I am very grateful."

The medicine people began to spread out, gradually circling the pillar. Margot smiled at them.

Just when they were ready to rush in and subdue her, they heard a hiss from behind them and, suddenly, the walls seemed to close in.

"She's coiled around us," yelled Geraldo. "Watch out!"

The warning came not a second too soon. As the heavy body of the serpent tightened around them, they leapt up and avoided the crushing contraction that followed.

Jeremy fired point blank with both darts and jumped up on the scaly hide at the last second. Trying to maintain his balance, he fumbled in his pocket and pulled out two more darts, slamming them home.

Something huge came down from above and only his quick reflexes kept him from the jaws that snapped on emptiness beside him.

He did, however, see the eyes. They were white and blind. It must be watching the struggle through Margot.

He fired one of the darts into its mouth and then jumped down to the floor near the pillar. In one fluid motion, he fired directly into Dr. Shayley's face and rolled out of the way as the giant serpent head struck again.

The creature hissed angrily.

"Get back!" he shouted. "I've blinded it, but it can still crush us in here."

He drew two more darts out of his pocket and jammed them into the gun. He feared he might take too long.

They scrambled out of the way as the huge reptile convulsed and whipped its body in a circle. James and Danny were struck and hurled across the room, but landed agilely enough to prevent any serious damage.

One after another, Jeremy pumped darts into the huge form that thrashed around him. After the seventeenth, it began to slow. By the time he had used all twenty-four, it lay inert.

Chapter Seventy-Four

Casa Malpais

The observation outpost across from the hill reported by radio that Dr. Myers had signalled from the entrance. In minutes, the choppers were back, landing on the road. Men poured out of them until it seemed half the military in the state must be present.

Myers and the shamans sat just outside the door where the breeze would carry away the stench spilling forth from inside. The temperature had risen and the overcast cleared.

Pierce came out of the hill, walked up to Jeremy and shook his hand.

"Hell of a job, Doc," he said. "How long do you think we have?"

"I don't know," replied the herpetologist honestly. "At least a couple of hours. I pumped twenty-four darts into her. The drug should hold her that long at least."

The scientists, including Dr. Sarno, were still below, examining the prize and setting up the cryonic chamber.

The specialists from the California lab had used sewer pipe wrapped in silver foil and heavy canvas. Section by section, they had encased her, packing more foil around her. The main artery had been tapped and they replaced her blood with glycerol. The process took time despite the tons of equipment the government had provided.

"How are we going to seal her up?" asked Myers, frankly curious. "I hear there's a spring that runs through the rock. You might be able to breach the wall and flood her chamber. It'll take a week and a lot more liquid nitrogen, but you could freeze that lower cave solid."

Matt looked uncomfortable. "That's what I tried to tell you before, Jeremy," he said. "This operation is out of our control now. The boys in Washington want her back there for study. We aren't going to bury her."

"What?"

The agent shook his head. "No, they're packing her up and icing her down, but there's a sky crane on the way that will hoist her aboard and fly her east."

Myers grabbed Matt by the collar and pulled his face close, the look in his eyes deadly serious. "You can't let that happen, Matt. There are other forces at work here as well."

Pierce broke the doctor's grip with surprising ease. "This isn't my project, Jeremy. I'm not calling the shots. You've got a genuine miracle here, a holdover from the ice age. The scientific community has already put in their bid. Everyone wants a piece of this."

"You'll kill it," said Myers. "Do you think I don't know the drill? You people are no better than my employers. Oh, it may be kept alive for a while to see what can be learned, but we already know it's dangerous. In time—short or long—they'll decide they've learned all they can from a live specimen and start hacking it up."

"That isn't your concern," said the agent. "This decision came from much higher up. There's nothing I can do and there's certainly nothing you can do."

Harold had drifted over when he saw the momentary struggle between the two. "What is it, Jeremy?"

"Fucking government wants to take it back for study," he said bitterly. "It'll be killed eventually and the skeleton will end up in the Smithsonian."

The Hopi turned to Matt and said, "You don't want to do that, Agent Pierce. We made a promise to one of our gods. You can't break it for us. If you do, you can write Arizona and New Mexico off the US map."

"What?"

He had gotten Matt's attention. "We may be a little dusty and dirty, Agent Pierce," said the Hopi in a reasonable tone, "but we represent the Hopi, the Apache, the Yaqui, the Zuni, the Pima, the Mohave, the Chemehuevi, the Tohono O'odham, the Maricopa, the Havasupai, the Cocopah, and the Navajo Nations. We are their spokespersons. All of us have made a sacred pledge to the Father of Serpents that we will return this creature to its sleep beneath the hill. Unless you want to find out how Custer felt, you would be unwise to betray us."

"Are you threatening the United States Government?" Matt sounded stunned.

"It isn't just us," said Rattle, who had come up with the others during the conversation. "The Father has commanded that we keep her alive. You wouldn't want to displease a god, would you?"

"Look," said the agent, "I'm sorry, but the government doesn't believe in Native American gods. There's nothing I can do."

"Agent Pierce," said Lotus in a pleasant tone, "I won't threaten you, but I do think you should reconsider. Do you remember what happened to the serpent slayer, Roberts?"

"Of course," said Matt. "What does that have to do with anything?"

"The Father of Serpents did that," said Geraldo. "He is very unforgiving of those who harm his children."

"He hunts them down," said Kade, still nursing his sore shoulder, "and you may have noticed that he has no mercy."

"We will have to act if you try to take her away. We are in Indian country." Gordon spoke plainly. "We could probably get a few thousand Indians here in the next thirty minutes."

Pierce looked at the surrounding countryside nervously.

"We would have to stop you or break our promise to the god," said Juan, "but he would not punish us. The Scaled One knows who is responsible when his children are taken and he acts alone. He has been here since the beginning of time, Agent Pierce. No one has ever captured him or stopped him from attaining his goals."

"Jeremy," said Matt, turning to the scientist for help, "explain it to them. I'm just following orders. I have no authority to act on my own."

"You don't understand," replied the doctor. "This is not a subject for debate." He grabbed Matt's collar again and pulled him close, whispering into his ear. "You saw Roberts, man. Do you want to end up like that?"

For the first time, it seemed to sink in. Pierce realized that he had gotten into something he couldn't handle. "I'll go and call it in," he said, and moved toward the choppers.

Harold looked at Rattle, Lotus and Danny. Without exchanging a word, the three nodded and began to move away, each taking different directions.

The Hopi leaned down and whispered into Jeremy's ear, "It would not do for all of us to be sitting here awaiting the decision." He sank to the rock next to the herpetologist and put his head down in his arms. "They will pick up John and Joseph, then return to our people." He chuckled. "If we do not return within twenty-four hours, the word will be spread."

The doctor shook his head and grinned back at the old man. "You guys are amazing," he said.

Greg Johnson chose that moment to approach and squatted opposite them. "You did well, my brothers." His tone sounded sincere, not mocking.

"All of us played our parts," agreed Harold, "but the game is not yet over." He looked at the Police Captain. "Will you join us on the 12th?"

"Of course," replied Greg. "I wouldn't miss it."

Jeremy must have looked confused, but Johnson smiled. "It is the anniversary of the defeat of the demon and the death of my friends Jack Foreman and Pasqual Quatero."

"We were lucky this time," said Juan from off to the side. "No one got seriously injured and you white men were able to do almost all of it."

Johnson grinned back at the Yaqui. "Not much supernatural about this one," he stated.

The shamans and Myers exchanged a knowing glance, but the Zuni shrugged. "Apparently not," said Geraldo, his tone milder than any of them expected. He looked at the policeman and smiled. "Otherwise you would have fucked it up royally and we would have had to save your butts."

Johnson stiffened for a second until he saw the glint of humor in the Zuni's eyes. Finally, he laughed. "You're probably right," he agreed.

Matt Pierce came toward them accompanied by some military officers and a group of armed soldiers.

Ramirez and Grimsley approached them from the other side with a number of DPS officers.

"I'm afraid we're going to have to hold all of you for a few days," said the agent. "The answer from higher up came back as no."

Lieutenant Ramirez cleared his throat, then said, "And I'm afraid I can't allow that, Agent Pierce. I have my own orders about this and I'm taking all the medicine people plus Dr. Myers back with me."

Pierce looked at the DPS Officer with real surprise. "Come on, Lieutenant. You know better than that. We're the government. We give the orders around here."

Grimsley smiled and laid a hand on his side-arm. "But this is Arizona, Agent Pierce. You've heard what crazy fuckers we are out here. We do things our own way, or have you forgotten how we lost the superbowl. No one in this state likes to be told what to do, especially not by the Feds."

The military men looked across at the police and one whispered in the agent's ear.

Matt grinned. "Okay, we have a Mexican stand-off. What do you want to do next? We're still taking that monster back to Washington with us whether you like it or not."

A loud explosion on the other side of the hill shook the ground beneath them and knocked more than one man off his feet. Smoke and debris flew out through the entrance, obscuring everything for a few critical seconds.

Within minutes, scientists and military personnel came pouring out of the hill like ants from a disturbed nest.

The shamans, too, had retreated across the road.

When everyone had made it out, a second—even larger—explosion rocked the earth beneath their feet. The hill rose up, then slowly sagged in the middle, settling, as every chamber and hollow within collapsed upon itself.

Everyone stood unmoving as an eerie silence fell over the site. It took almost a minute for the shouting to begin.

Jeremy and the shamans stood well away, close to the police helicopters. They looked at each other in puzzlement.

"Danny, Lotus and Rattle?" asked the doctor.

"No," said Harold. "They are long gone."

"Then who did it?"

Just at that moment, Dr. Sarno walked by. He held a bloody rag to his forehead and spoke animatedly to one of his assistants. "I tell you, I saw it. Huge and red. I've never seen anything like it in my life. It went past like a steam locomotive at top speed, just a blur. I'd swear that flame shot out of it."

Harold smiled at Jeremy. "The Scaled One," he said under his breath. "Of course."

The shamans exchanged knowing, satisfied looks. The god had helped again and this time they had no doubt of its power.

The complex at Casa Malpais now consisted of only a heap of sandstone. No one could explain the explosion, though some discussion of liquid nitrogen under pressure coming into contact with the underground spring followed. No one knew for certain why that should have produced such upheaval, but everyone felt sure there would be no digging it out.

The scientists were in agreement that the creature could not have survived. The freezing process had begun, but the equipment had not been set up with permanance in mind. They had planned to complete their work in laboratories.

There was no further discussion of detaining the shamans or Dr. Myers. The police offered to take those who wished it by chopper back to their respective villages, but they declined. They would return to Phoenix in their own vehicles.

Curiously, the ground temperature dropped significantly over the ensuing weeks. In subsequent spring seasons, the frost remained much longer than usual on the rubble that had been the Badland's House.

Wednesday, July 10th

Chapter Seventy-Five

Salt River Indian Reservation

All the shamans had returned to Tom Bear's home to finish their reunion. Jeremy Myers and their other white friends from DPS and the Tempe Police joined them. At the end of the day, they gathered out on the grounds beside the ravine, watching the colors of the sunset riot in the western sky.

"After all the discussion," said Jeremy, one arm around Rachel's waist, "I'm still curious about her. The Queen of serpents has been only a legend until now. Do you realize what she could have told us about the prehistoric world?"

"You can probably still ask her," said Gordon from where he sat, back to a mesquite post. "All you'll have to do is dig her up and thaw her out."

"Do you really think she made it?" Myers could not help wondering. "Though the scientists claimed they had her ready to transport when the explosion occurred, most agreed the work could not have been adequately done to preserve her for long underground. Remember, they planned to study her back in Washington."

"She lives," said Geraldo, reaching out to pat the herpetologist on the shoulder with uncharacteristic affection. His changed demeanor toward white men had been easy for all to see. "You did exactly what you were meant to do and so did we."

302   The Serpent Slayers

"Something that old," said Danny quietly from his place at Lotus' side, "it has a right to survive."

"In a way, I feel the same, but there are nearly two hundred people buried under that hill with her who might argue the point if they could," said Rod Grimsley. "I'm glad I don't have to judge her. That monster had no conscience."

"We can't think of her by human standards, Rod. She did kill a couple hundred people, probably no more than that," added Ed Ramirez. He and Faye sat together, arms laced comfortably around each other. "The Mogollons who walled off that section came along later, after she had been frozen. She had no experience of man. The impact is supposed to have occurred before we came to this part of the world. She retained her innocence until the end."

"Watch it, Ed," joked Rod. "You're becoming a scholar. We can't have that."

Ramirez made a face at his partner.

"We were fortunate," said Kade. "She could have emerged and dominated the earth again had we failed." Estelle sat a little behind rubbing his sore shoulder gently.

A silence fell over them as they watched the colors fade. All were grateful there were none of their own to mourn. Unlike their previous adventure, the gathering had survived intact and even grown. With the two additional Hopi priests, Maria and Estelle, plus the law enforcement people, Jeremy Myers and Rachel, they made a large and contented company.

"Life is meant to be this way," said Tom. "Perhaps we are finally growing up. We may actually be learning to live with each other." He looked around at their faces.

And what a collection of faces! Youth and age, white man and red, male and female—the gathering had become a blue print for peace.

"It looks as if we have plenty of reasons to do this again next year," said Michael. "Do you realize that both the demon and the queen appeared at mid-summer. It all occurred in the same month only a year apart."

"I hope that doesn't mean we have to go adventuring every July," said Gerry with a grin. "It's a terrible month for exertion—too hot."

Juan stood and moved over to Maria, putting his arms around her from behind and hugging her to him. "Did the agent make any more trouble, Jeremy?" he asked.

"No," answered the doctor with a wry smile. "I talked with Matt this morning. He really is an old friend. He appears to have developed considerable respect for this gathering. He actually seemed cheerful when we spoke. I'm glad he doesn't blame me."

"Did the final report determine what happened?" asked Cord.

Jeremy laughed. "Yes, and I chuckle whenever I think about it. The government made up its collective mind and decided how to handle it. They're blaming the scientists. No action is planned, of course, but they think one of the technicians must have set off the explosions through careless handling of the gasses. At least, that is what the final report will say."

"We should tell him about the Scaled One," said Rattle seriously. "It is not right that humans be blamed for the acts of gods. None of them could have known about the Scaled One."

"I did tell him," said Myers, "but he said the government wants nothing to do with that explanation. They couldn't accept it or, even more important, explain it to the public. No, they're actually happy about it. Blaming the scientists is a way to cover their own butts. It goes on all the time."

"Who would have thought that the god himself would step in when he did and take control of everything," commented James.

"I meant to ask you about that, Harold," said Jeremy. "Would you really have started a war if the government had taken her back for study? I mean, it turned out to be a great strategic move and all, but did you really mean you would enter into hostilities with the government?"

The Hopi had no trace of humor on his face as he replied, "You still don't understand, do you? The god would have expected it of us if we were to keep our bargain. It might seem strange to you that we honor the old gods, but our ways have been around considerably longer than yours. Yes, all of us would have returned to our people, explained it to the councils, and they would have battled to uphold our honor."

"I meant no offense," said Myers quietly.

"And none taken, my brother," said Harold lightly, "but you have only begun to realize how powerful the Scaled One is. He entered and destroyed the Badlands House with a hundred soldiers and policemen there. None of them saw. None of them would have been believed if they had. And, at that, we were lucky. He managed to blow it up with no additional loss of life. He is a god. It is not for us to question His will." He turned to Ed. "Do you agree?"

Ramirez nodded. "I guess I do," he said and looked to his partner.

"Of course," confirmed Rod. "But, remember. The idea of a real god—one that walks in physical form on the earth—hasn't been popular for a couple of thousand years in our world. Like the agent said, most people wouldn't be able to accept it."

"One thing," added Jeremy, "Matt did tell me that they found out where the hand came from. You know the one I mean? The one Roberts sent?"

"Where?" Ed asked.

"DEA found an unmarked truck and an illegal dump site near Springerville," answered the doctor. "The bodies of several men were there. One of them, some petty hoodlum, used to be the owner of the hand and forearm Roberts shipped with the specimen. The mutated snakes were coming from there too. Matt says DEA exterminated them. He said it took them a full day."

"I wonder how the Scaled One will view that?" asked Rattle.

A thoughtful silence followed. No one wanted to contemplate the wrath of the Scaled One or the consequences of that rage. Some of them had seen His handiwork and it remained too raw in their memories to even discuss it among themselves.

Rattle shuddered.

After a few minutes had passed, Tom stood and looked at his friends. "In keeping with what is obviously becoming an annual tradition, I invite you all once again to return a year from now for a second reunion of the Great Gathering. We will meet again in July and do honor to our departed brothers. Let us hope that the next is less strenuous than this one turned out to be."

Normal conversation broke out as some discussed plans for the following summer. Others talked of their just completed adventure.

As darkness struggled mightily with the dying sun, the guests of the Pima witch, Tom Bear, turned toward their barbecue and the warm fire of friendship.

All were content to spend this time at peace.

Few times in their lives would they enjoy such companionship and hard-earned satisfaction at a task well done. All gave thanks as the day faded.

But, then, that is the nature of man.

Thursday, July 11th

Epilog

Night had fallen on Casa Malpais and the Father of All Serpents sat cross-legged in the desert opposite the remains of the Badlands House.

He mused about the nature of humankind. They were such a mass of contradictions—inventive, independent, industrious, intelligent, courageous—all these descriptive terms applied. The two-legs had risen from a precarious and fragile beginning to truly rule the earth.

Yet there were other terms that could be used as well—stubborn, unaware, cruel, self-centered and destructive.

How strange, thought the god, that he should be enabled to save his daughter from herself by these strange, unpredictable and energetic beings.

Despite the hundreds of humans he had harvested through the years, the Scaled One's opinion of the creature that called itself man had been improving for centuries. Time, for him, had little meaning. He had seen many species come and go. These beings, too, would one day leave the earth, perhaps voyaging to the stars as they dreamed they would.

He looked again at the mound of ruined earth that blanketed and protected the slumber of the last of the great serpents and smiled.

He could still hear her calling to his mind just as the explosion sealed the chamber.

"Why, Yig?" She had cried. "Father! Why must I sleep in the dark?"

He had sent his thought to her mind, gently reassuring. "Because, my daughter, despite the centuries, your time has not yet come."

Silence had been the answer.

She would sleep and, in some distant future, when the earth had given up these two-legged humans, he would call her forth.

Together they would repopulate a world.

Meanwhile, he thought, *I have many other children to protect.*

But, then, that is the nature of Yig.

- The End -

Watch for the next novel in *The Shaman Cycle*
by Adam Niswander

THE HOUND HUNTERS

coming from Integra Press in October 1994

Novels in *The Shaman Cycle*

The Charm
The Serpent Slayers
*The Hound Hunters**

* Forthcoming